MAP'S
EDGE

Also by David Hair

MAP'S EDGE

THE TETHERED CITADEL BOOK 1

DAVID HAIR

Jo Fletcher
BOOKS

First published in Great Britain in 2020 by

Jo Fletcher Books
an imprint of
Quercus Editions Ltd
Carmelite House
50 Victoria Embankment
London EC4Y 0DZ

An Hachette UK company

A CIP catalogue record for this book is available
from the British Library

TPB ISBN 978 1 52940 193 6
EBOOK ISBN 978 1 52940 190 5

10 9 8 7 6 5 4

Typeset by Jouve (UK), Milton Keynes

Printed and bound in Great Britain by Clays Ltd, Elcograf S.p.A.

MIX
Paper from
responsible sources
FSC® C104740

Papers used by Quercus are from well-managed forests and other responsible sources.

Dedicated to all the health workers and essential service providers around the world who, as I type, are battling to keep us all going during the COVID-19 pandemic (and especially my nursing sister, Robyn). Your courage and humanity are deeply appreciated, not least by my mum, who had a critical operation during this fraught time and came through. Thanks to all of you.

TABLE OF CONTENTS

PART THREE: ANCIENT AND ALWAYS

THE MAP . . . AND ITS EDGE

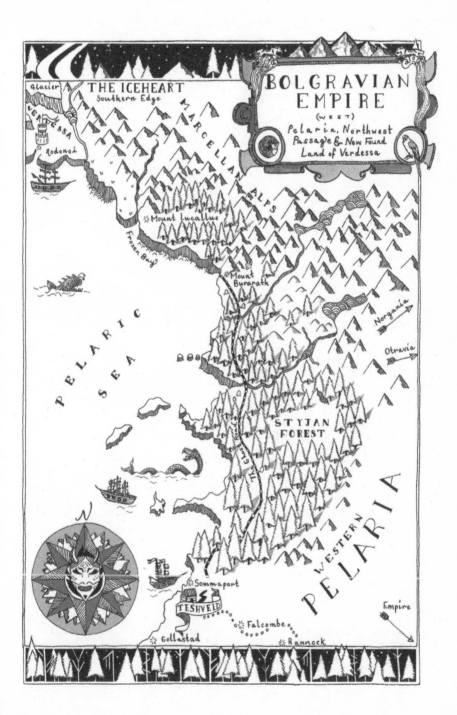

PART ONE
Out of Empire

1

Never open the door after dark

The crash of a mailed gauntlet on the door tore Dash Cowley from his dreams, and brought back another night when steel-clad fists ripped his life apart. For a moment he was back *there* and *then*, when doors crashed open and screams rent the air—

Then he woke fully, staring around the dimly lit cabin, blinking away those memories, but the fist kept pounding, and now a rough voice called, 'Oi, physicker: wake up!'

'Dad?' Zar called in a shaky voice from the loft.

'Shhh,' Dash hissed, peering at the door. He could see the flicker of torchlight through the cracks in the crude log cabin. It wasn't yet dawn and the wind was making the pines creak and hiss. Breakers boomed distantly, a mile away.

No one comes out here at this hour. Then a hundred potential reasons suggested themselves, all sinister. 'Stay hidden,' he hissed at Zar, as he hurriedly dressed. 'Keep your curtain pulled.'

'Oi, wake up!' that voice shouted again.

'Coming.' Dash staggered blearily to the door, bracing himself against the frame as he composed himself. His mouth felt sour, his head ached dimly.

Too much blasted rye last night.

Never open the door after dark in Teshveld, he'd been told within hours of arriving in this Gerda-forsaken seaside village. He checked the door bar was in place and called, 'Who is it?'

'It's Gravis, from the inn. I got lordships out 'ere, needin' a physicker.'

3

'What?' *There're no 'lords' in Teshveld.* But it was definitely Gravis' voice.

Then a cold male voice called in a Bolgrav accent, 'Open door or we break, yuz?' The voice was deep and atonal, every syllable laden with ponderous authority.

Shit, what's a Bolgrav doing here?

Zar poked a pale face through the loft curtain, Dash signed, *Pull your damn curtain shut,* then unbarred the door before it was broken.

A mailed fist flew through the opening and stopped an inch from his nose. Dash peered around it at a big, rugged man with greying hair and a beard like steel wire: a Norgan ranger, at a guess, in his forties or fifties. His pale blue eyes widened, but he didn't drop his clenched fist as he studied his host.

The Norgan didn't look impressed, which was understandable. Dash knew he didn't cut a heroic figure – just a slim man in his thirties, with intense eyes, greying black hair and a rudder-nose, passably handsome in a good light, but stubble-chinned and dishevelled right now.

'That's 'im, our physicker,' Gravis wheedled. The guttering torch he held cast everyone in a ruddy light. 'Dash Cowley, 'is name. Came 'ere four months ago. First proper healer we've 'ad in years.'

'Cowley,' the Bolgrav voice drawled; it belonged to a man in a noble's finery, standing behind the Norgan: clean-shaven and pristine, with a blond mane and haughty caste to his face. His pale cloak was collared with blue fox fur, elegantly out of place in this coastal backwater, but his clothing had a lived-in look, as if he'd been travelling a long time. 'You treat sick friend, yuz,' the Bolgrav told him.

Frankly, I'd rather cut your Bolgravian throat than tend your bloody friend, Dash thought, but the Bolgrav had three more soldiers – his own countrymen, judging by the conical helms and long flintlocks hanging over their shoulders – as well as the Norgan. One was a sergeant; the other two bore a stretcher containing a swaddled shape. Steamy breath hung over them; overhead, the planetary rings, silver bands of light that carved the sky in two, glowed like the blades of a sky-god.

Kragga, the Bolgrav probably is a lord . . . but what's he doing out here?

4

'He's right where I said, Lordship,' Gravis bleated, cap in hand. 'It's a cold night, an' a long walk.'

'Pay him, Sergeant,' the Bolgravian snapped. 'You, Physicker Cowley: where from is you?'

'I'm Otravian,' Dash said truthfully; his nose was proclaiming that for him anyway. 'My rates are –'

'We pay what you earn; what you deserve, ney?' the Bolgrav rasped, turning the 'w's to 'v's. He shoved Dash aside and stalked into the cabin, eyes flashing to the curtained loft. 'What is up there?' When Dash hesitated, he added, 'I send men anyway, so you tell now.'

'My, ah, child,' Dash admitted. 'Zar, show your face.'

She poked her head through the curtain, all freckled cheeks and big eyes.

'Ah, young girl, yuz?' the Bolgrav purred. 'You, girl, come down.'

'Get dressed first,' Dash called, gritting his teeth. *If this bastard mistreats her . . .*

But the best chance of getting rid of the Bolgravs would be to comply as quickly as possible, so he lit the oil-lamp, hurriedly cleared his table, then stood back as the soldiers hoisted the stretcher onto the table. It held a plump redheaded man who was flushed red, sweating badly and stinking of piss and faeces. His right side was encased in bloody, badly wrapped bandages.

'What's happened to him?' Dash asked, wondering if it was even safe to touch the man. 'Uh, my lord . . .?'

'Lord Vorei Gospodoi, am I. You speak Bolgravian? Be easier.'

Dash did have some Bolgravian, but he wasn't about to admit it here. 'Just Magnian, milord.'

The Bolgrav grunted in displeasure. His eyes fixed on Zar as the thin girl clad in a boy's shirt and trousers clambered down the ladder. He blocked her from reaching Dash, ignoring her flinch as he stroked her cheek. 'Mmm. Soft, like all Otravians, ney? What is name, girl?'

'She's called Zar,' Dash answered for her. 'She's my nurse. I need her help to treat this man.'

Gospodoi smiled coldly, but stepped aside, allowing Zar to dart past.

'Cowley, you will heal this man, or bad thing happens for you and daughter.'

Kragging Bolgravs, Dash thought. *We crossed a continent to escape arseholes like you.*

'I'll do my best,' he answered, 'but I need to know what ails him.'

'This man has unknown illness, from northwest.'

'The northwest? But there's nothing out there—'

Gospodoi fixed him with a frosty eye. 'I tell you this, you not repeat, ney? He fell ill in place across Narrows, name is Verdessa.'

The new-found land? Rumour had it there was nothing there but a thin band of rocky shore below the ice-cliffs, but of course, the empire was just getting started over there. Despite himself, Dash was interested. 'Verdessa – yes, I've heard of it.'

'Is new place.' Gospodoi smirked. 'All new places is found by Bolgravians. We are greatest nation, conquer all of Shamaya, yuz. Explore, expand, exploit. You will find, Otravian, no matter where you go – and whoever woman you meet – that Bolgravian man has been there first.' He chuckled, then jabbed a finger at the sick man. 'This man is cartomancer. You know cartomancer?'

Holy Gerda! 'Yes, I know what a cartomancer is,' Dash admitted.

'Excellent. You educated man, is good. So you must save him, yuz?'

'I'll do my best.'

'You will,' Gospodoi agreed, 'or I break your hands . . . and maybe hurt pretty daughter?'

Bolgravs: every other sentence a threat. 'How long has he been ill?'

'Two week.'

'That long? Was there no one in Verdessa or Sommaport you could take him to?'

Gospodoi went to answer, but the complexities of translating from his tongue to Magnian flummoxed him and he scowled at the Norgan. 'You tell, Vidarsson.'

The Norgan spoke up. 'I'm Vidar Vidarsson. The cartomancer's a

Ferrean named Lyam Perhan. He fell ill near the edge of the Iceheart, in northern Verdessa. We'd completed most of our work anyway, so we journeyed south to the coast and Perhan seemed to be rallying, so we sailed south for Sommaport. But he declined after we left Sommaport. Teshveld is the first village we found on this road.'

'Yuz, is as Vidarsson say,' Gospodoi put in. 'You medicate Perhan, make him healthful.' He stroked Zar's hair, then turned on his heels curtly. 'Vidarsson, you will stay and watch, with my men. I stay in tavern.'

Of course you will, Dash thought sourly, *and you'll probably drink their best grog and not pay.* But that was Gravis Tavernier's problem. His was to somehow save this cartomancer.

As Lord Gospodoi stalked off without a backwards glance, Dash turned to Zar and issued a string of instructions: for boiled water, for sedatives and for the herbal poultices he'd been preparing for the next slaan-fly outbreak. Outside, the Bolgrav soldiers were making themselves at home, pissing against his back wall and stealing his firewood while guffawing in their guttural tongue.

Once the Norgan ranger had taken in the lie of the land, including checking the two mules in the lean-to out the back, he sat at Dash's table, sniffing the wine jar. 'Rannock claret?' He poured himself a mug. 'You bring it with you from home?'

Questions weren't welcome, and nor was someone stealing his wine, but the Norgan was a hulking man with an air of violence, so Dash limited his response to sarcasm. 'I *traded* for that, Vidarsson.'

'Call me Vidar,' the ranger growled, pouring himself a mug of the claret. He had craggy features and a pulsing vein in his right temple. 'So what's an Otravian healer doing in this Gerda-forsaken hole?'

'I ask myself that every day. But we take oaths to heal where sickness is found.'

'Most healers I've met are motivated more by coin than oaths,' Vidar grunted. 'And most men who live in shitholes like this do so because they don't want to be found.'

'I bet most of those don't really want to talk about it, either,' Dash observed. 'Now, if you don't mind, I've got to look after your Bolgravian cartomancer friend if I'm to save my hands.'

'No friend of mine,' Vidar said, swigging his wine. He wiped his mouth. 'Good drop, this.'

'You're welcome,' Dash grunted. 'So why's a Norgan nursemaiding a bunch of Bolgravs?'

'Because I happen to like Imperial argents in my purse,' Vidar growled. 'And they're the only game in town.'

'You guided them in Verdessa? What's out there?'

'That's none of your concern, healer. Get on with it and I'll keep your wine company.'

Dash quietly fumed, but he and Zar began their task, removing the cartomancer's clothes, cutting away the soiled bandages and revealing the wound: a scab-crusted puncture that was seeping foul-smelling fluid. *That's no 'illness'*, Dash thought, having to stop himself retching at the stench.

'Never seen a healer get all spitty over a bad smell before,' Vidar observed sagely.

'I have a sensitive nose,' Dash replied. 'Aromatic herbs, Zar.'

'Maybe you're just a kragging useless healer,' Vidar sniffed. 'Or a fraud?'

That was too close to the truth, but Dash kept his composure. 'What happened to him?'

'Fell through some ice onto a buried branch,' Vidar sniffed. 'Useless outdoorsman, he was. Had to baby him through the journey. Reckon there's rotting debris in the wound.'

Dash poked around and nodded in agreement. 'The wound's become infected. His blood's turning septic. It's only the clotting around the wound that's preventing the poisoned tissue from circulating and killing him. What do you suggest, Zar?'

Zar's fifteen-year-old face was screwed up in horror at the foul-looking wound, but she managed a coherent response. 'We wash, cleanse, cauterise, then apply a poultice.'

'Good,' Dash said with approval, 'but consider his respiration and overall wellbeing: can he survive cauterisation, do you think? And what about sedation?'

Zar considered and they batted ideas back and forth, then set to work. Zar glanced sideways at Vidar, then softly asked, 'What's a cartomancer, Dad?'

Dash shook his head, but Vidar looked up. 'Well? Answer her question.'

It's not illegal to know, I guess, Dash decided. 'A cartomancer uses praxis to explore the world – specifically far-sight, foresight and earth magic – to determine the geological composition of a region.'

Zar's eyes shone as she looked at their patient anew. 'That's a good thing, right?'

'I suppose. But you have to remember, when they present their data to the empire, it usually leads to colonising invasions, the displacing of thousands of people to be exploited until they drop dead of exhaustion and kragging up the land for generations as they rape it beyond sustainability.'

'Oh.' Zar's burgeoning admiration evaporated.

'That sounds like Liberali talk, Cowley,' Vidar growled. 'The Imperium outlawed the old Liberali Party in Otravia nine months ago.' He added, 'They purged them with old-fashioned bloodwork.'

Gerda's Tits, people I used to know . . .

'I got out of Otravia years ago,' he replied, adding, 'in any case, I'm apolitical.'

'There are no apolitical Otravians,' Vidar snorted, then he sighed. 'Look, Cowley, or whatever your real name is, I sympathise. My country's been screwed over by the Bolgravs just as much as yours. So I'll stop asking questions you don't want to answer.'

They shared a more understanding look, then Dash turned to Zar. 'Let's get to work.'

They laboured for a couple of hours, cleansing and then cutting away infected tissue, before placing half a dozen leeches in the wound to suck up the infected blood. The cartomancer's breathing stabilised, but that was the only good news.

I'm sorry, Cartomancer, but the chances are, you'll never wake again. Dash hung his head, feeling that ache of not knowing enough, of not being enough. A real healer might have been able to save the cartomancer, but out here, knowing enough to cauterise a wound and sew up a cut made you the best physicker in the district. This was the western edge of the empire: the last place left to hide.

With a sigh, he plucked off the leeches, then mixed up a tonic, taking a moment to surreptitiously palm a tiny blue bottle and tip a drop into one of two clay cups. After he'd dosed the cartomancer, he pulled out a small keg and poured a thimble of amber fluid into each of the clay cups. He placed the tainted one in front of Vidar.

'This is Urstian rye, best in Ferrea. Surely that's worth some news?'

Vidar pushed the empty mug of claret aside, took the cup he was offered and downed it in one. Then he smiled. 'Now *that* was good. Where'd you get it?'

'From a trader in Falcombe, on the road here. Cost a fortune, because you just never see stuff like that out here: this isn't Reka-Dovoi or Kortovrad.'

'Tell me about it,' Vidar snorted.

Dash poured another round and the ranger related his tidings: more failed rebellions in the Magnian heartland; more political assassinations and intrigues. 'But we've been away over the Narrows for three months now, so I daresay it's all changed,' Vidar concluded, yawning.

'A successful expedition?' Dash asked.

Vidar chuckled. 'Tell you that, I'd have to kill you.'

They chatted away amiably enough for another few minutes, then Vidarsson began slurring his words. 'This rye . . . is . . . *kragging* strong, Cowley–'

'Oh, Urstian rye's a beast,' Dash agreed. He smiled, waiting as the ranger deteriorated quickly, his head nodding, until he slumped and began to snore.

'Gerda's Blood, Dad, you just drugged him,' Zar squeaked.

Dash went to the door and peered into the frigid night. The three Bolgrav soldiers were huddled over a blaze they'd made with his firewood. *If these bastards hang round much longer we'll be destitute again.*

'I want to read this cartomancer's notes,' he told Zar. 'You get some sleep.'

He tousled her hair and they shared a fond, anxious hug; they'd been through a lot together and their bonds were tight but she'd clearly guessed that as soon as Gospodoi's party were gone, they'd need to move again. If the Bolgrav gave their description to anyone with the wrong connections, the hunt would be on again.

Gerda knows where to next ... There're not too many other places to run, unless we leave the continent altogether ...

Zar went back to her loft and he returned to the unconscious cartomancer and removed the satchel under his head. With half an eye on the drowsing Vidarsson, he opened the leather bag and removed the journal all cartomancers carried, and began to read. He was interested to see that while the older entries were in Magnian, which everyone could read, the later writings were in Ferrean, a standard subject in Otravian universities – but not in Bolgravia.

I'm fluent in Ferrean, but I bet Gospodoi isn't. Most Bolgravs can't be arsed learning other folk's tongues. He read quickly, anxious to finish before his uninvited guest awoke.

I, Lyam Perhan, Imperial Cartomancer, do attest. In the year 1534ME, I accompanied Lord Vorei Gospodoi of Bolgravia on an expedition from Sommaport, across the Narrows, to the newly discovered land of Verdessa, which is claimed by Bolgravia.

The notes detailed navigational bearings, mineral readings and some sparse notes on flora and fauna. Perhan listed no native peoples, but he did mention a lake in the mountains at the edge of the Iceheart, the vast expanse of ice in the north. When Dash read the water analysis, one obscure chemical symbol, buried deep, leaped off the page.

Istariol . . . Gerda Alive, he found traces of istariol! And the readings hinted at far more: a lode bigger than anything discovered since the Mizra Wars. Dash's veins tingled at the thought of what such a lode could do in the right hands – it might even revive the fight for freedom in Otravia and across the Magnian continent. The call of home flared up inside him, together with the burning need for revenge on the Mandarykes and all the other turncoats who let the Bolgravs into Otravia.

He skimmed the rest of the journal, finding no other references to istariol, but he judged that Perhan was wilfully obfuscating. *The Ferreans have suffered as badly as the rest of us. Perhaps he didn't want to tell Gospodoi what he'd found, so he buried the information in such a manner that it was more likely a friendly eye would see it . . .*

He closed the journal and returned it to the satchel, then settled onto his pallet, closed his eyes and fell to dreaming of a glorious return to his homeland.

It felt like only minutes later when Zar shook him awake. 'Dad,' she murmured, 'he's waking – and the sun's coming up.'

Dash looked up blearily and rubbed his eyes. He might not feel rested, but excitement was tingling in his veins. After too many years of exile the sense of opportunity was beckoning, but he kept calm as he washed his face, re-lit the fire and put water on the boil, keeping one eye on Vidar Vidarsson as the Norgan snuffled his way back towards wakefulness.

The cartomancer's discovered enough istariol to start a war, but I'm almost certain he's not told anyone else. So does anyone *know about this find but him and me?*

He looked across the room at Zar, seeing her mother's face echoed there, and wondered if he had the right to drag her into one of his schemes. *Let it pass,* caution urged. *Keep your head down.* But the cartomancer's journal was a treasure map. Letting such a chance pass by would tear him apart.

And what's the alternative? To die in exile, while the Mandarykes ruin my homeland?

'Zar,' he asked, 'if we had a chance to return home, you'd want to take it, wouldn't you?'

'Of course. I'm sick of being nowhere.'

He winced. She'd be at home right now if he hadn't stolen her from her mother. *But she'd be living at the whim of the Mandarykes and their Bolgrav friends, just like her mother, and they'd soon have taught her to despise me.*

'It'd be for us,' he said, trying to convince himself as much as her. 'For all we once had.'

'I know, Dad,' she said, throwing him a warning look as Vidar stirred again.

Still undecided, Dash signed her to put the conversation to one side. 'Can you make us breakfast, please?' he asked, before turning to the Norgan. 'You all right there, fella?'

Vidar blinked awake, then peered at his empty cup. 'Deo's Balls, that stuff hits hard.'

'Just relax, friend Vidar,' Dash said. 'I'm sure it's been a trying journey for you.'

'You have no idea,' Vidar growled. 'The number of times I came close to knifing those pricks. Arrogant bastards think they own the whole kragging world.'

'They do: my land, your land, everyone else's land. They've got the most powerful sorcerers, they've got the biggest armies and the most gold: the three pillars of empire.'

Vidar looked at him steadily. 'Were you in Colfar's rebellion?'

Dash winked and threw the Norgan's words of the previous night back at him: 'Tell you that, I'd have to kill you.' They laughed, then he added, 'We lost. There's nothing more to say.'

'Aye,' the Norgan answered eventually. 'I just pray that one day there'll be a chance to strike back – a way that isn't just throwing my life away.'

'Don't we all?' Dash agreed.

13

The door swung open without warning, Dash flashed his hand to his dagger and spun round – to face a smug-looking Lord Gospodoi standing in the doorway.

The Bolgravian noble chuckled at the sight of bared steel. 'Physickers take peace oath, ney?'

Dash sheathed his weapon. 'Teshveld isn't safe, even for a healer.'

'Yuz, but maybe nowhere is safe for Physicker Cowley?' Gospodoi mused, allowing his cloak to fall open: he wore a twinned rapier and dagger, the gems on the hilts worth more than all of Teshveld, not that that was saying a lot. He ambled into the hut and studied the unconscious Perhan. 'How is patient?'

'He's alive, but I don't think there's much I can do,' Dash replied, wondering how good Gospodoi was with his sword. 'The infection's gone too deep.'

Gospodoi tutted, as if chiding a disappointing infant. 'I warned you,' he said, reaching out and grasping Zar by the hair. 'Maybe I make your daughter pay for your failings.'

'I can't do the impossible,' Dash replied, keeping his voice subservient despite his hammering heart. The Bolgrav soldiers were now pressed around the door, sensing the chance of violence. 'He was too far gone. You're not being fair.'

'Fair?' Gospodoi snorted, jerking on Zar's hair and making her squeal.

Then the Bolgrav laughed and let Zar go. 'Just joke, yuz? Is funny, seeing man sweat over nothing.' He put a hand on the back of Zar's neck and asked, 'So, you read Ferrean?'

Dash's heart thumped, but he kept his expression frozen. 'No one will harm my daughter.'

'Of course.' Gospodoi plucked the journal from the satchel under Perhan's head. 'You translate Ferrean words in this and all is well for you – and for little Zar-bird. Tell me about this "failed" expedition.'

Dash realised Gospodoi clearly suspected the cartomancer hadn't told him everything. *The empire doesn't like failure*, he thought.

So he took a deep breath, suppressed his worry about the threats to

Zar, accepted the journal and retreated to his desk. His mind wasn't on linguistics; he was trying to find a path he and Zar could walk that would allow them to get away unharmed.

'Zar,' he said firmly, 'no one's going to hurt you. Get up in the loft and clean up.'

'Yuz,' Gospodoi purred, 'put nice dress on.'

Zar shot up the ladder like a polecat, jerking the curtains shut after her. Dash heard her crawl to the chest against the back wall and open it. He pictured her tossing clothes about in silent fury.

Then he focused on Vidar Vidarsson. His presence here might just provide the tipping factor. *I can take one or two down, but not all these men – unless Vidarsson helps . . .*

They'd made only the beginnings of a connection, but they shared the same view on Bolgravs, at least. So he threw the ranger a grin and said, 'How's your head, my friend?' A plan began to form. He tapped the jug of rye. 'You had a little too much *moonfire* last night?'

In most of Norgania and Otravia, the slang for istariol was moonfire.

Vidar's eyes narrowed, then he stretched and stood. 'Can't ever get too much moonfire.'

'What is this moon fire?' Gospodoi enquired.

Dash handed him the jug. There was quite a bit of the rye left. 'This.'

Gospodoi sniffed it, then deliberately dropped the clay vessel on the stone floor, shattering it and spraying the precious drink among the rushes. 'I piss better drink than this,' he remarked.

You kragging arsehole.

'That's a waste,' Vidar muttered, his eyes glinting and the vein in his temple pulsing.

'I can get more moonfire,' Dash replied, discreetly tapping the diary, 'from an old flame.'

Message received?

He awaited some sign, but beyond that throbbing vein, Vidar's face was unreadable. *Tension, or dislike for his employers? Whatever, I'm pretty sure he's getting worked up.*

Deciding he needed more solid confirmation, Dash put one hand behind his back where Gospodoi couldn't see and traced a circle: Magnian finger-cant. *Are you with me?*

Vidar frowned.

Come on, man, are you in? Dash wondered. He thought they'd kind of made friends last night, even agreeing they'd both like to strike back against the oppressor. *But I doubt either of us thought that would mean here and now.*

Gospodoi went to the door and called in Bolgravian for his sergeant. *Are they suspecting something?* Dash worried as the sergeant came to the door and surveyed the small hut. Then he heard Zar moving above and glanced up.

'Girl is up there,' Gospodoi told the sergeant, this time speaking Magnian. 'If there is problem, we punish her.'

'Dad?' Zar called from behind the curtain.

'Make sure you're properly dressed,' Dash replied.

Tension settled like frost. Vidar went to the fireplace and warming his hands, said as if in afterthought, 'Tell me about this old flame, Physicker.'

He gets it. Dash stopped himself sighing with relief. 'Died of infection; there was nothing anyone could do. Then the damned nobles came in and took everything.'

'Too much you talk,' Gospodoi said. 'Stop now and read journal.'

Dash obediently began, 'I, *Lyam Perhan, Imperial Cartomancer, do attest –*'

'Ney, ney,' Gospodoi said impatiently, 'go to water readings, last entry. Tell me.'

Dash tapped a finger, thrice in quick succession, then twice, then once –

–and moved: his hand flew to the hidden dagger in the scabbard tacked to the underside of the desk, he drew it and thrust it into Gospodoi's kidneys, shouting, '*Now, Vidar!*'

Gospodoi convulsed in shock as the blade penetrated – but Vidar just stared, his mouth falling open, and Dash realised that the ranger hadn't understood any of his cryptic messages at all.

Shansa mor! 'Move!' he barked at the Norgan.

At the doorway, the big Bolgrav sergeant stood frozen, just as stunned – *no one* was *ever* stupid enough to attack a Bolgrav lord like this. But the two soldiers behind him were yelping and flailing for their weapons.

'*What the—?*' Vidar gasped.

'*Jou—*' Gospodoi grunted, reaching for his pistol, but his legs went and instead he staggered against the table.

The sergeant finally wrenched out his sword, but wavered, unsure whether to go for Dash or Vidar.

'*Kragga!*' Dash exclaimed, ripping his dagger sideways out of Gospodoi's belly, which sent blood spraying an arc across the room. The nobleman collapsed into the fireplace, sending ash and sparks spitting every-where. The flames quickly took hold of his clothing and as they blazed into life, he shrieked.

The Bolgrav sergeant made his decision: he raised his longsword and swung at Vidar – and the blade caught in the low rafters.

Vidar gaped at the blade, then at the sergeant, and now the pulse on his temple was really hammering.

Then he *snarled*.

Outside, the soldiers were shouting and waving their flintlocks around, but as they hadn't fired at anyone yet, Dash guessed they weren't loaded. But one had had the sense to ram a bayonet onto the muzzle and he burst through the doorway, lunging at the Norgan.

And still Vidar hadn't moved . . .

Then Dash suddenly realised this wasn't the paralysis of fear, but something deeper: Vidar's eyes blazed with amber light, then his spine twisted and he hunched forward, hands splaying as he vented a bestial roar. He battered the bayonet aside, then drove his fingers – no, there were *two-inch claws* bursting through his nails – into the man's throat and *ripped*.

Dash stared. *Kragga mor, he's a* bearskin!

The soldier collapsed in a haze of spraying blood as the second man appeared at the door with a loaded flintlock. He saw Vidar standing over his dying comrade and took aim – as the curtain in the loft jerked aside and Zar appeared, cradling a crossbow. With a sharp *thunk*, she discharged the weapon and the bolt slammed straight into the gun the soldier held, which jolted and roared flame. The lead ball pinged off the floor and lodged in the wall six inches from Dash's head, but he was already spinning and hurling his dagger, which buried itself in the man's left shoulder, sending the gasping Bolgrav staggering backwards.

With a furious roar, Vidar went at him, a six-foot leap that bore the soldier down. His teeth – now long, savage fangs – snapped closed in the man's neck. Vidar wrenched, the neck snapped and the soldier went still. But Vidar continued to rip at the flesh – then he turned his bloodied face back to the doorway . . .

In an instant, he'd launched himself back into the hut, straight at Dash –

–who leaped, pulled his old army falchion from the rafter where it hung and slammed the hilt into the bearskin's temple. Vidar folded, slumping stunned onto the bloody rushes. The pulse in his temple slowed and his claws and fangs began to retract.

In just ten seconds, the hut had become a charnel house.

Panting hard, Dash turned to the fireplace – and caught his breath in horror, for Gospodoi, who should at the very least have been unconscious, if not dead, was rising to his knees, his fingers tracing ancient runes that hung in the air, glowing, as he muttered, '*Skiamach! Animus!*

The stench of sulphur and smoke filled the room. The Bolgrav roared '*Impetu*–' as he punched his right fist towards Dash. The air *blurred*, then *rippled* – and blasted across the room –

–but Dash had already hurled himself aside. The ball of force still spun him round, but he kept his footing, and he still held his sword. He bounded forward and thrust it into Gospodoi's chest, sending him backwards into the fire again. The flames once again roared over

Gospodoi's charred silk clothing, but this time the Bolgrav had gone rigid.

Frightened the fire would engulf the whole hut, Dash lunged for the nearest liquid, which happened to be the piss-bucket. When he tipped it over the blazing Bolgrav lord, it sizzled and sent foul-smelling steam rising to the ceiling – but the fire went out.

Panting in relief, Dash wrenched out the sword, and just stood there, momentarily dazed by the chaos of the last few seconds.

But then Gospodoi sat up. His flesh was charred and his clothes were smouldering, but his eyes had turned the same bright blue as an azure light blooming from a necklace around his throat. He reached out blackened fingers and an unseen force gripped Dash around the throat, closing his windpipe and throttling him.

'*Skiamach, contundito!*' Gospodoi croaked, his face contorting with agonised rage. He tightened his grip, then twisted, trying to break Dash's neck.

'No,' Dash choked, dropping to one knee as his vision blurred.

'Father!' he dimly heard Zar shriek.

He almost lost the falchion as his limbs shuddered and the force binding his throat became unbearable, vaguely saw Gospodoi's hands swirl counter-clockwise and felt the unseen forces preparing to twist his head and rip it off. With what he knew would be his final burst of energy, he re-gripped the falchion and threw all his might into one movement, swinging the blade in an arc with all his remaining strength–

–and Gospodoi's head almost leaped from the neck, blood gushed and the torso crashed back into the fireplace, finally staying still.

All Dash saw was the blood, scarlet torrents sweeping across the world as the pressure on his throat finally took him down. Darkness roared in his mind as he toppled sideways.

Dash woke to find Zar cradling his head.

'Dad?' she said anxiously as he opened his eyes to find himself lying among the bloodstained rushes on the floor of his hut, his clothes soaking up spilt rye and urine.

'Ahhh—'

Vidar appeared over Zar's shoulder, peering at him with a mix of perplexity and anger. 'Gerda's Teats, what kind of blasted physicker faints at the sight of blood?'

'He . . . praxis . . . no air,' Dash panted. 'Blacked out.'

Vidar snorted, then grinned savagely. 'Well, that was fun. But you could've warned me.'

'I *did* warn you,' Dash croaked indignantly, then added, 'Well, I tried.'

'When?' Vidar demanded. 'Deo on High, Cowley, that man was a blasted praxis-mage – the whole kragging empire will come looking for him, and that means I'm a feckin' outlaw now – no, we *all* are. And to think I was going to retire on what he was contracted to pay me.'

'He wasn't going to pay you,' Dash replied. 'He was going to kill you.'

'How the feck d'you know that?'

Dash didn't reply; he'd just realised his daughter was in shock. He put his arms round her and pulled her close. Her eyes, round as saucers, were saying, *'Dear Gerda, I nearly killed a man.'* Practising with a wooden weapon was a world away from using a real one with intent.

He looked up at Vidar. 'I *tried* to tell you – I read Perhan's journal while you slept. There really was stuff he didn't tell Gospodoi – *big* stuff.'

Vidar stared. 'What the krag are you saying?'

'The "Moonfire"?' Dash said, 'the "old flame" – do you get it now?' He stroked Zar's back and kissed her forehead. 'Better now?'

Vidar was still looking puzzled. 'Nope. Don't get it.'

'I got it,' Zar sniffed. For a moment she brightened, then she caught a glimpse of the corpses again and went white.

'Got what?' Vidar demanded. 'This better be feckin' good, Cowley, 'cos we're surely going to hang for this when they catch us. I'd like to know why I'm dying an outlaw's death beside a man I don't even know.'

'Oh, it's good,' Dash replied, keeping his voice calm. *He's a bearskin: if he loses his temper again, he'll rip my head off.* 'Moonfire is slang for istariol and a "flame" is a nickname for a Ferrean. I was trying to tell you that this Ferrean cartomancer had found a lot of istariol he hadn't told Gospodoi about.'

Vidar stared. 'I thought you were telling me about some piss-headed girl you once shagged.'

Zar snorted.

'You, shut it,' Vidar told her. He fixed Dash with a glare. 'You, talk.'

Dash settled Zar in a chair, then picked up the journal. 'Your carto-mancer found istariol traces in a river in Verdessa, according to his personal diary. But he obviously didn't want Gospodoi to know, because he told Gospodoi his readings were negative and he wrote in Ferrean. The moment I confirmed Gospodoi's suspicions, he was going to kill all three of us.'

The Norgan started mouthing curses.

'I guess this means we're going to have to move again,' Zar grumbled.

'I'm sorry,' Dash told her, 'but I had no choice.'

'Then I'd better start packing – and just when I was starting to like it here,' she added sarcastically. She clambered up the loft-ladder, delib-erately avoiding looking at the bodies.

Dash turned to Vidar and, composing his words carefully, started, 'I'm sorry about your money, Vidar, but believe me, you weren't going to be collecting.' Then he fixed him with a confident smile. 'However, we can still come out of this rich beyond your brightest dreams.'

'My dreams can get pretty bright,' Vidar growled. 'Istariol, you say? That damned cartomancer found *istariol* and hid it from Gospodoi and me? That means that only he, you and I know . . .' He paused, taking that in.

'Exactly. But Perhan's beyond help now. I'm sorry if he was your friend.'

'Barely knew him, but he seemed a decent sort.' Vidar pulled a face then asked, 'So what about this istariol, then?'

'Well, I know where he found the traces: a lake at the foot of some mountain ranges. Does that sound familiar?'

'Aye – that's where the cartomancer hurt himself, right at the edge of the Iceheart. But the only thing he tested there were the waters at the mouth of a river running out of the Icelands.'

Dash thought about that. 'In that case, I reckon we need to follow that river to the source. There's a motherlode of istariol out there, Vidar Vidarsson. We can find it, mine it, sell it and make a fortune.'

'You're dreaming, Otravian,' Vidar growled. 'Verdessa is claimed by the empire and there's already a garrison there. Even if we got there undetected, how would we mine it? That takes men. And anyway, istariol is only valuable to a sorcerer and they all serve the empire.'

Dash whispered, '*Cognatus, animus,*' and felt the rush of energy as his familiar spirit sparked into life on his shoulder in emerald-hued Shadran parrot shape, invisible to anyone here but him. He traced a figure in the air: *Ignus*, the fire rune. Cognatus channelled energy and a tongue of fire formed on his fingertip, dancing prettily but not burning him.

'Not all sorcerers serve the empire,' he said, watching Vidar's reaction.

'I'm going to be a sorcerer, too,' Zar called, sitting on the top step of the loft-ladder.

Vidar stared from father to daughter, scepticism warring with greed. Greed won.

'Gerda's Fanny! You think we can actually do this?'

He said 'we', Dash noted. 'It's possible. Think, Vidar: we could be richer than kings.'

The bearskin looked skywards. 'You two are going to be the death of me, aren't you?'

Probably, Dash thought. *I've been the death of most everyone else.*

2

Who's with me?

You want to find bodies, follow the crows, Dash's father always used to say. The old man had fought the Urstian raiders twenty years ago, when Dash was a boy; he'd been a colonel when the Bolgravs tried and failed to conquer them the first time.

'They thought they could try us,' his father used to boast, 'but Otravia was ready.'

But we weren't ready when they came back, were we? Some of us even opened the kragging doors to them.

But that was of no moment now. What mattered was burying the bodies before the crows found them and brought other carrion-eaters. He and Vidar Vidarsson took the soldiers' standard-issue diggers and carved out a trench in the shade of the trees out the back, while Zar cooked a hearty breakfast from purloined rations.

It was hot work despite the cold and the two men quickly stripped to the waist. Vidar was thickset, a slab of muscle going to fat and scarred with a dozen old wounds, but whip-lean Dash had a few scars of his own.

'So,' Dash said, leaning on his shovel as he caught his breath, while the Norgan laboured on, 'who is Vidar Vidarsson?'

Vidar hesitated, then answered, 'I was a regular in the Norgania Royal Army – a scout – till I got into a stupid duel with a nob. Killed the fecker, then had to run. Ended up in Bolgravia, where they were re-tooling their army for conquest – I was there when Tempeskov came up with the idea of the rolling volley. Transformed warfare, he did. Turned the flintlock from a curiosity for scaring peasants to a decisive weapon.

I got officer rank – they used me to train the conscripts – but when they decided they were going to conquer the world, men like me got busted back to the ranks so that their gentry could get the glory.'

Dash spat on the churned turf. 'You fought for the *Bolgravs* during the conquests?'

'Nah, I left when it all kicked off. Never fired a feckin' shot on their behalf. Our unit came upon this village near Consadyne, in Magnia – it'd already been captured, but the Bolgravs lined up the survivors, men, women, children, even babes in arms, and speared every single one of them as an example to the rest of the old kingdom. So I settled some scores and got the hell out. Now there's a price on my head in half the empire.' He grimaced. 'It ain't much though, before you get any ideas.'

Not as much as my own bounty, I'd warrant, Dash mused. He nudged Vorei Gospodoi's body with his foot. The blackened headless corpse stank. 'Did he know who you are?'

Vidar gave a guttural laugh. 'Never used my real name in Bolgravia. He didn't know me from a turd and his argents were as good as anyone's. Or would've been – I was supposed to be paid when we got back to Falcombe.' He spat, then looked up. 'So what about you, Cowley? What's your story?'

'Short version: when the pro-Bolgravian faction seized power in Otravia, back in '30, four years ago, I took my daughter and got out.'

'You must've been pretty senior in the rebellion, being a sorcerer and all,' Vidar guessed.

Dash shook his head. 'No names is safer.'

'Fair enough. But why come *here*?'

He had a point: the Pelarian coast was as bleak a place as could be found on the mainland, a land of sleet in winter and creeping mould in summer.

'Feckin' miserable place to hide out,' Vidar added.

'I guess this is as close to the edge of the empire as you can get without leaving civilisation behind entirely. Out here, people don't talk to imperials, and they don't dob each other in.'

'So I'm guessing your head's worth more than mine – not that I'd cash you in, either.'

'Then let mutual silence be our bond,' Dash suggested drily.

'Aye, I'm all for that – and istariol. The price of the blood-dust never stops rising.'

'True, that.' Dash nonchalantly placed both hands back on the handle of his shovel, in case the next question caused offence, before asking, 'So you're a bearskin?'

Vidar's face hardened. 'Aye. Is that a problem?'

'It is with most folk – but I fought alongside one or two in Colfar's rebellion.'

'I got it mostly under control, if that's what you're wondering.'

Mostly . . . Dash gave the man a sympathetic look. Bearskins generally didn't live long. They were a dying breed, a legacy of the Mizra Wars, and those who were left were mostly to be found hiding on the fringes of society. Vidar looked to be in his forties, and that spoke of considerable self-discipline.

Although I still had to knock him out.

A bearskin was an asset though, by and large, and despite the confusion, Vidar had sided with him in the recent bloodbath. They weren't yet friends, but Dash felt they might become so. He slapped the shovel handle and said, 'Let's finish up here, then we can talk properly.'

They returned to work with grim energy, digging as deep as the root system permitted, then rolling the thoroughly looted corpses into the hole. Out of respect, they dug a separate grave for Lyam Perhan, the Ferrean cartomancer. He had likely been forced to serve; that was how the Bolgravs operated.

When he was patting down the cartomancer before burial, Dash made an important discovery: a tiny crystal vial of reddish water, barely as long as his little finger, pushed into the hem of his shirt. Behind Vidar's back, he held it up to the light and smiled, then pocketed it carefully.

When they had filled the graves, he said, 'Stand back.' With Vidar watching curiously, Dash muttered *'Cognatus, animus!'* and his familiar appeared to his sight, although not Vidar's. Cognatus, in his customary parrot-form, settled on Dash's shoulder, then plunged into him. Dash's vision changed, showing him an extra layer of life: the water seeping into the foliage, the insects and worms infesting the dirt and the sunlight pulsing through it all.

He traced *Terra*, the rune of earth, and said, *'Renovare, nunc.'*

The ground seethed with sudden energy: seeds burst into life and grass swelled up to cover the grave. Once he was satisfied, he concluded with, *'Abeo, Cognatus amico,'* dismissing the familiar, his magical guardian and partner.

The unseen parrot reformed on his shoulder and nuzzled his cheek as his sight returned to normal, then took flight, circling Vidar unseen and unheard before shooting into the trees. Dash had trained Cognatus to keep his distance, for one never knew who was watching: unless they took care, a sorcerer could sense another practitioner's familiar.

Vidar eyed the now-concealed graves uneasily. 'Ain't never been comfortable around sorcery,' he muttered. 'The Bolgrav military had plenty of enlisted sorcerers and damned scary buggers, they were.'

'I don't use it lightly,' Dash assured him.

Vidar ran his eye over the graves, which had all but disappeared; the next rainstorm – pretty well a daily event here – would render it invisible to even the most careful eye. 'Good work,' he conceded, offering his hand. 'If we're to be partners, best we shake on it.'

A partner . . . Aye, I'll definitely need one for this.

They clasped hands, then pulled their shirts back on before going through the loot: three flintlocks and a pistol, with plenty of powder and shot; the gemstones they'd prised from Gospodoi's rapier and dagger hilts; a few silver argents the noble had in his purse, and of course, Perhan's journal. Dash helped himself to the journal and gave Vidar the Bolgrav's purse. 'If you've been pressed into service you deserve it.'

Vidar gave him a grateful smile, then gestured at the guns. 'Two each?'

'Sure – you choose.'

'I prefer to get in close,' the bearskin growled, 'but I'll get a decent price for a couple of long-barrels.'

'I'd hang on to them – we'll need them if we're going to try for the istariol.'

'Fair enough.' Vidar picked up the flintlock pistol and tossed it to Dash. 'I s'pose a nob like you thinks a gun's a coward's weapon?'

Dash sighted at a nearby tree. 'I got over the whole "glory of war" thing years ago. All that matters on a battlefield is surviving.' He spun the pistol by the trigger-guard and thrust it into his belt. 'I'll take this and a musket. Haven't had a gun since I left western Pelaria.'

They were sharing out the gemstones when Zar, clad in a boy's travelling clothes, appeared with breakfast. 'If we're moving on, we may as well have a decent meal first,' she said.

'Don't s'pose you've got a second keg of that rye stashed away?' Vidar asked hopefully.

'Nope.'

'Then may Gospodoi burn for ever in the Pit.'

They wolfed down the food, washing it down with river water. There was no rain for a change, but the wind was surly and intrusive. There were good reasons why few people dwelt on this forbidding coast, and the climate wasn't the least of them.

When they were done, Vidar thrust his bowl at Zar. 'You go and wash this – your father and I need to talk.'

'I'm not a serving girl,' she flashed back.

'My daughter and I share domestic duties,' Dash told Vidar.

The Norgan frowned, then grunted, 'Huh. Otravians.'

'There's nowhere else where women are treated as fairly,' Zar declared, 'and–'

'Zarelda,' Dash interrupted, 'this is not the time to be playing "my country is better than your country". No one ever wins. Vidar's going to be with us for a while, so let's be civil.'

'Only civilised people can be civil.'

'*Zar!*' Dash turned to Vidar. 'Sorry. She's in a bad mood because we're going to have to move again. The last few years have been one long journey for us.'

'And wars,' Zar added tersely, then she *tsked* and said, 'Sorry, Dad's right.'

Vidar chuckled. 'I'm sure you'd be much happier at home in a castle with a dozen pretty dresses to your name,' he said, and when Zar began to flare up again, he barked out a laugh. 'Just teasing you, girl.'

'You and I are going to be deadly enemies,' Zar told the Norgan, but her eyes were twinkling. 'Well, unless you do everything I tell you, starting with serving me hand and foot.'

'Suspect it'd be easier to just be your enemy,' Vidar snorted.

'Let's stay on topic,' Dash interrupted. 'We really do have plans to make.'

'Fine,' Zar chirped, 'but does this primitive even know what istariol is?'

'Is she always this mouthy?' Vidar sniggered. 'Of course I know about the blood-dust.' Then he hesitated and added grudgingly, 'O' course, I don't know how much of what I know is true. But I do know that you need it for powerful sorcery; that it's worth more'n gold, and that you have to mine it. And it's rare.'

'That about sums it up,' Dash replied. 'If we can find even a small amount, the journey will be worth it. But Perhan's journal suggested a *lot* of istariol – a motherlode – and that could be worth a king's ransom. By the Pit, it could be a *country's* ransom!'

'Then it'd be too much to carry,' Vidar noted.

'True, but you won't make your fortune on just a sack-load,' Dash told him. 'And the Bolgravian Empire takes a *very* close interest in istariol. We start selling it, we need to do so from a position of strength or some bastard will just take it off us and put our heads on a block.'

'Then we just tap it occasionally,' Vidar suggested. 'Just enough to tide us over.'

'While tramping in and out of the wilderness?' Dash shook his head.

'No, that won't work either. From the moment we start selling, we're going to be marked. Istariol isn't a game you go into halfway. You're either all in, or not in at all.'

Vidar scowled and spat. 'Gerda's Tits, is it worth it?'

'Oh yes, for sure. If there's enough of it, we can buy ourselves a kingdom. But we can't do this alone. We'll need people. I've got a friend or two I can call on, but we'll need lots of bodies to make it work.'

Vidar looked troubled. 'We can't just noise it round that we've found istariol. Someone will go straight to the governor in Sommaport and we'll soon be hunted down.'

Dash had been thinking about this very thing himself. 'I'm not so sure,' he replied now. 'Teshveld is a frontier, of sorts: the edge of the world. This region is full of refugees, people who've lost everything. I reckon we can pull together enough folk to run a mine, and defend it too. There isn't a man out here – or a woman, from what I've seen – who can't handle a weapon, and none of them love the empire.'

Vidar looked sceptical. 'I thought you'd only just got here and were laying low? How d'you know anyone?'

'There's only one other local with healing skills and she's a church physicker, so I get to hear everyone's stories,' Dash assured him. 'Believe me, if we can convince folk that the venture is real and has a decent chance of success, they won't blab. We'll need to slip away on the quiet, and once we've got the stuff, sell outside the empire – to the Zarros Archipelago in Shadra, for example – they're still holding out. Play it right and we'll be sunning ourselves there inside two years.'

Vidar pursed his lips and gave a low whistle. 'Sun and sand and lithe, dark-skinned women? I'm in.'

'But what about home?' Zar asked. 'What about *Mum*?'

Dash gave her a warning look. 'While the Mandarykes rule, we have no home.'

'But—'

'Don't,' Dash warned, and his daughter fell silent. 'Istariol can change a lot of things. From Shadra, we'll be able to reconnect with the resistance movement in Otravia for a start.'

'What's this?' Vidar asked. 'If we're to be partners, I need to know what you're planning.'

Dash frowned at Zar, then explained, 'My wife divorced me on the eve of the Mandaryke coup – they're the traitors who seized control of Otravia, then sold us out to the Bolgravs. She's now married to one of them.' He was a little surprised at how much this admission still hurt him. 'She did it to protect her family, but mine went to the gallows. I took Zar and ran.'

Vidar took that in, then asked, 'Did Gospodoi recognise you, Cowley?'

'Cowley's not my real name – but I think he might have been starting to guess.'

'Fair enough. I won't ask more.'

'I'll tell you one day – I'll tell the world, when the time's right.'

'That's fine,' Vidar said, 'but let's be clear: I'm not going to be a martyr to your cause. I'm in this for the money and I can't imagine anyone else we recruit will feel differently. We band together and get rich, then we part and the rest of your quest for redemption is up to you. Understood?'

'Understood.' Dash kept his face stony as Vidar studied him.

Finally the Norgan sighed. 'All right, so what's next?'

'Next? We send out some messages, then we go to Gravis Tavernier's tap-house and buy some drinks.'

If Dash peered closely into the darkest corners of the tavern's rafters, he could see the glint of rat-eyes; he could certainly smell their droppings. The cockroaches were just about as big, and the wine was spit-worthy. But Gravis did brew the best beer for miles and he did decent business – or he would have, if any of his customers had been worthy of the credit he extended. The place was seldom full or boisterous, for half his clientele were fugitives from the empire with no desire to make an exhibition of themselves. Even so, it was by far the best tavern in the district.

Tonight, after Gravis had passed the word to certain people about Dash's desire to hold a meeting, it was packed. Dash lifted a hand in greeting to the publican as he entered, Vidar Vidarsson and Zarelda close behind.

His daughter looked round a little shyly; she'd never been allowed in Gravis' tavern before.

Dash scanned the room, picking out faces; a healer quickly got to know who was who in any community, even one as loosely knit and secretive as this one. There were all sorts here, from villagers to small-holders, mercenaries to hunters – and they'd pretty much all come to escape the empire. Most people here would rather slit a Bolgrav's throat than breathe the same air.

He'd already identified the opinion leaders: Sir Elgus Rhamp was a Pelarian knight and half the room would do whatever he did. Elgus, a barrel-chested, shaggy, thickset man with a ponytailed beard, had his usual coterie of his men around him, all drinking hard. Involving Rhamp was unavoidable, but he'd inevitably want to run the show – and take the lion's share. *I'll need to put him in his place and keep him there* . . .

The other person of importance round here was the local Deist priestess, Mater Varahana. In Magnia, taking vows was considered unmanly, so only women were entrusted – or condemned, in Dash's view – to intermediating with Deo. But Varahana was an old friend of his, something they'd kept very quiet.

He spotted the priestess, an angular, elegant woman wearing her hood up, sitting with the other healer in the region. In truth, Kemara Solus was the only *real* healer, as Dash had never been much more than a field surgeon.

Dash leaned over the bar and said, 'Gravis, beers all round, and three goblets of your best claret.' He slapped down half a dozen argents – most of his remaining coin – and as he'd expected, the clink of metal drew many eyes. 'And lemon ale for Zar.'

'Right you are.' He leaned in and murmured, 'Here, that Bolgrav lord – Gos-whateverthefeck – he ain't been back for his stuff. He staying at yours?'

Dash feigned surprise. 'He left three days ago – for Falcombe, he said. I guess he didn't value what he left behind.'

'Weren't much, to be sure. Just travelling gear and trinkets.' Gravis had clearly rifled through it all. 'Reckon I can sell it?' he asked hopefully.

Dash was no longer paying attention; instead, he was scanning the room again, looking around to ensure that certain people *weren't* here: specifically, Larch Hawkstone, the governor's warden, or any of his Borderers. He'd heard they were currently at the southern end of the district. 'I trust nobody we didn't invite is here?' he asked.

'Only folk here are those as don' like the empire, like ye asked,' Gravis told him.

'Good. Give me five minutes, then introduce me.' Dash thrust an ale at Vidar, scooped up the red wine and walked to the table where Varahana and Kemara were sitting. 'Mater Varahana, Mistress Kemara,' he greeted them, handing each a goblet. Keeping the third for himself, he added, 'Please – they're on me.'

Mater Varahana arched a perfectly curved eyebrow. 'Blessings of Gerda be upon thee,' she said formally, then she winked. 'I do like a good red,' she added, with a sideways glance at the redheaded Kemara that had Dash snorting into his wine. Then he did choke as Varahana dropped her hood, revealing a completely shaved scalp.

'Gerda's . . . uh . . .'

'Dash, darling, didn't you know that every six years all good priestesses shave their heads, to show our love of Gerda and our rejection of all earthly vanity?' Her eyes were twinkling as she chided him. She turned so her face was in profile and asked, 'What do you think?'

He stared, trying to see past the loss of the abundant auburn tresses he'd known during the wars. Her scalp was as pale as a newborn's, but her delicate features were accentuated and after a moment, he admitted, 'Actually, it suits you.'

'I know,' she purred. 'I take it you've met Novate Kemara?'

'I have,' Dash replied, turning to the lay sister. He'd always thought it iniquitous that male healers could operate independently, but a woman had no choice but to take vows. 'Mistress,' he said, dipping his head.

'Master Cowley,' Kemara Solus replied coolly. 'I hope whatever you've summoned us here to hear is more credible than your alleged healing skills?'

Kemara was a hard-faced green-eyed no-nonsense Ferrean in her late twenties. Her pugnacious face was framed by her scarlet ringlets. She had clearly been scarred by her past, but Dash approved of her no-nonsense air. His path had often crossed hers since he'd come to Teshveld – she'd quickly spotted his lack of formal training, but she'd been grateful for anyone who could lessen her burden, so they'd come to a cautious understanding.

'We all have to make a living,' Dash replied evenly, while Varahana snickered. 'I know my limitations. And yes, I do have a proposition, for everyone here: the chance of a new life.' He turned to the priestess and dropped his voice. 'I need your support, Vara – you're a known scholar and your help will be crucial.'

'You know I can't lie, dear.'

'You won't need to. I just wanted to warn you that I'll shortly be looking for your honest reaction to something I need to show people. Everyone here knows you're an educated woman.'

'Once a scholar, always a scholar,' Varahana agreed sadly. She'd been trained in Magnia's finest university before being forced into the priesthood.

'What's this all about?' Kemara demanded. 'If you're recruiting for another rebellion—'

'I'm not,' Dash interrupted. 'Those days are over. The empire won.'

They shared a bitter look – they agreed on the subject of Bolgravia, at least. 'The people of Teshveld came here to escape the fighting, and its aftermath,' Kemara said. 'No one wants to be dragged back into all that. We've all lost too much.'

'As have I,' Dash told her. 'I lost everything – except my daughter.' He glanced back at Zarelda, leaning nervously against the bar: a skinny teenage girl, a brittle mix of bravado and self-consciousness. The local lads were watching her with interest.

'She's growing up,' Varahana commented. 'She was such a little tearaway in Colfar's camp, wasn't she. Does she think before opening her mouth these days?'

'Sometimes – unless she loses her temper.'

'Like her father?' Kemara enquired.

'Me? No, I never lose my temper – I always know exactly where it is.' He touched his goblet to Varahana's and said, 'I'd better get this show underway.'

Halfway to the bar, he was intercepted by a smooth-faced man with lush black curls and bedroom eyes. 'Boss,' Jesco Duretto drawled, embracing him. 'Good to see you. I couldn't believe it when that messenger bird found me. Had to sharpen my blades again.'

'I doubt they ever got much of a chance to get blunt,' Dash replied, looking his old comrade over. Jesco was one of the few who'd got away from the messy end of Colfar's rebellion, but he looked much the same: the prancing duellist, always living in the now. But he was still the best swordsman and the best shot Dash knew. 'I worried the bird wouldn't be able to find you.'

'You can always find me, Dash,' Jesco said. 'Where's young Zarelda?' He peered about and spied her at the bar, wincing at her lemonade. 'My, hasn't she grown? When I was her age–'

'I don't want to know,' Dash interrupted. 'You're in the borders now, Jesco: rein it in or you'll have the whole room trying to rope you up.'

'Ropes, how exciting. So what's the gig, Dash?'

'It's about wealth beyond imagining – oh, and screwing over the empire to boot.'

Jesco patted his sword-hilt. 'You don't need to go on – count me in.'

Dash clapped his shoulder, then waved Vidar over. He introduced them, the silken swordsman and the hulking bearskin, before

34

continuing to the bar, nodding at a narrow-faced woman who threw him a wink: Tami, another face from his past. Then he took a swig of wine to wet his tongue before murmuring to Gravis, 'Let's do this.'

The innkeeper hammered on the bar, bringing the babble of conversation to a loose quiet. 'Folks, can I have your attention? You mostly know Dash Cowley, our physicker. He asked me to spread word of an opportunity for us all. Fill your cups – on Dash – then drink to his health and listen up.'

There was a low, attentive murmur of appreciation – a free drink was a free drink – and once all had been served, Dash stood on a bench and pitched his voice to the back wall. 'Folks, believe it or not, I didn't come to this place for the weather or the high life. I just wanted a bit of peace. I think most of you are here for similar reasons. Am I right?'

There was a cautious murmur of agreement, which would do for now. He pulled out the cartomancer's journal and brandished it. 'But sometimes, opportunities knock on your door anyway, and that's why I'm here now – with a proposal for all of you. It's a one-time *secret* proposition, so if anyone here can't swear to keep what I say next to themselves, please leave. I'll not judge – I just don't want you here.'

No one left, though he knew that didn't mean he could trust their silence. But he hoped he could trust their greed.

'I recently came into possession of this diary,' he went on. 'I'd even go so far as to call it a treasure map. You'll have heard rumours of the new lands the empire's opened up to the northwest, the place they're calling Verdessa?'

His listeners chorused agreement, sounding curious but still sceptical.

'The Bolgravs sent in a cartomancer to determine the potential wealth of those new lands.' He waved the journal. 'He didn't make it back alive, but his journal did.'

Gravis, putting two and two together, shot him a look, but the rest leaned forward, now fully engaged. 'How'd you get it?' someone called.

'The cartomancer gave it to me,' Dash replied. 'He didn't want the Bolgravs to know what he'd found, so he pretended his mission was a failure – but he told me the truth. I guess he must've liked my face.'

'It's a nice face,' Jesco couldn't resist throwing in. 'Honest, kind of.' It got a laugh, but everyone was clearly envisaging far bloodier ways by which it might have been obtained.

'How do we know it's genuine?' Sir Elgus Rhamp asked.

'How? We show a scholar, of course.' Dash jumped down and deposited the journal in front of Varahana. 'You all know Mater Varahana. She's not just a priestess, but a former Nyostian scholar. She can verify my claims.'

While Kemara eyed him with mute suspicion, Varahana opened the journal curiously and swiftly leafed through.

'Is it genuine?' Dash asked loudly.

'It carries the imperial seals. It looks genuine,' Varahana conceded.

'And what about this?' he asked, presenting her with the vial of reddish fluid he'd found on Lyam Perhan's body.

Varahana's eyes narrowed, then widened. She opened the vial, sniffed, then tasted the water. '*Istariol*,' she whispered.

The whole room went utterly silent.

Everyone leaned in towards the mater, straining to hear.

'How pure is that sample?' Dash asked.

'It's a high concentration – but one could create this with a pinch of istariol and some river water.'

'But I didn't – it came with the journal. May I guide you to the entry on the thirty-seventh page? I've marked it.'

Varahana leafed through and read. '*Truly? By the Lady Herself* . . . In *Verdessa?*'

'In northern Verdessa, taken from a river flowing out of the Iceheart. A no-man's land.'

'The Bolgravs claim Verdessa,' Elgus Rhamp put in gruffly.

'They have no right to,' Jesco retorted.

'Aye,' Dash agreed, 'but we'll obviously need to work around them.'

The look of naked greed was now present on almost every face save Varahana's; she just looked troubled.

Elgus Rhamp shouldered his way forward, visibly excited. 'You're saying there's istariol out there – and the empire *doesn't know*?'

'That's what I'm saying,' Dash replied. 'The most valuable substance in the world, just waiting for us to retrieve it. But you all know that the empire claims istariol as its own. If we have the vision – *and the courage* – to go after it, we will have to do so in *utter* secrecy. We mine it, then we get out, slip it in small quantities onto the black market and get rich. But I can't do it on my own: mining istariol is a large-scale undertaking. That's why I invited you all here. Let's find it for ourselves, not just blaze a trail for the Bolgravs to follow.'

That struck a real chord and in an instant, the taproom was buzzing with questions: how do they get to the istariol lode? How would they extract it? How would they get it back without the Bolgravian Empire smashing their operation?

Dash did his best, but he could tell there was still plenty of scepticism. Trust wasn't easily won in a place like this, but at least they were genuinely interested.

Or mostly interested. 'This sounds like horseshit to me,' Elgus Rhamp's eldest son, Osvard, called out in a loud, belligerent voice. He was the sort who thrived on conflict and dissent.

'What would Dash have to gain by lying?' Jesco asked loudly, eyeballing the young Pelarian mercenary coolly. Osvard sneered, but no one else appeared to have an answer. Everyone knew how much exiled Otravians hated the empire. Mutual greed did the rest: they *wanted* to believe, so that overcame any misgivings.

Dash threw a hopeful look at Vidar Vidarsson, who bared his teeth in a lupine grin.

It's really happening . . .

'What about when the empire finds out?' someone called.

'If they ever do – well, we'll have already gone,' Dash replied.

'So how do we sell it then?' another man asked.

'I'm sure one or two of you might know someone,' Dash answered wryly, knowing half the men here probably had black-market connections. 'Listen, I know this is no small matter: I estimate that we'll need fifty or sixty men to mine this vein, and they'll need their families for support. It'll take us months just to find the istariol, let alone dig out enough to satisfy us all, then get back to civilisation and sell it. You'll be uprooting your lives for at least a year, and it probably means you'll never be coming back here. But there are *fortunes* to be made. No one who embarks on this will ever know poverty again. Some of you will be able to return to your homelands and get your real lives back. If you've ever prayed for a better life, this is that chance.'

He looked around the room and finally asked the question. '*Who's with me?*'

Everyone fell silent, looking at each other.

Then Elgus Rhamp stuck his hand up and declared, 'I'm in, me and my folk. We've got enough muscle to get this done.'

That immediately brought half the crowd around – then Mater Varahana rose, silencing the room. 'Did not Deo place treasures in the earth for us all?' she said, her lilting, educated cadences a sharp contrast to Elgus Rhamp's rough accent. 'Did he not say unto his people, "Go forth, reap the harvest and pluck the fruits of my hand, for these things are for all men." *All* men, mark you, not just Bolgravs.' She pointed to Dash. 'I was a military chaplain and I know this man and I will vouch for him. I give my blessing to this enterprise.'

Her personal blessing might not mean that Mother Church as an entity was onside, but her approval won over the rest of the taproom.

Dash raised a hand in thanks. 'In token of your trust, I will reveal something that is not known to many. You know me as Dash Cowley, but my *real* name is Raythe Dashryn Vyre. Some of you might have heard of me.'

The low murmur that greeted this admission told him they did indeed know of Raythe Vyre, who'd been one of Colfar's commanders in the bloodiest insurrection against the Bolgravian conquest. *Raythe Vyre* was a name synonymous with rebellion and resistance to the Bolgravian empire.

'So whadda we call ye, then?' someone asked.

'I'll be "Dash Cowley" in front of the governor and his men, but otherwise, you can call me Raythe. So now you know my darkest secret,' he drawled, 'and just in case anyone's wondering whether it's easier to let the governor know about me and my crazy plan, well, let me just point out that a few argents for snitching won't bring you much, and it risks a knife in the back from someone who *really* wants to do this.'

Sir Elgus Rhamp hammered the nearest table. 'There ain't no one like that here,' he shouted, glaring about him as if his will could make it so. 'What's life for, if it ain't for chances like this?'

With that, his men shouted their approval, banging on tables, hooting and whistling, and the last objections were swept away amidst the resultant back-pounding and cheering.

Jesco was whooping along with the best of them, while Vidar was taking it more calmly, quietly supping on his ale and surveying the riotous drinkers. And Zarelda was also staring around the room, probably remembering similar scenes when Dash had recruited for Colfar . . .

And those folk who hearkened to me then are mostly dead . . .

An hour later, in the upper room of the tavern, it was as Raythe Vyre that he convened the first meeting of those he considered his captains. Sir Elgus Rhamp probably didn't see it that way, but that was just tough. The others were Jesco Duretto, Vidar Vidarsson, Mater Varahana, Kemara Solus, Gravis Tavernier – and at Rhamp's insistence, three of his people: his woman, Tami, and his eldest sons Osvard and Banno. Zar sat quietly in the corner, almost overlooked, but she was listening attentively.

Keep our connection secret, he signed to Tami, before clearing his throat to begin – but before he could start, Kemara stood.

39

'Get that pig out of here,' she snarled, jabbing a finger at Osvard Rhamp.

'What's the problem?' Raythe asked, as the belligerent-looking Osvard faced the healer, then he remembered: a month ago, she had broken Osvard's nose in the taproom after he'd groped her. The young thug had come to him to get his nose straightened. He'd not done a perfect job, but at least Osvard could breathe through it.

'Peace,' Sir Elgus growled. 'He's learned his lesson, Healer.'

'He's apologised – and we gave money in reparation,' the younger son, Banno, added. In contrast to his elder brother, he was a fresh-faced, earnest lad. 'It's all bygones.'

'Really?' Kemara sneered.

Osvard didn't look like he thought anything was bygone, but he lowered his head under his father's fierce gaze. 'I was drunk an' I got my dues,' he said sullenly, touching his crooked nose.

'It's all fine,' Tami put in, her hand on Rhamp's arm. 'Ossi will do what he's told.'

So that's the way of it, Raythe thought, keeping his face straight. *Tami's made her own bed – quite literally. But I guess she needed protection from somewhere after the rebellion failed.*

Noticeably, she hadn't come to him for that protection and for a moment, he missed her fiercely, though it'd been two years since they'd been lovers.

'Healer,' he said, turning to Kemara, 'are you content?'

'No, but I'll put up with him,' she replied.

'Forgiveness is divine,' Mater Varahana remarked. 'Need I remind you that *Novate* Kemara has taken her vows as a lay sister – which means she enjoys the *full* protection of the Church.'

'Noted,' Sir Elgus growled. 'Can we move on?'

'Excellent,' Raythe said, turning back to Varahana. 'What about you, Mater? I know you've given your blessing, but will you accompany us?'

'Well, Mother Church sent me here to shepherd my flock and here they are, about to gambol off the map. I must consider whether it's my duty to follow, or to continue my mission here.'

'Stay or go, there's also the matter of what you tell your superiors,' he reminded her.

'Aye, that's also my duty.' Varahana made a show of thinking deeply, then said, 'Let's not beat around the bush. I was banished from academia and my studies because I was outspoken about the Bolgravian Empire and its annexation of the Church. *Deo* is God, not any emperor sitting a throne in Reka-Dovoi. My heart and mind speak clearly on this. I will accompany your expedition and I won't betray it.' She swirled the remaining wine in her goblet, musing, 'Besides, it's when wealth and danger are present that men most need their god.'

'Indeed,' Sir Elgus put in, 'then, more than ever. I too know this from experience.' He looked suspiciously from the shaven-headed priestess to Raythe, and asked, 'I must ask: what is your history together, Dashr–ah, Raythe?'

No point trying to keep this quiet, Raythe thought. *They'll work it out soon enough.* 'Varahana, my friend Jesco and I all served in Colfar's rebellion. We all got out, as you see, and kept in touch since.'

'Colfar was a brave fool.'

'I don't disagree, but let's not speak ill of the dead.' Raythe lifted the journal. 'In any case, we've got more important things to discuss. If we're going to do this, we'll need to move fast. Most of the folk invited were selected because they're itinerants, hunters and trappers. They don't set down roots and they know how to move fast and effectively. So I reckon we should be able to vanish pretty quickly, but even so, the authorities are going to notice when some fifty families go missing, which means even if they don't know why we've gone, they won't like it. We'll certainly be hunted.'

'My men travel light too,' Elgus declared.

'But I've got my still and brewery,' Gravis pointed out. 'I can't just drop all that. I'm a brewer, not a miner.'

Elgus slapped him on the back. 'Don't worry, Tavernier: we'll not be going anywhere without you: your beer don't go, we don't go.'

'This won't be a jolly camping trip,' Raythe warned them. 'We're going to disappear off the face of the world. The cartomancer found the istariol traces in a river flowing out of the Iceheart, which means we'll have to subsist entirely on our own for a year or more. We're going to need wagons, horses, oxen, water-carriers and grain wagons, spare cloth and blankets, weapons, you name it – not to mention healers, smiths, craftsmen, bowyers, ropers, wheelwrights – all the key skills a village needs to survive and prosper.'

'How are we going to excavate the istariol once we find it?' Osvard demanded. 'We can't dig through solid rock and ice.'

Raythe went to answer, but Mater Varahana waved him to silence and her voice crisp and clear, an Academia lecturer to her core, she explained, 'The fact that such high istariol quantities are leeching into the river says that it's near the surface, possibly in natural caves. One of the properties of istariol is that its presence lends itself to geothermal activity that keeps the ground unusually warm.'

'What does that mean, practically?' Vidar asked.

'It means that where there is istariol, the region is warmer, wetter and more fertile,' Varahana replied. 'Explorers have found patches of lush, temperate land even hundreds of miles into the Iceheart, and that's due to the presence of istariol.'

Banno Rhamp gave a low whistle. 'So you're saying we'll follow a river through the Iceheart and come to a warm place in the middle of the ice? That'd be a sight to see.'

'There may even be rock islands floating hundreds of feet above the ground,' Varahana told them. 'Under certain conditions, istariol is lighter than air – in the old days, before the empire dug up all the istariol on this continent, floating rocks were commonplace. Some were as large as a hundred feet across.'

'Imagine,' Zar breathed.

Banno Rhamp looked at Zar as if seeing her for the first time and smiled.

Raythe pursed his lips when his daughter smiled shyly back, but right now he had more pressing concerns. 'So I've roughed out a plan of sorts. We'll spend two weeks getting ready to move, so the day after Hawkstone and his Borderers finish their monthly patrol at this end of the province, we'll vanish. We'll take the old coast road north.'

'The Ghost Road,' Banno murmured. 'Sounds appropriate.'

The Ghost Road was one of the lost and unlamented Magnian Empire's unfinished projects, before the Bolgravian Empire dominated the western continent; it amounted to miles of hard-pack winding north through the forest. No one knew quite where it ended, but there was no doubt it would provide them with the swiftest and least-suspected path out of Teshveld.

'We shall vanish like wraiths,' Raythe quipped.

'Or end up just as dead,' Kemara grumbled.

'Are you in or out?' Tami asked her bluntly.

'Oh, I'm in,' Kemara told her. 'I'm just not going to blindly accept everything I'm told.'

'That's up to you, of course, but my hand on it: I'll deal honestly with you all,' Raythe told them. He rose to his feet and facing Sir Elgus, said, 'And just so we're clear on this point: this is my initiative and I'm in charge.'

The knight stood to face him. 'I'm bringing five dozen trained warriors to this venture – that's pretty much the only muscle you've got. I acknowledge that it's your idea, but I should be an equal partner.'

Their eyes locked.

Sorcery required time and energy, words and gestures. In any fight, the vital seconds needed to conjure were the seconds in which sorcerers died: battlefields were for guns, not magic, unless you were well-protected and had plenty of warning. But not all sorcery was battlefield magic and Raythe had had Cognatus hovering unseen in the rafters above from the moment he convened the meeting. He made a gesture and the familiar dropped onto his shoulder, which opened up just enough of the Sight for him to see into the knight's soul.

He saw a man haunted by failure, pushed to the edge of the world by the ghosts of men he'd led to defeat against Bolgravia, battles lost and precious lives gone, trampled into the mud. He was a blusterer, present-ing an iron mask to the world, but cowering behind it.

Raythe's voice took on the cadence of *imperium*: control, 'I think we know that to lead this group will require knowledge as well as muscle. I know what we seek and how to use it. I'm a praxis-sorcerer and a noble of Otravia. I'm born to lead, and you should believe me when I tell you I have the wherewithal to do so. This is *my* expedition. We'll all share the spoils equally – and I mean equally, right down to the small-est family or lone trapper – but we leaders will make the decisions, and the deciding voice when we're not unanimous will be mine.'

He saw Elgus seek inside himself for defiance, but in the face of Ray-the's declaration, that resistance collapsed unvoiced.

'Aye,' the knight mumbled, 'it's your idea. We'll work with you.'

'Thank you,' Raythe said gravely. He glanced round the room, meas-uring reactions. Osvard and Banno Rhamp were looking puzzled at their father's unexpected capitulation, while the rest were visibly relieved that the moment of tension had passed . . . except for Kemara. Only another sorcerer would have been able to spot such a subtle use of sorcery, but she was watching him with a strange expression: he was sure she'd glimpsed something of Cognatus' presence.

Perhaps she's a latent talent? he wondered. If she was, that could be a boon. He made a mental note to speak to her when the opportunity presented itself.

But for now, he had what he wanted. 'So, we're agreed,' he said. 'We have two weeks to pack up our lives – and if anyone breathes a word to Hawkstone and his Borderers, you'd better believe me when I say the Pit will be too good for them.'

3

Hawkstone

Eighty-seven, eighty-eight, eighty-nine . . .

Kemara Solus tugged the hairbrush through her long scarlet ring-lets, wondering if she was doing the right thing in joining this mad expedition. In the distance, the half a dozen women of this tiny Gerda Convent chanted hymns; as a lay sister, she had only to take part in Matins and Vespers, the morning and evening prayers. And thankfully, she didn't have to shave her skull like the priestesses.

I thought this convent would hide me a while longer . . . But no, whether she liked it or not, the road was calling again.

'Dash Cowley', now apparently known as Raythe Vyre, clearly wasn't to be trusted, despite Mater Varahana's obvious affection for him. Otravian exiles wanted only one thing: to restart the rebellion, and Vyre was one of those who played the pipes and led the dance to hope-less war. And his eyes were unnerving: she didn't want those sorcerer's eyes pinned on her.

He's the last person I should be anywhere near . . .

But his mad plan did offer her hope. Only money could buy secur-ity, and istariol, the magical powder that fuelled big magic, was worth more than gold. If she let this opportunity pass, there'd never be another.

So while the hymns died away and the old sanctuary fell asleep, she packed up her herbs, readying herself for the road. 'Istariol,' she whispered, testing the word on her tongue. 'Blood-dust. Gerda's Tears. Moonfire.'

'Aye,' said a soft voice from the door. 'It's a dangerous quest, I fear.'

Mater Varahana had a soft tread.

'Mater, I didn't hear you,' Kemara said, as her superior entered and sat.

'You have lovely hair,' Varahana complimented, examining herself in the mirror. 'You know, I think I'll keep shaving mine. My hair was never more than a messy nuisance and this look accentuates all my best features.'

'I don't think it's supposed to be a fashion choice, Mater.'

'*Everything* is a fashion choice, darling.'

That was such an un-holy woman thing to say that Kemara blurted, 'Whyever did you take vows?'

'It wasn't my choice,' Varahana replied. 'My family didn't want a woman as the head, especially not a Nyostian scholar with *Liberali* views, so when my elder brother died they forced me into the Church so that my younger brother could take over as *paterfamilias*.'

'Not uncommon, sadly,' Kemara said, with grim sympathy.

'Oh, it got worse: I dared criticise the Church's accommodation with the Bolgravian emperor and was banished to here,' Varahana said, with brittle cheer. 'I had a library – now I have just one book, full of "divine truth". I'm a pig in mud, darling. But what about you? Will you take full vows yourself?'

Kemara snorted. 'I'm only a novate to get my healer's licence. And I like my hair.'

'As do I.' Varahana lifted one of Kemara's scarlet tresses and sighed. 'How are your preparations going?'

True to her word, Varahana hadn't told her superiors in Falcombe of Raythe's mission, or her convent's imminent departure – for the past few days, the nuns had been busy preparing to take the Ghost Road and vanish.

'I'm ready,' Kemara reported. 'The garden has been harvested, the roots, seeds and leaves are drying. The cart is oiled and ready and my mule is already eating like a horse.'

'But you don't trust Raythe, clearly?'

'I . . . well, he's a praxis-sorcerer.'

'And therefore blessed by Deo, according to the Dictate of Elymas,' Varahana chuckled.

'I don't believe in that.'

'That a sorcerer's gifts come from Deo? A dictate from the Arch-mater has the status of scripture, you know.' But Varahana's tone of voice suggested that they were on the same page, and it wasn't the one Archmater Elymas had written.

'I've met sorcerers before,' Kemara replied. 'They're some of the least godly people I've ever met.'

'Nonetheless, this is not ours to question,' Varahana noted with gentle sarcasm. 'In any case, Raythe was one of the better commanders during the rebellion. I trust him with my life.'

She spoke with such affection that Kemara wondered if the priestess was in love with Vyre. 'I had heard of him before now,' she admitted, 'but people spoke of him as a servant of evil.'

'Only his enemies,' Varahana said sharply. 'He led his division well, united men of at least seven nations into a fighting force and got us through some truly awful situations. I was his chaplain. His men loved him.'

'Well, I'm immune to his charm, but I'll take your word on the matter, Mater.'

'Scepticism can be healthy too,' Varahana observed. 'There's too little of it in this Church, even though we were all given brains as well as knees. But I'll leave you in peace now.' She made the sign of blessing over Kemara's head and left as silently as she'd arrived.

When she was gone, Kemara pulled up her right sleeve and studied the Rod and Crescent tattoo of a trainee sorceress, etched in faded ink on the underside of her forearm. For an instant, the roar of flames and the screams of someone she'd loved filled her ears. She whispered prayers until the suppressed hatred faded away, leaving her panting and sweaty.

I shouldn't join this expedition, she thought, worried. *It's going to drag back into the light all that should remain in shadow.* But to walk away now would be to invite other questions.

And where could I go? We're already on the edge of the map.

The two weeks flew by in a feverish rush. Teshveld was not so much a community, more a motley collection of hunters, trappers, fishermen, smallholders and refugees, all of them taciturn and wary of each other, but so far, no one had broken ranks and gone to the governor in Sommaport, at least as far as Raythe could tell. The imperial patrols came through on a regular and well-known cycle, which made secrecy easier.

Most of the forty or so individuals who had been at the tavern and agreed to the journey had families. Some knew others who hadn't been there, but would be interested, and they had to be approached and cautiously sounded out, then sworn to secrecy. Raythe worried, but as the days passed, he began to think their secret might hold. They grew to sixty families, plus many more single men, mostly hunters and trappers, as well as the mercenaries in Rhamp's service. In just a few days' time almost three hundred souls would be taking the Ghost Road.

But one cold afternoon, Larch Hawkstone, the captain of the Governor's Borderers – the thugs who passed as law enforcers in remote Teshveld – cantered into the yard outside his hut. He had a dozen men at his back armed with sabres and a few flintlocks. The air went still; even the birds in the woods fell silent.

Raythe was sawing timber, shirt off and sweat running down his back. His old wagon was spread out around him in pieces as he repaired the axle-mounts. There was no hiding what he was doing, so he straightened, mind racing. *Why's Hawkstone here? He should be down in Sothlyn this week, squeezing the crofters for tax they can't pay.*

'Master Cowley,' the Borderer captain called, his suspicious eyes resting on Zar, who was shelling peas on the porch. 'What're you up to?'

Raythe put the saw aside and faced him, flexing his aching hands. 'Repairs, Captain,' he answered, assessing the riders. The Borderers had a bad reputation at the best of times and their demeanour today suggested that they were anticipating trouble. There surely would be if Hawkstone found the looted Bolgravian flintlocks inside.

'Has someone taken ill?' Raythe asked, hoping against hope for a simple explanation.

Hawkstone, a burly man with leathery skin and a thick beard, leaned forward in the saddle. 'More like taken leave of their senses,' he drawled. 'I was speaking with Orban Croft and he says there's folks here are packing up on account of Dash Cowley, but he dinnae know why. An' now here's you, fixing up your wagon.'

Orban Croft, that nosy prick . . .

The question was, had someone dropped the word 'istariol' in Larch Hawkstone's ear, or the name 'Raythe Vyre'? Croft hadn't been at the meeting, though – what had he been told? And by whom?

'First I've heard of it,' Raythe replied genially, hiding his alarm. His sword and pistol were inside and his limbs ached from the effort required to get his wagon fit for travel again, even though he was used to hard work. 'This old thing's been crying out for attention all summer.'

'Skinny runt, ain't he?' one of Hawkstone's men snickered.

Piper, isn't it? Raythe thought. Yes, he was lean, but he was muscular, and there were plenty of scars earned in battle, including one left by the lead ball they'd cut out of him after Colfar's last stand. He didn't think Hawkstone's men could boast much in the way of honourable wounds; they just chewed on the fat of the land. But thirteen against two – and one of those a teenaged girl – were the sort of odds Hawkstone's men liked.

'I expect Orban Croft got things garbled, as usual,' he remarked. 'I'm here for the long haul.'

Hawkstone studied him dubiously, then asked, 'Do you know the name "Gospodoi"?'

'Of course. He was the Bolgrav lord whose party called on me a few weeks back. One of them was sick, but I patched him up.' Raythe stopped for a moment as if thinking, then added, 'I'm pretty sure they were heading east when they left.'

Hawkstone screwed up his face in puzzlement. 'Governor Veterkoi just received a letter from his counterpart in Falcombe, asking why Lord Gospodoi hasn't returned.'

'I have no idea – that was the direction he was heading. But the roads aren't exactly safe between here and Falcombe.' *And how would the governor even know he was coming?* he wondered.

Hawkstone answered his unvoiced question. 'Lord Gospodoi sent a bird ahead, to ensure his lodgings were ready.' He stroked his beard as he added, 'We'll just have a look round, shall we? Make sure there's none of the lord's belongings lying around here.'

Zar shot him a fearful look, which didn't go unnoticed.

'The girl worried about something?' Piper sneered. 'Hey, Twig-legs, what's your problem?'

'I've got no problems,' Zar shot back rashly, 'but yours are obvious.'

'Don't give me mouth, girl,' Piper snarled, swinging from the saddle and advancing on her. 'Your girl needs a good slapping, Cowley – I'll do it myself.'

Raythe stepped in front of Piper. He came up to the man's chest. 'Hawkstone,' he called, 'call off your dog.'

Piper bunched a fist and Raythe fixed the Borderer with a baleful stare. 'Don't.'

The thug wasn't at all fazed. 'Or what, little man?'

'Sure you want to find out?'

'Feck off!' the Borderer snarled, splaying his fingers and shoving at Raythe's chest—

—except that Raythe wasn't there: he'd stepped away and twisted to one side, letting the man's hand flash harmlessly past him – but he'd simultaneously brought up his knee and now he slammed it straight into Piper's crotch, even as he grabbed the Borderer's arm and hauled it round. As Piper gasped explosively and jack-knifed, Raythe flipped him onto his back and slammed a foot down onto his throat. Convulsing and turning purple, Piper tried in vain to inhale.

Half a dozen blades were already out and three men were unslinging their flintlocks and priming them – as the front door of the hut opened, revealing Jesco Duretto, cradling his own flintlock, the hammer cocked, with a big smile on his face. A moment later Vidar Vidarsson appeared from behind the hut, hefting a huge woodsman's axe with a deep, throaty growl.

'Bet that hurt,' Jesco snickered at Piper. 'You'll be singing falsetto for a week, I'll wager.' He levelled the gun at the nearest Borderer. 'But at least he's alive, eh?'

The Borderer froze.

'Hold!' Hawkstone barked and his men had enough discipline – or maybe a sense of their own mortality – to stop where they were. Jesco's gun was just one against three, but Vidar's growl sucked the air from their lungs and they froze like deer before a wolf, primordial fear overriding natural belligerence.

'There's no need for this, Captain,' Raythe said calmly. 'Your Bolgravs aren't here. Try the Falcombe Road.'

Jesco switched his aim to Hawkstone himself. The Borderers, faces strained, counted the odds: they might be in their favour, but if it did kick off, some of them would definitely die.

For a moment, pride warred with fear on Hawkstone's face, then he spat, 'You've overstepped, Cowley. The governor grants us the right to go where we want.'

'And does he give you the right to bully children, or is that just for your own amusement?'

Piper made a growling noise and Raythe pressed his foot down on his windpipe again. 'I've nothing to hide, Hawkstone – but you don't *ever* unleash this pig on my daughter.'

'She needs to show respect,' Hawkstone muttered.

'The pig didn't earn any,' Zar sniffed.

'*Zar*,' Raythe warned, before adding, 'She's right, though.'

Hawkstone's eyes narrowed, but he made a gesture and his men reluctantly lowered their guns and sheathed their blades – not that it made Raythe feel much better, for swords could be redrawn in seconds. But Jesco's gun and Vidar himself were a clear and present threat too, so he took his foot from Piper's throat and picked up his axe from the woodpile.

Piper rolled over, dry-retching and gasping for breath. When he got his breath back, he glared murderously up at Raythe, his hands twitching towards violence.

'Is it really worth dying over?' Raythe asked quietly, smacking the axe haft into the palm of his left hand.

Glowering, Piper lurched dazedly to his feet. 'You shouldn't–' he started, but his voice came out in a breathless, rasping squeak and he shut up.

Raythe turned back to Hawkstone. 'Shall we start this conversation again, Captain?'

Hawkstone considered his options. Legally, he could do whatever he damned well liked; usually anyone who stood up to him was dragged off to the cells in Sommaport after an educational beating – but those were mostly villagers with no martial training, not an exiled Otravian who was clearly more than a healer. He scowled, ordered Piper to remount, then faced Raythe again.

'You're out of line, Cowley,' he rasped. 'All of you are.'

'I saw a man menacing a young girl,' Jesco broke in. 'I think it's your rabble who are out of line.'

Hawkstone grunted, then hauled on his reins and turned his horse. 'We'll be back,' he promised, before raising his hand and cantering away, his men at his heels.

Raythe didn't react, other than to mutter, 'Zar, what have I told you about provoking those pigs?'

'I think you said, "Don't provoke the pigs",' she drawled.

Jesco ruffled her hair. 'She's like you a few years back, Raythe,' he chuckled. 'Mouthy.'

'Please Deo, not,' Raythe muttered, watching the Borderers riding away. He noted they were now strung out and slowing down, not speeding up as they receded . . .

'Stay alert,' he warned. 'Zarelda, get inside.'

'But Da—'

'*Get inside!*' Raythe snapped as the riders suddenly hollered, wheeled their horses and came streaming back down the track, blades flashing in the dull light as they cleared scabbards.

Battle-honed reflexes instantly took over: Jesco aimed and pulled the trigger, the hammer fell, igniting the powder in the pan, and it boomed, gouting flame and flooding the air with black smoke. An instant later one of the Borderer gunmen flung up his arms and went over the back of his mount. His gun discharged harmlessly into the air, making the horses screech and recoil.

The remaining two gunmen immediately fired back, but under cover of the smoke of Jesco's shot, Raythe had already ghosted to one side. One ball struck the wall and the other flew through the open door of the cabin, making Zar shout in alarm.

Jesco drew his sword. Vidar, growling like a wolf, hunched over, baring his teeth.

We've got about eight seconds before they're on us, Raythe calculated.

He dropped to one knee, shouting, '*Cognatus; animus!*'

His inner senses roared, the inside of his skull flashed with light and he felt Cognatus plunge into him. His familiar filled his senses, peering through his eyes and engaging with his mind. Potential crackled around him, but he was still vulnerable to blade or ball.

The Borderer gunners peeled away to reload, but the rest barrelled onwards, brandishing curved sabres.

'*Praesemino!*' Raythe shouted, *prepare*, and as Cognatus poured energy through him, the air temperature palpably dropped.

But the enemy were closing in . . .

Jesco stepped in front of him, as he always did – and to his surprise, Vidar did the same, even as the human mask he kept over his bearskin nature slipped and his features contorted.

'I *always* have to do this,' Jesco complained, as the riders bore down on them, 'but good to have company. Welcome to the team, Vidar – just think of yourself as Raythe's shield.'

Vidar hefted the axe and roared as his mouth filled up with very sharp teeth.

'That's the spirit,' Jesco said chattily. 'Though it's a pretty thankless task, I should warn you.'

A moment later the attackers were on them, the horses rearing up while the riders hacked downwards. 'Here we go,' Jesco cried, parrying a blow, then thrusting his blade into his foe's side. The man shrieked, jerking on his reins and sending his horse off-track. Vidar, bellowing in fury as another horse reared over him, steel-shod hooves flailing, slammed his axe into the beast's throat and it went down, crushing the rider beneath; there was a sharply cut-off howl.

Zar shouted something from the doorway and loosed her crossbow, but the bolt flew wide and she yowled in frustration.

Finally, Raythe and Cognatus were ready. '*Paratus!*' he shouted, as he traced *Caeli*, the rune of air: '*Impetus potentia nunc!*' A burst of force slammed from his palm and hit the knot of riders like a herd of run-away bulls, sending beasts and men flying; limbs snapped and heads thudded on the ground with a sickening crack.

'It's rewarding, though,' Jesco went on, talking to the heedless Vidar as if they were sharing a tankard at Gravis' tavern. 'I love it when he does that.'

Vidar roared and the horse coming at him suddenly shot sideways, clipped another and went down, dragging its rider with it. Now, with only half a dozen still mounted, Hawkstone was revealed, lining up his pistol.

'*Habere scutum!*' Raythe cried, and this time Cognatus sent rippling, translucent energy outwards to form a glass-like shield. Hawkstone's gun barked, but the ball hit the transparent wall, lost all impetus and dropped to the turf to lie harmlessly among his broken men and beasts.

'Yee-ha!' Jesco crowed as he charged into the chaos, hacking down anyone who was trying to get to their feet. Then Vidar leaped – a gigantic bound of fully ten paces – and bore another man to the ground. When the bearskin ripped out his throat with a single swipe of a massive claw, the few remaining mounted Borderers broke and went galloping away with Hawkstone at their head. Those on the ground still able to move clambered slowly and painfully to their feet and limped off, leaving seven dead, one man with a broken leg, and four horses who would never walk again.

Raythe groaned as he saw the damage, momentarily hating his powers. 'Abeo, *Cognatus, amico*,' he muttered, and the link to his familiar spirit dissipated, leaving him feeling like he'd taken a punch to the throat. The invisible parrot reformed and settled on his shoulder, cawing excitedly at the carnage.

Jesco, noticing Vidar about to chase after the Borderer captain, grabbed the bearskin's axe-haft and shouted, 'Vidar, *Vidar* – they've gone – that's enough!'

The berserk ranger's eyes were blazing amber and his bestial face contorted . . . but he seemed to hear Jesco through the red haze and he dropped to his knees, panting and staring down at his bloodied hands, and then at the dead and broken lying around them.

They say a true bearskin hates what he is, Raythe remembered.

It didn't appear to bother Jesco, though. 'There, Shaggy, we're all done,' the Shadran chirped. 'Better now?'

The Norgan ranger gave him a haunted look, then shuddered.

Jesco patted his head cheerily. 'Don't try telling me it wasn't fun,' he remarked, walking over to the Borderer with the broken leg. 'What do we do with this poor chap?'

The terrified man was holding one knee and sucking in agonised breaths as he stared at his lower leg hanging at an unnatural angle. His other leg was far worse, though, with the calf-bone jutting through the flesh and blood pumping out in a gushes.

He died before their undecided eyes.

Holy Gerda, Raythe thought, *we haven't even left and the killing's begun.*

Jesco shrugged. 'Problem solved.' He turned to Raythe. 'How long before more come back, Boss?'

'At the rate they were running, they'll reach Sommaport by nightfall, so it's conceivable the good captain will be back by midday tomorrow,' Raythe said with a sigh. 'He'll probably have a squad of fifty backing him up – that's too many for us to deal with. On the other hand, my wagon's all but ready; I only need to bolt it back together. I say we just go – everyone's more or less ready anyway. Let's bring our departure forward a day. We'll move to Gravis' tavern and send the word around.'

'Good. I'm sick of this dump,' Jesco declared. Clapping Vidar's shoulder, he said, 'Well fought, brother.'

Vidar rose shakily. 'Aye, and you. You called me back – I'm in your debt.'

'You killed a man who wanted to kill me: I'm in yours.' Jesco grinned. 'Evens, then.' He walked over to a broken-legged horse and pulled out his blade, ready to put the beast out of its misery, when he stopped and asked, 'Raythe, can you heal these poor brutes?'

Raythe frowned. 'Not instantly, no.'

'Shame we don't have that sort of time,' Jesco remarked, and plunged his sword through its chest. He dealt with the rest of the injured horses, then pointed to the one remaining, which had bolted a few dozen yards but was now watching warily. It was unharmed. 'That one's mine.'

Surveying the battleground, Vidar asked, 'I thought you needed istariol for sorcery?'

'Only for the big stuff,' Raythe told him. 'Little spells like this, I can power myself.'

'*Little*,' Vidar echoed, his eyes widening. 'No wonder the Bolgravian sorcerers ripped our armies apart.'

They all set to work and an hour later, the wagon was loaded and Jesco, settling himself on his new mount, was needling Vidar about the fur cloak he wore. 'Was it your father? Or your mama?'

Raythe left them to it and walked over to his shaky-looking daughter. Putting an arm round her shoulder, he said quietly, 'You all right, Zar?'

'I hate this place,' she said, her nose wrinkling at the stench of blood. 'I'm glad we're going.'

Her bereft voice belied her words.

We haven't lived in the same place longer than a year since we started running, Raythe thought. *She really needs stability.*

'Unless we do this, nowhere will ever be safe and there'll never be a hope of anything better,' he told her. 'Sometimes you have to leave to find the way home.'

'I know. It's just . . .' She bit her trembling lip, then blurted, 'I miss Mum.'

She'd always adored Mirella. She'd been twelve when they'd escaped the Mandaryke coup. Now she was nearly sixteen.

'We'll get her back,' Raythe promised her. 'I swear we will.'

Three days later, Larch Hawkstone nudged his mount into motion and the sixty Borderers at his back followed him in a heavy thud of hooves, flowing down the slope towards the clearing where Dash Cowley – *or whatever his real name is* – lived. Eight dead men and four dead horses lay scattered about the yard, stripped of weapons and left to the elements and the wild dogs. There were a dozen of those, snarling at the newcomers; they only scattered when he fired his pistol over their heads. Birds rose from the trees, squawking indignantly, but no one appeared from the hut.

'As I thought,' he grumbled. 'The bastard's legged it.'

The governor, unnerved by the news that Cowley was a sorcerer, had dithered for a day, and another full day had passed while he'd authorised the release of men and a pair of praxis-sorcerers, summoned from the nearby Bolgravian port of Gollostrad.

Hawkstone wasn't overly troubled by Cowley's absence – in truth, he'd not been overly anxious to face the sorcerer again – but what did alarm him was that most of Teshveld appeared to have vanished as well.

We've seen no one in the last five miles – every farmhouse and hovel we've passed has been deserted, he worried. *What's going on?*

This was serious: by his count some forty or fifty families were missing, and that meant lost tax revenue for the governor: it meant no provisions for winter, fodder for men and beasts, or tavern girls to make this Deo-forsaken place halfway bearable.

Even my daughter has vanished . . . That thought rankled, even though the girl was a burden on Hawkstone's purse. Though he'd never have admitted it, the few times her mother had allowed him to hold her, to be a father to her, were like balm on his chafed soul. That he might never see her again was a hideous thought.

I don't mind never seeing Cowley again, but I want my girl back . . . And I want to know where everyone is.

Sweat formed on his brow as he reined in before the hut. The door was hanging open and the wagon was gone.

Governor Veterkoi's going to blame me for this, I just know it.

'The feckers 'ave feckin' run off,' Piper wheezed through his bruised windpipe. 'All've 'em.'

'Obviously,' Hawkstone growled. 'Search this place – rip it apart. I want to know where they've gone.'

While his men dismounted, he turned to the praxis-sorcerers the governor had assigned him: surly blond-haired Bolgravian brothers just out of the academy. 'Can you find them, Lords?' he asked, hating having to be deferential to the foreign conquerors.

The young men glanced at him. 'Yuz,' they chorused in low, accented tones, before going back to their own discussion and pointedly ignoring him.

Fuming, Hawkstone directed his men, but the search was brief and fruitless. Cowley was gone, but who knew where? Morosely, he went from corpse to corpse. These were men he'd led: yes, for the most part they'd been mindless thugs, but he was accountable for them.

Veterkoi's going to have my warrant for this.

Just then, hooves thudded and he turned to see a lone horseman coming down the slope towards them at a gentle trot. The rider wasn't a big man and he was unarmoured, but even confronted with sixty heavily armed men, he appeared utterly indifferent, and that gave Hawkstone pause.

'Halt,' he called, glancing at the Bolgravian sorcerers, who were muttering and tracing finger-patterns on the air. His Borderers grasped hilts and unstrapped weapons, but the rider didn't react, just continued his slow advance.

'I said, halt!' Hawkstone warned.

This time, the rider reined in and raised his right hand, displaying an iron medallion.

He wasn't close enough yet for Hawkstone to make out the two-headed eagle of Bolgravia engraved on the metal but he had no doubt that's what he would see.

'Which one of you is Capitan Hawk Stone?' the stranger asked, his voice wooden.

He was both ordinary and strange: not high Bolgrav, but one of the lesser tribes of that vast land, with dark hair and a pale, sunburnt face. He was clean-shaven, with big watery grey eyes and an oddly guileless expression, as if he didn't appreciate the danger he was in.

'It's Hawkstone – I'm he,' Hawkstone said. 'Who are you?'

The rider looked him over unhurriedly, as if considering whether he was worthy of that information. 'My name is Toran Zorne,' he said at last, in well-enunciated Magnian. 'I am an Under-Komizar of the Ramkiseri.'

The Bolgrav secret service—

Hawkstone saw the two sorcerers exchanging a worried look, then they touched their right fists to their hearts, and that was alarming because usually sorcerers deferred to no one, not even the governor. But of course, Ramkiseri agents were also sorcerers – and they were infamous.

This Toran Zorne is probably four times the magician my Bolgravian twins are.

'How ... uh ... how may we serve?' Hawkstone croaked, noticing that his men had already found other things to look at.

Zorne gazed about him, his expression as flat as his voice. 'I am seeking a man named Jesco Duretto, a Shadran mercenary. He was under surveillance in Falcombe until recently, when he disappeared. Have you seen him?'

Hawkstone didn't know the name, but there'd been a Shadran here a few days ago, an oily, olive-skinned killer with a smarmy tongue. 'I may know him,' he said carefully.

'There is no "may": you know him, or you do not. Which is it?'

Hawkstone swallowed his impatience; you didn't lose your temper around a Ramkiseri agent. 'There was a Shadran here a few days ago, but I never learned his name.'

'It is your business to police this land,' Zorne replied, in that strange, disconnected manner he had. 'Why did you not identify him?'

Because he had a flintlock trained on me . . . 'I'm sorry, Komizar –'

'*Under*-Komizar. Why was he here?'

'Uh, he was with a man called Cowley – Dash Cowley, who lives here with his daughter, a skinny girl, about fifteen.' The Bolgravian gave no indication of knowing the name. 'There was a Norgan as well.'

'Describe these people.'

'Cowley's a physicker, dark hair, lean build, nose like a rudder on a riverboat. His daughter's called Zar – she's a skinny reed. The Norgan was a big bastard, over six foot tall – oh, and he was a bearskin, by Gerda.'

'Dash Cowley.' The Ramkiseri agent pondered, then said, 'That is not his name, but I believe these are the people I seek. Where are they now?'

'Gone.'

The Ramkiseri agent looked at him like he was a stupid child. 'Gone where?'

'We don't know.'

Under the man's expressionless gaze Hawkstone found himself blurting out the whole sorry story, concluding, '—now it looks like the whole damned district's gone missing. Could be as many as three hundred folk.'

'And you let three men face down you and your men?'

Hawkstone swallowed. 'You weren't there.'

The Ramkiseri man heard that in stony silence, then, somewhat surprisingly, said, 'You did right to withdraw. They would have killed you otherwise, because they are more *competent* than you.' He looked around the circle of hard-faced men, then focusing on the two Bolgravian sorcerers, fired a string of curt, atonal phrases in their native tongue at them.

Turning back to Hawkstone, he asked, 'Why did you confront this man in the first place?'

Hawkstone flushed, unused to being questioned like this by anyone but the governor, and never in front of his men. There would be heads cracked if anyone thought this meant a lessening of his authority. But that was for later.

'A Bolgravian lord named Gospodoi was reported missing and it is known that he visited Cowley.'

'I know of Lord Gospodoi.' Zorne frowned. 'What business would he have with Cowley?'

'Someone in his party was ill, according to the innkeeper. Cowley is a physicker.'

'He's not a healer. He's a dissident and a rebel. Where is this tavern owner?'

'Gone, with the rest.'

The Ramkiseri agent's face flickered with mild annoyance, the most expression he'd hitherto shown in the conversation. He dismounted, reverted to Bolgravian and conversed with the young sorcerers. After a minute he turned back to Hawkstone and said, 'Take your soldiers one hundred yards down the road and out of sight, Captain. Then return here with one of your men. On foot.'

Hawkstone noticed his men watching beadily, to see if he'd take the order. He ached to refuse, but keeping his anger hidden, he said curtly, 'You heard the Komizar—'

'*Under*-Komizar,' Zorne interrupted.

'*Under*-Komizar . . . Come on, you lot, shift your arses.'

He herded his men up the road and over the rise. The first person to say anything about taking orders from that fish-faced Ramkiseri prick was going to get a fist in the ear, but he hoped they knew better. Foreign lords came and went, but he was still their captain.

Piper threw a look over his shoulder, then snarled, 'Hope that bastard strings Cowley up by the balls.'

'He will,' Hawkstone growled. 'Those Ramkiseri agents are trained trackers and master torturers. Cowley's got a world of hurt coming. So, I've got to go back and help out the Under-Komizar. You lot wait here and don't do anything stupid.' He scanned the faces and picked the one he'd miss the least. 'Piper, with me.'

Piper gave him a nervous look. 'Er . . . what d'you want me down there for?'

'Because that Under-kragging-Komizar wants someone with me, and I want my best man.'

Piper wasn't even close to being his best man, but he was too stupid to know that.

Hawkstone put Simolon in charge, then led the way back down.

'Damned praxis gives me the shits,' the burly trooper whined, dragging his heels.

'Both of us,' Hawkstone muttered. 'Keep your mouth shut and do whatever Zorne says.'

Whatever that is. He licked his suddenly dry lips. *Nothing'll happen. We're all on the same side here . . .*

They re-joined the three Bolgravians in front of Cowley's abandoned hut, nerves jangling even more when they saw that the two young sorcerers had carved a triangle within a circle in the dirt. Hawkstone felt sweat bead on his forehead, but Piper was visibly trembling.

'Ah,' Zorne said as they approached, 'come. You, Captain, stand here.' He indicated a spot outside the shapes carved in the dirt. 'And you, your name?'

'Uh, Piper . . . Piper.'

'Then come, Piper-Piper,' Zorne said, his wooden voice stripping the misunderstanding of mockery. Some other quality had crept into his voice though, because Piper obeyed unhesitatingly, and Hawkstone almost followed. The two blond brothers took up positions on the points of the triangle, leaving the third one free.

Zorne walked Piper into the middle of the triangle within the circle.

Hawkstone had a horrible sense of foreboding. He went to speak, but found he couldn't.

'Stand here, yes, just here,' Zorne said, looking up at Piper's rough, battered face with his bland eyes. 'We are going to find Lord Gospodoi, but I fear that if he came here, then he is dead. The man you call Cowley, he is not a good man. I am commanded to find him. I have never failed. Never.'

'Uh . . . good–' Piper began.

'Silence. You will listen. We are all capable of a higher purpose: this I am taught and I believe it. Mine is to find and eliminate wrongdoers. Yours is to shed blood for your lord, yes.'

'Yes,' Piper repeated blankly.

'Yes, we are agreed. But Lord Gospodoi is missing and I must find him. Will you shed blood, Piper-Piper?'

Don't, something screamed in Hawkstone's mind, but his throat – and his whole body – had gone rigid. The two young blond Bolgrav sorcerers leaned in, chanting under their breath.

Zorne's eyes flashed pale blue, like a beam of sunlight through ice.

'Uh, yes . . .' Piper mumbled.

'Excellent.'

Zorne's gaze didn't move – but his right hand slammed up under Piper's jaw, his hand folding under as a punch-dagger emerged from a concealed forearm sheath and impaled the Borderer through the bottom of the mouth and into the brain from below. He was dead before he hit the ground.

Shansa mor . . .

If Hawkstone could have run, he would have, but his feet were rooted to the spot. He could only watch as Zorne laid Piper on his back and calmly slit his throat. Blood pumped from the gash and ran into the furrows in the ground until a wet scarlet circle and triangle were fully formed.

The chanting of the sorcerer twins rose as Zorne took his place at the third corner of the triangle and added his own voice to the ritual. Hawkstone knew little of the praxis, but he'd heard of spells requiring blood or even a life. Minutes passed while he trembled on the edge of flight, terrified that he'd be next and petrified that the only way to stay alive was to not draw attention to himself.

Though it was mid-afternoon, the air around them darkened, the light becoming hazy and dim and shadows forming, though there was nothing to cast them. Piper's body visibly withered as he emptied of blood, becoming a dried husk, parched skin stretched over bones, eye sockets empty and teeth bared to the sky.

Then the ground shuddered and a path of sunlight formed, running straight towards a copse behind the hut.

'Ah,' Zorne said, with satisfaction, lowering his arms.

The two young sorcerers reeled, sagging to their knees and breathing hard as Zorne stepped from his position and came to Hawkstone's side. 'Blood price will be paid for your man,' he droned. 'Regrettably, necromancy requires a death, and only such magic can find the dead.'

'So you knew . . . Gospodoi was dead?' Hawkstone stammered.

'I suspected.'

Only suspected – so Piper would've died for nothing if he was wrong. Holy Deo —

64

'What now?' he managed.

'We will see what we have found,' Zorne said, and led the way to a pristine-looking clearing. He spoke a praxis-spell while tracing a dark pattern that hung in the air – and the ground suddenly churned as if pierced by a giant plough, sending dirt and leaves swirling up to clog eyes and noses.

Then the sickening stench of rotting flesh struck them; even Hawkstone, used to such things, found himself retching, but by the time he'd recovered, the spell had done its work and the dust and debris had flowed fully aside, revealing a tangle of bodies: Lord Gospodoi and his party, still clothed. Feeding beetles swarmed over them. The head of the Bolgravian lord's corpse was lying beside his body in the pit.

'See, Captain – your man Cowley? He is not a good man at all,' Zorne said. 'I will bring him to justice – and you will help me.' Turning to the Bolgrav twins, he said, 'Find their trail,' and the two young sorcerers began to trace new furrows in the dirt.

For a horrible second, Hawkstone feared that this next spell would require his death, but Zorne said, 'Captain, you now serve me. Bring your men. We have work to do.'

Looking into his emotionless, implacable face, Hawkstone was struck by the notion that the man had been born without a soul.

'Did you feel that?' Kemara Solus blurted, then she flushed.

Interesting. Raythe looked at her. 'Aye. I'm surprised you did, though.'

They were standing at the lip of a rise, looking at a dirt trail winding into the northern forests. Below them spread the Teshveld Valley, a patchwork expanse of fields hemmed into the coastline by rugged, forested peaks. The sea was a distant glimmer of grey-green beneath a sullen sky. The trail, the beginning of the Ghost Road, wove into the trees in a general northwestern direction; the caravan of wagons and mounted men and women was following it into the valley below. Kemara's small overloaded cart, drawn by her recalcitrant mule, waited beside Raythe's, with Jesco, Vidar and Zar loitering nearby. They were at the rear for a very specific reason.

Kemara looked like she wished she'd kept her mouth shut. 'Before I entered the Novitiate, I studied in a Nyostian Academia,' she admitted.

Ah . . . Now her bitter manner felt explicable. 'You're a failed sorceress?' Raythe exclaimed, immediately wincing at his thoughtless words.

'Feck you very much for the reminder,' she snarled, glowering. 'Yes, that's why I'm just a lowly backwater midwife and healer and not some preening hollyhock with a free pass from Deo to do whatever I fecking like.'

'I'm sorry. Sometimes my tongue works before my brain.' He thought of Zar and smiled. 'It's a family trait, you'll have noticed.'

'And is sorcery?'

'Not usually.'

While sorcery did very occasionally run in families, it was more likely to crop up randomly. The talent for sorcery came from personality and drive, not blood: it required a certain type of mind, one which could reconcile a kind of crazed conviction that one could alter reality with the analytical discipline and imagination to make it happen.

In many ways I'd prefer Zar not to have this 'gift', he admitted to himself, *but of course I'd be proud if she did.*

'I take it they cauterised your gift when you failed the tests?' he asked.

'Aye. I have no regrets, mind – the whole thing gave me the shits.'

He wondered at that. For one thing, Cognatus was fascinated by Kemara. The invisible familiar, in cat form today, was slinking around her, sniffing. Non-sorcerers were usually of no interest to him.

Perhaps they botched her cauterisation?

But before he could enquire further, Jesco sauntered up, cradling his flintlock, his hair immaculate as ever. 'What's happening?' he purred. 'Anything exciting?'

'Someone just used the praxis,' Raythe replied. 'Possibly at my old hut.'

Zarelda edged closer. 'What did they do?' she asked.

'It's impossible to say, but the governor has a pair of Academia graduates – twin brothers called Jorl and Karil,' Raythe answered. 'They might have been trying to find us. What I just sensed was High Praxis, something big and involved. I think it's safe to assume that they've realised that most of Teshveld has vanished and they probably want to know where to.'

'Are they going to chase us?' Jesco purred. 'Won't that be fun.'

'I hope not,' Raythe said, pretty certain they would but hoping to reassure Zar. 'Stand back everyone. I've got work to do.'

Jesco ushered Zar, Vidar and Kemara to a safe distance, allowing Raythe the space to focus.

The caravan of seventy wagons, one third of which contained their stores, had left the imperial roadway leading into the east a mile back. There'd been little sign of their passage on the well-travelled, hard-packed surface, but here on the little-used Ghost Road their passing was clear. He'd asked some of the hunters to ensure that there was no tell-tale debris left behind, but the land itself marked their direction. That had to change.

He marked out a sign on the turf – *Terra*, for earth – then, calling Cognatus to him, began his spell. The white cat became the parrot, which flew into his chest and they became one being. His vision blurred, then sharpened into beautiful intensity.

He ran through the words and symbols he needed.

Cognatus was energy and he was the channel: their bond made magic real.

It was the same spell he'd used to conceal the mass grave back at his abandoned hut, but done larger: a powerful but subtle ripple of energy, slowly expended and with little to show for the exertion until at the very end, when a rush of wind blew in from the north and rustled through the trampled grass in a rippling wave that swept for miles back along their route.

When it was gone, the ground had been restored to pristine wilderness, without a hint that even a single hoof or wheel had once been imprinted there. Dung pats had been swallowed by the swathe and not a blade of grass was broken. Then he sent a second pulse that swept away any trace of magical energies.

He'd kept it all as discreet as possible; with luck, there were no sorcerers nearby who would have sensed what he did, but it took its toll and he sagged, barely able to hold himself up and feeling like someone had just sucked the marrow from his bones. Jesco appeared and propped a shoulder under his arm. He'd done this several times already and each time was like being bled by a hundred leeches.

'Well done, Boss,' Jesco murmured. 'Let me carry you off to your boudoir.'

'Just the saddle will do,' he mumbled. Looking at Kemara he asked, 'How much of that did you see?'

She hesitated, then said, 'I saw your familiar enter you. I sometimes see him with you – and other times I've seen wild spirits, especially near streams and old boneyards. But I told you, I failed the tests.'

'Cauterising should have blinded you to seeing spirits.'

'So I understand,' she snapped, 'but the people who dealt with me weren't the most diligent.'

That rang true: only one in ten with the potential ever amounted to much, and too often graduated sorcerers had little interest in fostering the gift in others. 'If they didn't completely seal your gift, you might still develop a useful talent,' he told her, thinking to give her hope. 'Some people are late developers.'

'And some have no desire to meddle with nature,' she replied.

'Come on, *everybody* wants to be a sorcerer.'

'No they don't. I'll stick to healing. Someone has to in this expedition, now that you're too busy.' She tossed her head and stalked away.

'You'd have to be really unwell to ask her for help,' Vidar grumbled.

'Actually, she's fine with her patients,' Jesco replied. 'It's just Raythe she's grumpy around.'

Failed sorceress, poorly cauterised, bitter. 'I imagine she's had a hard life,' Raythe mused. 'It's tough for those who fail the tests: from having the world at their feet, suddenly no one wants to know them. I probably remind her of all she's lost.'

He put Kemara's problems aside for now; he had three hundred others to worry about. 'Let's get going.' He pushed off from Jesco's shoulder and went to Zar, who was staring out over Teshveld with a faraway expression.

'Time to move on.' he said. 'You ready for an adventure?'

'Teshveld was a shithole, but I wanted to go home, not further into the wilds.'

'We have no home, not until the Mandarykes fall,' he told her yet again. 'To have any chance of that, we have to do this.'

When I return to Otravia, it's going to be at the head of an army. We'll find this istariol and use it to break the Mandaryke cabal and restore freedom and justice. He gazed down the slope at the train of wagons and carts, each person drawn by the hope of something better.

I hope they all get to fulfil those dreams – and that mine don't cost them everything.

4

Feral

If there were ghosts on the Ghost Road, Kemara saw none, though there were plenty of grave markers. Every few miles there'd be a dozen or more, the final resting places of the prisoners of war and slaves who'd laboured here long ago, before the old Magnians had abandoned their dream of linking their empire from the furthest north to the deepest south. They'd never settled here; the soil was too thin and the weather too bleak, nothing but a desolate sea of trees. Only a few trappers braved the harsh terrain to collect the furs so beloved by the Bolgravian nobility.

Despite this, she found her own spirits were lifting. As they wound through the mist-wreathed forest, the dark, brooding beauty of the sea of pines spoke to her, for all that it was an eerie place. The road appeared to have some property that kept the creeping undergrowth at bay, but it didn't appear to deter the wildlife. The sea was out of earshot, but bird-song filled the air and the wind sang in the treetops. For Kemara, whose eyes were open to the spirit world, there were other glimpses too, of birds and beasts that weren't really there, and sometimes tiny shaggy goat-footed men or graceful water nymphs, glimpsed behind a branch or beneath the surface of a stream, watching her curiously as she went by.

It pained her to see them, for she would invariably start to reflect on all she'd lost.

But there was plenty going on in the newly formed travelling community to distract her. The first few days were awkward and fractious, with disputes breaking out between drivers over precedence in the order of march or the rate of travel, while others were already lamenting – loudly – the necessities they'd foolishly left behind, and demanding that others share.

Arbitration fell to Raythe Vyre, Elgus Rhamp and Mater Varahana, but Kemara heard all about it. Almost everyone called by the healer's cart at some point of the day, seeking lotions, potions or advice. Fourteen of the wives were pregnant and those approaching term were anxious that the travel would induce the babes to come too early. She soon grew short of sleep and patience too, and often napped in the back of the cart whenever she had a moment, leaving her sure-footed mule to find her own way.

She'd not even realised how deeply she'd fallen asleep until she was jolted awake by someone shaking her shoulder and calling her name.

'Mistress Solus?' a young voice repeated, drawing her from the depths of a lurid dream, 'Mistress Healer?'

Kemara struggled awake, breaking through into a gentle light filtered through green leaves, and found Zar Vyre hovering over her. The cart had come to a stop off the track and Beca the mule had her head down and was grazing furiously. She could see the rest of the caravan a hundred yards ahead, scattered across a clearing.

'Uh . . . guess I am now,' she yawned. 'What's happening?'

'We've reached a river, so we're setting camp early. We can finally wash,' Zar added, in a fervently thankful voice.

'Praise be.' Kemara eyed the coltish girl and asked, 'What's Zar short for? Zara? Zarette?'

'Zarelda.'

'That means "Warrior Woman" in Old Otravian, doesn't it?' Kemara looked her over. 'How can I help you?'

The girl looked around to ensure they were alone before leaning close and, though there was no one near, murmuring, 'I'm having really bad headaches and I'm seeing stars, like someone hit me. And I'm feeling really sick, you know?'

'Hmm.' She fixed the girl with a stare. 'Are you pregnant?'

'No – *No!*' Zar looked appalled. 'I've never even . . . um . . .'

71

'Okay, okay.' Kemara considered her for a moment, then said slowly, 'I've heard you say you want to be a sorcerer like your father . . . well, this is how it starts – although don't go getting too excited, because it's not the only possibility.'

The warning was too late, for Zar's eyes were already widening until they were round as saucers. 'It's actually happening? *Finally?* Oh, oh–'

Clearly there were no other possibilities as far as she was concerned. She burst into tears, hugged Kemara, then danced a jig.

'I'm sure it's exciting,' Kemara remarked drily, 'but maybe best keep it quiet until we know for sure, yes?'

The girl looked about to burst with excitement, but she said dutifully, 'I won't tell a soul, promise – apart from my father.' And she bounded off like a deer towards her father's wagon.

Gerda protect her, Kemara thought, crossing fists over her chest. *Please don't put her through what I endured.*

Every wagon rolling towards their unknown destination was a world of its own. *A true metaphor for life,* Raythe decided as he watched them rattle by. *Life is transitory, and so are we.* Each unit was separate, unique, an individual or a family with their possessions pared down to bare necessities, but each had their own personal flourish. The blacksmith Lynd Borger was hauling his anvil and bellows, as well as his wife and seven children. Gravis Tavernier's wagon had been kitted out as an inn on wheels, while Kemara's cart was also her apothecary. Some travelled with friends or like-minded souls; others kept themselves to themselves, as if the caravan was merely coincidental to their own journey. And yet all were part of the greater whole.

Raythe's own mid-sized wagon was sparsely packed; what few mementos of their old life back in Otravia he'd brought were carefully concealed. At night he slept beneath the wagon, with Zar tucked up in the back, the old loft curtains giving her a little privacy. He barely saw her during the evenings now; she barrelled around the campsites with the others of her age, eager to be accepted. She'd never really had friends before, so it was nice to see her beginning to blossom.

But she's also beginning to develop the praxis. One way or another, her life's about to change completely.

Even though both he and her mother were sorcerers, and despite Zar's unwavering certainty, the chance of her developing such powers had still been against the odds. Even now, until she manifested and gained a familiar, it was just potential. But Cognatus was now watching her avidly, as were other spirits, wisps of energy that took form as tiny animals or diminutive human forms, invisible to anyone except him – and maybe Kemara.

During the day, he left Zar in charge of the wagon, while he rode up and down the lines, ensuring all was well and learning names and faces. The order of march had swiftly been established: Sir Elgus Rhamp's outriders cantered ahead on their war-bred steeds like they owned the land, but they ensured the river-crossings were passable and although most of Rhamp's mercenaries were young and arrogant, seeing manual labour as beneath them, sometimes they would even lower themselves to clear the frequent falls of tree or rocks blocking the way. They followed orders grudgingly and got into fights at the drop of a hat, particularly after yet another night flocking about Gravis' wagons, carousing with the tavern women until they fell over. They'd already drained half of the innkeeper's beer and now refused to let anyone else near. Most of the disputes in the caravan concerned their behaviour.

The second group were the villagers and farmers who'd left land and homes behind to follow Raythe's mad dream. Mater Varahana spoke fluently about faith and togetherness and the ordinary folk, all pious, hardworking followers of Deo and Gerda, who'd wound up at the edge of the map following dreams that life had continually crushed, rallied around her. They were banding together increasingly to protect their womenfolk from Rhamp's predatory men; Raythe had noticed that at the priestess' suggestion, they had started ringing their wagons in the evening to look after their wives and daughters.

Not a stupid decision, he admitted, unhappy that there was so little he could do about the mercenaries right now.

The third group were the hunters and trappers, around forty of them, most of them single. Solitary men by nature, they loosely followed a hunter by the name of Cal Foaley, whom Vidar was cultivating. Some were dangerous, damaged men, and even Rhamp's mercenaries recognised that they weren't to be messed around with.

All told, he had around three hundred people, two-thirds of them grown men, with around sixty wives and as many children. At times, when Raythe was trying to conceal their trail, or deal with disputes, it felt like there were far too many of them, but when he worried about what they might face on the road, they looked pitifully few. Privacy was negligible and arguments were constant as the new community tried to learn how to live together. He swiftly got sick of having to calm everyone down, but if he could keep a volatile group of refugees, many with their own epic tales of trauma and despair, from each other's throats, the effort would be worthwhile.

By the end of the first week, they'd covered a hundred miles, helped by the Ghost Road easing their passage and thanks to the spells to stop overgrowth laid down by the ancient Magnian sorcerers who'd helped build it.

One hundred miles – but we're still hundreds of miles from Verdessa and it'll be high summer by the time we arrive . . . if we can keep together. I guess that's my job.

'Mistress Kemara?'

This time it was Mater Varahana's voice dragging Kemara out of the deepest slumber.

The last few days had been exhausting, for she'd been inundated by the sick and the injured. She rolled over, saw that the sun was barely above the horizon, the air was cold and the dew still thick on the ground. The wind moaned through the pines covering the inland flank;

the west was open grasslands extending to the coastal ranges some twenty miles distant.

'What is it?' she asked anxiously; being woken by others always brought back bad memories.

'Bess Shapple's having abdominal pains,' the priestess told her. 'She's asking for you.'

'Aren't they responding to prayer?' Kemara asked, stifling a yawn and sitting up.

'Hilarious,' Varahana said dourly. 'She's frightened she's losing her baby.'

That killed all levity and though Kemara's tiredness remained, sleepiness vanished. She sat up, struggled to her feet and dragged her bedroll into the back of her cart before hauling on her boots and grabbing her bag and a shawl. She turned to the priestess and said curtly, 'I'm ready. Lead the way.'

They hurried through the waking camp as the earliest risers rekindled cooking flames, or stumbled into the bushes to perform their ablutions. They'd been two weeks on the road and covered nearly two hundred miles, according to Raythe Vyre's estimation, but the Ghost Road would end soon and travel would become harder.

Ronno Shapple, a paunchy trapper with a mane of grey curls, hurried to meet them. Seizing her hand, he babbled, 'Bess is cramping, she can't hold down food – I'm worried–'

'Of course you are,' Kemara cut him off. 'I'll look after her; you keep the gawkers away.' She made her way into the canvas tent where Bess lay groaning beneath a blanket, sweaty despite the chill in the air. Half a dozen women swarming around her parted as Kemara swept in.

'Bess, what's up?' she said, dropping beside the bedroll and taking the woman's hand.

'She's got–' Jayne Ruelle began, but Kemara was shaking her head.

'I'll hear from Bess, please,' she said crisply. They undoubtedly meant well, but none had anything like formal medical training. 'Everyone out except Nella.'

Nella Baird, a solid farmer's wife, took some relish in ordering the rest away, before muttering, 'Silly bints.'

'Fresh water, please, Nella,' Kemara ordered, more to buy herself a moment's peace than for real need. Once she'd gone, she gave Bess an encouraging smile. 'Now, what's the matter?'

Bess, a blunt-faced woman with a lived-in air, gave her an exhausted look, laced with fear. 'Somethin' ain't right inside,' she groaned. 'It's like birthin', but I'm months away. An' somethin's wrong in my back. I keep getting these shootin' pains like knives down my thighs, then numbness, and I can't move. I'm scared I'll end up a cripple.'

Kemara kept her demeanour positive as she asked a few questions and moved her arms and legs, trying to gauge how much movement the woman had. After a few more questions, Kemara had the trapper's wife hike up her skirts and they joked about cold hands as she probed the woman's swollen belly and her genitals. When she pressed her ear to her belly, she could sense a heartbeat, rapid and weak, but not unduly so. 'She's a little lively, for sure, Bess. No bleeding?'

'None,' Bess grunted. 'I'd be bloody hysterical were it that.'

'This is what, your third pregnancy?'

'Fourth. Miscarried my first.'

'Lots of women miscarry their first,' Kemara reminded her. 'It doesn't mean you'll lose this.'

Nella returned and began to boil some water, while Kemara selected some soothing herbs. *It's likely just sciatica, and pinched nerves around a spinal disc,* she thought, but she couldn't be wholly sure, and the baby's heartbeat was a little concerning. So she gave herself over to easing her patient's pains, while outside, the usual morning routines were followed; cattle rounded up, horses and mules hitched to wagons and carts, while the children squalled about, blowing off steam before another day of being bumped around in cramped wagons.

Then Raythe Vyre poked his head in. 'A word, Mistress Kemara?'

Kemara scowled as he withdrew, which made Bess chuckle, despite her discomfort. 'You don't like him, do you?'

76

'Sorcerers give me the creeps,' she told Bess, which was certainly true. 'That's all.'

'But you still came?'

'Couldn't let you go off without a midwife, Bess, you and all the other lasses who'll end up carrying before this is done.' She sighed. 'Better go see what his Lordship wants.'

Bess gripped her hand. 'What's goin' on inside me, Kem? Gimme truth, not sops.'

'Truth is, I don't really know. Could be a problem, or could just be stomach gripes or whatever. Time'll tell – but I can deal with most things. Hold steady, girl. We'll get you through this.'

Kemara extricated her hand, rose and went outside the tent, where Raythe Vyre was listening to Ronno Shapple. 'My wife is nae right,' the trapper was saying. 'We got tae get 'er back tae civilisation and a real healer.'

'*Real healer?*' Kemara grumbled as Elgus Rhamp stomped up, a sour look on his face.

'You must be joking, Ronno,' Raythe replied. 'We're two hundred miles from Teshveld, let alone anything approaching "civilisation". We aren't going back, and that's a fact.'

Ronno's face was anguished. 'I should'nae ha' come.'

'You'll get the same care, here or in Teshveld,' Raythe pointed out, not unkindly. 'There was only ever me and Kemara – oh, and the governor's physician, who never tended the likes of you anyway.'

'Aye, that's as maybe, but we cannae move 'er. You got tae stop the caravan.'

'We're not stopping for one sick woman – nor man, neither,' Elgus Rhamp rasped. 'Gerda's Teats, if we'd been doing that, we'd still be ten miles out of Teshveld with the governor's troops massing round us.'

'But we're not,' Ronno snapped back. 'We're in the middle of bloody naewhere and the scouts all say the back trail's empty. What's a day or two for a life?'

'It's a precedent we can't afford,' Rhamp retorted.

Raythe noticed Kemara and asked, 'How is she?'

'Her belly's stirred up and she's feverish and there's a pinched nerve in her back, at the least. I can't say more than that at the moment.'

'See?' Ronno exclaimed. 'Can ye look at her, Raythe?'

Kemara bridled, but Raythe was already saying, 'Kemara knows more about healing than I do, especially when it comes to childbirth. I have every confidence in her.' He turned to her. 'What's your diagnosis?'

'Best case, she's hurt her back and got a fever. Worst case, her back is gone and her unborn is distressed and feverish. I would like to keep her here for a day or two.'

Rhamp went to bark something at her, but Raythe raised a hand. 'Elgus is right, we can't stop for sickness. Can you tend her while we move?'

'Not if there's a real problem.' She dropped her voice and turned her head away from Ronno. 'It's not impossible she's miscarrying. Move her and we risk losing her and the child.'

Raythe sighed. 'All right, so what if I assign guards for you and you catch us up once she's right?'

Kemara bit her lip, trying to think it through. The surrounding land was inhospitable, but even though they'd seen no sign of human life here, that didn't make it safe. Wolves roamed in packs and there were likely to be mountain lions and bears. And while she was devoting all her time to one patient, she'd be neglecting the dozen other pregnant women, not to mention the daily array of broken limbs, diarrhoea and myriad other vexations plaguing the caravan.

But right now, Bess needed her most.

'If you can handle the healing for a couple of days, then I think it is for the best,' she told Vyre. 'Making Bess move right now would be torture for her.'

'I have men I can spare,' Elgus Rhamp put in.

Kemara watched the mutual lack of trust play out in the eyes of Raythe and the Pelarian knight. When Raythe glanced at her, she thought, *Not Rhamp's men – not after what Osvard did.*

Clearly understanding her fear, Raythe said, 'I'll assign Jesco and a couple of hunters.'

'It's important that my people contribute,' Rhamp said gruffly.

'Then you should have made your son keep his hands to himself,' Kemara snapped.

'When are you going to get over that, Healer? My lad came off worst.'

'And if he hadn't?'

'I'd've made amends.'

'There are no amends for what he tried to do,' she shouted at him. *Don't you get that?*

The Pelarian gave Vyre an exasperated shrug. 'You're the boss,' he said pointedly.

'Elgus, your lads have taken Osvard's side to a man,' Raythe pointed out. 'I'm not alone in hearing whispers of "setting things right" and "eye for an eye". I'll not be imposing anyone unwanted on Mistress Kemara.'

Rhamp drew himself up to his full height and growled, 'You speak grand about building trust, Raythe, but you're all talk.' He stomped away.

Kemara let out her breath. 'Thank you.'

'I've been trying to build bridges with him, but I'm getting nowhere,' Raythe muttered. 'I sympathise with Bess, but we can't afford to leave anyone behind, or get too stretched. We've been lucky so far: empty lands and decent weather have meant no one's tried to turn back, but it would take just one deserter to get back to Teshveld and start talking and we're all screwed.'

She didn't have to like it, but he was right. 'So the men you're leaving are more to make sure we keep coming than to protect me,' she observed.

'No, your safety matters,' he reassured her. 'Take a day and a night and try to resolve this, will you? But no more than that. Do your best – but remember, the most important thing is that no one goes astray.'

79

Then he looked around, trying to see who was hollering his name. 'Ah, there's Vidar – that'll be the scouts' report. I have to go.' He faced her and said softly, 'Be safe, and good luck.'

Then he hurried away.

An hour later, the Shapples' wagon, her own cart and the three guards who'd been assigned stood on a wide plain at the edge of a sea of pines watching the clouds blowing in from the coast twenty miles away. They were alone, and miles from help.

Shut inside the tent to avoid the drizzle, time seemed to drift, the minutes measured by Bess' pained breathing in between bouts of uneasy sleep. Kemara brewed herbal teas and other elixirs to ease the pain, massaged and manipulated limbs and provided what comfort she could with constant murmuring conversation and encouragement.

It was mentally exhausting.

Outside the tent, she dimly heard Jesco Duretto, Cal Foaley, a weathered, lupine man who she gathered was something of a legend among the hunters, and a young tyro called Eidan Marr come and go. Sometimes rain sleeted in, then it would suddenly give way to sunlight blazing through the tent flap. Ronno came and went, mucking around with his children, Benji, five years old, and Kan, who was three, in that distracted way men had when forced to do something they considered a woman's task. But he cared deeply; that was clear in his agitation and the way his voice cracked a little each time he asked for news.

Around evening, smelling food, she crawled out of the tent, stretching and wincing at the way her joints cracked from the hours spent kneeling or squatting by the sickbed. It was dusk and the rain had finally blown over, leaving clear skies. The planetary rings arched above, almost close enough to touch.

'How is she?' Jesco asked, looking up from the spiced vegetable mashcakes he was cooking; the other two guards were out of sight. His long flintlock was loaded beside him and he was sitting on a saddle beside the fire. Sunset was imminent, the slow descent into night well underway.

'Asleep.' Kemara yawned and stretched again, feeling her muscles pop. 'Where's Ronno and the bairns?'

'Fetching more water from the stream over the way,' Jesco replied, pointing north. 'Foaley's off down the back trail and Eidan's watching at the edge of the trees. We're pretty sure there's nothing on the coast side to trouble us.'

'Any sign of trouble?'

'Foaley reckons there's wolves about: that's why he's gone scouting behind us.'

She gazed about. The horizons were wide here at the edge of the plains, although the sea was out of sight behind coastal hills. The snowy peaks to the northeast scraped the clouds.

'I'm a little surprised no one lives out here,' she commented. 'It's really beautiful.'

'Koh nomads use these plains as winter grazing, but they're away northeast of us by now, behind those peaks there. Come winter, they'll be back – but trust me, you don't want to be caught by them.'

'But none right now?' she clarified.

Jesco shook his head. 'Their migration cycle is sacred to them, so you won't see the Koh back here until autumn.' He glanced towards the stream. 'Here's Ronno and the lads. Good timing. This food's about ready.'

With the two hunters still away, they fed Ronno, Benji and Kan, while Kemara wolfed down her own food and readied a mashcake for Bess. Then young Eidan hailed them from the trees, waving cheerily as he emerged. The sun was about to touch the western hills and the clouds were limned in red and gold.

He was still a hundred yards away when Jesco suddenly shouted, '*Eidan, run –!*'

Only then did Kemara see that dark bipedal shapes had detached from the gloomy trees and were racing towards the young man. Jesco grabbed his flintlock as Eidan broke into a panicked run.

She squinted, trying to make out what was pursuing him – then Jesco's long-barrelled gun cracked, belching flame and black smoke, and one of the pursuers threw up his arms and dropped to the ground. But the others were closing in, making weird braying noises.

'Oh Gerda–' Kemara heard herself gasp as Jesco frantically reloaded.

Eidan, realising he was about to be overtaken, spun round, whipping out his blade.

'Ronno, grab a weapon,' the Shadran snapped. 'Kemara, get these lads to the wagon.'

The trapper shouted at his boys as Eidan drove back one attacker with a series of slashes, but another was closing in on his flank. Then Jesco's gun blasted out another gout of flame and that second attacker roared and spun away, clutching a shoulder.

Eidan whooped, cut down his foe then turned and came pelting back towards them, while the attackers – seven or eight hairy, unkempt men clad in ragged uncured pelts – hesitated, perhaps deterred by Jesco's marksmanship.

The young hunter burst away from them, running hard–

–but even as Kemara shouted a warning, one hurled a javelin–

–that slammed into Eidan's back, sending him ploughing into the turf, transfixed through the back.

Oh no–!

'Boys,' she shouted to Benji, who was holding his younger brother's hand and backing away, 'get in the wagon – *now!*'

Jesco was cursing as Ronno fumbled an arrow into place and fired wide.

Kemara collared little Kan, hoisted him over her shoulder, then grabbed Benji's hand and ran for the wagon, her heart pounding. She recognised their enemy now: wild men, known as ferali, who were surging towards the stricken hunter, howling triumphantly. Jesco fired again and another went down, but the rest fell on Eidan. Their primitive clubs rose and fell, then three of them dragged Eidan away, while Ronno, babbling in terror, shot wide again.

A few seconds later, the ferali had vanished into the trees, taking Eidan's body with them.

Kemara swallowed bile as she thought about what that meant. 'Stay *here*,' she told the boys, glaring them into obedience, then running to the tent.

'What's happening?' the pregnant woman demanded. 'I heard shots.'

'There's ferali out there,' Kemara hissed. 'Can you move?'

Bess clutched her breast. 'Where are my boys?'

'In the wagon, and that's where you have to be,' Kemara told her. 'Sorry, but we have to move you.'

Bess groaned, but she obeyed, fear for her family outweighing the pain. Kemara heard Jesco's gun bark again as she helped Bess crawl from the tent, then hauled her to her feet. She threw an anxious look towards the forest, where she could see ferali were still milling beneath the trees. Another was crawling for cover, wailing thinly.

'Stop shooting,' Jesco told Ronno, who was too scared to shoot straight; he'd already wasted half his arrows without hitting a thing. 'Hold, man!'

Adrenalin pouring through her, Kemara helped Bess hobble to the wagon and hoisted her into the back with her sons. Jesco was close behind, pulling Ronno with him, and just in time, for a volley of arrows suddenly sleeted from the trees, only just missing them as they ducked into cover. Kemara's mule and the horses, Jesco's Boss and two other riding animals and the two big draught beasts, were tugging at their ropes, but perhaps the ferali wanted the animals alive, because so far they hadn't targeted them.

What if they rush us again? Kemara wondered.

'Mistress Kemara, have you ever fired a gun?' Jesco called, his voice doubtful.

'As a matter of fact, yes.'

The Shadran grinned. 'Excellent. Eidan's pistol is in his saddlebags.'

He indicated a pile of gear, halfway to the horses. He looked calm, despite their precarious position.

'I'll take it,' Ronno blurted.

'You stick to your bow,' Jesco answered. 'Hit something and I might reconsider.'

The trapper hung his head, scowling and ashamed.

'Go on, Kemara,' Jesco urged. 'I'll shoot if they break cover.'

Kemara nodded, then ran for Eidan's gear and swiftly located the small wooden-handled pistol from under the canvas cover, along with his powder and shot. She glanced towards the pines, saw nobody emerging and decided she'd load before returning to the wagon.

Now, how did this go? Powder – ram – ball – ram again.

It'd been two years ago, in another life entirely, a fleeting respite on the road. She thanked that benefactor now, if not for all that he'd done. But she was partway into the routine of loading when one of the horses whinnied and she turned to see *someone* was standing among the beasts, loosening their tethers.

She froze – and so did he.

The ferali was clad in just a loincloth; he was holding something that was more butcher's cleaver than sword, discoloured by rust and old blood. He was lean to the point of skinny, but corded in muscle. His straggling beard and hair were filthy and the only pale thing about him was his eyes, so burned by the sun was he. Even across the thirty yards between them, she could smell his rank, humid odour.

Then he screamed, scattering the beasts, and roared towards her.

Dear Gerda –!

Reflex took over and she muttered, 'Ball . . . ram . . .'

He launched himself at her, that brutal blade raised to strike, as she wrenched back the hammer with both thumbs and from barely three feet away, jerked the trigger.

The gun roared, bucking in her hand and jarring her wrist – and the ferali was slammed backwards. Her eyes were dazzled by the flash and her eardrums reverberated, blotting out all other sound.

Blood splashing from a crater in the man's sun-blackened chest, he stumbled backwards, clutching the wound and gasping for air, while she overbalanced and found herself sitting in the wet grass and staring at him in shock.

He fell, choking, and died in front of her, his despairing face etching itself into her future nightmares. She realised she was breathless and dazed to the point of fainting, but somehow she found the strength to reverse the rammer, thrust the brush down the barrel to clean it, then bite open another twist of powder and reload.

Only then did she think to look back, and found Jesco watching. He gave her a casual thumbs-up, then turned his attention back to the woods, while she scanned the grass for other attackers.

Seeing none, she tentatively called, 'Beca—'

Being a mule, Beca ignored her.

Every nerve jangling, she crept towards the beast, petrified in case anyone else was lurking in the grass. Beca baulked when she grabbed her reins and hauled, but then – *miracle of miracles* – she came, and the horses followed. She led them back to their camp, her heart thudding in her chest at every step.

'You all right?' Jesco called.

'Aye,' she replied, and she was surprised to find she really was: she felt vividly alive, every nerve awake and her senses on overload. 'Aye, I'm fine.'

I killed a man – but I'm fine.

She tethered the animals to the wagon, then hoisted herself up beside Bess, who was grimacing and clutching her belly with one arm, but she was holding her sons against her with the other and looked as calm as could be expected.

Kemara flashed what she hoped was a reassuring grin. 'You okay?'

'Of course,' grunted Bess, then she whispered, 'Kem, you've got blood on you.'

Kemara looked down and saw splattered scarlet spotting her bodice. 'It's not mine.' She scanned the plains, then trained her eyes on the forest, which was now descending into darkness. There was no sign of the ferali, but they were surely still out there.

Unless they've taken poor Eidan away to cook him. Her hand suddenly began to tremble and she shook herself angrily.

Ronno darted to the side of the wagon and grabbed at his wife's hand. 'We shouldn't have come,' he moaned. 'It's too dangerous.'

'We're going to be fine,' Kemara told him.

'No, we're—'

'Shut it, Ronno,' Bess growled. 'We're here and we're staying.' She looked at Kemara. 'Give us a moment, will you, Kem?'

Kemara was grateful to clamber out. Staying low, she ran to Jesco, who was huddled behind his saddle beside the fire. The handsome Shadran flashed her a grin. 'Good work. How're they doing?'

'Bess is good. Ronno, not so much.' She glanced around and wondered aloud, 'Where's Cal Foaley? Shouldn't he be back by now?'

'As I hear it, if anyone can look after himself, it's him.' Jesco peered along the barrel of his gun, frowning. 'We're losing the light and there's a good number of those bastards left. If they rush us under cover of darkness, we're screwed.' He pulled a sour face. 'It's exactly what they'll do, if they can still think things through.'

That was how Kemara saw it too. 'Can they?'

'Definitely. They were like us, a few generations ago. But some folks let the wilderness into their souls and end up no better than the animals they hunt.' His expression was somewhere between pity and revulsion.

'Then what do we do? We can't hold them off if we can't see them coming.'

The Shadran considered, then replied, 'We move.'

Kemara shook her head. 'It's a clear night and I'm guessing their night sight will be better than ours. And I don't know if Bess can move at all.'

'She might have to.'

Dear Gerda, must we decide between Bess and her unborn, or the rest of us?

Then she looked up at Jesco as inspiration struck. 'I've got an idea.'

*

To her surprise, Jesco approved her plan, even though it meant staying put and taking the ferali head-on. Or it was maybe *because* of that; he seemed to live for danger.

It didn't take long to ready their little surprise, then they pulled Kemara's cart back about thirty feet behind a makeshift rampart of saddles, baggage and the Shapples' wagon, picketing the animals behind them. They let the fire burn low as the darkness deepened, to aid their night-sight. Above, the planetary rings cleaved the sky in two, lighting the stark plains and deepening the shadow of the forest. The air cooled, the birds fell silent and the wind dropped away entirely.

Ronno took cover under the wagon, while Jesco and Kemara huddled behind the saddlebags.

'Hey, Healer,' Jesco said, 'seeing how we're all about to die, why not tell me your story?'

She gave him a dubious look. 'You first.'

The Shadran chuckled. 'Sure. Born in the south, orphaned by Bolgravian cannons, grew up sleeping rough in the markets. Survived by . . . well, you can guess. I was a pretty boy, in demand. Then a rich man took me in, taught me the blade and found I was good. You can make a real living that way in Shadra, fighting duels of honour on behalf of nobles and merchants. In the end I had to run. I came north, got caught up in the Pelarian wars – that's where I met Raythe and Varahana. The war was fun, but we lost, so we came west.'

The lack of self-pity or relish in his voice, the sheer matter-of-factness, struck a chord in Kemara, reminding her of herself, or how she'd like to be – only he had a charm she'd never had. Even her friends thought she was a grumpy so-and-so.

'And what about you?' he asked, smiling in that heart-melting way – although he clearly wasn't interested in melting her, or any other woman.

'Well . . .' She hesitated from habit, because she wasn't used to revealing her past. She had rehearsed versions of the truth for such moments, but somehow, she suspected he'd quickly see through them. And she was scared, and talking did help.

'I was born in Ferrea, obviously.' She displayed a thick tress as evidence. 'I was going to be a Sister of Gerda, but then—' She stopped abruptly, wondering if she should actually tell him.

'Then?'

She swallowed, gathering her nerve, and repeated, 'And then—'

—and then someone shrieked savagely and what looked to be a dozen feralis came howling out of the darkness. She blurted a curse, mixed fright and relief, and snatched up the taper she'd kept smouldering, while Jesco thumbed the hammer on his flintlock.

She touched the taper to the thin trail of powder at her feet and a line of fire instantly shot off into the darkness, setting light to the grass at the feet of the charging wildmen, dazzling their eyes and exposing them in the light. Their savage cries changing from bloodlust to alarm, they recoiled, automatically bunching together.

Kemara snatched up her pistol and fired at the same time Jesco did, while Ronno's bow snapped into life, and this time his arrow struck home. Three of the attackers were knocked off their feet and sent sprawling on the ground; they cried out in pain, but the rest came on.

Jesco touched the torch he'd prepared to the embers and made it roar to life, then brandishing the flaming brand in his left hand and his blade in his right, he launched himself at the half-blinded wildmen, slashing the belly of one, then opening the throat of the next, before slamming the torch into the face of another. In seconds, half the attackers were down.

But the rest were swarming past him, coming full tilt at Ronno and Kemara. Ronno shot again, his target folding in two over the arrow in his belly, but there was no time to reload her pistol, so Kemara had only her dagger. She drew back her arm and threw it at the man coming at her, a tower of sweaty muscle and leering eyes. It flew straight and true, embedding itself deep in his chest, making him stagger. His face crumpling into disbelief, he ripped it out – but as he sucked in a wet, choking breath, he crashed to the ground, gasping like a beached fish.

But the next man was on her, hitting her like a charging bullock and knocking her onto her back. She flailed weakly, gasping as her lungs emptied, unable to catch her breath and utterly dazed. Engulfed in his meaty stench and crushed by his weight, she wondered if this was it – only then realising that he wasn't moving.

Tentatively running her hands over his body, she discovered an arrow buried in his left side. She thrashed out from under him and only now did she catch sight of Cal Foaley, who was sweeping past and first hamstringing Ronno's attacker, then slashing open the ferali's throat as he turned.

Jesco gutted another – and at last the remaining two fled, wailing. The first got ten paces before Foaley snatched Ronno's bow from his shaking fingers and shot him. The second managed another dozen paces until he was barely visible in the smouldering grasslands, but Foaley's next arrow took him cleanly in the back and he went down like a felled bull.

Kemara rose to hands and knees, gasping until her lungs filled again. The fight had taken about thirty seconds in all, and somehow, they'd killed ten men and emerged relatively unscathed. Jesco's coat was slick with blood, but he was moving freely, as if none of it were his.

Jesco gave Cal Foaley a broad smile – a genuine knee-trembler, if Foaley had been that way inclined. He clasped his hand and pounded his back, exulting, 'I knew you'd be out there – I was counting on it.'

'If I'd been standing with you, it still wouldn't have deterred them,' Foaley growled, 'so I waited, downwind and out of sight, to take 'em by surprise. These animals are predictable.' He turned to the trapper, clapped his shoulder. 'Good shooting, Ronno. You found the rhythm of it, right on time.'

Ronno mumbled shyly, then hurried to his wagon, leaned in and hugged his family.

Jesco strode to Kemara, pulled her upright and embraced her, and for a moment she wished he was another, before just enjoying the physical contact and the relief of survival. 'This one's a warrior too,' the Shadran said grandly. 'No one I'd trust more at my back.'

Cal Foaley gripped her shoulder in turn, his weathered face not unlike those they'd slain, but there was intelligence and humour in his eyes, not just that blank hunger. 'I saw it all. Fine work, Mistress.'

She gave them a grateful look, then looked round.

Dead eyes caught her gaze, and mutilated bodies, sprawling in unnatural poses, soaking the ground in gore. All of a sudden her knees went, her gorge rose and she was vomiting up her dinner, despite having seen plenty of blood in a life dealing with illness, injury and childbirth.

Jesco knelt beside her and laid a sympathetic hand on her shoulder. 'It's normal, a reaction to the violence,' he told her. 'We all go through it.'

'I know,' she told him, still humiliated. 'You'd think I'd be fine, given that giving birth is at least as gory.'

He shuddered. 'You're not wrong. But listen, I'm sorry about this but we need to move, in case more come back.' He looked round at the bodies and added, 'Besides, I'm too lazy to bury these bastards and they already stink.'

Kemara sighed, washed her mouth out with water and went to the wagon, where the two children were sitting, staring out with terrified, awestruck eyes. She dreaded to think how much they might have seen. But Bess was sitting up and before she could say anything, the trapper's wife said, 'I heard. Let's just go.'

'My cart's got springs round the axle,' Kemara told her. 'It'll be a gentler ride for you.'

Ronno replied gratefully, 'Aye, let's do that, then.'

As they moved off into the night, with Bess in the back of Kemara's small cart and Ronno driving his big wagon, Jesco trotted by on Boss, his warhorse. Leaning down, sounding deeply conspiratorial, he said, 'I believe you were just about to tell me your deepest secrets when we were so rudely interrupted?'

She clicked her teeth and Beca began to move, then she poked out her tongue and said, 'Missed your chance. You'll have to wait until the next time we face certain death.'

'Can't wait.'

Kemara snorted. 'Maybe not, but I'm in no hurry.' Then she tapped the pistol in her belt. 'Do you think I can keep this? Did Eidan have, um, kin?'

Jesco shook his head. 'Just a few friends.'

She tried not to think about that poor young man and what would still likely befall his body. But perhaps when the wildmen didn't return, the ferali tribe would move on and his body would lie undisturbed in the woods.

' "If I die alone, let the wolves devour my bones",' she quoted from an old poem. ' "Let the crows eat my eyes, and the starlings take my hair to nest".'

' "But give my sword to my son, so I'll be with him when the fight is won",' Jesco added, concluding the verse. 'Keep Eidan's pistol, Kemara. He'll be with you when you next fight.'

'May that be many, many years from now,' she wished.

'Somehow, I don't think we'll be that lucky.' Jesco nudged his horse into motion. 'Come on, if we push it a bit, we should catch up with the rest of the caravan by dusk.'

Raythe raised the sextant and took his sighting along the dimly visible arch of the planetary rings. He jotted down the readings. They now twenty-three days out of Teshveld: three weeks and more than three hundred miles from their starting point. They'd made excellent time, aided by the Ghost Road and good weather. Jesco, Kemara, Foaley and the Shapples had rejoined them after only a day, and thank Gerda, Bess' condition had stabilised. Kemara reckoned it'd been mostly a trapped nerve, made worse by a touch of stomach illness.

But that was a week ago and now a new problem faced them. Here, where snow-tipped mountains hemmed in the north and east, the Ghost Road abruptly ended. It ran up to a cliff overlooking the sea – and stopped. A mountain loomed above them, the final tooth of a jawbone of peaks running all the way from the northern alps to the breakers. There was no obvious path forward.

'What the krag were they thinking?' Elgus Rhamp complained, as the leaders convened to view the dismal outlook. 'Who builds a road up to the edge of a fecking cliff?'

'The Magnian Emperor probably thought if he built a road, the sea would get out of his way,' Jesco chuckled.

He was the only one smiling. Elgus looked bewildered, Vidar was mumbling into his beard and Mater Varahana was looking skywards, as if she suspected Deo of personally testing her faith. Beside her, Kemara was glaring at Raythe as if this were entirely his fault.

He cast about for some clue as to why the empire would run the road up to the edge of a sea cliff which fell hundreds of feet to a rugged, boulder-filled shore where waves hammered the rocks. A mountain range blocked their way, and trying to pick a path under the overhanging cliff would be impossible, even for those climbing, Vidar had reported. There was no clear way forward.

Surely this route was surveyed before they started work – why start a job you can't finish?

Varahana joined him and gazing thoughtfully about, suggested, 'Maybe they intended building the road around the western flank of that peak there, but the land fell into the sea? They had no other route, nor means of getting past here, and abandoned the project.'

'Likely,' he agreed. 'How long ago, do you think?'

'Eighty years.' She indicated a nearby boneyard. 'The dates on the gravestones are likely the year the road was abandoned. I don't think they went further.'

'Damn.' Raythe gave a deep sigh. 'Perhaps there's an inland route the surveyors missed?' he said, although he doubted it.

'How did your cartomancer's party get to Verdessa?' Kemara asked, joining them diffidently.

'They sailed directly. That was never an option for us.'

'But we set off not knowing whether it was passable,' she noted sarcastically.

'It will be,' he said firmly, 'even if we have to dismantle each wagon and reassemble it on the other side of these mountains.'

Sir Elgus waggled his fingers in a pseudo-magical way. 'Can the praxis aid us?'

'Perhaps,' Raythe replied. He'd been mulling over the same thing. 'I'll work something out. Let's set up camp: we're due a rest day or two anyway, and it'll give us a chance to think.'

There was clear ground atop the cliff, levelled by the road-makers long ago, and the rocky ground and coastal aspect had limited the regrowth. The wagons fanned out, the travellers claiming spaces and bustling through the myriad domestic chores. Raythe saw to his own tent, chivvying Zar into her chores, then they joined the throng around the main campfire, where the day's catch was being cooked alongside a spiced root stew and loaves of flatbread.

A few men brought out musical instruments after the meal, led by a skinny young harpist called Norrin. Jesco was among them with his fiddle and without need for discussion, the musicians led off with a series of gentle jigs and reels, while those listening clapped along and sang if there were words to the tune.

Then, amidst boisterous applause, Kemara rose and swayed through a gypsy havasi, sweeping her hands about her gracefully while her hips and shoulders quivered and gyrated. The single men – the majority in the caravan – watched hungrily. She was one of the few single women here, a volatile gender imbalance on such a journey, and already she was fighting off suitors, despite her status as a novice of Gerda. Then other women, mostly the married ones, joined her as the wind rose and sparks flared from the bonfire. The next dance was a polka and men flooded the space, seizing hands and spinning their partners energetically.

Raythe saw his short-haired, boyish daughter watching the dancers wistfully and slipped an arm over her shoulder as he sat.

'I wish I could dance,' she said.

'I haven't said you can't.'

She shot him a look. 'You've never taught me.'

'It's not exactly High Praxis – figure it for yourself.'

She twitched, vacillating between the desire to join in and fear of making a fool of herself.

'Go on,' he urged. 'Remember, in a few days you'll likely manifest and gain your familiar, and after that you'll be so caught up in new things you'll forget what relaxation is.'

'I can't wait.' Her aura was growing stronger every day and if he were to exercise witch-sight, he knew he'd see all manner of spirits flitting about her, invisible, bodiless bundles of energy and will seeking a host and partner. The one she chose would become closer to her than a husband or lover.

Cognatus fizzed into being, landing on his shoulder in parrot form and cooing at his daughter.

Yes, I know, Raythe agreed, mind to mind.

The familiar shrieked excitedly, flapping ghostly wings. It might not understand his words – praxis-spirits understood only Old Magnian – but it caught his mood.

His gaze shifted to Mater Varahana, who was also watching the dancing with a wistful expression. Under the Deo Orthodoxy, single women weren't permitted to dance in front of men, let alone priestesses. The Vara he knew was cultured, educated and aloof, but she'd once waltzed in Magnian royal palaces. He wondered what she'd have become if her family hadn't pushed her into the Church.

Someone he'd have liked to know; that he was certain of.

After a few dances, the priestess rose and called out, 'Tomorrow morning, an hour after sunrise, I will hold a service for the faithful. I expect to see you all present.'

There were a mix of dutiful and fervent declarations of attendance, then someone called out, 'Let's have a tale of the Second Age.' Varahana frowned, then gave a nod of agreement: the Second Age ended with the rise of the Holy Church after the fall of the pagan Aldar and most tales of those times held a strong moral lesson.

Jesco leaped to his feet and putting aside his fiddle, declared, 'A tale of the Second Age? I know just the one. Gather round, and I shall tell you of Vashtariel, last God-King of the Aldar.'

This roused a cheer and in moments, Jesco was in the midst of the encircled crowd, the centre of attention and in his element. He smoothed back his hair, struck a pose and began.

'Mother Church teaches that there are twelve marks of damnation – twelve horrendous sins, any one of which will send us to the Pit for all eternity, should we die unshriven.' Jesco winked broadly and said, 'See Mater Varahana for details.' That got a laugh.

He struck his declamatory pose again and went on, 'But in the Second Age, the Aldar who ruled acknowledged no such sins. To them, *honour* was all, a special kind of honour they called *mana*. To be known as fearless, magnanimous, lusty and eloquent enhanced your *mana*. They strove with rivals in ritual contests. Insults were answered in blood. Humility was weakness, pride was strength. And sorcery was the highest art of all: a terrible form of sorcery known as *mizra*, so powerful it could tear the world apart.

'In truth, the Aldar were raised to break every stricture we live by: they killed, they stole, they ravished, they boasted, they preened and they shone. They sought not to serve their gods but to *emulate* them in arrogance and hubris. Better to be renowned in sin than for-gotten in virtue, they said. Being of both genders at once, every sensual pleasure and vice was open to them. And Vashtariel, King of the Aldar, lived a life of infamous excess, even by his people's standards.'

By now, the travellers were completely caught up in Jesco's story – he never wasted a crowd. Raythe smiled at the wide-eyed faces. Even Varahana was enjoying herself. Then he glanced at his daughter and noticed that her gaze wasn't on Jesco, but on Rhamp's son Banno – who was staring back. He tapped Zar's shoulder while giving the young man a hard look, breaking up that little mutual admiration society, at least for the moment.

Unaware of the minor drama being played out, Jesco went on, 'Vashtariel's palace – his *rath* – was built on rock so full of istariol that it floated above the earth and had to be chained to the ground by huge links of metal. Rath Argentium, it was called, the Silver Palace. He had thirty consorts, one for every day of the month, all of surpassing beauty, and he bedded each in turn on a giant bed of silk and pearls. He used sorcery to create dragons on which he rode as other men rode horses. Every day, he trained with bladed weapons against the city's best gladiators, and after slaying them, he would breakfast on the liver of the fallen. His favourites were lavished with luxurious gifts, but his enemies were invariably left broken and enslaved.'

Jesco reached down for his goblet to wet his throat before continuing, 'Oh, to be a god-king, to live each moment to the fullest, without fear of recrimination, reproach or censure.'

The crowd made jest and called encouragement and Jesco started strutting about like a preening Aldar lord, bantering with his audience before resuming his tale.

'Vashtariel's courtiers grew sick of the king's mad excesses and began to dream of bringing him down, but such was his prowess at arms that none dared take him on. However, his most devious foe was his closest advisor: his brother and high vizier, Tashvariel, who had always been jealous of his elder brother and longed to surpass him. One of his duties was to prepare each consort for the royal bed, and he ached to possess them, especially silver-tongued Shameesta, the chief among them. But the court was full of watchers, no consort was ever left unattended and so his obsessions went unsated – and being unsated, they consumed him.'

The listening crowd, murmuring in anticipation, reverently made the sign of Gerda the Intercessor, for this was also her tale.

'Tashvariel began concealing istariol powder in the livers of the dead gladiators, the only part of Vashtariel's meals that the tasters were forbidden to eat. As the istariol crystallised in him, the god-king became ever more convinced of his own divinity, and his already strong sorcerous powers became even more powerful – but they also became noticeably erratic.

'With the first part of his plot going according to plan, Vizier Tashvariel started on the next. He raised up his chosen champion, a gladiator named Gerda, and taught her a secret path of sorcery: a counter to the mizra called *praxis*, and when he was certain she was ready, he staged a series of gladiatorial games. Without any intervention on his part, Gerda easily triumphed in every one. To honour her prowess, God-King Vashtariel chose Gerda as his next prey.'

Jesco drew his blade and whisked through a series of theatrical fencing moves, making his audience cheer and jeer, before going on, 'On that fateful morning, Gerda was brought to the palace's sacred arena, destined to be the god-king's sacrifice – and his breakfast. Clad in imperial purple, with his flowing black locks and skin gleaming like copper, he was a vision of dark majesty – but Gerda, pale of skin and hair, shone like a fallen star.

'Vashtariel strove against the gladiator, battering at her defences, but Gerda was different from all of his previous opponents for, unknown to him, she was filled with the might of her human god, Deo. She countered his every blow, until he decided he must cheat and bring her down with his sorcery – but when he tried to destroy her with the mizra, she countered with the unknown praxis, undoing his magic. He barely recognised the emotion filling him, for it had been a very long time since he had last felt fear, as he tried ever more frantically to slay her.

'Every clever ploy and subtle technique failed, even brute force falling away before her skill and agility, and at last her weaving blade pierced his heart and the god-king fell at her feet.'

A hush had fallen, but at those words everyone made the Sign of Gerda.

Jesco struck his heroic pose again before resuming his tale. 'But Vashtariel refused to die! He sought to restart his own heart with the mizra, a sorcery requiring such strength and skill that only a madman would have dreamed of essaying it. With his power dangerously augmented by the excessive istariol he'd been unwittingly consuming and his control undermined by delusions and fear, his spells were both blindingly successful – and disastrous.

Invoking his gods, he opened himself up to the full might of the mizra – and it consumed him! This unleashed a vast explosion that brought rack and ruin upon all his kind, ending the era of the Aldar and plunging the land of Shamaya into eternal winter and centuries of misery. Indeed, the Ice Age Vashtariel summoned grips us even now, half a millennia on.'

A hush fell on the circle, although everyone here knew the old tale.

Jesco waited for a few seconds, then asked, 'Did Vashtariel survive? No: the god-king who had destroyed so many of his own people was consumed utterly. Did his treacherous brother Tashvariel profit from his perfidy? No, for he too was consumed, along with glorious Shameesta and all the other queens.

'Did any Aldar survive?' He looked around, shaking his head sadly, and whispered, 'No, the Aldar perished, from the oldest man to the youngest babe in arms. They are gone, leaving the world to us humans.'

Utter silence fell as everyone there contemplated the passing of the dread Aldar.

It was broken by Mater Varahana, who put in piously, 'But let us not forget Gerda, who was shielded by Deo and taken to sit at his side, on the right hand of the Sacred Throne, where she serves as his maiden: ever virgin, ever our champion.'

'No good deed goes unpunished,' quipped Jesco, before giving everyone a flourishing bow. 'Thus ends my tale of the fall of Vashtariel, last god-king of the Aldar.'

He was warmly applauded, though Varahana threw him an arch look at that final aside. After that, the musicians struck up another reel, Jesco helped himself to some of Gravis' ale and the night's informal festivities went on.

'Is that really what happened?' Zar asked Raythe. She'd been too young for school when they'd fled Otravia and since then her education had concentrated on reading, writing, counting, map-reading: the necessary skills of life; with little time for history.

'So Mother Church would have it,' Raythe replied carefully.

'Not really, then?' Zar said, matching his tone.

'Who knows for certain? If it is true, then who survived to tell it? But it neatly justifies all manner of things, the rise of the Church, most of all, and the usage of praxis-sorcery.'

'Then what do you say happened?'

Raythe thought about how to reply. Church orthodoxy was strict in the empire – in Bolgravian territories, Jesco would have swiftly found himself surrounded, marched off his stage and locked up for such an impious rendition of the tale – and one day they'd all return to that strict world. But he wanted his daughter to grow up with a questioning mind.

'What the historians taught us in Otravia, before the Church took over the universities, was that the Aldar were humans, like us, just a different tribe. But they misused their sorcerous power – mizra – and the istariol during their dynastic wars and that's what destroyed our climate. The polar caps swallowed up the deep north and south and the world became much colder. There are archaeological finds I've seen that back this theory. But as for the rest . . .'

Zar took that in as Norrin and Jesco struck up a lively jig and suddenly most of the crowd were bouncing around. She stood and stretched. 'You know, Dad, I think I do want to dance.'

Looking around, he smiled; it was the happiest evening of their journey so far. 'Then off you go,' he told her.

She offered a hand. 'You coming?'

His smile vanished, because suddenly it wasn't Zar standing there but Mirella, imperiously demanding that he waltz with her: their first dance. 'I . . . I think I'll sit this one out,' he stammered, shocked at the wave of emotion rushing over him. 'Go on, have some fun.'

She pulled a face, but an instant later she was standing amidst the women, quickly catching the rhythm of the dance as they spun and twisted, moving forward to meet the line of men, dipping, then retreating. When, moments later, Banno Rhamp appeared opposite her in the male line, her face lit up.

Raythe could feel himself quietly fuming, but it was all part of her growing up, so he let it go and instead, enjoyed the sight of her joyous face. She'd not had many such moments in recent years.

Soon almost everyone was up and the ground was quivering at the enthusiastic stamping of so many feet.

'Do you dance, Master Vyre?' a woman drawled and he turned to see Tami standing over him, a hand on her hip.

'I used to,' he said tersely. 'Shouldn't you be with Elgus?'

'The old fart's too deep in his cups to dance, and his sons are idiots.'

'You got yourself in there,' he said unsympathetically. 'I didn't even know you were with him.'

'No, you didn't, did you?' she noted. 'You sent a bird to Jesco, but not to me. Lucky I was close by, hmm?' She patted his arm slyly. 'Don't you miss *us*, Raythe?'

'Not really,' he said without thinking, then cursed himself for his bluntness.

Tami winced. 'I'm crushed.'

'Sorry, that came out worse than it was meant. But life goes on.' He met her gaze. 'I'm glad to have a sympathetic ear inside Rhamp's pavilion. I trust he treats you well?'

She gazed across the camp to where the big mercenary was drinking with his bearded henchmen, shaggy giants like the trollochs of Norgan legend. 'Oh, you know. It's not love, but he keeps my arse warm at night and he doesn't call me "Mirella" in the heat of passion.'

This time it was Raythe who winced. 'Aye, well . . .'

'Let's keep to business, shall we?' Tami smiled lazily as she withdrew her hand from his arm. 'It's a shame you don't dance any more, though. You used to be good.'

He swallowed an old ache as he watched her sashaying away, remembering how they'd sparked before it all went wrong, just before Colfar's rebellion collapsed into anarchy. And that took him back to Mirella, and the trail of destruction he'd left behind ever since he lost her.

Dear Gerda, let this expedition give me what I need to put it all right . . .

Wood-smoke was rising sluggishly in the cold air, while the sea crashed against the rocks below the cliff. The noise and smells dragged Zarelda back to wakefulness and she rolled over, smiling.

It was not quite morning and her father was still wrapped in blankets and snoring softly under the wagon. She rubbed grit from her eyes and peered out to see the horses grazing on the dew-laden grass. Steam was rising from their nostrils in the bitterly cold air and she could barely feel her toes.

But last night she'd actually *danced* – and mostly with sweet, handsome Banno Rhamp.

Is he too old for me? she wondered. He was twenty, five years older than her, which felt like an enormous gap – but when he'd taken her hands in the dance and their eyes met as he spun her round and round, it seemed like no barrier at all.

I'm nearly sixteen, she reminded herself. *Most girls are married by then.*

Not that marriage was something she wanted right now, not with the imminent awakening of her praxis, but she was sick of the solitary life she and her father lived. Father worried too much, and maybe that was sensible in an imperial-held village, but out here everyone was on the same side, weren't they? *And I've missed out on so much.*

Feeling wide awake, she pulled on her socks and boots, then clambered down and crept through the maze of wagons for the women's trench. After peeing, she scurried to the cliff, rubbing her forearms, trying to generate a little bit of heat.

Banno had said he'd be on watch in the morning – and there he was, his handsome face creasing into a grin as he caught sight of her. He quickly shed his heavy fur-lined leather cloak and draped it over her shoulders, a courtly gesture that sent a thrill through her.

'That was fun, last night,' she told him shyly. She'd felt so free and daring for once, like a normal girl.

'It was. Best night of the journey. It feels like we're becoming a real community at last.'

'Well, it's your father's people who are mostly keeping to themselves,' she pointed out.

'I know,' he confessed. 'The truth is, some of our soldiers aren't exactly civilised. Just keeping them from committing hanging offences is hard enough – believe me, Pa's cracking skulls every night trying to keep them in line.'

She laughed. 'That I can believe.' She'd been very conscious last night that while Banno and most of the villagers were gentlemanly, many of the knight's men just stared at her with blank hunger. 'Some of those hunters are just as bad,' she said, trying to even up the conversation. 'Vidar and Foaley really have to push to keep them in line too. But last night was different. It felt good to be together.'

The sun was coming up now and she admired the way it basted his face in rose-gold light. He looked like a young pagan god of dancing and music. 'What do you think about this whole journey?' she asked.

He grinned. 'What do *you* think?'

'That my father's insane,' she exclaimed. 'He thinks he can go back to Otravia and drive out all the Bolgravs and that Mother will just collapse back into his arms. He thinks everything can be like it was before.'

'And you don't?'

'Mother married a Mandaryke,' she admitted. 'Nothing can ever be right again.'

'She *married* one of them?' He gave a low whistle.

'I guess it was that or die. Father always says she's fighting from the inside.'

'I'm sure she is.'

'I miss her every day. It's been four years of fighting or hiding and pretending to be nobodies.' She blinked away tears crossly.

'Then before this, you were somebodies?' he asked curiously.

'We were Vyres,' she harrumphed. 'Grandfather was in the Assembly and Father was going to stand at the next elections – so yes, we were somebodies.' She realised how boastful she sounded, so she asked, 'What about your family?'

'Well, we're not rich, but House Rhamp is an old line in Pelaria,' Banno replied. 'We fought when Bolgravia invaded, but our cavalry got shot up and our footmen broke and ran. I lost two of my brothers that day. We fell back, hired more men and Father took those of us who were left into Vassland, but the other captains turned their coats and we barely escaped. We turned ourselves into a mercenary company and we've been guarding wagons and keeps for petty barons since then. Father thinks this is our last big chance for freedom.'

'I'm sorry for your losses,' she said formally, adding, 'It's good that you still have brothers.'

'Aye, that's true, but there's a Bolgravian governor living in my family's castle in north Pelaria: they've stolen everything of value and quadrupled taxes.' He glared out to sea. 'One day I'm going to kill every damned Bolgrav in Pelaria, or die trying.'

Why do boys always say things like that? There will always be more Bolgravs – isn't it better to be alive?

But she didn't want him to think her weak, so she nodded emphatically.

They fell silent until Banno flashed his cheeky grin and asked, 'So, do you own any skirts?'

She snorted and flicked a pebble at him. 'One or two, but they're hopeless for riding and doing anything practical. And anyway, I'm going to be a sorceress, so soon I'll be wearing apprentice robes.'

He gave a low whistle. 'You'll be well above me, then,' he said wistfully. 'You'll be needing servants and all, to do your cooking and chores.'

'Ha! Chance would be a fine thing. I've had to be mother, daughter, maid and every other *bloody* thing ever since we left Otravia,' she grumbled, before realising she'd sworn. She defiantly doubled down. 'And that's not going to *damned* well change any time soon, is it?'

'I reckon Mater Varahana will want you for the convents,' Banno said, grinning. 'Quiet, pious girl like you.'

They both burst out laughing at the thought.

Then her father's voice cracked out from the edge of the camp. 'Zar, get the horses fed and the breakfast fire underway. Banno, get back to your post.'

She exchanged an unrepentant look with her new friend and scampered away, glancing at her father as she passed and trying to assess if he really was cross.

Not really, she decided. *Maybe a little.* She went to tease him when the world wobbled and in a slow blur, she tumbled into oblivion . . .

Kemara leaned over her cooking fire, holding the handle of a black-iron pan in which cured sausage sizzled. Her stomach moaned as she inhaled the aroma. Such luxuries would begin running low soon and then what?

Will we all turn into ferali, eating raw meat with fingers and teeth?

She got lost in that thought as she ate, drifting through her worries until she heard movement and looked up to find Raythe Vyre staring down at her, an anxious look on his face.

'What is it?' she demanded, more brusquely than intended, but she hated being surprised and his penetrating eyes always unsettled her. 'What's wrong?'

'It's Zar – I think she's manifesting.'

She grimaced, remembering her own experience. 'I suppose you need someone who does actually know what they're doing when it comes to medicine,' she remarked caustically, but he didn't even notice the sarcasm.

'Yes, indeed – please?'

'Because you asked so nicely,' she muttered, hurriedly banking the fire before picking up the satchel of essential herbs she kept ready at all times. She checked to make sure she'd packed enough pots of calming unguents, then turned to face him. 'At your service, Lord Vyre.'

'It's just Raythe.' He led the way back to his wagon, where Jesco Duretto was sitting beside a blank-looking Zarelda, while Vidar, looming over them both, watched anxiously.

She went to the girl's side, flapped Jesco away and knelt. Zarelda was unconscious, her mouth slack and skin pale and clammy, but her blank eyes were glowing and she was shaking. Kemara took her hand, counted out the rapid pulse then looked up. 'Yes, she's manifesting. Have you done this before?'

'No,' Raythe admitted. 'The Church always step in at home. But I know the theory.'

'That's a comfort. We'll need blankets and broth.'

'But she's already too hot—'

'Blankets! Broth! And boil some water – lots of it.' Once she'd sent the men off on tasks designed to keep them from under her feet for as long as possible, she sorted through her herbs, running over everything the Nyostians had taught her about this process.

'Your core will go cold, but because your pores will open, you will start losing heat too fast. We have to trap that heat,' she said out loud, 'so we'll need warm infusions, woollen blankets – and hyosca oil for the skin.'

Once they'd delivered the things she'd demanded, she shooed the men away, then undressed Zar down to her small-clothes and laid her in a nest of blankets beside the fire, which was now roaring. She massaged in the hyosca oil and fed her the broth Raythe had prepared, talking to the girl all the while, for she remembered that she'd been paralysed but lucid throughout her own manifestation and she guessed Zar was fully aware too.

'You're going to be fine, lass, just stay alert. Your father's been through this, and so have I.'

She summoned Vyre with a wave and while she kept Zar comfortable and calm, he started carving symbols into the soil around them until they were enclosed in a circle of runes that glowed with the same pale blue light as the energy bleeding from Zar's eyes.

'*Cognatus, ministro*,' he murmured, and his familiar, the Shadran parrot she'd glimpsed before, appeared on his shoulder.

'Hello there,' Kemara said in greeting, and it turned a curious eye her way. Then it became a green cat and jumped down so it could start circling around outside the protective wards. 'Yes, I can see you,' she told it, making it hiss. 'And hear you.'

'You must've got a long way through the initiation before they failed you,' Raythe commented, clearly fascinated despite his worry for his daughter.

It wasn't a conversation she wanted to have, not now – or ever. 'Failed is failed,' she said curtly, closing the subject.

He went to reply, but Cognatus turned and yowled as pale shapes began to appear all round them. Raythe extended a hand and called, '*Cognatus, veni.*'

The familiar flowed into him and vanished, sending his aura pulsing, but Zar whimpered and he and Kemara turned their attention to the girl.

'Stay calm,' Kemara said, ignoring the spectral shapes outside the protective circle.

Raythe took his daughter's hand. 'Zar, listen to me: this is the moment I've been telling you about, okay? Your soul is opening and it's wanting to bond with a spirit – but you have to choose the right one, remember? I wish I could do this for you, but I can't, and it's not going to be easy. You need to *listen* to them, to get a sense of their nature before you choose, so take your time, wait until there's only two left, then signal me and I'll open the circle – then it'll be done.'

There was no sign the girl had heard, but Kemara could remember her own awakening. She'd been overwhelmed for much of it, her body and brain overstimulated, but she'd been aware and able to move at the end. *When I messed it all up.*

'Be strong, girl,' she whispered, sharing a taut look with Raythe. He was much more sympathetic when he was scared, she decided, and he clearly loved his daughter. 'It won't be long now.'

Outside the circle, shadows were dancing, glimmering eyes trained fully on the girl whose soul was opening up. They were all hungry to get in.

Too much, too much – it was a flood of light, an ocean of fire, all frozen heat and searing cold. Every breath Zarelda took carried too much information, the smells so overpowering they nauseated her, the tastes filling her mouth and drowning her – but through it all, the voices of Father and Kemara kept her anchored to the here and now.

You have to let the right one in . . . Her father had told her that, and she'd read it too, but she'd not really understood. For one, how would she know which was the right one? As she stared unmoving out of the circle into the night, she saw the spirits gathering there, shimmering blurs of light and energy forming and reforming as birds, as lizards, as cats and grasshoppers and even fish, or half-human hybrids, tiny part man, part mythical beast, all floating around the outside of the circle. They looked entirely real to her, but she knew that only a sorcerer could see them, and for the first time she noticed that none of them bent even a blade of grass when they moved. They were here just for her, and that was wonderful and terrifying.

She had read the textbook Father had given her cover to cover and even started to understand some of it. *Magic is achieved by symbiosis,* the first chapter told her. *The spirits are pure energy, but they can't discharge that power, so we sorcerers must be the conduit for that energy. By bonding with a spirit, we become their channel for interacting with the world: we direct them with words and signs. But you must choose a spirit whose nature most accords with yours to be fully effective, to achieve the most stable sorcerous partnership.*

It had sounded natural and easy, reading those words, but as the spirits closed about her, she found herself paralysed by their multitudinous eyes, their hungry mouths and reaching paws and claws. *Choose me,* they all called. *Choose* me.

107

She closed her eyes.

Fail to choose and your gift will fade. Choose awry, and the mismatch will poison and consume both you and your wrongly bonded familiar. Your gift will turn to destructive mizra and you will become anathema.

For all that, failures were rare, Father had reassured her. 'When I saw Cognatus, I just *knew*. Trust your heart, Zar.'

Now she gazed silently out into the night as the shadows danced in the light flowing from her eyes, parading themselves and tasting *her*. They knew the stakes as well as she did: they didn't want an unsuitable bonding either. So as time passed, those morphing shadows became fewer and fewer.

In the end, she'd read, *there will be two remaining: the closest matches, those most aligned to your soul. But one will be better attuned to the powers that nurture life, which we call the praxis, while the other will be more attuned to destruction, or the mizra. The last two are twins, light and dark. Choose the light.*

So she waited until finally there were just two still wooing her: a red fox cub and a brown one, circling intently. Both were utterly enchanting, winsome bundles of soft fur. Their big eyes promised love as they morphed through shape after shape, from lambs to cats to puppies to frogs and back to foxes, which had always been her favourite creature.

The red one was *adorable* and she almost reached for him – but then she saw that it was never the first to take a new shape; it was measuring her reaction to the other: it was *calculating*, while the plainer brown one had a lustrous innocence to it.

She signed to her father and he made the magical circle fade, then she reached out to the little brown fox. It cooed and dissolved into her, and her soul *chimed*.

An instant later, the red one nearly took off her hand: it started shrieking and snarling as it hit the wall of air above the protective circles and for a few seconds all she saw were flashing teeth and claws that tore at the wards, while knives of fury bored into her soul.

Then her father snapped something and swatted it away and there was just her chosen, a little brown fox cub, beaming up at her and snuggling into her lap. She fell in love.

'*Ego nomine vos "Adefar",*' she remembered to murmur. *I name you Adefar*: the diminutive of Adela, the name her mother had chosen for her own familiar.

Father and Kemara, on either side of her, were looking down at the little creature, then Father's Cognatus nuzzled Adefar, who responded with deference, like a child to a grown-up. Zar smiled at the parrot and fox cub, thinking what an incongruous pair they made.

'Well done,' her father said. 'You got the right one. Now you've got to learn how to live with it.'

Zar stroked her new companion, feeling happier than she could ever remember being. Her father grinned and hugged her hard. When he finally released her, she turned to Kemara, expecting a hug.

Instead, the healer rose, mumbled, 'Congratulations—' and strode off. That was odd, but really, nothing more than a small blemish on an otherwise perfect moment.

'So,' Father said, patting her knee, 'back home, you'd have been tested for suitability the moment you revealed any potential, taken in by an Academia and guided through your manifesting – but out here, you've done it all yourself. The important thing to remember is that right now, you are entirely capable of killing other people – and yourself. I know you'll be burning to try things out, but you need to remember, *restraint* is the defining characteristic of every good sorcerer. You need to master your spirit and your power before you start using it.'

She nodded dutifully, but she was practically purring as she stroked the fox cub.

'Learn the words, learn the runes,' her father went on, sounding very serious. 'Learn what you can and can't do. Of course, I'll be here to guide you through it.' He tousled her hair and added, 'And don't ever forget that your familiar is invisible to anyone but another sorcerer, so if you start petting it or talking to it, or reacting to it in any way, that will just annoy people.'

'He's *so* cute,' she said, gazing down at her new beloved.

'He's being precisely what he thinks will appeal to you,' her father pointed out, 'but you have to remember, "he" is probably centuries old and doesn't really have a gender – spirits can take whatever form they like. He'll test you, trying your patience and your will, but show him love, and he'll repay it in kind. With a strong bond, you'll have a friend like no other.'

'I'm ready,' she said proudly. 'I've been waiting for this all my life.'

'I know.' He put his arm round her and hugged. 'You've done well, Initiate Zarelda. Welcome to a larger world.'

'So, Master Vyre, have you worked it out?' Mater Varahana asked, joining Raythe at the edge of the sea-cliffs where the road fell into the sea.

'Not yet,' Raythe admitted.

For three days he'd been standing up here, looking over the edge at the wave-drenched boulders below, and he was conscious that people were beginning to doubt him. He'd been constantly turning the problem over in his head, but the only plan he'd come up with so far was to collapse the cliff and use the rubble to create a path along the foreshore. But he had to admit it wasn't a very practical solution, and in any case, he doubted he had the strength required.

Cognatus squawked disapprovingly at the Mater from his perch on Raythe's shoulder and took to the air. The parrot circled the priestess then landed, unseen and unfelt, on her head and mimed pecking at it like an egg.

Raythe wiped the smile from his face and signed the familiar to return. Cognatus blurred to his shoulder and becoming a cat, hissed at the priestess. He was always jealous of the people Raythe liked most.

Varahana threw him a quizzical look. 'Is something the matter?'

'Not at all. Do you have any ideas?'

The mater's demeanour suggested she had. 'Have you looked closely at the headland itself?'

Raythe turned to the hill above them, an almost sheer protuberance anchoring the mountain range to the coastline. 'Vidar's hunters have been looking for a way over these hills,' he replied, 'but so far, they've only found wild goat tracks.'

The bearskin, standing nearby with Jesco, gave a grumpy harrumph. 'This range is a spur of the Great Northern Barrier,' he growled. 'So far I've found nothing a horse could comfortably traverse, let alone a fully laden wagon.'

Varahana smiled quietly. 'Then let me show you what I found this morning.'

With Cognatus flitting above, Raythe, Jesco and Vidar followed the priestess into the shadow of the headland. She led them up a steep slope through the pines, pushing aside the encroaching undergrowth. After a few minutes' climb a shallow stream appeared, running through a narrow crevice. It wasn't wide enough to walk more than two abreast, but if they were careful, a wagon would fit, Raythe estimated. When Varahana pulled off her sandals and started to wade upstream, graceful as a heron, the men had no choice but to follow, grumbling about the chilly water.

The rivulet got deeper the further they went, until about sixty winding yards in, they reached a small pool half-hidden beneath a curtain of thick vines tumbling from the rim of the ravine more than fifty feet above them. The holy woman posed dramatically and gestured upwards. 'Ta-da!'

Raythe narrowed his eyes and followed her pointing finger – and exclaimed in surprise, for the vines were coiled around a fallen metal portcullis some twenty foot across. Studying it from this angle, he could see the cliff-face was unnaturally square.

'What is this?' Vidar asked.

'It's a *rath*: an Aldar place,' Mater Varahana replied, in rapt tones.

'Aldar?' Jesco squeaked, making a sign against evil.

'Isn't it wonderful?' Varahana trilled, clearly unconcerned about the reputation for curses and hauntings such places invariably attracted.

Raythe gave her shoulder a squeeze, then, drawing his falchion, took the lead, hacking a path through the tangled vines covering the cliff until they clambered in behind the curtain of foliage. There, they found the remains of an ancient wooden doorway, smashed open and exuding a dank draft that smelled of decay.

'Feel that? The air's moving in there – so there must be other openings,' Varahana said. 'I have long dreamed of finding such a place. With any luck, it's not been touched since the Vanith-Aldarai age.'

'Have you been inside already?' Vidar asked.

Raythe noticed the bearskin was looking nervous, his temple pulsing.

'Not yet. I thought I'd better summon some big, strong men to look after me first.' Then she laughed and added, 'And I didn't have a light.'

'Speaking of which, it's too dark to go inside –' Jesco began. He hated caves.

In answer, Raythe murmured, '*Cognatus, animus: lumis*,' while tracing *Flux*, the rune of energy. When his familiar entered him, he got the sense that Cognatus didn't like this place one bit, but a globe of pale light formed in the palm of his left hand, lighting the interior of the cave and revealing a dark tunnel behind.

'There, now we can see,' he told Jesco brightly.

'You can be such an over-achiever at times,' Jesco muttered. 'Who broke the door down?'

'It could have been anything – an animal, bandits, or just time,' Varahana replied. 'The Aldar died five hundred years ago, after all.'

'Everyone knows raths are haunted,' Vidar growled. 'That's why the Ferreans call ghosts "wraiths".'

'Nonsense,' Varahana said briskly, 'A rath was just a dwelling place. The Aldar built to last, and in their latter days they lived mostly underground, trying to escape the devastating storms they'd unleashed upon the world. Not many dwellings escaped the Mizra Wars, but some were so well hidden they were never found. This might be one.'

Raythe had seen the remnants of two Aldar strongholds in southern Otravia: both were little more than devastated stonework, mostly reclaimed by nature and well picked over by fortune-hunters and thieves, but what if this wasn't? Aldar relics were always in demand, and some could be worth *thousands* of argents.

'Let's explore,' he said. 'Perhaps there's a way through the headland – that stream might actually be the remains of an old road. And raths were often also mines, with passages wide enough for wagons.'

'I could stay here and mind the door,' Jesco suggested.

Vidar looked at him quizzically. 'Are you scared?'

'Scared? *I'm terrified!*'

'You? The fearless Jesco Duretto?' Vidar scoffed.

'I know, I know: best swordsman in Creation, best shot too, and I came through the rebellion without a scratch – you want to know how? *Fear.* I'm so terrified that I dodge faster, fight harder and kill quicker than anyone else. How about you, big man?'

'A Norgan knows no fear. We come to kill.' Vidar gave Varahana a toothy grin. 'If you say there's no ghosts in there, then there's no ghosts.'

'I didn't say that at all.' Varahana smiled. 'But we have a sorcerer with us. I'll be hiding behind him.'

'And I'll be hiding behind Jesco, as usual, to square the circle,' Raythe said briskly. 'Shall we get on so we're not late for dinner?'

They put their boots back on, then Raythe led them forward, his praxis-light burning steadily, his steps sure. At first the floor was covered in rotting leaves and detritus like the bones of long-dead animals, but as they progressed, that lessened until there was little more than a fine layer of dust over everything. The air was cold, a breeze brushing constantly at his skin. He could see vast cobwebs in the higher alcoves, but they looked lifeless, as if the spiders had long-since eaten out this place and moved on. After a few dozen yards, they found no animal droppings and the few bones they did come across were ancient, crumbling away where they lay. The rath had been lifeless for a long, long time.

Then the tunnel opened into a larger chamber with a broken fountain lying shattered in the centre. Varahana gasped and striding forward, exclaimed, 'Great Gerda, look at this—' Her voice echoed down the tunnels.

On the ground was a broken life-size statue of a robed male, marvellously wrought in cream and golden marble. The finer features of face and clothing had been smoothed by age or damage.

'Is it an Aldar?' Jesco squeaked.

'I think so. It looks like the Church did get here first, a long time ago,' Varahana said regretfully, as if she weren't a church-woman herself. 'After the Mizra Wars, all images of the Aldar were smashed and their dwellings comprehensively looted, then abandoned. No one was permitted to live in the raths.'

'Who'd want to live in such dark, creepy places anyway?' Jesco muttered.

'Oh no, once they were full of light and colour,' the Mater replied, gazing about avidly. 'They were beautiful.'

There were four exits from the courtyard and they had entered from the southeast. To their left, another stair descended, perhaps to the seashore, judging from the sound of the waves. The path to their right was blocked, but the path they wanted: opposite them and exiting the chamber to the northwest, seemed open.

'Let's go forward,' Raythe decided. 'Vidar, mark our path, please.'

The next corridor became a stair, ascending through the rath. They began to find rooms: most were empty, but some contained the rotted debris of centuries-old furnishings. Then Jesco exclaimed and bent to pick up a square copper coin.

'An Aldar *ravok*,' Varahana proclaimed, pointing out the crowned head on the reverse. 'They're rare now.'

Jesco grinned, until Raythe added, 'Some say they're haunted.'

The Shadran stiffened and dropped the coin – which Raythe neatly snatched from the air. 'They're also worth a small fortune at home,' he chuckled, pocketing the coin and winking at Jesco. 'Cheers, my friend. Too kind.'

The passage took them past a stairway going up that was mostly blocked by a rock-fall, then in a large chamber they discovered the desiccated bones of a huge beast that Vidar identified as a shingar lizard.

'Shingars can grow more than eight feet long – they eat people,' Jesco noted. 'And I'm the tastiest person here.'

'Excellent: if one appears we'll feed you to it,' Raythe replied.

'These're very old bones,' Vidar rumbled, 'and there's not even a smell of dung here. This place is deserted.'

'Except for ghosts,' Varahana put in lightly, grinning at Jesco.

With that reminder, their banter died away and they pressed on, shuffling through the darkness and dancing shadows thrown by Raythe's praxis-light. Despite education and experience, they'd all heard tales of old Aldar at their grandmothers' knees: about vengeful, inhuman wraiths with poison breath whose mere touch could draw the soul from the body. Such stories weren't easily dismissed in this ancient emptiness.

'How did there just happen to be an Aldar haunt, right where the road ended?' Jesco wondered.

'The Aldar built strongly and in tune with nature,' Varahana replied. 'It's probable that the coastline here is anchored by this rath and that its presence protects the hills behind it. Off the coast of Magnia, there are rath ruins that are now islands because they've remained intact while everything around them eroded into the sea.'

'Who exactly were the Aldar?' Jesco asked suddenly. 'I heard they were eight foot tall and came from the stars. The tales say they had wings, and eyes that could burn a man in an instant.'

'That's nonsense,' Varahana replied. 'They were men like us, and they used the mizra to make their lives easier, until it turned on them and destroyed them. They were arrogant slave-masters who warred for pleasure.'

'So do I,' Jesco said slyly, then he mock-gushed, 'Oh, sorry – I thought you said "whored for pleasure".'

Varahana gave him a prim look, but the wonder of the place quickly stole her attention back. 'Of course I'm glad the Aldar are gone,' she said, adding longingly, 'but I would dearly love to see one.'

'Be careful what you wish for,' Raythe advised as they entered the next chamber. 'What do we have here?'

His light revealed another courtyard with a dried-up pool and fountain in the middle, but this one had a domed canopy, an actual skylight to the world above. The dome was mostly intact, except where vines hung through the occasional broken pane of coloured glass. There were small piles of rotting leaves and silt mounds on the cracked stone floor underneath, but most remarkable was an almost intact statue a dozen feet tall presiding over the space. Four arms were spread wide, but they had all been broken off at the elbows, and the head, now just a shattered lump of marble, sat at its feet. The statue was of a slender female with winged feet, her robe tied with a snake-girdle.

'Is this an Aldar?' Vidar growled. 'See, I told you they weren't human: it's got four arms.'

'No, it's one of their goddesses,' Varahana replied, her scholar-self utterly intrigued. 'Perhaps it's Kiiyan; she was the most revered. The dying prayed to her for mercy in the afterlife. The extra arms were symbolic of her attributes. They would have held lanterns or flowers or the like.'

'Ki-ee-yan,' Jesco pronounced the new world reverently – he collected gods to pray to in battle. He bowed and intoned, 'We mean no harm here, Great Lady.'

Raythe snorted and advanced further into the room, wanting to examine a plinth in front of the fountain, where a stone box had been smashed open. He tentatively prodded a copper disc glinting among the wreckage, and for an instant, a faint red light pulsed beneath his fingers – and a moment later, a panel in the wall collapsed inwards, revealing a gaping rectangular-shaped hole behind them. The crunch of the falling stonework echoed through the chamber.

They all jumped in shock, raising their weapons as the sound reverberated through the silent ruins and dusty air washed over them. Raythe glanced again at the copper disc, but the faint glimmer he'd thought he'd seen was gone. Although the new opening exuded menace, nothing else stirred.

'We should go,' Jesco suggested. 'This whole place could collapse on us.'

'No,' Varahana replied, 'just think: whatever's down there has never been looted. *Imagine!*'

'I *am* imagining and *that's* why I think we should leave.'

'We'll be fine,' Raythe said. 'They're all dead and gone. But we should investigate. If we're going to bring the caravan through here, we need to know it's safe.'

Jesco groaned, but Varahana grabbed Raythe and pulled him forward, as he had the light. Vidar followed, his craggy features wary, but resolute.

Raythe and Varahana shared a look of mutual intrigue, then together, they stepped through the broken arch. 'Look,' he said, examining the broken seals, 'see this? It was closed from the *inside.*'

'That's not good,' Jesco squeaked, sounding very different from his normal assured self.

'Aldar royalty were buried with their chief servants,' Varahana lectured. 'They were expected to seal themselves in with the body.'

'Cheery,' Jesco said. 'Raythe, just saying: when you die, you're on your own.'

Raythe laughed and moved into the passage beyond, where stairs led them deeper into the earth. There were cracks in the plaster, but they could still make out the remains of a mural in which multi-armed Aldar gods vied for supremacy, or doled out judgements in courts filled with tall, slender, pale people – the Aldar themselves, perhaps? The gods all wore masks, some fierce, others serene, variously coloured in primal red, white, black, blue or green, while the Aldar had pale, narrow faces.

'It's so beautiful,' Varahana breathed. 'Look; that's Kagemori, the Death God in the demon mask; and Kiiyan with the doves. And the Jade Emperor in the emerald dragon-mask . . . Dear Gerda, I've never seen such a large Aldar mural.'

Gazing at the red-eyed, black-masked Kagemori, Raythe shuddered.

The Death God was in the process of beheading a supplicant, while fiery beast-men feasted on the carcases of those already judged and found wanting. 'What are we walking into?' he asked Varahana.

'I don't know,' she confessed, drinking in the mural avidly, trying to commit it to memory.

Further in, the barbaric murals grew ever more disturbing, showing dismembered bodies at the feet of executioners, and the wretched faces of the condemned: who had tanned, human faces.

Vidar, examining the opposite wall, growled, 'Look at these.'

'It shows the Paradise-Hall of the Jade Emperor,' Varahana exclaimed as they examined a courtly scene in which Aldar musicians played for performing dancers. Then she moved to the next panel and laughed aloud, the sound echoing merrily in the near-dark. 'Well,' she exclaimed, 'they were unashamed sinners, clearly.'

They all studied the scene, in which most of the guests in the Jade Emperor's palace were naked and engaged in the sorts of things that priestesses of Deo and Gerda frowned upon, even for reproductive purposes.

'There's rumping in Aldar heaven?' Jesco snickered. 'I want to go there when I die.'

'*Jesco, that's blasphemy*,' Vidar warned, offended more on Varahana's behalf than his own.

'We know that the Aldar had quite different mores,' Varahana said loftily, though her eyes were twinkling. 'Sexual congress was not considered sinful, and they were quite–' She had stopped before a panel where the lovers were clearly both female. She coloured and completed her thought. 'Erm . . . quite liberal.'

'No wonder they're all burning in the Pit,' Raythe drawled sarcastically. 'Let's move on, shall we?'

'You'll notice the nobles were paler of skin,' Varahana said as they descended the next flight of stairs. 'Pale skin implied a life free of toil. The Aldar believed only those of noble birth ascended to Paradise; lesser beings were reincarnated, seeking betterment. That's why their primary religious symbols were the Sacred Wheel and the Uros, a snake devouring its own tail.'

'Reincarnation,' Jesco mused. 'I'd like to come back as a queen.'

'I think that's already happened,' Varahana quipped, and the Shadran burst out laughing.

'You're quite fun, for a priestess,' he said. 'How seriously do you take your vows?'

Varahana threw him a forbidding look. 'As seriously as I take my rank.'

Only a virgin could aspire to be a mater.

'Just asking,' Jesco replied, batting the ridiculously long, thick eyelashes over his big, lustrous eyes. 'Really, I'm enquiring on behalf of a friend. Fur-clad man, tall, bit of an animal.'

Vidar gave a small growl of warning.

'See what I mean?' Jesco laughed. 'You have an admirer, priestess or not.'

'I'm going off you rapidly,' Vidar told him, while Varahana gave them both a rather nonplussed look.

'Enough,' Raythe interrupted testily. 'Let's keep our minds on the job, shall we?

Varahana gave him a grateful look and, preening unconsciously, pushed forward.

The passage switched back in the other direction as it descended. Now the murals were depicting an undersea realm presided over by a blue-masked goddess with tentacles for hair, but they weren't in good condition as they'd suffered from water seepage through the rock. This tunnel ended in an archway and a small chamber beyond. Outside the chamber lay two slumped-over skeletons wrapped in cloth that fell to dust when Varahana touched it. She made the sign of Gerda over them and breathed, 'Rest, faithful ones.'

'Kragging idiots,' Jesco sniffed.

'They likely had no choice, and their families would have been rewarded for their sacrifice,' the Mater replied, her voice sad, before suddenly blurting, 'Dear Gerda, this really is an Aldar tomb – I am in Paradise!'

She skipped into the next chamber, Raythe followed, his praxis-light illuminating a minimally adorned oval space, a dozen feet in diameter. Within lay a larger-than-man-sized coffin, the lid covered in dust. According to Varahana, the mural on the sides depicted the Jade Emperor and Lady Kiiyan, receiving the homage of a kneeling, masked warrior.

Varahana went to the box, which was surely a sarcophagus, and brushed the dust off it with her hand, then she gasped and recoiled. When Raythe stepped to her side, he saw the lid was glass and with the dust smoothed away, they could clearly see a being in sumptuous robes, wearing a demonic mask. The corpse's visible skin was dark with age and desiccation, the fingers just bones, but gold gleamed from a ring on his right index finger.

'It's the man – or woman – in the mural,' Varahana breathed, pointing at the kneeling drinker. 'See, it's the same mask. This must have been an Aldar king or queen, to have such a tomb.' Her voice was awestruck. 'I've heard that Aldar skeletons remain intact for millennia, but in their campaign to eradicate all memory of the Aldar, the Church burn them. To find an intact tomb like this is *incredible*.'

'They say the Aldar could be man or woman at will,' Jesco breathed. 'Imagine that.'

Varahana looked at him. 'You know that's just an old wives' story, don't you? It's based on bad translations of old texts. The Aldar didn't use gender-specific terms like "he" or "she" in their writing and they never appeared unmasked before a human, so the story grew that they had no gender. It's all bunk – and that's a fact.'

'Facts are overrated,' Jesco replied. 'I prefer my own sweet fantasies.'

Varahana waved him off and went back to studying the entombed Aldar. 'This is magnificent, Raythe,' she said, studying the scroll-work embossed on the side, then sounding out symbols: 'Bu-ra-ma-na-ka . . . Buramanaka. Loosely, it means "Devouring Wind".'

'Nice,' Jesco drawled. 'Clearly a lovely fellow, fond of children . . . for breakfast.'

'We should burn him,' Vidar growled.

'*Never!*' Varahana exclaimed. 'This is a treasure beyond price.'

'Shouldn't a priestess be exorcising this place?' Raythe asked, amused by Varahana's passion.

'Exorcism is rot; it's just window-dressing for commoners,' the mater replied, trampling over centuries of Church tradition. 'Dear Gerda, I could learn so much from examining the skeleton, and his clothing and gear – look how well preserved it all is in there. If we leave it and someone else finds it, they'll likely destroy it, and who knows what knowledge will be lost for ever? Raythe, can we take it with us?'

Raythe looked from the priestess' excited face to the dead Aldar's mask and back. 'I understand, Vara, truly I do. But think of the practical issues. How could we transport it safely? It would crumble the moment we tried to move it. And possessing one Aldar artefact is illegal – think of how we'd suffer if we were caught with an actual corpse! Even researching them is forbidden except under Church guidance.'

'I know, believe me,' Varahana murmured, then she brightened. 'But *I'm* the Church out here.'

'I'm not sure Archmater Elymas would sanction grave-robbing – and even if we did manage to get it back to camp intact, there's no way we could transport it further without damaging it – just the movement of the wagons will wreak havoc. And if anyone found it, there'd be utter panic.' He studied the chilling corpse, then gave her a sympathetic look. 'Those rings are valuable. You can take them.'

Varahana looked stricken. 'But the mask—'

'Not that,' Raythe insisted. Aldar masks had an uncanny reputation.

Varahana sagged, but she didn't argue. 'All right, if you insist.' She turned back to the coffin, found the latch and unclipped it, then gripped the side and lifted.

Fear . . .

'Did you hear that?' Raythe asked. It sounded like someone had whispered the word 'fear' – or maybe it was 'Vyre'? But no one else had reacted, and he instantly doubted his ears.

'Hear what,' Jesco squeaked, 'a ghost?'

'No,' Raythe replied, engaging his sorcerer's sight and looking around. 'There are no spirits here.'

Varahana made the sign of blessing over the dead Aldar, then reached in and pulled the rings from the bony fingers. Handing them to Raythe, she said sternly, 'These are not for selling.'

'I know,' he told her, handing them back. 'Keep them, to remember this place by.'

She positively glowed in response, then turned back to the mask and gazing longingly at it, started, 'Can't we –?'

'Aldar masks were sorcerous artefacts,' Raythe reminded her.

'Then we should smash it,' Jesco chimed in.

'That wouldn't be enough. I know they require specific rites to render them inert.' He shut the glass lid and let out his breath. 'We should re-seal this tomb,' he said. 'We don't want anyone else down here – especially as they'll see that it's recently been disturbed.'

Vidar frowned. 'Let's make sure there's a path all the way through this hill before we get too far ahead of ourselves. That's why we're here, remember.'

'Good point,' Raythe agreed. 'Onwards.'

When they got back upstairs, he called upon Cognatus to hide their disturbances, then, using earth magic, he did his best to repair the shattered stone seal. Even after applying the spells, it remained cracked and weak, so he traced the rune *Visu* – the eye – to conceal it with illusion. 'That'll have to do,' he told them. 'As long as no one actually leans against it, it'll remain hidden for years.'

Varahana looked ready to cry, but Jesco was clearly relieved to be moving on.

The next passage ascended in a series of switchback ramps into more formal areas until they emerged into a burnt-out entrance hall with giant double doors partially broken and open to the elements. Birds were roosting in the upper decorations of the columns and there were all manner of leaves and twigs and old bones, the accumulated debris of centuries. The ceiling had partially fallen and the air stank of rot and decay.

Jesco, sweating profusely, hurried to the doors and climbed through, returning just a few moments later to report a clear paved road and a wooded valley beyond. 'Looking back, the entrance is clearly visible,' he said, 'but I don't think anyone lives out here. I can't see any trace of cooking fires in the valley below.'

'The Ghost Road has been closed to all-comers for decades,' Raythe reminded them. 'No one's supposed to be out here, and in any case, it's not fertile land.' He considered the way they'd come. 'We'll have to navigate a few stairs and there are some narrow places, but I think with a bit of effort, we can get our people through, wagons and all.'

'As long as they're not too superstitious to try,' Varahana said. 'They'll need reassurance.'

'I'm sure you'll convince them, Vara. And well done for finding this path.'

'Deo will always light our way,' Varahana quoted, 'even in the darkest cavern.' Then her face brightened. 'Isn't this the most wonderful place? I can die happy now.'

'Governor, your people have vanished. What are you doing about it?'

Toran Zorne's voice seldom varied, Larch Hawkstone noticed. Whether he was questioning a peasant with the help of a heated knife or dealing with the governor of the province, that same inflexible monotone prevailed. There was an almost childlike simplicity to it, as if he didn't have the emotional range to support his vocabulary.

The man has no soul, he thought yet again.

Governor Milek Veterkoi seemed to feel the same way. The empire's chief local bureaucrat, a fat, greasy-looking man, was slouched in his seat of office, flanked by grey-haired functionaries who were taking turns to murmur in his ear. The Governor's Manor was in Sommaport Town, fifteen miles from the mysteriously abandoned village of Teshveld.

'I don't care where they've gone, Master Zorne,' Veterkoi repeated. 'Keeping order in Teshveld costs more than we take in tax. The empire is better off without them.'

'They are imperial subjects and may not depart our borders without your leave.'

'They have it,' the governor snapped. 'I didn't want those bastards and their whore-wives anyway. They can journey to the Pit for all I care.'

'The Ramkiseri does not approve of fugitives,' Zorne said firmly. 'And I have reason to believe that numbered among them are several wanted men and women.'

The governor sniffed. 'They're *all* petty criminals and scum, Zorne.'

'There are Otravian rebels among them who are wanted by the Lictor. He has offered a substantial reward for their recapture. One in particular, known here as Dash Cowley, carries a price on his head of one hundred thousand argents.'

The governor's eyes bulged, and so did Hawkstone's.

Gerda's Tits, that's enough to retire on thrice over, thought the Borderer captain.

'I, uh—' Governor Veterkoi stammered, then managed, 'Who is this man?'

Bloody good question, Hawkstone thought. *And what'd he do, to whom?*

'His real name is Raythe Vyre,' Zorne responded flatly.

'Colfar's right-hand man?' Veterkoi exclaimed. Then he asked, 'Who gets the reward?'

'Any rewards will accrue to those key to the successful conclusion. We of the agency do not profit from our work; our reward is the maintenance of the imperial peace.'

The Ramkiseri are as corrupt as any other ministry and the only peace they offer is the grave, Hawkstone thought, but he had to admit that Toran

Zorne did appear to be something of an exception: a man who lived up to the ideal, accepting no bribes and cutting no corners. *It's a miracle he hasn't been knifed yet.*

'Key to that success will be the official who takes responsibility for resourcing my investigation,' Zorne added, looking meaningfully at the governor. 'That person will also have to take responsibility for distributing the reward.'

Veterkoi leaned forward, determined that he would be that man. 'So if I give you soldiers and you find this miscreant, I get the reward – to distribute to those deserving of a share, of course.'

'Correct,' Zorne said stiffly.

'Then I think we have an understanding, Under-Komizar Zorne. Make free with my province. Just find the fugitives and collect that reward for me.'

Zorne's expression didn't change. 'I need a ship – or better, two – readied for me, with a detachment of marines.'

'Two ships?' Veterkoi raised his brows.

'Vyre's people haven't gone east, back into imperial lands: it's too well-populated for concealment. We would also have known if they had taken ship. That means they have either gone south into Shadra, or fled northwest into the coastal forests. There are fleets between here and Shadra and the imperial governor there is vigilant.' *Unlike you*, his tone implied.

'Therefore,' Zorne went on, 'I conclude that Vyre has taken the Ghost Road north, and if that is the case, I will need ships to overtake him.'

'But where are they going?' Veterkoi asked, bemused.

'Verdessa,' Zorne replied. 'That is where Lord Gospodoi returned from, only to be murdered by Vyre, and from that incident I must infer that Lord Gospodoi found something of value in Verdessa.'

'Then you will have your ships,' Veterkoi said, his voice grudging. 'It will take me a week to recall them from the south. They'll need to be refitted – and then you'll be battling northerlies all the way. You might be better off riding after them,' he concluded hopefully.

Zorne considered, then shook his head. 'No, I will take your ships, despite the delay. If I'm wrong, they will enable me to correct my course without leaving us stranded in the wilds. And I wish to retain Captain Hawkstone's men as scouts. We will depart tomorrow.'

Hawkstone remembered the lethal violence Vyre and his friends had unleashed on his men. He had no desire to take them on again. He glanced at Veterkoi, shaking his head faintly, but the Governor completely ignored him and instead waved his hand airily.

'Of course, Komizar. Hawkstone and his men are yours,' he said, making Hawkstone's heart sink. 'I myself will select your men and requisition ships. And thank you, Komizar.'

'Under-Komizar,' Zorne corrected.

With a silent sigh, Hawkstone saluted his old and new commanders, but Zorne was already striding away with barely a nod to Veterkoi.

Hawkstone scurried to catch up. 'This Vyre must be an evil bastard,' he ventured, as they descended a flight of steps.

'Evil?' Zorne looked puzzled. 'I do not acknowledge the concept. Men of base types are ruled by animal urges and self-interest. Only higher men act according to principles. Like most, Vyre is of the base type.'

As are you, Hawkstone, his blank grey eyes seemed to add.

As they left the governor's mansion, Hawkstone couldn't help thinking that Zorne was likely going to be the death of him – and that he'd be better off putting his dagger in the man's back before that happened.

Although perhaps that's just my animal urges and self-interest . . .

5

Through the rath

The journey through the Aldar rath wasn't difficult, but their guttering torches were a paltry ward against the dark and the sheer menace of the passages seemed to suck the air from the travellers' lungs. The Aldar's legacy of desolation crushed hope like an avalanche. The travellers whispered, crept and prayed their way through the maze.

Kemara Solus didn't enjoy having to cajole Beca through the gloom, both of them sweating from claustrophobia. She wasn't superstitious or scared of the dark, but confined spaces always triggered her worst memories.

But she had more to worry about than some ancient ghosts. A month ago Osvard Rhamp had put his hand on her breast in Gravis' tavern, trying to feel her up, so she'd broken his nose. The matter was supposed to be done, but she knew Osvard wasn't the sort to let things go and of late he'd begun to hang around her again. Mater Varahana had warned Sir Elgus for her, but she was pretty sure the old knight had just ignored her.

He'll try something again, I know it. Her mother had taught her that an unmarried woman must face the world boldly, presenting a mask of fearlessness, or men would trample her into the muck. *You have to fight for yourself, because no one else will.* Her mother had died alone, though, because she'd not learned the other lesson Kemara had taken to heart: in unity is strength. Kemara had always made sure to befriend other women, for mutual protection.

Men didn't understand that to be a woman – especially a solitary one – was to be always on watch, to be always guarding yourself. It was oppressive, all that fear, but she tried not to succumb to it, taking pleasure in company and music and dance, the things she loved, refusing to live with one eye always glancing over her shoulder, watching the shadows.

Some men could be trusted for a night or two, but only a woman could be a friend. And the only person she'd ever truly loved had died horribly, and she'd done nothing but watch.

'Solace . . .'

She started at the darksome voice that whispered in her ear as she entered a larger chamber where a great fountain lay in dry, dusty ruins at the feet of a headless statue. An arched opening on the far side showed the way forward. Beca quivered nervously and the cart rumbled to a halt. She saw a torch in a wall-holder, marking the exit to take, but that whisper had seemed to come from the direction of the fountain.

Solace – or Solus?

A moment later there was a sharp cracking sound to her right and amid a great puff of dust, a concealed passageway was revealed. For a moment she feared the whole tunnel would collapse.

Then a shadowy shape formed in the new opening and a woman's voice whispered, *'Kemara.'*

The voice tugged at her heart, reminding her that there were worse things than Osvard Rhamp in the darkness after all.

'Ionia?' she whispered, then she shook her head, thinking, *Ionia's dead. She's ash.*

But the cowled shape beckoned, then turned and vanished into the darkness. She stared after it, unexpectedly stricken by grief and dread.

Then the next wagon caught up and Relf Turner shouted, 'Move your kraggin' beast, Healer!'

She threw him a caustic look, drew Beca to the side, tethered her and waved the Turners past. Relf peered at her curiously, until his wife slapped his arm and told him to stop gawping.

Once they'd gone, Kemara took the torch from the front of her cart and darted to the new opening – but it wasn't normal. There was a translucent film hanging in the air that distorted the opening, but she could see right through it to a passage beyond.

It's an illusion, she realised. Someone had placed a veil over this section of the wall and she'd have driven right past it had not she heard that voice. *And seen Ionia . . .*

She hesitated and glanced back, but the next wagon wasn't yet in sight, so holding her torch aloft, she stepped through. Within, she found a dusty hall with debris strewn across the floor and decayed murals everywhere of ancient gods and people at war and play. She paused to look, then that voice whispered from the next doorway, '*Kemara . . .*'

She spun round and glimpsing a wispy shape, she hurried after it, but it kept flitting ahead, always just out of sight. She followed recklessly, until she found herself descending steps to a small room, guarded by two skeletons and dominated by a glass-topped sarcophagus. There was no sign of the ghostly woman any more, and the voice had become androgynous, with a distinctly alien lilt.

'*Koni'ka, Kemara*,' it said. '*Toru gigaku ka.*'

She knew the language: it was Aldar, just as Ionia had taught her, and the voice had said, *Greetings, Kemara. Take the mask.* Her heart thudded at the thought that she had been recognised, and knowing by what. Years of dread welled up, freezing her in place, for *this* was what she'd been running from, ever since she'd fled Ferrea.

No, she corrected herself, *I ran from the empire. This is what I've been running to . . .*

She looked into the shadows, hoping to glimpse her former mentor, though there was no one there. But then the ancient ash encrusted on the roof sparkled and shifted to a woman's face – to Ionia, gazing out at her with reassurance and want.

'*Kemara, dear heart, take it*,' she whispered. '*It's been waiting for you.*'

Kemara went to reply, but the face vanished and her words died stillborn. With her heart thudding painfully, she examined the sarcophagus. A desiccated old skeleton lay there, stripped of rings or other jewels, but in any case, they would not have been the real prize, which was still there.

A *gigaku*: an Aldar spirit mask.

It was a fearsome thing, lacquered in deep scarlet, its features neither male nor female, with a maw that was all teeth, a wrinkled nose, big eye sockets and goat horns. It was undoubtedly a historical treasure, if you didn't know exactly what it was – but she did. Gigaku were used for channelling spirits: wearing the mask created a bond similar to those shared by praxis-sorcerers with their familiars.

I should leave this well alone . . .

But Ionia wanted her to take it, and it wanted to be out in the world again. It was also intrinsically valuable, especially to certain people – it was probably worth more than she could ever hope to make from this journey, even if Vyre's promises came close to reality.

I don't have to wear it, she told herself. *I could sell it and have a life of my own choosing . . .* There was a thriving black market in such artefacts, and she knew people . . .

I won't wear it, she told herself. *I'll just sell it.*

Greed was ruling her, she knew that, but she was more troubled by the knowledge that she wasn't entirely sure what it was exactly that she was greedy for. But she lifted the lid and plucked the thing up, and for a moment she had to really fight not to fit it to her face. From somewhere she found the strength to bundle it into her mantle.

She closed the sarcophagus, bowed her head and hurried away.

'*Solace,*' the voice whispered.

Solus meant 'Sun Child', nothing to do with consolation or mercy, but this felt like some consolation for all she'd been through. *I won't use it,* she told herself. *I'll just sell it and move on.*

She refused to look back as she left the chamber, even though she knew she'd see Ionia standing there with *that* look on her face. Blinking away tears, she took to the stairs and fled.

A few more wagons had passed Kemara's as she explored, but no one seemed at all suspicious and nor did anyone appear to notice when she slipped out of the concealed passage, untethered Beca and re-joined the column on its dark passage through the rath.

Twice she had to get out and lend her shoulder to the wheel to help Beca up flights of stairs, each step a battle. None of Rhamp's men offered help as they passed. They all blamed her for Osvald's actions. She and the mule were both perspiring heavily as they reached the entrance hall above.

As she led her mule through the broken doors and into the light again she glanced at the sun, shocked to discover they'd been only a few hours underground – it had felt like for ever.

Raythe Vyre's boyish daughter, standing near the doors, gave her a shy wave – then Banno Rhamp strutted by and Zar's attention went entirely to him.

Kemara snorted in gentle derision; Raythe had better stop that fast, if he didn't want to be a grandfather before his time.

She guided Beca into the press of milling wagons, to hear the travellers loudly marvelling over the old Aldar ruins and their own daring in traversing them. The idiots had clearly expected boghuls and nashreks to assail them at any moment. She suspected she'd been the only one to see a real ghost.

It was a cold, clear day, made colder by the wind blowing off the snow-covered peaks to the north. Her eyes were drawn to their jagged edge, the southern border of the Iceheart, the vast untracked wastes where nothing and no one had lived since the Mizra Wars. They really were approaching the edge of the map, the edge of where humans could live.

Then like a hot cattle-prod to the back of her head, she felt eyes on her and when she looked back, she saw Osvard Rhamp a dozen yards away, leaning on a spear and chewing redleaf, staring at her. When their eyes met, the pig made a stroking gesture along the shaft of his spear and grinned, licking his lips.

Her whole skin prickled and her perspiration went cold, making her damp clothes clammy.

She turned away and hurried Beca to a clear spot surrounded by people she knew well, and made a point of calling greetings to her neighbours, to make sure they all knew she was there.

He'll try something again, and soon, she worried. *He doesn't care about the consequences.*

But right now there were her patients to see to, dinner to prepare and a camp to ready. She rubbed down Beca and fed her, then walked her to a nearby stream, where she found herself alongside the heavily pregnant Regan Morfitt, who was due in a month or two.

Even though it was only midday, they wouldn't be moving on today, not when more than half the wagons were still making the slow underground journey through the hill. Several of the larger carts had had to be broken down to fit through; they needed to be reassembled before they could move on.

When she returned to camp, it was immediately clear that someone had rifled through her possessions – no, more than that: they'd slashed the bodice strings on her other two dresses, and hacked the word 'slut' into the front panels with a knife.

She checked her secret cache and found the mask still there, along with her paltry stock of jewels, her tarnished silver earrings and bracelets. She'd not been robbed, but she felt *violated.*

No matter what I do, he's not going to leave me alone . . .

'What now?' Raythe yawned, as yet another person loomed over him with yet more problems to unload.

'Hey, Grumpy,' Zar said, crouching beside the embers of their fire and prodding it into life.

He jolted up. 'Zar! Sorry, darling, didn't realise it was you. I thought it was Gravis again. By Deo, he can complain when the mood takes him.' His eyes narrowed. 'Where've you been?'

'Huh. You didn't even notice I wasn't here.'

Too true. 'I'm sorry, Zar. I've had people coming to me constantly, like I can solve everything.'

'It's your expedition,' his daughter pointed out. 'What'd you expect?'

'Perhaps a little more self-sufficiency?' He sighed heavily. 'Rhamp's bullies think they can do what they like, half the woodsmen are almost feral and the ordinary villagers don't feel safe – and I'm horribly sure they're right to feel that way.'

'Not all of Rhamp's men are bad,' Zar replied. 'Banno –'

'You keep away from him. He's ten years your elder.'

'Five.'

'Whatever. His older brother is a thug and I warrant he's no better.'

She stood, hands going to hips – *so like Mirella* – and snapped, 'You know nothing.'

'You're the one who knows nothing,' he retorted. 'Banno might be "nice", but he has a long way to go to prove himself worthy of trust, and given that his father will probably stab me in the back the moment we find the istariol, I'm not holding out too much hope.'

'Yeah, like your judgement of character's so damned good.'

'*Zarelda!*'

For a moment they glared hotly at each other, then his anger broke. 'Look, sorry, sorry. Just be careful, all right?' When she still looked fit to stomp off, he said, 'Why don't we see what that new familiar of yours can do?'

Her face immediately softened, though she was still cross, but she made an imperious gesture and her familiar streaked in from the dark, still in fox cub form, and nuzzled her calves.

Raythe called Cognatus to him and he and Zar watched the two familiars tread carefully around each other, shifting from shape to shape – cat to hound to wolf to bear – and then suddenly they pounced on each other and began flailing furiously.

Zar squealed, but Raythe interjected. 'Leave them. They won't hurt each other.'

'Are you sure?'

'It's just play . . . well, more like they're testing each other out.' They watched the pair wrestle, a blur of speed and shapes and silent snarls and squeals, then Raythe conjured a little raw energy, enough to link to Cognatus.

'*Opperio, Cognatus*,' he called, and the familiar immediately flashed to his shoulder and perched in parrot shape.

Zar's familiar snapped at him until she also called, '*Opperio, Adefar—*'

But instead of obeying her, the spirit flashed up into the nearest tree and sat staring down at her with beady eyes.

'*Opperio!*' Zar snapped again, pointing to the ground at her feet – but her familiar tittered like a mischievous child and vanished. '*Adefar – Adefar?*'

She went to chase him, but Raythe laid a hand on her arm. 'Wait. He's testing you.'

'But *why*?'

'Remember what I told you? Whatever he looks like, he's *not* a cute fox cub. He's a wild thing that has never had any limits placed on him before now. He doesn't want to serve you, or even be your friend – he wants to *be* you. So you have to establish the boundaries, just like you would with any pet.'

'But he's not just a pet,' she blurted. 'I want us to be *partners*.'

He stroked her arm. 'And you will be, Zar, but right now, he wants to be the boss and you can't let that happen.' He smiled, remembering his own struggles. 'Remember, at best a spirit is about as bright as a really smart dog. They can recognise commands and they're sensitive to mood, but they're not smart enough to be in control. *You* have to be the leader, and that means you need to win the battle of wills.'

'I'm not a bully,' she told him grumpily. 'I want him to love me.'

'Of course you do – and you know what? I went through exactly the same thing. So here's what you need to remember: some sorcerers react by trying to bully their familiar into submission – that can work, and those who take that route will be quick to tell you it's the only way. But a familiar who resents you will get you killed in the end. It'll wear you out, it'll be inefficient and malicious: it'll become the thing you make it. But if you're patient and firm, and do everything with love, it'll reward you with the same.'

She thought for a little, then asked, 'So what do I do?'

'Just wait. Don't be angry, don't try to pull him in or punish him. Wait, be open, and he'll come back to you.' He ruffled her mop of unruly hair. 'Patience.'

'I'm not a patient person,' she muttered.

'But you can be.'

She groaned, then sighed heavily. 'I suppose if you can do it, I can do it better.'

He snorted. 'That's the spirit.'

She hugged him briefly, then rose. 'I need to go for a walk.'

He frowned – it was late evening, and the camp was almost fully asleep. 'Don't go far,' he warned. 'Stay inside the perimeter.'

'I'm only going to pee,' she told him tartly. 'Is that all right?' She spun on her heels and stalked off, leaving him floundering, as she increasingly did these days. She was growing up and changing fast and he didn't really know what to do.

Cognatus chirruped impatiently and he stroked his soft feathers, then sent him off to do whatever he wished. It was tempting to set him to watch Zar, but he'd have quickly forgotten the task anyway.

She'll be fine, he told himself. *She'll have her familiar mastered by dawn.*

Five minutes later, as he poked at the smouldering fire, a girl's scream ripped the air and his heart almost stopped.

Kemara glared out at the night from her tiny circle of light, refusing to cry like a kragging baby over what had been done to her clothes.

What are *you going to do about it?* the darkness asked, a dark that now wore a lacquered face.

She'd asked around and found out who'd slashed them: one of the

Rhamps' camp-women. 'Osvard didn't even have the guts to do it him-self,' she muttered. Confronting him would do no good; he'd just tell her to krag off – and what could she do about it anyway?

Vyre won't do anything and Elgus will shield his son, no matter what.

She'd spent the evening among other women, even singing vespers with the Sisters of Gerda, anything to avoid being alone, but the camp was falling asleep and her companions had all retired for the night.

I should have set up next to Varahana. It's too late now – but I've camped alone before, and anyway, I'm only a few dozen yards from Relf Turner's family. I'll be fine.

Rhamp's people, over by the open doors to the Aldar fortress, had been singing and drinking to their own dubious courage. But soon that racket had settled down and she began to breathe more easily. Finally, exhausted, she closed her eyes and almost immediately fell into a dream where a masked being like a bipedal panther stalked her through the ancient Aldar ruins.

She woke sometime later, cold because she'd fallen asleep before properly bedding down. All was silent; the planetary rings arching above looked so close she might almost be able to stretch out and touch them. She shook out her blanket and rolled onto her back, settling into sleep again –

–when she jerked up, because someone was moving through the grass just a few feet away. She slipped her knife into her hand, although it was more utensil than weapon, and sat up.

'Who's there?' she called, but of course no one replied.

The air seemed to drop in temperature, sending a cold pulse through her skin – then someone did move, off to her right – and as she spun, a man chuckled from somewhere on her left and she whirled again and saw a big shape loom out of the shadows and her mouth flew open, because she wasn't too proud to scream.

But the shadows blurred, a rough hand clamped over her face, chok-ing off her cry, while another hand fastened around her wrist and *twisted.* A spasm of pain shot up her arm and the knife fell from suddenly lifeless fingers. She tried to fight, but though she was strong for a woman, against a man trained to the sword, with shoulders like rocks and muscles she couldn't span with two hands, she was borne down, her face planted into the dirt and a heavy, stinking weight crushed her flat, jolting the air from her lungs. She dimly sensed another man appear – then he crunched his boot down on her hand, but her sharp cry was stifled by dirt.

Red pain burst through her skull and blood flooded her nostrils.

'Not so high and mighty now are you, *Healer*?' Osvard Rhamp snarled in her ear. His free hand gripped her skirts and yanked them up, baring her thighs as she thrashed beneath him.

The other man blurted, 'Ossi, you said you wouldn't–'

'Shut the krag up,' Osvard snarled, pushing her face back into the earth. 'Relax, *Healer*. It's the last bit of fun you'll have before I send you to the Pit.'

She managed to turn her head aside enough to prevent him breaking her nose as he slammed her head down again, but that left her so dazed that she just lay there as he tugged at his belt and breeches. Her whole body clenched in terror . . .

Then someone did scream, only a few yards away, her shrill, piercing cry ripping the night in two. *A young girl's scream.*

Osvard growled like the beast he was, but he didn't get off. However, the second man whirled and hurtled towards the sound.

Zar had drifted around the fringes of the camp fires, thinking hard. *Patience.* She hated the word, but by Gerda she'd surely learned it in the last four years: in the squalor of the rebellion's camps and during their flight afterwards. She'd grown up in a mansion in a big city, but four years of poverty and fear had taught her perseverance, too.

And of course, there was that interminable wait for the praxis to manifest. She'd never doubted it would happen: she'd woken each morning expecting some sign, but every day had been a disappointment, every morning a dawn of hope.

I waited for that and it came. I can outlast a little familiar spirit . . .

After she'd peed, she headed in the direction she'd last seen Adefar, not calling but just being visible, avoiding the distractions of other people, skirting the Rhamps' encampment, even though she really wanted Banno's reassuring presence.

She could sense Adefar was hovering nearer and nearer, losing the contest of will by degrees, and decided she could stay out just a little longer, to see if the familiar would return of its own free will.

But then she heard a woman's gasp of pain and revulsion, and dark, hot male voices, and she saw movement beside the nearest camp fire: Kemara's little camp – and that *someone* was lying on top of the healer, grunting and pulling at her clothing.

For a moment she didn't comprehend and went to turn away in embarrassment at interrupting something – then the man slammed Kemara's face into the dirt and she realised what it was she was seeing.

Zar's reaction was instant, the gut response of seeing someone afflicted by what every women dreaded: she screamed like a washer-wraith, the sound bursting from her lungs and ripping through the silence.

The man on Kemara jerked his face towards her and she recognised Banno's older brother – then a man she'd not seen stormed towards her, growling, 'You, shut the feck up!'

In her terror, her mind froze – but her body responded, jerking her backwards as she shrieked, *'Father!'* She tried to dart aside, but the man was on her in an instant and bearing her heavily to the ground.

He landed on top as her back struck the turf, crushing the air from her lungs, and inside her head something seemed to tear loose, while he babbled, 'Shut up, shut up, shut up –' and his flailing hands tore her blouse . . .

Then Adefar flashed into her like a torrent of fury, light and heat boiled up in her right hand and she thrust it into her attacker's face. Something like a river of icy fire streamed through her, exploding through her palm in a flash of livid heat that seared her attacker's cheek.

His body spasmed away from her and he jack-knifed over, wailing in agony as she tried to rise, but her legs wouldn't respond and her whole body was shocked into immobility by the aftermath of that explosion of energy.

But even in the heat of terror and revulsion, part of her was exulting: *Adefar came for me.* She cradled him against her soul as the night burst into life around her.

Raythe was up and running in an instant, powering through the darkness, calling Cognatus to him as he hurtled towards the echo of his daughter's voice, while all around him, the camp shook itself awake. Torches were flaring and voices shouting – then another cry erupted, but this was male and he recognised a blend of panic and pain. He headed for that wailing, and now he spotted the small fire still burning, and someone was moving on the ground and a man was climbing off a woman – and steel was glimmering cold in the firelight.

He bounded in, caught the wielder's wrist and twisted, hard, then hammered a fist into the man's jaw, sending him staggering. The knife went flying off into the dark, but the man came back at him, and now Raythe recognised Osvard Rhamp, his face rendered copper-red by the flames, and he was wrenching out his sword as he came.

Raythe threw himself aside from a wild swipe and lashing out with a double-legged scything sweep of the legs, tangled Osvard's limbs and sent him sprawling. He rolled away from a swinging sword that bit the turf beside his head, ripped out his own falchion from his scabbard and rose.

On the ground, Kemara Solus was also rolling away, pulling her skirts down. Her face was a mess of blood and dirt and the tale of what he'd interrupted was utterly clear. But there was no sign of Zarelda.

Osvard was coming at him again, lining up a deadly thrust which Raythe parried aggressively, then whirled through a high cut that became a feint so late it defied sight, turning the blow into a slash that opened up Osvard's arm. The mercenary howled, dropping his sword into the fire, and Raythe released one hand from his falchion, clenched his fist and slammed it into the mercenary's jaw.

Osvard went down hard, out cold before he hit the ground. Raythe whirled, paused an instant to ensure Kemara wasn't bleeding out, then spun to face the shadows.

'Zar?' he shouted in terror.

'Father!' His daughter's voice was strangled but somehow triumphant and he stumbled through the darkness until he found her on the ground, cradling her familiar. Beside her was a young man clutching his face, writhing and whimpering, oblivious to everything but his pain.

Raythe gathered up his daughter in his arms and clasped her to him as she sobbed.

Then Vidar Vidarsson and Jesco Duretto burst into the light of Kemara's cooking fire, weapons drawn, and other voices demanded to know what was happening.

'I've got you, I've got you,' he told his daughter, before asking, 'What happened?'

'I . . . I—' Zar stammered, and then she writhed in his grip and showed him her left hand: it was glowing, pale orange licked with scarlet, but the light was fading even as he stared at it.

He understood at once. *She's used sorcery, without any training . . .*

She was pale and frightened, her blouse was torn and she was in shock, from both the aftermath of using the praxis for real and the assault. But she was also excited. He pulled her to her feet and hugged her hard, while glancing down at the man at his feet: Poel, the young-est of Rhamp's feral sons.

'What happened?' he demanded again, although he was shaking with fury, for the story was clear. The real question was, what should he do about it?

'Rhamp!' a voice shouted, out of the darkness. 'Elgus, get out here, *now!*'

The knight was already awake and arming himself, roused by the alarm spreading through the camp. He threw a grim look at Tami, who was also up and belting her sword-belt over her nightdress. 'What's this about?' he asked blearily as he stamped outside and watched his camp lurch into wakefulness. The lads had grown slack on the road, losing their discipline, and he made a mental note to set that right.

Then he glared about, picking out faces. *There's Banno . . . Nesto and Falgram, there's Semus . . .* Then, *Kragga! Where're Osvard and Poel?*

He'd only bred sons – his wife used to jest that he was compensating for something. Mind, she'd been the only one who could get away with that sort of lip. Birthing Poel had killed her, and his boys had grown all the wilder for that loss. Tami had been warning him for days that his eldest and youngest were plotting something stupid.

I should've listened.

'Rhamp!' It was Raythe Vyre's voice.

As Bloody Thom and Crowfoot, his lieutenants, joined him, Tami patted his shoulder, then darted into the shadows, a crossbow in her hands. He smiled. She was a keeper.

'What is it, Vyre?' he shouted back defiantly as the bonfire roared back to life, revealing a group of fellow travellers at the edge of his camp: Raythe Vyre, with Vidar Vidarsson and the Shadran, Jesco Duretto. Vyre had his daughter with him, pale as a wraith. And the Ferrean bitch Kemara Solus, the likely cause of all the trouble, was there too, her face roughed up.

But what froze him was that they had Osvard and Poel with nooses round their necks, the loose ends cradled by Duretto and Vidarsson. The ropes, he suddenly realised, were slung over a branch of the tree they all stood beneath. His hand flew to his pommel as anger belched in his belly.

No one treats a Rhamp like that . . . He made a sign to Crowfoot to prepare for mayhem. *Maybe it's time to put Vyre in the dirt?* He heard the whores squeal as they were shoved to the back, and the rasp of steel clearing scabbards, the growls of readiness. So he strode out to meet these *bastards* who *dared* threaten his boys.

But by the time he'd reached talking distance, he'd schooled his face to geniality. A smile could mask a blow better than most other ruses. 'Raythe,' he drawled, 'what *appears* to be the problem here?'

Vyre wasn't fooled for a moment. 'What's the punishment for rape, Elgus?' He gestured and Duretto and Vidarsson hauled on the ropes, bringing Osvard and Poel to their tiptoes, eyes bulging. Osvard was bleeding from the arm and Poel had a livid red hand-print burned into his face. 'It's hanging, I believe.'

'In Shadra, we cut a man's cock off,' Jesco put in, tugging Poel's rope. 'We leave him an inch, for pissing.'

'In the uplands of Pelaria, we leave a man tied to a stake, for the wolves,' Vidar growled.

Elgus placed a mark against both men's names, but for now, he pushed his anger down and feigned confusion. 'Come now, Raythe. This is the wilderness, not the empire. We all know the Solus woman has been leading Osvard a dance – and she spreads for anyone else to spite him–'

'Liar!' Kemara snarled.

'I never did a thing to her, Pa,' Osvard called, straining against Vidar's noose. 'I done nothing, nor did Poel. We was just putting her in her place, that's all.'

Beside him, Poel made squeaking sounds of agreement. He'd never got over being his own mother's death: he clung to Osvard like a parasite. But he was still flesh and blood.

'It's not clear to me what's happened, Raythe,' Elgus said, injecting more command in his voice. 'We don't hang a man when there's a doubt – and my sons are entitled to more than a lynching.' He spread his hands. 'Let's talk this out, man to man.'

'No,' Kemara snapped, 'I know what happened. Hang the stinking bastards.'

Bloody Thom murmured, 'Boss, there's fifty of us and three of them. Let's kill the feckers.'

It was tempting, but even as Elgus considered, there was a stir on both flanks. Mater Varahana arrived with her flock of townsmen and their families, their faces blanching as they beheld the confrontation. But a quick glance was enough to see that most of the men held weapons.

At the same time, Cal Foaley and his hunters appeared on the other flank, bristling with blades and bows, a far deadlier threat.

That cast enough doubt for him to hesitate, but the bigger issue was that he still needed Vyre, until they found the istariol. *Stand down*, he gestured to Crowfoot, and the men at his back carefully moved hands from hilts.

That done, he advanced and Vyre came to meet him. 'Raythe, this is nonsense.'

'Osvard tried to rape Kemara – and Poel went for my daughter.'

Shit, his kragging daughter, Elgus thought. *What the krag was the little snit thinking?* He rapidly revised his approach. 'What's *alleged* to have happened?'

Vyre met his eyes. 'The whole camp has seen how Osvard harasses Kemara. I do not accept that she leads him on. She is blameless in this matter.'

'She broke the lad's nose,' Elgus retorted. 'He takes a Pit-full of lip over that – he's had a rough time of it.' He raised a hand. 'Not that that makes retribution right. But he's young.'

'Old enough to hold her down with a knife to the throat and begin to strip her, with Poel's help. When Zar came upon them and tried to raise the alarm, Poel attacked her.'

It all rang true, but Elgus seized on the opening: 'You said "began" – so that's not the deed itself. Osvard only wanted to scare her, I'm sure of it. He's all bark and no bite, that one – and as for Poel, I doubt he could even get it up.'

'Osvard told Kemara he was going to rape her, then kill her. Poel pinned Zar down and tore her blouse.'

'Words and fumblings, Raythe. Words aren't deeds – if he even said them at all.'

Vyre's face hardened. 'He meant every word. They both did.'

Elgus fumed inwardly, *I should beat the pair of them to pulp.* But he couldn't be seen to back down here. Leading a warband required absolute authority.

'Raythe, we're in the wilds now. Imperial statutes mean nothing out here: you and me are the law. My boys aren't bad, just fecking stupid. By the Pit, I'll bet we were just the same at their age! You think a girl wants you, then they get the jitters and where are you? Dick hanging out and looking like a raper, that's where. And at the end of the day, who's been harmed? Your daughter looks fine, and the healer will have nothing but a black eye come morning. My lads have had the worst of it and that's natural justice.' He dropped his voice further and added, 'We need each other, Raythe. You need my men, and we need your leadership. Cut my lads loose and let's put this behind us.'

Or else I'll kill you and yours and manage without you, he resolved.

Raythe's mind raced, seeking some middle ground that would extricate them all from this, a way for everyone to back away from the precipice, because the threat was none too veiled: right now: only his sons' plight was holding Elgus Rhamp back. That and the hope of istariol.

They could go on a rampage at the drop of a hand and they'd turn this place into a slaughterhouse. Though plenty of them would also die, they'd triumph, I don't doubt it . . .

But letting Rhamp's sons go would break his own authority. He had to come out of this with his standing enhanced and his relationship with Rhamp intact, or this expedition had already failed.

He could think of only one way.

'They'll have the Otravian punishment for attempted rape,' he told Elgus. When the knight tried to interject he raised a hand, silencing him. 'Tie them to the tree,' he called to Jesco and Vidar. 'Then bring me a horsewhip.'

'Vyre—' Elgus began.

'They're getting off lightly,' Raythe snapped, and stalked away, deliberately exposing his back, knowing Cognatus would warn him if the worst happened.

The entire camp was here now, with lit torches illuminating every face with a ruddy, infernal glow. Mater Varahana bustled in, but Raythe waved her away, murmuring, 'It's not your business, Vara. No one blasphemed.'

She held out a horsewhip. 'Your every need anticipated, darling.'

He gave her sideways look, concealing a smile as he took the whip. 'Aren't you the wise one.' He turned to Foaley, and murmured, 'How much authority have you got over the hunters?'

'I wouldn't call it "authority" at all, but they listen.'

'How do they feel about Rhamp?'

'They think he's an arse.'

'Good.'

'They think you are too, but not so much.'

'Excellent. Glad I can count on someone. Can you watch my back? Tami's out there somewhere and who knows who she'd shoot at in a crisis?'

Foaley nodded as Raythe stripped to the waist, revealing the scars and pockmarks of old wounds, and enough muscle that most could see he wasn't a pushover. Then he flicked the whip, getting the feel of it as he stalked to the tree where Osvard and Poel's backs were being bared.

'I'm not scared of you, runt,' Osvard barked, but Poel, beside him, was whimpering. Everyone knew that a prolonged whipping could destroy the back muscles completely, leaving a man crippled and in pain for the rest of his life.

'Mater Varahana, what's the normal number of lashes for attempted rape?' Raythe called.

'Twenty lashes,' the priestess replied, her austere features neutral.

'Twenty it is.'

He touched the whip to Poel's back, at which the young man, who was still in his teens, burst into tears. Ignoring the ring of people pressing closer to see blood, Raythe steeled himself for what must be done.

'Vyre . . .' Elgus Rhamp began, his voice strained.

'Touch Poel and I'll kill you,' Osvard snarled.

Raythe paused. 'What's the penalty for threatening an official, Mater?'

'Er, twenty more.'

'Thank you.' Raythe turned back to Poel. 'Did you go with Osvard to Mistress Kemara's campfire with your brother? Did you stamp on her hand to keep her down? Did you bear my daughter to earth and rip her clothing?'

The sobbing young man broke down, moaning, 'I'm sorry, I'm sorry, I'm so sorry . . .'

All round the circle, the men and women of Varahana's flock hissed and *tsked* grimly.

'This will remind you *never* to do any such thing again,' Raythe said gravely.

Then he brought the whip arcing round and slashed it down, cracking it on the boy's pale, pimply back and breaking the skin in a welt running from right shoulder to left hip. Poel shrieked and collapsed against the tree trunk, held up only by the ropes knotted about his wrists.

Osvard roared like an angry leopard, '*I'll kill you—!*'

'Shut the krag up!' Elgus bellowed at his son. He stepped into the circle and looking at the precise lash wound, stated, 'You've done this before, Vyre.'

'I have administered my own discipline, as a good officer should.'

'A man should always wield his own justice,' Elgus agreed. He touched his blubbing son's shoulder and murmured, 'He's learned his lesson. Don't break him. *Please.*'

Raythe sensed his plea and he lowered the whip, not in fear, but in understanding. They'd reached middle ground on this point, at least. 'Very well. Jesco, cut him down.'

'I'll do it,' Elgus grated, pulling a dagger and slicing the ropes, then lowering his weeping child to the ground . . . then he properly saw the handprint burnt into the young man's face. 'What in the Pit . . .?'

'My daughter used the praxis, an accidental discharge of power during the assault,' Raythe told him.

Elgus stared at Zarelda and Raythe feared violence, but instead the knight made the Sign of Gerda. 'No one will ever touch her again,' he said solemnly. 'This I swear.'

Raythe believed him – but did Zar? She looked like she wanted to spit, but for once she swallowed her words and nodded, before her eyes flickered elsewhere – to Banno Rhamp, who was looking utterly wretched.

Perhaps this'll ram home for her what the Rhamps are like?

But there was still Osvard to deal with. He hefted the horsewhip again, then a hand closed over his wrist.

'Let me,' Kemara demanded. When he went to pull away, she kept hold. Up close, she was perspiring heavily, but her eyes shone like moons. 'Give the whip to me.'

The intensity in her face overrode Raythe's objections. He looked at Elgus, who grunted, 'If that's what she wants.' He clearly thought it would lessen Osvard's punishment.

So did Osvard. 'Sure, let her. She's can't hurt me,' he sneered. 'Took her down one-handed.'

'Shut up,' Elgus hissed again. 'For krag's sake, boy, *shut up!*'

Raythe reluctantly relinquished the whip. 'Listen—' he began.

'I know what I'm doing,' she snapped, as she confronted Osvard's mocking face.

'Come on, then,' the mercenary jeered, 'or better yet, why don't you ram that whip handle up your—'

The lash slashed through the air, a rush of gelid blue light burning Raythe's retinas as it flew, the sinuous knotted cord of leather bit into Osvard's back and he *screamed* as his skin and muscles parted to the very bone and all along the wound, ice formed, blackening the skin.

'Gerda's Teats,' Elgus gasped. 'What in the Pit–?'

Raythe was almost as astounded, even though he'd guessed at her potential, but he'd sensed no build-up of energy, seen no spell-work – and Kemara looked utterly horrified at what she'd just done, which wasn't a good thing.

Uncontrolled sorcery – mizra – *is the power that destroys civilisations.*

Osvard fell to his knees, hanging from his bound wrists, writhing as the ice spread and burrowed, and Raythe realised that this could kill him. He knelt and laid a hand on the man's back while calling on Cognatus and muttering a counter-spell. Kemara's magic collapsed and Raythe looked at her. She was just staring, terrified, as people backed away from her.

She lost control, he realised. That happened occasionally in teenagers with sorcerous potential, but she was close on thirty. *She needs real training, or to be cauterised properly, before it goes bad.*

But from the murmurs around them, everyone thought she'd done it deliberately. 'Another sorcerer,' he heard from all around them. 'She's an Arcanus too.' Many made reverent signs, for the Church maintained that the praxis was Gerda's gift to the world.

Just as many looked scared and hostile.

Osvard was now unconscious, but when Raythe checked his pulse and respiration, he was still alive. He stood. Taking the whip from Kemara's unresisting hand, he told Elgus, 'I think the punishment is served. And I think you've seen ample reason why your followers should give Mistress Kemara – and *every* women in our caravan – the respect they're due. Do not the knights of Pelaria pledge to serve and protect all women? Then honour your vows, and see that your men, the extensions of your will, do likewise.'

Elgus looked at his son, then at the whip. 'We've all learned a great deal tonight,' he said, in a strained voice. 'I'll control my people.' Then he looked hard at Kemara. 'You control yours.'

'I'm answerable to no one,' Kemara retorted.

The knight bunched a fist – but then he turned it into a dismissive gesture and strode away, his fighting men picking up Osvard and Poel. There were all sorts of backwards looks, blends of fear and malice. Everyone knew of the praxis, but only a sorcerer knew what it could and couldn't do, and that amplified the natural dread of the uncanny. It would take real courage for anyone to assail Kemara after this.

But that didn't mean she was safe. 'Perhaps you should move into my camp, Mistress Kemara?' Raythe suggested, as everyone left.

'Why, so you can protect me?' she sneered.

'Evidently you need protecting–'

'He caught me by surprise – it won't happen again.'

'But I could teach you–'

'I'm not interested. I've got it leashed.'

'But–'

Then Zar's voice cut in. 'Kemara, you could learn with me?' she suggested.

When she went off, why did Zar go to Kemara? Raythe wondered suddenly. He'd not sensed any bond between them. *But if she hadn't, Kemara might well be dead.*

Kemara stopped, clearly thinking that same thing. Uncertainty creased her angry visage. But then her eyes tightened. 'I'm not learning it. I don't want it.'

She whirled and stormed away.

For the next few days, the tension in the caravan was like a tightening noose round Zarelda's throat.

Rhamp's soldiers and camp-followers refused to mingle with the other groups, but there was no more carousing in their camp, for Sir

Elgus had laid down the law. Things had changed, that was clear. She ached to see Banno, but he appeared to be confined to his camp.

She also badly wanted to speak to Kemara. She felt like the attack had formed a tenuous bond between them, and sometimes she caught the redheaded healer watching her.

There was a wonderful compensation, though: Adefar was hers again and their bonding felt complete. Her peril and his immediate response had overridden the stupid little power-plays and now her familiar was devotion itself, protective lest she be assailed again. Every moment she could spare was spent trying safe little spells to deepen their mastery, like braiding ropes, igniting twigs and dousing them, or conjuring puffs of wind. It was wonderful, and almost enough to compensate for the nightmares of being crushed under Poel's body . . .

It was from just such a dream that she jolted awake one night. She joined her father, sitting beside the fire, and looked up at the glittering stars and Shamaya's planetary rings. Jesco and Vidar were sleeping, and so was Kemara, beneath her cart nearby. Her father was gazing at the Ferrean woman with an odd expression.

'Hey,' she mumbled, poking the fire with a stick, 'd'you fancy her?'

He harrumphed. 'She'd bite my head off.'

'I kind of like her. But I wish she'd learn the praxis.'

Her father sighed. 'Aye, me too.'

They watched Cognatus and Adefar skirt each other, then blur into bird shape and soar off into the dark, flitting above with sense-defying speed and agility, vanishing, then reappearing. That got her thinking.

'How come I can sometimes see Adefar – and Cognatus – but other times not?'

'Spirits are little bundles of intellect and energy,' her father replied. 'They can hide from us or each other at will, and we can command them to do so as well. In Teshveld, I had Cognatus conceal himself most of the time, in case someone had the witch-sight and realised what I was. You can conceal your aura too. Often it's best if no one knows who or what you are.'

'So there could be another sorcerer among us, but if they hid their aura and familiar, we'd never know?'

'If they're skilled enough, yes.'

'That's a little scary,' she admitted.

'It is, but the truth is that magic is slow, and in any case, I'd back myself against most other sorcerers. I'm more scared of an assassin with a gun or a bow.'

She shuddered, unused to thinking of the world in such terms.

'In time you'll learn to assess every situation for danger, and how to counter those threats,' he said. 'I'll teach you what spell to conjure in a crisis, which way to move, who to deal with first.'

She remembered how dark her father's hair had been, and how clear his complexion when they fled Otravia, and compared it to the greying temples, brow and strain lines that marked his face now. If he spent all his time thinking like that, it was no wonder.

'I miss feeling safe,' she admitted.

'Me too.' He hugged her close. 'Me too.'

At dusk on the fifth day out of the Aldar rath, Raythe was sitting with Zarelda, taking her through her praxis words, while Vidar and Jesco diced and joked. Kemara was a little way away, sitting alone, hunched over her own fire, with them but apart.

Then someone coughed diffidently at the edge of their circle of light: Sir Elgus Rhamp, unarmed, with a small keg under either arm. 'Raythe,' he called, 'can we talk?'

They all rose and Raythe peered into the shadows, but Rhamp looked to be alone.

'Come ahead,' he called.

The knight entered the circle of warmth and handed over the two kegs. 'We've reached the end of what Gravis had brewed,' he rumbled. 'The last two ale barrels are being rolled into Varahana's and Vidar's camps right now, but I figured you might like the good stuff.'

151

Finally, a peace-offering.

This was necessary, but Raythe was conscious that Zar mightn't see it like that. He looked at her enquiringly and she murmured, 'Make up if you have to. Just don't forget what he's like.'

She went to go, but Sir Elgus blocked her departure, dropping to one knee. 'My sons did wrong and I humbly apologise. I am your servant, Mistress Zarelda.'

'Uh . . . thank you,' she stammered, and hurried away, before stopping and calling, 'About kragging time,' over her shoulder. Raythe signed to Jesco and Vidar that all was well and he motioned for Elgus to sit.

They had a couple of ryes, and spoke of the daily goings-on of the expedition, a subtle reminder to each other that they needed to cooperate to make this work. Elgus told him that Osvard and Poel were recovering, and extremely penitent, which Raythe doubted, and they talked through the provisioning, which needed to get tighter.

Finally, Elgus brought up the praxis, and more particularly, the revelation of two more practitioners. 'You've got two sorceresses on your hands, Raythe. As I understand it, until they're fully trained, they're a danger to us all.'

'It'll work out,' Raythe replied. 'You keep your sons under control, I'll worry about them.'

Elgus frowned. 'So does the praxis run in the blood?'

'Not really. In theory, anyone can use magic. But it takes a certain intellect and attitude to master it: complete conviction in your ability, a capacity to visualise that verges on a waking dream, a facility with language, to communicate with the spirits in their language, and an understanding of how nature functions – animal, vegetable *and* mineral. Not many folk can handle all of that.'

'But you and your daughter both have it? Surely that's blood?'

'Zarelda thinks like me,' he told Elgus. 'Magic's something she's aspired to all her life and she knows she can do it because I can. She'll master it in no time. And Kemara's had some training – her control isn't perfect, but we'll remedy that.'

Better he believes that, than the truth.

'She's a sharp-tongued bitch,' Elgus muttered, before raising a placating hand. 'I'm not saying what happened was her fault – but there's folks wondering why a sorceress would pretend to just be a healer.'

'In Teshveld I was doing exactly the same,' Raythe pointed out.

'But since then, you've been using your talents to help us. What's she been doing?'

'Saving lives. Healing people.'

The Pelarian knight grumbled, then shrugged. 'Well, maybe now she's known, she'll do more. Isn't there some kind of thing where two sorcerers are more powerful when they work together?'

Elgus clearly had a brain behind that brawny exterior. Perhaps he was still plotting, but hopefully this talk had changed his thinking.

'You mean the meld,' Raythe said. 'It's true that in the Arcanus Academia, we're paired at an early age, if we're compatible. A strong meld partnership can do much more than either sorcerer on their own. If I can forge a meld with either Zarelda or Kemara, it'll be well worth the effort.'

Though I've not melded with anyone since Luc Mandaryke and I fell out . . .

'So what's next, Raythe?' he asked. 'When do we reach Verdessa?'

Raythe signalled to Vidar and Jesco to rejoin them, then said, 'We're a few days from the Bay of Shardak. Gospodoi's ship passed it on the way west. The bay is hemmed in with mountains, but it's completely iced over, according to the journal, so we'll be able to drive our wagons right across into Verdessa.'

'Where we run the risk of imperial patrols,' Elgus commented.

'True. But the river we seek is this side of the imperial garrison at Rodonoi, in the foothills of the mountains. The imperials don't know we're coming and with luck, they won't know we passed.'

Elgus toasted that, then turned to Vidar. 'Are you a genuine bearskin, big man?'

Vidar's smile faded. 'I am.'

The knight whistled softly. 'Had one in my company for a while. But the rage took him during a scrap with imperial cavalry and he wouldn't – nay, *couldn't* – run. Killed a dozen of the bastards before he went down, mind.'

Vidar looked away into the gloom. 'There's a beast in every man. It's how we control it that defines who we are and what we become.'

Elgus sighed. 'A lesson I hope my sons will learn. Look, I'd better get back to my men. It's been good to talk,' he added, offering Raythe his hand.

They rose and clasped hands. 'Your son Banno is courting my daughter,' Raythe noted. 'I don't mind the friendship, but it's to go no further.'

'I'll talk to the boy,' Elgus said. He nodded his shaggy head to Jesco and Vidar. 'Gentlemen.'

As they watched him go, Raythe thought, *I still don't trust you, but I reckon you'll keep the peace, for now.*

6

Sickness

Mater Varahana lifted her head and hands to heaven and made the Hand of Gerda over her congregation, feeling a sense of serenity and oneness; that always surprised her.

Then she scanned the gathering: she normally had sixty to seventy people at the morning service, but today there were only forty, and most of them looked worried. She didn't know why that was and their anxiety was beginning to infect her. She knew all of their life stories by now, felt their needs as her own.

Kneeling in the front were her six Sisters of Gerda, anonymous in their shapeless cowled habits. The ethos of the Sisterhood was to vanish into servitude: names were rarely used and every Sister was expected to be able to perform any task they were called upon to do. To Varahana it was a kind of madness.

But then, isn't that what religion is? Mass self-delusion, willing yourself to believe the impossible in the face of all reason, because you're scared that otherwise, your life has no more purpose than that of an ant. Yet, here I am, passing down the fairy-tales . . .

Then she chided herself, because she was wool-gathering while her congregation waited for words of encouragement and inspiration. So she snapped into the present and began, 'Dear Brethren, we gather as always on this beautiful morning' – in truth, it was dreary, grey and foreboding, but she'd been preaching of late about the virtues of seeing beauty in all things – 'to contemplate the gift of a new day. Life is eternally renewing, and . . .'

Her voice trailed away as Carroda Layle appeared at the edge of the gathering, a pleading look on her face.

'Mater,' she called, 'I'm sorry to interrupt, truly, but please come – my Shana, she's so sick–'

This caused a stir, with the more self-righteous harrumphing over having their worship interrupted, while others burst out, 'She's not the only one, Mater.'

As if to emphasise the point, Lew Fulter bent over and vomited into the grass.

Varahana gestured at her Sisters to rise and hurried to Carroda. 'What's the matter with your daughter?' she asked, as her congregation crowded in to hear the news.

Carroda, a farmer's wife who'd argued strenuously against joining this 'mad trek into nowhere', seized her hands. 'Shana's been sick all night.'

'So's me boy,' Ardo Myle put in, flapping his hands excitedly. 'Me missus is with him now.'

'Has anyone told Raythe Vyre?' Varahana asked, extricating herself with some difficulty from Carroda's sweaty grip.

' 'is Lordship's off first light with the scouts,' someone replied.

'An' Rhamp's closed off his camp,' Lew's brother Tawyn put in. 'Reckon them's sick too.'

'Raythe needs to know,' Varahana said firmly. 'Someone find him. Carroda, take me to Shana.'

'But what if ye get sick too?' Tawyn demanded. 'We can't risk ye, Mater.'

'Gerda will protect me,' Varahana stated, though she believed no such thing. 'Carroda, show me. Everyone else – a little privacy, please?'

That helped keep the wall of people back a few paces as Carroda dragged her to her family's wagon. Carroda's husband gave her a dirty look, as if the illness was Deo's fault, but Varahana ignored him as she ducked under the awning they had fashioned from a blanket to create more living space.

The stink of sickness inside was stomach-turning, but Varahana knew how to keep nausea at bay, even when others lost their fight. Shana, a ghostly-faced girl clinging to a battered doll, was whimpering dazedly, her eyes unfocused. Her skin was cold, but dripping sweat, her pulse rapid and weak, despite her slow, shallow breathing. Vomit crusted the front of her nightdress and blanket, her arms were bruised and her sinuses were blocked and swollen. There was no one symptom that confirmed the identity of the ailment – and nothing fatal, she hoped most devoutly.

'Shana?' she called, but the girl didn't react. She tapped her cheek, then pinched it, gently first, then harder, but she got no reaction other than a faint twitch of the eyeballs; it was as if the girl were trapped inside but unable to make anything work.

What is this?

All the while Carroda hovered, her habitual sour face despairing. 'She's a healthy girl,' she hissed. 'What's wrong with her?'

'It's too soon to say,' Varahana replied. 'Has Mistress Kemara seen her?'

'We looked for her, but she weren't in her camp, nor at yer service.'

'I expect she's seeing other patients. Keep Shana warm, despite the sweating. Her body's ability to regulate temperature is awry. I'm going to see if anyone else has the same symptoms.'

Carroda seized her shoulder. 'Mater, won't you say a prayer, to keep her safe?'

It's knowledge that'll save her, not prayers, Varahana managed not to say. 'Of course,' she said, schooling her voice into calm. She recited a prayer and although Carroda wept, the rote words seemed to help her, if not the girl.

Varahana checked first on Lew Fulter's boy and was unsurprised to find the symptoms were the same. 'Keep him warm and hydrated,' she recommended, then moved on from wagon to wagon, finding the same thing, over and over. At the fifth, she found Kemara Solus, administering a herbal steam treatment to unblock a young boy's nose.

The healer looked up. 'You spoken to Vyre?' she asked, her brusque tone no doubt the result of the exhaustion written across her face.

'Not yet.' Varahana blessed the boy, then pulled Kemara aside. 'When did you learn of this?'

'About midnight – I haven't stopped, I've just been going from case to case. There are no bites or cuts that I can see, they've not been eating the same foods, there's no one person who everyone's had contact with . . . I'm wondering about contaminated water, maybe?'

'Have you seen anything like this before?'

Kemara screwed up her face. 'That's the problem. As well as the respiratory problems and the nausea, there's a lot of bruising too, although I can't see what anyone's been bashing themselves against. There's nothing that identifies this sickness positively, and too many things it could be.'

'That's just what I've been thinking, too,' Varahana admitted, and they both sagged a little.

'Is Vyre going to be any use in this?' Kemara asked, her expression sceptical.

'I've never heard Raythe claim that the praxis can heal sickness. I've seen him use it to seal wounds and the like, but the humours that cause illness are usually too small to deal with that way.'

Kemara sighed. 'Then it's up to us. I've been trying to stop the vomiting and clear their airways, but nothing's really working. If anything, it's getting worse. If we can't find a way to treat this disease, whatever it is, people are going to start dying.'

Raythe trotted back into camp, already briefed by Jesco, who'd found him. They went straight to the central fire, where the villagers and farmers had gathered. Varahana, their main spokesperson, was waiting with Elgus Rhamp and one of his advisors, the scar-faced man known as Crowfoot. The preserved bird claw that gave him his nickname hung round his throat.

'Sir Elgus, is your camp similarly afflicted?' Raythe asked, as he drew the knight and the priestess aside.

'Aye,' Rhamp growled.

Good, you'll be in no position to try anything while we're weak, then, Raythe found himself thinking, possibly uncharitably. Aloud, he asked, 'How many cases?'

'About one in four, same as the rest of the camp, I gather.' The Pelarian knight glowered at Kemara as she strode to join them. 'Healer can't find cause nor cure.'

'But I'm working on it, rather than standing around griping,' Kemara replied. 'Lord Vyre, is there anything a praxis-mage can tell us about this?'

'I wish there was. I can't manipulate what I can't see, as I'm sure Varahana's explained. But there are things I can do, like using heat to dry up certain fluids. But you've both got the knowledge; I've just got the tools.'

'I'd have thought ye'd be more use, to be frank,' Elgus grumbled.

'Give me a line of fighting men or a wall to break down and I'll gladly show you what I can do,' Raythe answered tersely. Intimidating Rhamp remained his number one priority.

Elgus raised a placating hand. 'Sorry, Raythe. My worry's doin' the talking. No offence.'

'None taken,' Raythe lied. 'Kemara; set me to work.'

Varahana left Kemara and Raythe plotting possible remedies for the congestion. *That's just treating the symptoms,* she decided. *What's causing it?*

That thought stayed with her, although it wasn't until late afternoon, after another round of blessings and prayers, that she was able to act on it. She put on a shapeless robe and cloak and slipped out, leaving her six Sisters to lead the next round of prayers. Following Kemara's comments on the possibilities of a bad spring, she went to the stream, where even now, women were filling up water containers. She peered over their shoulders and tasted the water – it was very cold but there was nothing out of the ordinary that she could taste. She wondered if she should ask Raythe to forbid drinking there, just in case, but without any evidence, that felt premature.

A group of Rhamp's men were watching, and she heard some ribald comments about the proclivities of bald priestesses – it never ceased to amaze her that even in a crisis, people could remain completely mule-headed – but then Tami appeared and berated them until they left. Varahana thanked her, then pulled off her boots and hung them by the laces around her neck before she headed upstream, wincing at the cold of the thigh-deep water and pushing against an increasingly strong current as the banks, tangled with weed and shrouded by the leaning pines, closed in.

She continued a hundred yards upstream, through a series of gentle bends, pools and shallows, seeking clues. A rotting animal carcase might have explained things, but she couldn't find anything, nor any dangerous plants, and frequent sips of the water revealed nothing untoward.

The small river was frigid, despite the warmth of the day, and her legs soon went numb with the cold, despite the effort of moving against the flow. Needing respite, she waded towards the bank, where a small patch of flat mossy gravel worn smooth by the water was bathed in a patch of late sunlight.

She was about to step onto dry ground when she paused, because there were clear signs of something having trampled and churned the muddy gravel, although no clear boot or footprint remained. She bent and peered, finding smears in the mud, as if something had been dragged, but there was no blood, just those marks in the mud.

A hunter, using a branch to obscure his tracks?

She immediately began to feel uneasy. The low hills, dotted with scrub and windswept pines, provided ample cover for a stalker, and the shadows were lengthening. Every time she turned around, the sense of being watched grew.

Then her gaze caught on something in the water and she frowned. A trail of dark fluid had suddenly erupted through the silt and begun diffusing into the stream. She took a glass phial from her pouch and held it over the pin-hole through which the fluid was still emerging until it filled up with a greenish liquid.

Emerald green . . . from beneath the riverbed . . .

It reminded her of something, some obscure lecture, or maybe something she'd read too many years ago, before she was forced into the Church. She held it to her nose and sniffed, but there was little odour, just a faintly unpleasant tang to the scent.

What is it I'm trying to remember?

She had no laboratory to test it out here, nor reference material to research. And she was half a mile from camp and would be losing the light in a couple of hours' time. If this wasn't the answer, walking it back to camp to puzzle over it would be wasting valuable time.

Much though it went against her training, sometimes you just had to trust to fortune. So after another look over her shoulder, still unable to shake the feeling of being watched, she took a tentative sip . . .

Bitter, herbal . . . unpleasant. And not anything she recognised.

She stoppered the remainder in the phial and contemplated the tingling on her tongue, the only notable lingering property of the fluid.

Then it hit her – both the taste, and the answer.

She went to speak, just to vocalise her anguish, but her tongue went numb a moment before she lost all feeling in her mouth. She should never have tasted the fluid –

'Oh . . . no . . .' she mumbled, swaying as the ground seemed to shift beneath her. She went to cry out but her throat had locked up, even as her sinuses blocked, bile rose in her throat and her strength went. Her knees gave way as the ground tilted and slammed into her face. Feeling no pain, she tried to roll over, only managing to get into a foetal position before her muscles locked. Sound distorted and her sight dimmed to a wavering blur; her gorge filled, she convulsed and started vomiting, the foulness pooling before her mouth.

And from beneath the riverbed, where the fluid had erupted, a dozen shapes began to writhe up through the gravel, and skeletal hands burst through . . .

The fluid gripped her throat and she felt her airways clog. She couldn't move her legs, but her fingers had some life left: she desperately thrust them down her throat to make herself vomit again, even as the dark shapes clawed their way out of the riverbed. Then her stomach contents, green and foul, burst from her mouth. She tried to rise as more shapes rose around her, hissing voices and slime-covered shadows running with water closed in.

She heard a harsh cry, and something crunched heavily in the gravel as she toppled sideways, already fading out.

Raythe Vyre stepped outside the latest foetid tent where another villager lay dying and looked at the sky, guessing at the hour. It was twilight and in the northern summer, daylight lingered long; it would be hours before it got truly dark. He placed a hand on his sword hilt, frustrated at his helplessness, wishing this was a problem that he could stab.

But no weapon could fight this sickness, it seemed. All through the day, those afflicted had been getting worse and worse, in many cases their breathing so shallow that it wasn't clear if they still lived. Several times he'd used the praxis to clear breathing passages, but they just refilled. Thrice he'd restarted the heartbeat of dying patients, including young Shana Layle. Half the camp was ill now, with the other half working feverishly to save them. And he and Kemara were no closer to learning what it was infecting them.

If it was the water, some of them must be immune; that was the only conclusion they could draw, having eliminated any other suspects: it wasn't anything anyone had eaten, not mushrooms or herbs, and rotten meat never had this effect.

But he himself had drunk the water and he was fine. *Perhaps it's only intermittently dangerous?*

Seeing Kemara Solus emerging from another tent, he strode to meet her.

'Any the wiser?' she asked, her voice subdued.

'No,' he confessed. The illness was still a mystery – and so was she.

They'd worked all day, often side by side, but even now she'd been slow to unbend. His usual charm wasn't working – not that he was flirting, not in such a crisis. But he could admit to himself that he had been trying to befriend her, with absolutely no visible sign of success. Perhaps it was a matter of trust.

She ran through the latest names to succumb, concluding, 'We've got half the camp down.'

'I know.' He glanced towards Rhamp's enclave. The Pelarian had closed it to outsiders, but the illness was just as prevalent there. 'If a ferali horde found us now, I doubt we could hold them off.'

'We can't move,' Kemara replied quickly. 'It'd kill half the patients immediately.'

'I know that too. I need to find Varahana – I warrant she's been trying to think this through.'

Kemara gave him a betrayed look – no doubt she just saw him as backsliding from the real work of saving lives – but he didn't let that deter him. Sometimes you had to deal with the big picture, not just fight fires.

Varahana might have discovered something.

He headed for Varahana's wagon, where he immediately found himself surrounded by terrified men and women, all demanding he see their wife or husband or child next, and it took some time to determine that Varahana had last been seen going upriver, alone.

'Please – listen to me! Mater Varahana is investigating the cause of this outbreak and I must find her. When we return, I'll see to your sick, I promise.' He thought about asking them to stop using the water, but in truth, they had no other option. Then inspiration struck: many healers believed that boiled water was better to clean wounds.

'I want you to boil all water before use, do you hear me? *Boil it* – and pass the word round the camp for me, will you? All water for drinking and cooking and washing wounds must be boiled.'

Giving them a task worked: those belabouring him for aid were put to work and he was able to grab Jesco and Vidar. Together, they trotted to the stream, where people were filling buckets for the evening meal. Raythe wasted more time to ensure they understood they needed to boil every drop before using it, but at last they were able to set off upstream. Darkness was beginning to cloak the wooded gully and pine-covered slopes: the long twilight was coming to an end.

'Mater Varahana?' Vidar kept calling, but no one replied.

'We'll need light,' Raythe muttered, then switching to the praxis-tongue he muttered, '*Cognatus, animus . . . praesemino lumis.*' The usual rush of energy coalesced into a globe of brightness in his left hand, which gave them twenty feet or so of clear vision, but beyond that, the shadows swarmed in as if mustering for battle.

Vidar growled and shed a layer of humanity. Hunching over, he started sniffing the wind, while Jesco, completely unperturbed by his comrade's wilder side, drew his sword and made the sign of Gerda.

Raythe went to speak, when from somewhere ahead, a burning arrow shot into the air, fell and was gone . . .

'What's–?' Jesco began.

Vidar snarled again and hunched over still further, his face contorting into a savage, muzzle-nosed visage, his limbs bulging and his spine arching. Cloth began to tear and he shed it. Snarling and stalking forward, he started sniffing the air loudly.

Jesco threw Raythe a bewildered look.

'Like that, he can smell someone a mile off,' Raythe murmured. 'Maybe . . .'

'Aye, and hear them, too,' Vidar growled, barely able to form the words. Then he howled, a word just about discernible as *Vara!* and went storming upstream into the darkness.

'Shit,' Raythe exclaimed, and took off after the bearskin with Jesco bounding along behind – but in moments, Vidar was out of sight and all that was left was the stir he'd made in the dark waters of the stream.

Varahana came to her senses to find flames streaking the air around her, flaring and roaring above her head. Someone was panting above her and dancing some kind of polka around her body. Stones had embedded themselves uncomfortably in her wet skin. A heartbeat thudded like a drum, pounding the inside of her skull.

Then she realised that the heartbeat was her own and that it was Tami standing over her, flailing about her with a torch in one hand and a sword in the other. On every side were vaguely human-shaped beings shrouded in riverweed, circling like vultures around a dying cow.

Dying cow ... that's me ...

She tried to rise, but it just wasn't in her. But her tongue loosened enough that she could slur, 'Ver ... de ... ghul ...'

'I know,' Tami snapped, pirouetting again and thrusting the torch at the nearest circling verdeghuls. The flames caught it and the thing shrieked and backed away into a deeper part of the stream. For a moment Varahana glimpsed a face like dead leaves pasted over a human skull, with eyes like slimy pools.

Verdeghuls – green ghouls – were relics of the old wars, plant-based lifeforms bred to kill. They excreted poison, then feasted on the paralysed and dead.

The mystery was solved – as long as she or Tami lived long enough to tell anyone.

But that wasn't looking likely. She tried again to move, this time almost entangling Tami's legs. They were surrounded by a dozen ghouls, barely kept at bay by the flames, although two lay dead in the shallows by the flat bank.

Redoubling her efforts, Varahana retched until she expelled nothing but bile. She blew mucus out of her nose until she could breathe freely again, then threw her cloak into the fire, where it began to smoulder. All the while, Tami fought like a lioness, driving the attackers back over and over. She cursed and babbled as she fought, berating her foes – it was pointless, but perhaps she wasn't able to fight with her mouth shut.

'Back up, krag it ... and you, *ha!* Got you!' she crowed, as another ghoul caught alight, setting the rest to hooting and shrieking. Baring yellowed teeth, they recoiled out of reach, their burning comrade yowling as it was consumed by flame.

Finally, Varahana was able to roll onto her knees and pull herself up. She grabbed the now-burning cloak by its singed collar and flapped it about, helping Tami to drive the verdeghuls back. The creatures snarled, but gave ground.

Then suddenly they all closed in, shrieking as one. Riverweed snaked out like tentacles and even as Tami immolated another ghoul, her wrist was caught and she was wrenched off her feet. Varahana tried to reach her, but something slammed into her from behind and she went down beneath at least three of the ghouls, the stench of rotting weed filling her nostrils as she struck the gravel. Teeth snapped behind her neck, then bit into her flesh at shoulder and left thigh, making her shriek in pain and desperation.

Her cry of anguish filled the air – and was swiftly drowned by a beast's agonised howl–

–then something struck the press of verdeghuls, smashing the bodies sideways. Bellowing in rage, the creature, something between a bear and a wolf, straddled Vara's prone form, lashing out to left and right.

One ghoul was still fastened to her leg, but she was getting her strength back, more every minute, and she was able to draw the dagger she'd completely forgotten about and stab it straight through the eye. She kicked it away the instant it lost its grip and it fell into the flames, shrieking.

More torches suddenly blazed into life and now she could see Raythe and Jesco too, and another three ghouls were writhing in the growing conflagration. A globe of light burst over the little pool, illuminating Raythe and Jesco as they forced the remaining verdeghuls back with blade and fire.

With a wail, the surviving ghouls spun and fled into the undergrowth, angrily thrashing through the scrub – and then everything went quiet . . .

They didn't go far, she thought fearfully, trying to peer through the darkness.

She'd just managed to get to her knees again, when Vidar – or the beast that he'd become – engulfed her, hugging her forcefully, then lifting her up and throwing her like a child over his shoulder. With a mighty howl at the planetary rings above, he went hurtling downstream, and she found herself battered against his mighty shoulders as the blood rushed to her skull.

Mercifully, she blacked out again . . .

'Move, move,' Raythe shouted, getting the caravan lurching into motion. 'Get those wagons moving – and stay together, you hear me? *No one* gets left behind.'

Those of his leaders who could – Elgus Rhamp, Cal Foaley and Jesco Duretto – echoed his words from up and down the forming lines in between the sounds of whips cracking and beasts sounding their displeasure at being awoken at midnight. Riders flanking them held torches aloft to light the way through the darkness and to spot for dangers.

Raythe's praxis-sight told him that the night was very much alive: the verdeghul nest numbered at least fifty beings, maybe more, and they were near and hungry. They preyed on the dead and dying, but normally shunned open conflict, so as long as he could get his people out of their territory, they'd be fine – but it meant those families who'd been entirely incapacitated by the venom the ghouls had trickled into the water needed someone to step in and drive their wagon. Those hunters and mercenaries who were well enough had been split among the afflicted families to protect and move them, and they were doing a good job.

'So far, so good,' Raythe muttered to himself as the line of wagons began following Foaley's outriders roughly northwest. He trotted back along the line, his praxis-light showing the way and eliciting awed sounds from those who saw it.

'Can I 'ave one o' those?' Gravis Tavernier called.

'Sorry – I can only create one at a time, and I need to be present,' Raythe called back. 'Keep it moving.' He pushed on, mentally ticking off names until he was at the rear, where Varahana's wagon was being driven by Vidar, fully restored to himself, sitting beside one of the mater's anonymous Sisters. For some reason, the nuns didn't look happy to have the big Norgan ranger driving their wagon.

Raythe gave Vidar a wave, then peered in the back, where four of the sisters were huddled around a prostrate Varahana. She was still fighting the verdeghul venom, for she'd been bitten badly, as well as tasting the sample she'd collected in her phial, which he now had in his own pouch.

Now I know what it is, I might be able to distil an antidote, he thought. *If I can, some of the worst cases might be saved, like Shana Layle . . .*

Then he pulled up short, realising that he'd not seen the Layles' wagon yet.

'Who's behind us?' he asked Vidar.

'The rearguard, and maybe a few stragglers. Jesco's back there.'

'I'll go and check on him. Take care of Vara.'

'I will,' Vidar replied, in a voice that said a lot more than his words.

Raythe gave him a salute of thanks, tugged on his reins and went looking for Jesco. He found the Shadran a few hundred yards back, with a cluster of men, and a pair of wagons, including the Layles', to Raythe's relief. *That's everyone, thank Gerda.*

'So, verdeghuls,' Jesco remarked, as Raythe joined him. 'I never thought they were real.'

'They used to lurk around the battlefields of East Otravia,' Raythe said with a shudder. 'I suppose this lot usually prey on animals that drink from their stream. Is everything okay here?'

Jesco hung his head. 'Shana died while we were out looking for Varahana.' He indicated the Layle wagon, a few dozen yards ahead. 'They're grieving hard. She was their only child, centre of their lives.' Jesco choked up a little, looking away. 'Can't imagine that sort of loss.'

'Ah, damn it . . .' Raythe's throat caught too. 'What a waste.'

Behind them, the verdeghuls shadowing them were receding into the distance, happy to let these dangerous interlopers pass; they would no doubt loot the camp of whatever had been left behind.

'Was Shana the only one to die from the venom?'

'Seven others.' Jesco reeled off the names of the victims, men, women and children. 'Many are still sick, but now we know what the affliction is, most are recovering. Kemara is performing miracles.'

'Aye,' Raythe conceded, 'she may be a grumpy one, but she's tenacious and knows her work.'

'Aye, and she's a good way with the patients, especially women and children.'

'So it's just men she doesn't like?'

'Nah, it's mostly just you,' Jesco chuckled. 'And speaking of women we admire, I think Varahana has a beau. Our shaggy Norgan went positively feral the moment he realised the good mater was in trouble.'

'I noticed,' Raythe replied. 'A strange couple.'

'The sophisticated scholar and the savage bearskin?' Jesco grinned. He liked nothing more than to gossip about romance. 'He can go a day and not speak; she can't go ten seconds. I can't see it happening.'

'Oh, I don't know,' Raythe replied. 'Most couples are basically similar, but some look for opposites: people who're things they aren't. And he's a good man.'

'I agree – but she's our Mater: there'd be uproar if anything happened between them. And she takes her vows quite seriously.'

'Aye, that's truth.' Raythe sighed. 'But out here, maybe we can rewrite the rules a bit. I'd like to see her happy.'

'Even if it's with someone else?' Jesco asked slyly.

'Aye, even then.'

'Tami did well,' the Shadran added.

'Aye – and then she went straight back to Elgus Rhamp,' Raythe noted. 'Anyway, it's none of my business what they all get up to. I'm doing this for Mirella.'

'I know, Raythe – but what's she doing for you?'

Who knows? Raythe thought, not wanting to speculate. 'Come on, let's go before more of those kragging ghouls come.'

They dug in their spurs and trotted back to join the caravan. It was going to be a long night and many miles before anyone would feel safe enough to make camp again.

7

The frozen bay

'Dear Gerda, it's been what . . . two months?' Raythe remarked.

'Feels longer,' Jesco replied. They'd been sharing the driving and were at last nearing the end of another long, exhausting day's travel. 'We've done – what d'you reckon? About four hundred miles?'

'Aye, but since we left the plains behind that Aldar rath we're only averaging five miles a day.' Raythe pointed to the north. It might be late summer, but the heights still glistened with snow. 'At this rate, it'll be autumn before we reach the place where Perhan found istariol.'

They'd had a hard couple of weeks since they'd escaped the verdeghuls: the weather was fickle up here, as changeable as a Pelarian spring, which was bad enough, and the old Aldar road had been swallowed up, leaving them mired in a dark, wet, trackless forest. But the scouts pushed on and returned with news of a coastal plain ahead. It took a few days of hard work to hack a wide-enough passage through the giant trees so the expedition could pass, but the shared labour helped to rebuild some of the camaraderie between the travellers, with the hunters pitching in alongside Rhamp's mercenaries and Teshveld villagers. The reward was gaining access to open ground again, even if it was a windswept, bitterly cold wedge of tundra.

Jesco pointed at another line of ranges arching down from the north. 'Look at those: are we going to find our way blocked again?'

'Don't worry – see that spearhead-shaped peak, the southernmost one? That's Mount Lucallus and it marks the point where the mountains hit the coast. That's where we'll find the frozen bay, and once we cross that, we're in Verdessa.'

'Mount Lucallus?' Jesco echoed, wrinkling his nose. 'You mean it's named after –?'

'Luc Mandaryke? Yes.'

'I'll piss on it specially,' Jesco promised.

'You do that. Hopefully it'll crumble into the sea.' Raythe tossed Jesco the reins. 'Here – I'm going to go and find my daughter. She's been gone too long.'

'You're her father, not her nanny.'

He ignored that, leaped off the rolling wagon, trotted to the back and unhitched Jesco's warhorse, a gelding he called Boss. As he moved back along the column, people called greetings and shouted complaints; for those serious enough, he paused to hear the whole story. Stores were getting low and they were now entirely in the hands of the hunters, who searched daily for plants, bulbs and roots, fish and fresh meat.

One of Rhamp's outriders passed him, careful to give him a salute. Kemara Solus was engrossed with the pair of pregnant women currently riding in her cart; she'd handed over Beca's reins to a young boy who was taking his duties very seriously indeed. Three carts down, he found Varahana's wagon, driven by a villager while she sat in the back teaching half a dozen children aged around six or seven their letters. Her usually ironic expression had vanished; she looked cheery and animated, reflecting the lively joy on the children's faces. It made him smile to see it – and again when he spotted Vidar riding nearby; more puppy than wolf when Vara was around.

I still don't think it'll happen . . . She's a priestess first, and however she ended up in the Church, she does take her vows seriously.

Beyond them, he found a cluster of younger horsemen gathered around Cal Foaley, listening avidly as the hunter gave them their orders for the day. Amongst the dozen or so riders was Zar, dressed like a young man, as always. His frown deepened when he saw that Banno Rhamp was beside her. He watched silently as Foaley rattled out a string of orders, dividing them into fours and sending them out to relieve the wider patrols for the afternoon, then called, 'Zar?' as she readied to leave with her patrol.

She glared back, a defiant *Don't you dare embarrass me* look on her face.

Foaley joined him. 'Raythe, what's up?'

'Morning, Cal. What's Zar doing here? I told her she was to stay in camp today.'

Foaley scratched his nose thoughtfully, then said laconically, 'She's as good a rider as any. Better'n most.'

'That's not the point. There are men in this camp I'd as soon she was nowhere near.'

'She holds her own. The lads are giving her a wide berth: they know she's got the praxis and fact is, they're scared of her now – and more than a little proud, most of 'em.'

Raythe frowned at Banno. 'Some aren't giving her a wide enough berth at all.'

'Him? He's a good lad. How old's the girl? Fifteen? Most folks would call that a good age to be wed. Best way to stop worrying about your daughter is to marry her off, make her someone else's problem.'

'*Marry her off? Are you mad?* Do you know—Never mind. Listen, we've been travelling since she was twelve and I won't countenance such a thing until we're back where we belong.'

'Could be a long old wait,' Foaley remarked. 'You want to end up with no grandchildren?'

Raythe bit his lip. He'd not really thought of it that way. But Zar was noble-born, and Otravian nobility at that, far above some Pelarian mercenary. 'When the time and place – and the suitor – is right, I'll consider it.'

'Good. Then in the meantime, I've some outriders who need relieving.'

Raythe harrumphed, then relented. 'Very well. But keep an eye on her.'

Foaley gave him a wry salute, then trotted back to his protégés. He placed Banno and Zar on different patrols, so after a sharp staring contest with his daughter, Raythe let it go.

She's going to grow up, whether I like it or not.

With a sharp '*Yar!*' Zar spurred her mount and pelted off, and Raythe watched them go with an odd sensation in his heart. She might be his fledgling, but she'd fly away all too soon.

Freedom was a galloping horse tearing across the plains. The other riders in the patrol were left far behind as Zar sped over the frost-rimed gravel. She'd been petrified her father would order her return to the wagon in front of everyone and been ready to erupt with defiance – but thankfully, Foaley had stood by her and her father had backed down.

With Adefar swooping alongside her, she felt like her life was her own now, that things were finally turning her way. 'Whatever the world throws at us, we're ready,' she told the spirit, even though she knew it wouldn't understand her.

After a while she slowed and let the others catch up. Their leader, a straggle-haired hunter called Xan Lynski, called, 'Stay with the group, girl,' with nervous authority, as if he feared what she'd do, but she recognised that Lynski knew more about the trail than she did, so she obeyed with good grace.

The other two finally steamed up – Rolfus Bohrne, one of Rhamp's men, and the blacksmith's third son, Ando Borger, flushed with exertion and the sting of the frigid wind on their faces.

'We've got the vanguard today,' Lynski reminded them, 'so we'll relieve Morro's patrol and scout ahead through the afternoon, camp for the night and re-join the caravan tomorrow morning. First though, I'm going to say this straight up: anyone laying a finger on Zar will lose their fecking hand. You want a woman, you pay one of Gravis' women. Got it?'

'We get 'em for free,' Rolfus Bohrne smirked. 'Anyways, money's changed hands on her already.'

'What?' Lynski snapped.

Zarelda stared as Bohrne kicked his horse into motion and rode off, crossing paths with another rider who appeared over the ridge to their north. Her heart thudded as she recognised Banno's brown mount, but her initial exultation blended with indignation as she thought, *So, 'money's changed hands', has it? We'll see about that.*

Lynski looked like he was contemplating putting a shaft in Bohrne's back, then he turned his simmering glare on Banno as he cantered up. 'By the Pit, what's going on?'

'Change of plan,' Banno said. 'I've been reassigned to your patrol.'

Lynski scowled, then looked skywards. 'Right then, follow,' he called, leading the way towards the coastal range.

Banno fell in beside Zar. 'Hey there.'

'What are you doing?' she asked. 'I know Foaley didn't sanction any change of patrol.'

'What he doesn't know, he doesn't have to.' Banno smiled. 'I just wanted to be with you.'

Her heart thumped and she had to swallow before asking, 'Are your brothers healing?'

'Poel is fine. Your father was merciful. But he's got your hand-print on his face for life.'

She coloured and admitted, 'It was an accident – I thought I was fighting for my life and it just happened.'

'Honestly, I don't blame you,' Banno said. 'It's good you can protect yourself.'

'I've barely dipped my toes in the water,' she answered, not wanting to scare him off. 'I have a million things to learn.'

'What sort of things?'

'A whole new language, for one, although really, I've been learning it for years. Old Magnian's the language of the praxis, and I need it to command my familiar.'

He looked around. 'A familiar?'

'He's called Adefar. He's being a bird at the moment. You can't see him, but he's circling above us.'

Banno looked around blindly, then asked, 'Why Old Magnian?'

'So Adefar knows I'm talking to him. Otherwise he'd act on everything I said, which would be disastrous.'

'I guess it would!' Banno laughed. 'What can you do?'

'Not so much, right now.' She paused, then asked shyly, 'Do you really want to know this stuff?' At his eager nod, she grinned and started, 'Well, there's three parts to the praxis: Proteus – that's about one's own body; Menteus, which is about our mind, and Mundius, which is about our world. An initiate like me starts with one, but eventually I'll learn them all. Some specialise, others stay general.'

Banno looked both impressed and apprehensive. She decided she quite liked that.

'Which are you learning first?' he asked.

'Mundius. Soon I'll be able to make fire and quench it, purify water, shape the earth, make plants grow, that sort of thing. In the empire, I'd have been sent to an Arcanus Academia to learn it all, but out here, it's just Father and me.'

'And the healer too,' Banno reminded her.

She didn't understand Kemara's reluctance to learn, but she remembered just in time to pretend that she was already fully trained. 'Kemara keeps to herself.'

'Did you always know you'd be a sorcerer? Is it because of your parents?'

'It sounds weird, but it doesn't run in families. My father says it's a personality trait, not a blood thing: you've got to be crazy enough to believe you can change the world, but disciplined enough to control it.'

'What happens if you can't master it?'

'The power dies.' She thought about Kemara. 'Or it kills you.'

Banno gave a low whistle. 'Then I hope you master it.'

'I will.' It had never crossed her mind, even for an instant, that she wouldn't.

They rode on in silence for a time, then Banno asked, 'Where did you live before Teshveld?'

She didn't really like talking about her past, but Banno had a nice, earnest face and tousled hair she longed to tame. 'All over Pelaria – but mostly I wasn't allowed to leave the house, and if I did it was as a boy.

Father always pretended to be a healer or a builder or a trader and somehow we'd scrape by – until someone got suspicious and we had to move again.'

'Must've been hard to make friends.'

'Friends?' she echoed, unable to keep the bitterness from her voice. 'I never got to make any.'

Ignoring the sudden change in her mood, Banno laughed. 'Hey, me neither. We've been travelling since before I was born too, hiring on to whoever pays us. The locals usually hate us, so we mostly keep to ourselves.'

'It was like that when we rode with Colfar in the Otravian rebellion,' she told him. 'I didn't get it, you know? These towns we were supposed to be "liberating"? They didn't mind if we died for them, but half the time they just refused outright to let us in. What was that about?'

'It's amazing we've not met before, when we're so alike,' he mused aloud, and only then did she realise that she was grinning at him like a brainless hollyhock – exactly the sort of girl she despised, who only thought about boys and pretty dresses.

'Have you ever killed someone?' she blurted, her tongue flapping out the first thing that popped into her brain, and she immediately cringed at the blunt, thoughtless question.

'Just once. We were guarding a wagon-train and bandits hit us. I was beside one of the drivers and he took an arrow in the gut. One of the bandits tried to leap aboard, but I cut his hand and he went under the wheels. Mind, he nearly tipped me off too, and the wagon damn nearly went into the ditch, but I righted it in time. Deo, I was scared.'

Somehow, that admission was more endearing than any claims of heroism. 'Sorry for asking.'

'It was a fair question,' Banno told her. 'I've never wanted this life. Whenever I see builders, I always think, "That's what I want to be." One day, maybe.'

'I always thought being a soldier was quite glamorous,' Zarelda admitted.

'Hardly! We just stand around looking tough. Smart mercenaries don't fight: we just take contracts and pray we don't have to. Pa's real good at picking sides and getting us out fast if it turns to shit.'

'Father's good at that too. I guess they're not so different. But my father is a praxis-mage and he's not a good enemy. I really hope your father remembers that.'

'I hope so too.' He went red, then gestured towards the horizon, where the patrol they were relieving was just coming into sight. By now the coast was closing in on one side and the mountains on the other. The peak they were calling Mount Spearhead was growing huge as they approached.

They reached its skirts by sunset, pulling up their horses on a ridge overlooking the bay. On the near side a gentle slope dropped to a desolate stone beach, but the mountain ranges blocked the way forward. This had to be the bay her father had talked about, the frozen bay they had to cross to reach Verdessa, which lay dark and green on the far side, just a mile or two away.

There was only one problem. The bay wasn't frozen any more.

'*Damn it*,' Raythe muttered, staring down from the ridge overlooking the bay while wind laced with tangy sea-spray buffeted him and his leaders. The sea, a mess of whitecaps and dirty grey-brown waves, hammered into the rocky shore in giant surges that shook the ground.

He looked again at Lyam Perhan's journal as if the words written there – *the bay looks to be permanently frozen, year-round* – would somehow magic the seawater back to ice.

The cartomancer had clearly miscalculated.

To his right was a river which poured out of a ravine on the near side of Mount Lucallus, which was the southernmost tip of a spur of mountains; they had no chance of crossing it, not with wagons and livestock. His caravan was stranded with no way forward.

Just half a mile across the bay, Verdessa sat mocking them, its lush loamy greens in stark contrast to the lifeless, scoured brown tundra on which they stood. Over there, rich hunting in fertile forests probably meant they could eat like lords. Here, they'd starve.

Mount Lucallus, he thought bitterly. He'd laughed when he'd heard that kragging Luc Mandaryke had a mountain named after him, but right now, it felt like his old nemesis was up there, looking down on him and mocking his failure.

Basically, we're well and truly kragged.

Behind him, Sir Elgus Rhamp stood rocking in the wind and staring blankly across the bay. Mater Varahana was gazing skywards, her lips moving, praying for enlightenment, perhaps. Kemara Solus had her hands on her hips, her face closed up. Even Jesco looked a little helpless, faced with an obstacle he could neither charm nor stab.

Behind them were the men and women and children who'd followed them from Teshveld: they were all looking for a solution from their leaders.

'Well, Lord Vyre?' Kemara called. 'How're you planning to get us out of this one?'

I have no idea ... 'I imagine it'll freeze over in a few months,' he muttered.

'We've got about a month's supply of food,' she snapped.

'Tell me something I don't know.'

'What, like "you've screwed up"?'

He ignored her and went back to trying to work out some way to get across, but even a sorcerer who'd mastered the winds couldn't fly, and there was nothing in the shape of Mount Lucallus that suggested another hidden Aldar fortress – and anyway, it was on the far side of the torrential river gorge. 'Perhaps we can build rafts and float across?' he wondered out loud.

'Really?' Kemara snorted. 'I assume it's escaped your notice, but the wagons are made from short planks – nothing we could build would hold more than a few people or horses at a time. And the seas are wild enough to rip apart whatever we build, anyway.'

'There'll be calm days,' Raythe replied hopefully, his thoughts beginning to move again. He pointed to the thickly forested far shore. 'We could send a team across to cut longer timber.'

Elgus Rhamp was nodding slowly. 'Maybe.'

'No, rafts won't work,' Varahana said. 'There's no way to steer or propel them, and each return trip would take most of a day – even without mishap we'd be here for a month at least.'

'Then we need a faster solution,' he conceded, looking at Kemara. 'That means the praxis.'

'What, you can just magic up a bridge or something?' she asked, her voice a mix of sarcasm and curiosity.

So she is just a little interested in what she might be able to do.

'Well, I could get the spirits to build a causeway from rock and earth, but they wouldn't be able to do it any faster than a gang of men. And any wooden bridge – even assuming we could cut the timber to shape – would only take us onto the near flank of that mountain, which is so steep only the most agile could climb it. We'll see if there's a gentler crossing inland, but we're running out of supplies, and therefore, time.'

'So you're saying you're really no use at all?'

What happened to her, that she's so scared of her own powers? he wondered. 'No, only that we need a smarter solution. There'll be a way, I'm sure of it.'

The watching crowd fell silent, and then got bored – there was nothing interesting in just watching a man think – and started drifting away, followed by his leaders.

Finally just he and Varahana were left. 'Any ideas?' he asked her.

'Can you call down the planetary rings to make a bridge?'

They shared a smile, gazing up at the dim light of the rings half-hidden behind the scudding clouds. 'If only.'

Then inspiration did hit. 'I'd need timber and a sextant – and I'd need to work out the equations,' he muttered. 'And it'll burn up the last of the istariol I've hoarded. But the direction is right, and I can cope with the distance, I think.'

Varahana had no idea what he was on about.

Another look at the alignment of the planetary rings and he was sure it could work. With rising satisfaction, he called Jesco and Vidar over. 'I've got a solution,' he told them. 'You need to find the best young carpenters we have and we'll have to get a team across the inlet.'

'What do you intend?' Varahana asked.

'There's a way of using the praxis to open a gate between two places, but it's tricky, and when it's activated, it creates a kind of sensory explosion that any other sorcerer for at least a hundred miles in every direction will feel: it'll be like sending up a gigantic torch saying "Here we are!". There's bound to be praxis-wielders at the imperial garrison in Verdessa: they'll sense our activity and they'll want to investigate.'

'Is there no other way?' Vidar asked.

'Not that I can think of, not in the time we have – or rather, don't have.'

'Provisions are getting dangerously low,' Jesco agreed.

'But there'll be game in those woods over there,' Raythe pointed out, 'so if we can find a way round the cliffs, we can send our hunters ahead while I work on the gate.' He clapped Vidar's shoulder. 'I'll have to send Zarelda across, so make sure whoever goes with her can be trusted.'

'Raythe, relax,' Varahana said. 'She's way more mature than you credit.'

'Aye,' he agreed, 'that's what worries me.'

Zarelda had been expecting the whole 'Lord Protector' spiel for days, but when her father finally cornered her on the slope overlooking the inconveniently melted bay, it didn't go at all as she expected.

'Look,' he started, 'I'm not going to lecture you about men in general or Banno in particular. We've been through all that before and it'll bore us both. Just, *please*, be careful. I'm too young to be a grandfather.'

She pulled a face. 'Dad, that's the *last* thing I want.'

'Good.' He sighed heavily, which made him look older still, and at thirty-six he was already *ancient*. 'One day we'll settle down properly, somewhere secure, and then you'll be free to be your own woman.'

'We weren't even secure at home,' she muttered.

'True, but that wasn't normal. It's usually only once in a century that the Great Houses face a purge like that.'

He tousled her hair and she wondered if he'd actually noticed she was growing it out; she was tired of looking like a boy.

'In time, we'll have our real lives back,' he promised.

'But what if that day never comes? Do you want me to spend my life as a spinster?'

'Well, yes, ideally,' he replied, then winked at her. 'I just want you to be careful, and not just with your body, but your heart. You're only fifteen.'

'Nearly sixteen—' she began.

'Indeed,' he interrupted, smiling suddenly and fishing in a pocket, pulled out a little box. 'When I said "only", I meant "Happy birthday for tomorrow, sixteen-year-old".'

She couldn't believe she'd lost track of the days. Her heart thudding, she felt a burst of joy and love for her father.

'I'm of age tomorrow,' she realised, throwing him a teasing look.

'Try to ignore that fact. You're still under my protection.' He looked her in the eye. 'Zar, let's find this istariol, become filthy rich, topple the Mandaryke cabal and get Mother back. Then you can do what you like. That's all I ask.'

'That's all?' she echoed sarcastically.

'I reckon it's do-able,' he insisted. 'Friends?'

As usual, that crooked grin which had been her beacon from her earliest memories, won her over. They hugged hard and everything was right again.

'Friends,' she repeated, and crooked her little finger.

As he linked his with hers, he grinned. 'Good. By the way, I have a job for you, my sorcerer's apprentice.'

'Catch!' Ando Borger called, and the rope came snaking across the rock-face.

Banno Rhamp caught it left-handed, clinging by his right to a stone nub at eye level. His boots were wedged into barely-there toeholds, the river surging past furiously just a few feet below them.

The previous afternoon, Foaley and Vidarsson had marked a crossing place between the rocky cliffs. At low tide the current was treacherously swift; at high tide a backwash created a confusion of whirling counter-flows that reduced the current to a sluggish swirl laced with sea-spume and driftwood.

There was no way to get wagons, horses or gear down here and across, but anyone lithe enough for the climb could manage. The far riverbank was some forty yards away and just as steep, but there were plenty of fractures providing hand- and foot-holds in the cliffs on either side.

Banno secured the rope to a log trapped at the water's edge, creating a guide for the climbers following him. Most were younger men from Teshveld, sons of sons of craftsmen who'd grown up with hammers and saws in the their hands. Even young Norrin Harper was there, with his instrument strapped to his back beside a satchel of hand-tools.

And Zar's with us. That thought made him smile.

She appeared behind the last man, her face taut with concentration as she found the crevices, then, grinning impudently, she leaped down to join the young men.

'Easy,' she said. 'Don't see what you needed a rope for.'

'We've got packs full of nails and tools and shit,' Rolfus Bohrne growled. 'Men's work.'

'Labourers' work,' she retorted. 'Follow me.'

Banno had been lectured about Zar being sacrosanct by Raythe Vyre himself. That had been embarrassing enough, but afterwards, his own father had pulled him aside. 'Court her if you want, boy, but keep it seemly,' Elgus told him. 'I like watching Vyre squirm over his daughter, but I need his goodwill for now, so keep it chaste.'

That was fine. He liked Zar a lot, but no way did he want Raythe Vyre coming after him. It was enough to be with her, for now.

The next part, crossing the river, was the most dangerous. Although it was high tide and the water was almost unmoving, there was plenty of debris to snag clothes, hair and limbs and drag a swimmer under.

Ando Borger, who was nominally in charge, began giving orders. 'One at a time, and *be careful*. Watch for driftwood and don't get snagged. First one over strings the rope for the rest of us. First one ready gets the honour of leading us over the river.'

The young men pulled off their shirts, all clamouring to be first – and then turned expectantly to look at Zarelda, a few flexing muscles to provoke a reaction.

But she didn't even blush: just laughed, took a coil of rope and tossed Banno one end, then dived fully clothed into the river. A moment later she came up and her arms began to churn as she headed for the far side.

'Look at her go!' Ando Borger exclaimed.

She swam well, powering through the eddies until she found her footing just short of the far shore and waded to the narrow strip of gravel, water streaming from her clothing.

'Nice arse, if you like 'em skinny,' Rolfus Bohrne chuckled.

'You mind your tongue,' Banno told him.

The other man gave him an 'I'll say what I bloody well like' look, but shut up. Banno was his boss' son, after all.

Zar tied her rope to a rock and Banno did the same at his end, tightening it until it was taut enough for those following with the heavy satchels of gear to cling to.

It was almost an hour before they were all standing on the far bank.

Banno joined Zar as she sat on a rock drying in the sun. 'Congratulations,' he said. 'First into Verdessa.'

'I know.' She gave him a satisfied grin. 'I win again.'

Zar felt like she was floating on a heady sense of freedom. She knew Father loved her, that he was trying to protect her, and that necessitated hiding and anonymity and constantly moving on, but it was so *wearying*. Being given licence to do this was wonderful.

What's the point of being alive if it's just to live in a box?

Feeling exhilarated, she bounded on ahead of the others and clambered up the rockface, then helped Banno secure the rope for the others, before setting off along the clifftop, climbing along the edge of the ravine all the way to the sea-cliffs, then around to those with the ocean below. Adefar was with her, darting hither and thither, shapeshifting from reptile to bird to goat and back to fox for sheer joy.

The young men, weighed down by their tools, were left well behind, all except Banno, who strove manfully to keep up with her, panting under the weight of his burden. By the time he caught her, he was perspiring heavily, his cheeks bright red and hair slick with sea-spray.

'Wait!' he called, sounding exasperated.

Zar sped up again, freedom and the joy of life giving her wings, but finally she came to a notch in the cliff where another small stream cascaded off the edge, a small, erratic waterfall that fell all the way down into the breakers below. She peered over the cliff and saw waves breaking around a ring of rocks, dozens of yards below. But the space inside that ring was still, and it looked deep. Her imagination began to feed her wicked thoughts.

Banno appeared behind her and stopped, breathing hard. 'Gerda's sake, Zar,' he puffed. 'Slow down. We don't know what's out here – and you might fall–'

'Fall?' she said, with a sudden laugh. 'What, like this?'

Turning, she pretended to lose her balance and plummeted over the edge as Banno shouted in alarm.

She dropped through the waterfall towards the swirling ocean below.

With Adefar swooping alongside protectively, she breathed deep, pinched her nostrils shut and slammed feet-first into the water, right in the middle of the ring of rocks. When at last she struck the stony bottom, she kicked off back to the surface, gasping at the freezing cold.

Okay, this is stupid – but dear Gerda, it was fun to see the look on his face.

A moment later, Banno hit the water beside her in a huge splash. She squealed as he plunged past her and then erupted from below, grabbing her forearms as they trod water and shouting, 'What in the Pit are you—?'

She grabbed his face, kissed his mouth, hot and salty in this freezing place, then pushed him under and thrashed away. By the time he spluttered up again, she'd climbed onto a rock, laughing hysterically.

'Zar!' he shouted, red-faced now.

She dissolved into giggles at the sight of him, as he kicked towards the rock, but as he tried to clamber up beside her, a wave hit the pool and knocked him off his feet. He vanished, then came up choking with water and laughter, and she felt a wave of vivid affection.

A man who laughs is a treasure, her mother had said, almost the last thing before they parted, which was odd, because Mirella had never laughed once in the brief time Zar had been with her and her new husband, while Raythe had made her laugh all the time.

But that was another time and place, and this was the first real fun she'd had in weeks, since the dance. Banno clambered up beside her, shaking with cold and laughter, his eyes fixed on her, and she met him, grasped his shoulders and kissed him again, half in and half out of the water, savouring his taste while his lips explored hers, and then as their mouths opened, their tongues coiled together and a surge like praxis-energy jolted through her. She moaned softly into his mouth and felt her soul adhere to his.

'This is wonderful,' he told her, as their lips parted, 'but we're going to freeze to death.'

She shivered in response, but it wasn't from the cold. He was right, though: the chill was going straight to her bones, despite the burning in her heart. 'Let's get ashore,' she panted.

To her surprise, he picked her up and waded to the beach, a tiny strip of sand beneath the cliffs – cradling her against his chest. His big, beautiful brown eyes were full. Then he lowered her to the sand, rolled against her and kissed her, drinking her in.

'Do you know what today is?' she whispered. 'It's my birthday.'

He pulled back and looked down at her, filling her sight and senses. His strong body felt solid as the cliffs, but gentle and warming as the sun. Their wet clothes barely felt present as they clung together. 'How old?'

'Sixteen. Of age, by Imperial Law.'

He swallowed. 'Deo on High, your father would kill me.'

'Me too,' she giggled, then she kissed him again. 'I don't care.' She stared at him, willing him to take the lead, to take control.

He groaned and looking away, murmured, 'It's not right, not without our parents' consent.'

Her disappointment in him was crushing. A moment she felt like she'd been building up to for months was evaporating, making her doubt everything.

'Are you afraid of my father? Or yours?' she demanded, more bitterly than she'd intended.

Aren't I good enough for him? Or is he not who I want him to be . . .?

He sat up, looked at her and said, 'Zar, you're utterly glorious. But I want to be better than my father and my brothers. I don't want to be just another mercenary who takes everything and leaves a trail of girls in trouble. I want this to be right, and I'm prepared to wait.'

His restraint softened her disappointment.

'And,' he added, 'I want it to be somewhere nice, not at the bottom of a cliff in freezing saltwater with Rolf Bohrne and Ando Borger and the rest watching from the cliff.'

Fair enough.

That killed most of her remaining ardour and restored her faith in him. *He can think as well as feel,* she thought admiringly, and her spirit was suffused in warmth despite the cold wetness.

'How come you're not married?' she blurted. At twenty, he was past due.

He pulled a face. 'I was going to be, several times, but the wars got in the way. First time, alliances shifted and it got called off. Second time, we had to flee after a defeat. Third time, my betrothed caught the plague when her father's castle was besieged. Since then, we've been moving too much.' He threw her an anxious look. 'I guess I'm bad luck.'

'Not to me,' she told him.

He kissed her again, and for a long minute all she could do was devour him hungrily, until they disentangled and made their way along the narrow shore, clinging to rocks as the waves pounded in, delighting in the power of the waves and their own ability to resist it.

They emerged on a long beach on the western side of the bay, shivering in the cold wind and their salt-stiff clothing, and found a driftwood log to sit on and warm themselves until the others arrived, soldiering down the slope with their heavy packs. Ando Borger had brought Banno's as well as his own; he'd left it at the waterfall where Zar had jumped in.

'Don't think I didn't see you two,' the blacksmith's son told Banno and Zar quietly. 'Think of your virtue and of Gerda watching on high,' he advised. 'Restrain yourselves.'

'We are,' Banno replied, 'but Zar is going to be my wife, one day – you'll see.'

Ando's eyebrows shot up and he backed off, shaking his head.

Zar turned to Banno, struck dumb by his words. From first kiss to secretly – or not so secretly – betrothed in a matter of minutes? It felt giddy and mad, but somehow it didn't feel *wrong*. Most girls were betrothed to virtual strangers before they were sixteen, and some were married off even earlier, regardless of Imperial Law.

Chimes rang in her heart as she gazed at *her man* and imagined the life they would have together.

I can wait, she thought tremulously. *But not too long.*

'You're looking a touch put out, Boss,' Jesco drawled. 'Anything on your mind?'

'Nothing but the task before me,' Raythe lied.

When Zar had vanished around the headland across the river mouth, he'd felt like he'd lost her, regardless of their words before they'd parted.

Telling her to go forth wasn't the same as actually letting go. She was the centre of his world, the only part of Mirella he still had. If he lost her, he didn't know what he'd do.

To love is to trust, Varahana had told him, and she'd given him a hug. He'd needed that.

He'd spent the last few days trying very hard not to think of what might be going on across the bay – although he'd still kept a distant eye on them. Zar's young men seemed to be working hard, for through his spyglass he'd seen the trees being felled and trimmed. Each evening their cooking fires gleamed in the twilight. But he still worried about what might be happening after the fires burned low.

Then Varahana and Kemara arrived, barely looking at each other. 'I'd better see what these two want,' he told Jesco apologetically.

Varahana began talking the moment he was in earshot. 'Raythe, how long are you going to let this go on?'

He knew what she meant. Despite sharing his camp, Kemara still refused to train. She wouldn't learn the praxis language or undergo a manifestation, and that meant her gift was festering inside her, and that would end badly. If a mizra-spirit entered her, she could lose all control – people could get hurt, or even die.

'It's not my choice,' he replied. 'You can lead a horse to water . . .'

Vara's normally serene features creased in annoyance; the way she was glaring at Kemara told Raythe that she was jealous. Some scholars couldn't conceive of why they, with their huge intellect, couldn't grasp sorcery. 'She had a whole past she never told me when I took her in. I thought she trusted me, but now . . . I'm vexed, Raythe. She's exasperating.'

'Welcome to my world.' They turned and looked at Kemara, who'd heard every word.

'Mistress Kemara, we owe it to our fellow travellers to either train you, or attempt another cauterising. We can't just let this go on.'

Kemara scowled, then asked, 'What's involved in trying to cauterise my potential again?'

Raythe *tsked* in disappointment. A sorcerer's gift was rare and he felt personally betrayed by her refusal to embrace her gift, but tried to understand. *Maybe what she went through the first time traumatised her too much? What a waste.*

He shared a resigned look with Varahana and said, 'Kemara, I've never done it before, but I know the theory. At the moment all my energy must go into the crossing, but after that, I'm sure we'll find an opportunity.'

Looking relieved, she curtseyed ironically, then stomped away.

'I've never met someone with that potential who doesn't want it,' he commented.

'Some must be thrust into it all unwilling – like me and the Church,' Varahana replied.

'You've come to terms with your lot, though.'

'Most days, Raythe, but not all. It's hard to put aside that it wasn't my choice to begin with. I miss my books, my friends . . . I even miss my family, sometimes, and they're the bastards who made me take vows.'

'Then leave,' he urged. 'We're in the middle of nowhere and this isn't even imperial territory. If you don't want to be a priestess any more, then defrock yourself. Grow your hair, go mad.'

She laughed, her voice cracking a little. 'How could I do that, Raythe? I'd be letting so many people down. I'm Gerda and Deo's representative here – I can't betray that trust. They're my flock, my people.'

'You've got six Sisters of Gerda. Promote one of them.'

She gave him a sour look. 'That lot are only good at singing and praying, Raythe, dear. They've known nothing but a nunnery since they were young, and most of them are past sixty. Why do you think I'm in charge?'

He sighed and tried again. 'Well, Elgus and I are making up the law as we go. Why can't you make up Church laws too? New lands, new rules. Abolish the stupid stuff like shaving heads and chastity.' Then he went red, afraid he'd said too much.

But Varahana just laughed. 'It doesn't work that way, darling. The Church is all about tradition and ritual and shared beliefs. I can't just change something that doesn't suit me. My flock have placed their souls in my care.' She looked away sadly, towards where Vidar was sawing timber for the gate. 'So even if I wanted to "go mad", I can't.'

As they fell silent, Raythe felt a sense of shared burdens, and shared sorrow.

She's right, they did all put themselves in our care, even Elgus and his men.

He'd been resisting feeling any real responsibility by telling himself that everyone was here out of greed. But each day of shared perils added an extra weight to his shoulders, reminding him of Colfar's rebellion and the men he'd commanded, most of whom were dead now. He still felt a lingering guilt that he'd not died with them. Perhaps one day, he'd think back on the people of this caravan in the same way.

Varahana squeezed his hand. 'Bear up, Raythe. You can't make everyone's decisions for them.'

'True.' He gave her a fond look and changed the subject. 'By the way, Vara, I'm hoping I can draw on your scholarship. I need someone else to work with me on the praxis-gate to get us across the bay. Will you help?'

Varahana looked astounded. 'I'm not a sorcerer, Raythe, much though I wish I was.'

'But you have mathematical training and I'm guessing you know how a sextant works? Your knowledge and skills are exactly what I need for the calculations.'

The lure of using her education won out over priestly duties in seconds. 'I would be delighted to help,' she exclaimed. 'So long as I can fulfil my ritual duties, every other moment I can spare will be at your disposal.' She battered her long eyelashes at him. 'What a pleasure to give my brain something to do.'

'You're welcome. Glad to provide a modicum of pleasure in your dry and dusty life.'

'Raythe, darling, I have a stash of communal wine and my own fair hands, so my life isn't as dry as you might imagine,' she said, with a wicked chuckle.

'You just destroyed my faith in Deo,' he exclaimed, his cheeks suddenly burning.

'You didn't have any, dear,' Varahana tittered, completely unashamed. 'When do I start?'

'How about tomorrow morning? Bring paper, if you have any.'

'I'll rip some blank pages out of a hymn book,' Varahana replied, sashaying away.

He realised he was still blushing and hastily turned his mind to the task he faced.

A Westgate: Deo on high, do I even remember how?

Kemara woke lying amidst saturated grass and staring at the underside of her cart, shivering at the cold air whistling through her dew-sodden blanket. She shuddered, thinking how bleak this coast would be in winter, once ice and snow covered the rocks and coated the stark pines.

Her eyes flicked to the nearest fire, where Raythe Vyre was poking the embers to life as his comrades woke. Seeing the Otravian sorcerer took her mind straight back to her rejection of praxis training.

He doesn't know what he's asking of me.

But it was a relief to have finally got him to agree to cauterise her, though deferring the moment until after they crossed the bay felt cruel, as if he were stringing her along, hoping she'd change her mind. 'But I won't,' she muttered.

She stared at the bottom of the cart again, where a concealed compartment housed the stolen artefact. *Koni'ka, Kemara*, the Aldar mask whispered in its cold reptilian voice. She blanked the insidious sound with a shiver. There was an illicit dealer back in Pelaria who'd give her ten thousand argents for it. *It's insurance, in case this trail of istariol runs cold, that's all.* So she refused to respond or to elevate it further into her consciousness.

Abruptly she scrambled out, hung her sodden blanket over a guy rope to shelter her as she undressed and put on a dry smock, then laced her bodice and pulled her tangled hair into a loose knot. She felt hor-ribly grimy, her eyes gritty and sore, as she trudged into the trees and peed, then stumbled back to camp.

'Mistress Kemara,' Raythe called, 'would you like some coffee?'

Her whole being groaned with want. 'You have coffee still?'

'We've been padding it out with chicory, but it's just about palatable.'

'Sold.' She accepted a mug and sipped slowly, letting the warmth and flavour seep into her as she admired Jesco Duretto, cooking hotcakes in a small pan. The handsome Shadran was, as always, freshly shaved and groomed and pleasing to the eye. Priests might decry vanity, but he lived by it.

Vidar's horse was gone and Raythe was sitting on a log, glowering across the bay at where his daughter was encamped with all those young men. *Just the sort of reckless thing I did at her age*, she thought. It amused her to watch Vyre's discomfort.

'When I was young, I defied my parents and ran away to join the Nyostian sisters,' she commented and when he looked at her, she added, 'You didn't think I came from a family that actually wanted a scholar daughter, did you? My folk wanted me pulling pints in a tavern. Some-times children see more clearly than their parents.'

'But most times they don't. Banno's a mercenary's get.'

'He's the son of a Pelarian knight. And from what I've seen, Zar wants to be a sorcerer more than *anything* else. She won't throw that away.'

'But in the heat of the moment—'

'Oh, stop torturing yourself. She's a sensible girl and he's a surpris-ingly decent boy. And what's the worst that can happen? She's not fertile for another two weeks.'

'Argh!'

Torturing Vyre is quite fun, she decided. 'Really, what does it matter? I tried it when I was her age and it was quite off-putting. I didn't do it again for years.' She winked at the amused Jesco, who grinned back.

Raythe counter-attacked. 'I don't understand you. Who in the world rejects sorcery?'

That killed her mood. 'I was treated like shit by the Church when I failed my tests. They dragged me through the Pit and I won't go through that again.'

'You wouldn't – I'm not the Church, and I desperately need a fellow practitioner. I'm exhausted and I really need help. You mightn't believe it, but I'm a good teacher. The Church sorcerers deal in absolutes, but I don't.'

He actually sounded like he meant it, but it was too late.

'You're right, I don't believe you,' Kemara lied. 'And I don't want to talk about it.'

The Otravian fell silent, to her relief. They munched on Jesco's hot-cakes and watched the women making their way down to the river mouth with pails for drinking water. On the beach, Mater Varahana was leading matins and Kemara realised that yet again she'd forgotten to attend. Her vows didn't feel relevant out here. People came to her for healing anyway, regardless of the Church's blessing.

But Varahana's protection matters, especially while Osvard still holds a grudge.

She put that aside and distracted herself watching Cognatus leap after birds that flapped aside when they saw him coming; they never went far as he couldn't hurt them anyway.

'So, Raythe,' Jesco said, breaking the silence, 'what's a Westgate?'

Raythe's expression shifted from morose to attentive. 'Well, you know – I hope? – that our world, Shamaya, is a sphere floating in space?'

'That's what my Nyostian tutors taught us,' Kemara put in, interested despite herself. 'They said Shamaya spins around the sun, but the planetary rings spin around us.'

Jesco blinked. 'Bullshit! I've heard some crap in my time, but that's just plain silly.'

'Why?' Kemara asked, surprised at his ignorance.

'Because clearly everything has to revolve around the centre of the universe, and that's me.' Jesco slapped his thighs cheerily as she burst out laughing. 'We all had an education, Raythe, so just get on with the lecture.'

Raythe snorted, then went on, 'Okay, so Shamaya spins eastwards, towards the sunrise, on an axis that runs from the poles through the centre of our world.' He picked up an egg and slowly spun it. 'Like this. We calculate that it spins at more or less a thousand miles an hour, but we don't feel a thing, because the whole planet is moving, including the air – and we don't fly off because of gravity. But imagine if you could momentarily *not spin* with the rest of the world, so that instead of moving one thousand miles an hour east, you just hung in place. Effectively, you'd be travelling one thousand miles an hour *westwards*.'

'And getting flattened by every hill and tree and passing thing,' Jesco snorted.

'Of course – but what if you were insubstantial, so that nothing harmed you? Sorcerers discovered that spirits, the beings we use to make magic, exist in a field of energy called *aether* or *nebulum*. By infusing something with nebulum, we make it insubstantial for a time.'

Kemara leaned forward. 'So that it travels west at a thousand miles an hour, safely? That's impressive,' she conceded. 'Is that what a "Westgate" does?'

'Exactly,' Raythe said. 'You set up an archway that will infuse anything passing through it with nebulum, holding it in stasis in the spirit realm. If I set up another gate across the bay, *exactly* westward of the first gate at *exactly* the same elevation, and infuse it with the counterspell, the infused object or person will effectively be propelled through that second gate across the bay, be stripped of the nebulum and step onto that far shore, inside' – he raised his eyes, silently calculating – 'roughly three and a half seconds.'

Jesco whistled. 'Why don't we do that all the time?'

'Because it's very costly in time and energy, and every sorcerer for miles can sense it,' Raythe replied. 'The Bolgravians tried it once, to move a force of men into Pelarian territory – they had concealed sorcerers set up the gate to exact calculations and they managed to move about a thousand men through before the Pelarians realised and destroyed the host gate. But the Bolgravs didn't realise they'd been found out for another two hours, by which time not only had those men they'd sent ahead been surrounded and massacred, but everyone else they passed through the opening gate in those two hours was trapped in the nebulum, which made them a meal for the hungry spirits. It was an utter disaster, so it's almost never done, and very seldom with more than a handful of people. The only reason it'll work for us is that we're hundreds of miles from civilisation, and our destination is only a mile away and exactly west of us.'

'It sounds horribly dangerous,' Kemara said.

'It's probably our only choice right here and now.'

She considered that, then reluctantly admitted, 'I suppose. Do you have everything you need?'

'I do, but it'll take all my remaining istariol. I have just a couple of pinches left.'

'And you'll need to get those calculations absolutely right,' Jesco commented.

'Aye: longitude, latitude, axis tilt, time of year, velocity, timing,' Raythe agreed. 'I've got Varahana working on it. I'll set up this gate while Varahana's working on the positioning of both mine and the gate Zar's working on.'

'You're entrusting our safety to an untrained novice?' Kemara exclaimed. *Gerda's Blade, he's reckless.*

'I'll double- and triple-check everything Zar does, but I needed her to make a start. The receiving gate is very simple to charge, but it takes a long time. It's the positioning that's crucial, and Varahana and I will be calculating that. I could use help to infuse the first gate, though.' He looked at Kemara. 'You could do that, if you were willing. It would save us days of effort.'

She bit her lip, then conceded. Raw energy was increasingly spilling from her – this might even release the pressure. 'I'll do it,' she agreed.

It was dusk, a grey day slumping into night, and in the camp below, Zarelda ignored the men watching her in bemusement as she manipulated a six-foot-long wooden rod with a circular disc of metal affixed to the top. Across the bay, her father had conjured a bead of orange light. It was just an inch in diameter, but the minute alterations he was making at his end sent his light dancing thirty or forty feet away every time. She'd been chasing that light for the past twenty minutes and was growing increasingly ratty about it.

'Keep the kragging thing still,' she swore, enjoying the freedom to curse to her heart's content. Her father couldn't hear her, of course, but she liked to imagine his ears crisping at her increasingly colourful collection of obscenities.

The button of glowing orange settled on a rock above her and she bounded up the slope, caught it on the disc, then, keeping the orange light centred, pushed the rod into the turf. It jerked around a little and she had to adjust, but then it steadied and a light flashed across the bay.

Adefar, in sparrow form, flashed down and danced gleefully in fox-cub shape, then leaped onto her shoulder and nuzzled her.

'Yes!' she crowed.

'What just happened?' Banno asked, oblivious to Adefar and much else that she was doing.

'We have the position of the gate,' she said, peering across the bay and waving wildly. Father was lost in the gloom, but she knew he'd have his spyglass trained on her. 'This is where we need to build the frame, to the *exact* dimensions I tell you.' She piled stones around the pole to make sure it stayed on the exact spot.

'Why?'

'Because, *magic*, duh.' She was feeling very pleased with herself: here she was, just sixteen and already helping perform praxis-sorcery, and with a handsome, admiring young man watching her every move. With that in mind, she stuck out her chest and peered mystically into the distance, going for 'soulful yet alluring', the sort of person she pictured her mother as, only less of a treacherous bitch, of course.

'This going to be *amazing*,' she boasted. 'We're going to move everyone from there to here in an eye-blink.'

He certainly looked impressed – until Rolfus Bohrne ruined the moment.

'Oi,' he called from below, 'are you going to take a turn cooking tonight?'

She relaxed into a slouch: posing like a preening hollyhock was too uncomfortable to keep up for long. 'Sorry, I'm too busy.'

'You too good for the rest of us, Ladyship?'

'I've always been too good for you,' she retorted.

His eyes narrowed, but all he said was, 'Fine. Banno: your turn.'

'He's busy too.'

'Is he just?' Rolfus growled. He turned to Ando Borger in exasperation. 'Ando, I thought you were in charge—'

'I am,' the smith's son said, 'I'm in charge of supporting Mistress Zarelda. You're cooking tonight.' He turned back to Zar and asked, 'Okay, so what do you need?'

Basically, I'm in charge, Zar thought, glowing a little. She smiled at Ando in gratitude. 'I need men who don't need their fingers and toes to count, and timber, cut to the specific lengths I'll give you. That's tomorrow's job.'

She worked her charges hard after that: getting the timber lengths cut right and fitted precisely together, then erecting their gate exactly facing the one her father was constructing across the bay. She knew she was annoying the shit out of Rolfus in particular, but she didn't care. Three days passed in a cascade of small victories and aggravating miscalculations, but Adefar was attentive and obedient and so were her coterie of young men. Life wasn't comfortable on this windswept, frigid shore, but it was very satisfying.

But all too soon came the moment she'd dreaded. She was standing at the wooden erection, trying to work out if it framed the middle point to the exact inch, when a new voice spoke behind her.

'It needs to be taller by at least a foot,' her father remarked.

She froze, her mouth suddenly dry. Her adventure had ended. She was no longer the boss, no longer free – and she'd got it wrong. Behind him she could see Jesco, stroking his sword hilt as he eyed up the half-dressed young men in the camp.

'Uh, good morning,' she mumbled.

Rolfus and the others were all eyes and ears, waiting for her to be taken down a few pegs.

'The shape's wrong, too,' her father added. 'It's supposed to be an equilateral triangle.'

'It *is* equilateral,' she started, 'but the bottom ends are buried.'

'You were supposed to allow for that.'

'I did, but we needed to go deeper for stability.'

'Then you should have recut the timbers.' Raythe glanced at the young men, who were watching with a certain vindictive amusement. 'You . . . Ando Borger, yes? I put you in charge here – where are the food stockpiles? Where are the spare timbers?'

The young men, after a careful look at the smiling Jesco, mumbled, 'We'll get right on it.'

'Excellent. I see no reason for more than four of you to be here.' Raythe eyed them, then chose Banno, Rolfus and Norrin. 'Right, let's get this sorted out.'

They worked all morning until the tilt was exactly right, a matter not of inches but fractions of an inch. Finally, Raythe placed his sighting gem inside the frame. Hovering in mid-air, it flared to life; a moment later it was speared by a beam from the other side.

'They're aligned,' he announced, smiling finally. 'We can begin empowering it today.' He waved the others away. 'Daughter, a word, please.'

She exchanged an anxious look with Banno, then followed her father down to the shore, where waves hissed between the driftwood piled up on the smooth grey pebbles. She waited until the silence became awkward then blurted out, 'Dad, *nothing* happened.' She stared at the spume and mumbled, 'We've kissed, that's all. I'm not Mother.'

'Good, but that's not what I was going to ask.' He ruffled her hair. 'How's Adefar? Are you fully bonded?'

'It's wonderful,' she beamed. 'He's like a part of me.'

'You're a natural,' he said, making her heart soar. 'I think you're ready for this next task.'

He took her back to the triangular arch and bade her lay her right hand on it, then he placed his fingers over hers and said, 'Close your eyes and concentrate on the sensation of touch.' She did so, conscious of Banno and the others watching curiously. Adefar, in fox-cub form, perched on her shoulder, watching avidly.

With an effort, she managed to shut out her awareness of them all and declared herself ready.

'Good. Now call Adefar into yourself and trace *Flux*, the energy rune,' he commanded.

She traced the rune in pale light, which made the watching men murmur, and as she did so, her soul seemed to swell inside her. 'Done,' she muttered, gazing at her father's hand on hers.

'Good. Now, feel the heat of my palm on the back of your hand. Sense the roughness of the timber beneath your fingers. *Listen and feel*, Zarelda,' he repeated, then he broke off and muttered something in the runic tongue. She tried to follow his words, but lost track and reverted to doing as he bade her and just *feeling*.

After a moment she realised a current was flowing from him into her and on into the timber. The wood was beginning to vibrate faintly.

'Do you feel that?' he murmured. 'I need you to take over. Adefar is already part of the chain, so all you need do is maintain the same low, slow energy.'

The strange thrumming sensation was now permeating her entire body. 'Yes, I feel it!'

'Good. Get to know it – *become* it.'

She did as her father said, and as she attuned all her awareness to it, the world dropped away.

'Now,' Raythe said, 'you take control.'

That was harder, but there it was: energy crackled through her into the wood.

'Well done.' Raythe removed his hand, but the current went on flowing through her and into the timber. 'Any sorcerer for miles can now sense us, but don't hurry – getting it right is the most important thing. Take your time: you've got all day.'

'All day?' she blurted. 'What if I need to pee?'

Her father chuckled. 'You can walk away for a few minutes and the connection will stay live. Just relax – there's nothing you need to do that's more important to the expedition than this.'

She felt a thrill of pride and anxiety, but she pushed it away to focus on the task. Everything else faded into the background. She dimly sensed her father depart for the other side of the bay once more, although Jesco remained. Sometime around mid-afternoon, she came out of her trance to find herself wrapped in a blanket, with Banno sitting nearby, watching protectively, and she felt an even greater sense of rightness.

I'm doing this: I'm becoming who I always wanted to be.

The exhilaration carried her through the day.

'Do you feel that, Captain Hawkstone?' Toran Zorne's voice, usually so monotonous, rose fractionally in surprise. It was the most animation Larch Hawkstone had ever heard from the Ramkiseri agent.

'I feel nothing,' the Borderer captain answered, puzzled, looking around the forecastle of the frigate, one of the two ships Zorne had requisitioned. The frigate was equipped with a dozen bombards, iron-barrelled cylinders designed to propel metal balls packed with explosive powder for hundreds of yards; the second vessel, a troop-carrier, was packed with Hawkstone's men and a contingent of Bolgravian marines.

Zorne had made the frigate his flagship, leaving Hawkstone on the troopship with the men, but that evening, when they'd moored in a sheltered bay beneath the distinctive peak of Mount Burarath, Hawkstone had been summoned to join Zorne.

'Someone is drawing heavily on the praxis,' Zorne intoned, pointing west along the coast.

Although well aware that all Ramkiseri were sorcerers as well as implacable killers, Hawkstone found the reminder unnerving. Goosebumps rising, he murmured, 'If it's Vyre, he's ahead of us.'

Zorne considered this. He seldom consulted with anyone, not even the two Bolgravian sorcerers the governor had loaned him. Hawkstone couldn't read his moods; in fact, he was becoming increasingly sure that humanity was just as much a mystery to Zorne as the Ramkiseri was to them. He behaved as if everything was black and white, a strange flaw in this world of grey duplicity.

'Tomorrow we will sail towards it,' Zorne announced. 'If it is Vyre, well and good: it means we will have found him. If it isn't, then he's still behind us.' He looked up at the mountain. 'After the delays, storms and contrary winds, I hoped to find them here – this mountain range looks impassable to me. If they've bypassed it, how?'

Hawkstone peered around. 'Perhaps there's a track inland?'

'Perhaps,' Zorne echoed, leaning against the rail with the sea breeze stirring his hair. Since taking to sea, he'd let his hair and beard grow.

Sailors of the Bolgravian Navy were traditionally bearded; Hawkstone wondered if perhaps Zorne wished to blend in.

The under-komisar pondered the shore, then straightened. 'We have two hours of daylight. Have the captain lower the coracle. You and I will go ashore and seek clues of Vyre's whereabouts.'

Hawkstone shipped his oars as the boat grounded on the gravel shore and the sailor they'd brought with them, a dour man named Trimble who constantly chewed a wad of redleaf, steadied the boat so Hawkstone and Zorne could disembark. Hawkstone sucked in his breath as the frigid water covered his knees, but the Ramkiseri agent didn't even flinch.

Still, Zorne had mucked in, rowing just as hard as Trimble and Hawkstone, and now, without a word, he helped haul the boat up the beach with no airs of rank or superiority.

'Wait here,' he told Trimble.

'How do we climb up?' Hawkstone asked, gazing up the rugged cliffs overhanging the bay.

'We don't need to,' the Bolgrav replied, striding towards a rocky outcrop battered smooth by the sea; rubble was piled at the base. 'Wait there,' he said, raising his hands and weaving patterns with his fingers while muttering a torrent of strange words. The air hissed and shimmered and shadows danced along the broken cliff-face. For a minute, nothing happened – then the pile of boulders crumbled and Hawkstone found himself staring at time-worn steps and what might even be an arch in the stone face.

Zorne's face took on a fleeting look of satisfaction. 'I was right,' he said. 'Mount Burarath is a former Aldar stronghold.'

Hawkstone made the Gerda sign to ward off evil.

'I saw regularity in the shape of the stone, albeit distorted by time,' Zorne added, before resuming his spell-work, which sent the rocks blocking the tunnel flowing down and into the waves, revealing a dark opening. 'It's been blocked from within and concealed by rockfalls,' he intoned calmly, as if this were a daily event for him. Maybe it was.

Real Aldar artefacts could fetch thousands, although markets were filled with fakes, gulling the unwary. Greed warred with fear in Hawkstone's chest, but Zorne didn't hesitate.

'Let us see what's to be seen,' he said, conjuring a glowing orb of light about his left hand and leading the way up the stairs.

Hawkstone glanced back at the two ships floating offshore. Even from that distance he could see the decks were lined with watching men. Then he looked up at Zorne, already at the arch, and started after him, knowing he had little choice but to follow.

Once inside, Zorne's glowing orb provided illumination enough to proceed up more ancient stairs. There was even an old handrail carved with flowery flourishes and curves, and at the top, a hall with rooms on either side was strewn with the wreckage of broken pottery which looked well picked over.

'It's been looted before,' Hawkstone observed, disappointed.

'That's to be expected,' Zorne replied, unmoved. 'Come.'

He led them along the hall and up another stair, wider and more ornately decorated, but also more damaged, as if someone had been so offended by the beauty that they had to destroy what they could. Hawkstone saw him occasionally trace a swirl with his fingers. Then they reached a giant chamber filled with layers of silt and dust.

Hawkstone started. 'Wheel ruts – and recent, too.'

Zorne knelt and studied the line of a wagon's passage through the detritus. 'Vyre's people are travelling west.'

They followed the tracks, stopping now and then to examine their surroundings, until they reached another hall where they could see daylight ahead of them, revealing two giant doors opening out over a wooded valley.

'They passed through the whole blasted mountain,' Hawkstone breathed.

'An act of some courage – or perhaps desperation,' Zorne replied. 'They are motivated by more than just escape. There are a dozen vales east of here where a viable settlement could have been established if they merely sought a home outside imperial jurisdiction. But they are pressing on.'

'To Verdessa?'

'To wherever Gospodoi's mission went,' Zorne predicted. 'He travelled into the Verdessan hinterland and I'll warrant that is where Vyre is going. Come, let us retrace our path.'

Winding back through the darkness, they passed the hall they'd first entered, then traced a long but relatively straightforward descent though the mountain until Zorne paused, staring at a wall. He muttered something and an arch appeared where there had just been stone.

'An illusion, to hide this arch,' Zorne commented. 'And see, the seals are recently broken. Curious.' He went through, Hawkstone reluctantly trailing behind him, into a chamber of murals. They had arcane symbols traced above, perhaps narrating the scenes.

'Can you read those words?' Hawkstone asked.

Zorne shook his head. 'Only a scholar could do so.' He raised his light orb and walked on, past increasingly lurid murals, although he didn't appear to notice them much. 'Multiple languages are an inefficiency,' he commented at last. 'There should be only one language, written in one script. Everything else is a hindrance.'

'Language makes us who we are,' Hawkstone said. It was something his father used to say.

'Dividing what should be one,' Zorne droned. 'One day, there will only be one people, one language, one culture, one empire. This is destiny and those who resist it are misguided. Do you understand?'

Not really, was the honest answer. But Hawkstone replied, 'Aye, we should be united: by the sword,' because it seemed the sort of thing to say.

'If necessary, but war is also wasteful,' Zorne replied, cocking his head. 'Be silent.' He listened to the air and Hawkstone could almost fancy he heard something whispering.

I hope I'm imagining that . . .

'Follow,' Zorne commanded, and although his feet dragged, Hawkstone did as he was bidden, down another set of steps and into a chamber that held a massive glass-lidded sarcophagus containing the bones of some ages-old figure.

An Aldar, Hawkstone guessed fearfully.

'Someone found this recently – see, the dust is disturbed. One of Vyre's people, I must presume,' Zorne noted. 'They took the death mask.'

Hawkstone shuddered. 'Souvenir?'

'Perhaps. This was a great lord or lady of the Aldar. His people hid his resting place, so they must have perished at the end of the Mizra Wars, knowing their age was no more and any public grave would surely be robbed. Ordinarily, the Aldar did not separate the living and the dead: one buried one's kin in the family home.'

'Heathens.' Hawkstone made the sign against evil again.

Zorne raised the orb of light in his hand and surveyed the walls, then shrugged. 'The Aldar are gone and so are their gods. They have nothing to teach us.' He lowered his orb over the desiccated corpse until it touched the skeleton, which promptly ignited, burning with a hungry blue fire that swiftly engulfed the dried-up bones, tissue and cloth.

And he speaks of waste, Hawkstone thought. *I'm right: he has no soul.*

The Ramkiseri agent turned to the heathen murals, muttering words that caused the plastered walls to crumble and collapse in choking clouds. 'Better such artefacts be lost,' Zorne intoned, and started striding back to the main passage again.

Hawkstone stumbled along behind, completely lost, but Zorne led him without error back to the shoreline, where Trimble waited, sitting on the rim of the boat, still mechanically chewing his redleaf.

Not all men would have stayed at their post after sunset on a dark and hostile shore. Zorne gave him a small nod of the head. 'Trimble, yes?'

'Signalman Moss Trimble, sir,' the sailor mumbled.

'You have done your duty,' Zorne told him, likely his highest words of praise. He turned back to Hawkstone. 'As Vyre's people have passed through here, I must presume it is his use of praxis I have sensed. They're within one hundred miles of us, northwest of this place. We set sail at first light. We should find them within two days.

'And then?'

'They will be wiped out.'

Hawkstone faltered, 'There are families with him . . . women, children.' And one of them was Angrit, the mother of his daughter, Rosebud. He'd been paying gild, right up until she vanished. 'Surely they deserve mercy—'

Zorne looked puzzled. 'Laws must be upheld, Captain Hawkstone. We must exterminate them all. It is our duty.'

'This is it,' Raythe muttered, sighting through the triangle on the eastern shore to Zar's identical structure on the western promontory. They might look the same outwardly, but the spells on the far gate were less complex: it was really just a net for catching whatever passed through this gate and stripping it of nebulum, returning it to its natural state.

He'd spent a full day building on the able work Kemara had done readying the timber, spending hours chanting instructions, tracing myriad runes from every discipline of the praxis.

Only a Master sorcerer could do such a thing. *And I can* do this, he reminded himself.

Everyone was watching; they all knew there was no going forward unless he got this exactly right, and likely no going back.

He took his time, checking and double-checking all the calculations with Varahana, but at last the moment could be delayed no longer.

Right . . . He put on thin gloves before reaching into his belt-pouch to retrieve a small corked pot. He broke the wax seal to reveal about a thimble-full of crimson istariol; it smelled like ammonia. Adding water, he churned it to a paste, then began daubing it onto the frame while everyone watched anxiously. It took five minutes to use up every grain.

Time was of the essence now. He pushed aside his compulsion to recheck everything, knowing that was just procrastination, and spread his hands, shouting, '*Cognatus, spiratus igneous; spiratus aerium, qesta mei imperandi!*'

His sight blurred, showing him shapes and shadows rushing in, inhuman eyes and mouths painted across the air like shifting watercolours. Those watching in perplexed silence saw nothing as he bound these lesser spirits to the gate, but when he ignited the istariol, there was a gasp of awe as the space inside the portal *wavered* – and now anything seen through it looked milky and distorted.

He sucked in his breath, but it held . . .

So far, so good. Without taking his eyes from the now shimmering, fire-fringed arch, he called to Jesco and Vidar, 'First, the barrel.'

The two men rolled an empty wine barrel forward and positioned it in front of the arch. On his signal, they pushed it gently through the gap. It sparkled as the glistening film suspended in the arch ate it up – and it vanished. Everyone held their breath as Varahana put Raythe's spyglass to her eye and looked across the bay.

One . . . two . . . three . . .

Across the bay, a torch ignited and waved: the signal of success.

'They've got it – they've got it,' Varahana called.

'Yes,' Raythe breathed.

Jesco and Vidar whooped, and the watching travellers burst into cheers – then Jesco recklessly stepped through the arch himself. Raythe froze in alarm, his gaze flying to Varahana: this was not what they'd planned.

The next three seconds felt like a lifetime – until Varahana shouted, 'He's made it–' adding under her breath, 'the bloody idiot.'

Her words brought a fresh cheer from the watchers, as well as audible relief: the magic gateway worked.

'And Jesco just got out of all the hard work,' Vidar noted.

'He'll be busy enough on the far side,' Raythe replied, 'and he's answered the question everyone was afraid to ask: it's quite safe for the living. Get them moving, Vidar: this gate won't burn for ever.'

In moments, the beach became a hive of activity. A dozen men had already clambered around the cliffs, ready to pull the gear and people through the other gate. Those young women and children fit enough to cross the river had also set off, leaving the able-bodied adults to start pushing the wagons through the arch one by one. Gravis' brewing wagon was first, followed by the grain stores, then Varahana herded her Sisters through, waving as she vanished. A sense of accomplishment grew as the minutes passed without mishap, but so too did the apprehension as each new traveller readied themselves for their turn to face the gate.

Raythe was maintaining the flow of energy, but he was worried the istariol was being consumed too quickly; he still wasn't certain everyone would get through.

The horses were skittish, sensing the thrumming energies; they had to be blindfolded and manhandled through. The minutes were passing and the istariol fires fuelling the arch were burning ever lower.

'Go, go!' Raythe urged those remaining. 'Get the rest through – *hurry!*'

Then Vidar gripped his shoulder and pointed east. 'Raythe,' he murmured, 'two ships just rounded the headland.'

Raythe turned, his heart leaping to his mouth, to see a frigate off the point. Behind it was a vessel with high sides: undoubtedly a troopship. Both ships were flying the Imperial Blessed Orb.

Damn it, they've found us – at the worst possible moment. And we're so close!

He propelled Vidar towards the gate, snapping, 'Get to Zar and Varahana and protect them!'

The Norgan bearskin hunched over, snarled and leaped through the portal. As he did, the troopship veered towards the far side of the bay – but the frigate swung into the near shore and ran out its bombards with chilling efficiency.

8

Bombards and balls

The taste of the redleaf spread through Moss Trimble's body in gentle waves of stimulation, sharpening his focus as he watched the shoreline grow. Like most of the crew, Trimble was Pelarian and he'd as soon as not serve these damned Bolgravs, but the empire ruled now and it was throttling the life from his country. Everything of value was shipped east, leaving the natives to live hand to mouth. Any job was worth it, even one serving the Deo-be-damned Imperial Navy.

Trimble had been a signaller for three years, but thanks to his chief vices, grog and redheaded streetwalkers, he'd accumulated barely more than a few argents. That was going to change, he'd resolved. *Two more years until I can go home and I want be rich.*

So he eyed Toran Zorne suspiciously. *You better get us back safe, you bastard*, he thought, though he doubted the Ramkiseri gave a shit about anything but his kragging empire. *That's prob'ly why the damned Bolgravs always win.*

As if conscious of his regard, Zorne turned to him. 'Trimble, yes?'

At least he speaks Magnian, Trimble reflected. *Most Bolgravs can't be arsed.* 'Aye, sir.'

'Tell the captain to take us as close to shore as possible and to prepare the bombards. And signal to the troopship to land the men on the western side of the bay.' He extended an arm. 'See, there are also people there, with wagons and horses. We have found our quarry.'

Trimble saluted, ran up his signals, then peered towards the eastern shore, where a cluster of people, horses and gear were gathered on the beach beside some kind of triangular wooden edifice. Then he stared at the distant but more numerous group to the west. When he returned his gaze to the eastern one, a spark of red hair caught his eye, streaming in the wind like a banner, and he felt that familiar surge of predatory emotion that redheads always engendered in him.

A nice, tasty Ferrean bitch . . . that would make this all worthwhile . . .

No doubt these mad fugitives had seen them by now – them, and the Bolgravian flag, the Blessed Orb, flapping in the freshening breeze. He could picture the panic.

Dumb bastards, he thought. *You're all going to die.*

'Master Trimble?' Zorne reminded him tersely.

'A Ferrean redhead,' he growled, gesturing towards the shore. 'Likes me a redhead.'

Then he headed along the deck to deliver Zorne's message, hoping the redhead would survive long enough for him to reach her.

Zarelda was first to see the two ships as they rounded the headlands. After ten years of living in fear, she knew instantly what the Blessed Orb meant: *run.*

But half the horses were still across the bay, and most of the older men, and the women and children were spread across a mile of coast. And even to her untrained eye, neither shoreline looked defensible.

'Vidar,' she called urgently, 'what do we do?'

The Norgan had come across moments before, snarling and spitting in fury. Around them, people were crying out in alarm and searching for their families. One man tried to run back through the portal, but Jesco and Banno smashed him to the ground an instant before a horseman came through, his beast rearing and bellowing.

'Kragga,' Jesco screamed in the man's face, 'are you trying to kill us all?'

'You can't go back through, it's a one-way gate, you idiot!' Zarelda shouted. She threw a frightened look at the far shore where her father was. *I have to keep this gate open, no matter what*, she realised. *It's the only thing I can do to help him.*

She threw a look at Banno for strength, and anchored by his anxious but composed features, told herself, *I can do this.* She gripped the wooden support again and felt Adefar inside her, pouring energy in waves. There was a sudden surge from the gate as a knot of women and children came stumbling through, one after the other, and hope waged war with fear.

'Get ready to move,' Banno was shouting. 'Get those wagons hooked up!' *If we all get across, we can flee inland where the ships can't follow.*

But there was a great *boom!* as the bombards spat and smoke enveloped the leading Bolgravian ship as it closed in on the far shore. A few moments later, she saw explosions on the beach where her father was standing next to the Westgate.

The next few women and children came through her gate screaming, while the second ship sailed right on towards their beach, its decks filled up with men waving weapons at them.

Kemara Solus watched the men push Beca and her cart through Vyre's portal with trepidation. 'Knowing my luck, if anything does go wrong, it'll happen to me,' she muttered, but the torches kept waving across the bay, signalling success, so she had to assume all was fine.

She'd been intending to take the cliff and river crossing herself, rather than trust Vyre's sorcery; although she'd helped power up the Westgate, she felt horribly uncomfortable around the praxis – even a few seconds inside the spirit realm felt too dangerous for her. She'd removed the mask from its hidey-hole in the cart for just that reason, scared of what might befall it in the nebulum. It was tied up inside her skirts right now, a guilty presence.

But when the imperial ships appeared, her fear went visceral, screwing up her insides and taking her back to that awful, blank room, the glowing irons and that sadistic beast of an Invigilator . . .

Fighting the terror, she strode back through the panicking knot of women and children massed before the gate and bellowed, 'Move! Get yourself through – you'll be safe on the other side –'

For an extra few minutes, maybe.

She caught sight of Raythe Vyre, his face pale and drawn, one hand on the frame of the portal and the other conjuring frantically. 'Go,' he was roaring, 'go –'

She joined him, still screeching encouragement at the travellers waiting take the plunge, for many were as frightened by the portal limned in crimson flames and that uncanny opaque film that swallowed people as they were the Bolgravian ships. Some two dozen were still dithering, the infants were screaming in terror as they watched the gate eat people up . . .

'Move –' she and Raythe shouted simultaneously, 'go –!'

Then she saw flashes from the side of the frigate standing just beyond the breakers.

'Get down!' she shrieked as the air boomed and smoke billowed, but she didn't follow her own advice, instead clutching the support as some threw themselves through the gate while others dropped to the earth. She found herself beside Raythe, staring in horror as three bombard balls ploughed into the beach in a spray of pebbles just a dozen yards from where they stood, while others flashed past and buried themselves the hillside. One mowed down a mule, splattering blood over the shingle and tussock.

Raythe spun and roared, '*Cognatus – aqua morai!*' and a rogue wave swept up the beach and drowned the three balls in spume. One still exploded, but the water absorbed the force in a burst of salty spray. An instant later, the balls that had struck the hillside exploded, sending metal whining about them, and someone bellowed in agony.

Then everyone tried to pile through the portal at once, one terror outweighed by another.

Raythe shouted, 'One at a time – don't overload the gate –' while hauling people aside, trying to regulate the flow. Kemara held back one man until his wife had gone through, then propelled him forward.

Another explosion detonated nearby, sending shrapnel whistling past her face. Then Raythe shuddered, his face contorting as a blossom of blood soaked his right side. *Oh krag,* she thought, stumbling towards him. His eyes glazed over, he swayed and almost fell. 'Raythe!'

'Kemara,' he croaked, 'need . . . help—'

She pressed her hand to his side to try and staunch the bleeding. 'Come on—' she began, trying to pull him through his own portal.

But Raythe remained rooted to the earth, solid as a tree-trunk, and his free hand closed on her throat, his desperate eyes boring into hers. Then something like a knife plunged through her brain and his voice, his heartbeat, his *everything,* thundered through her in a forced rapport that swept her up in a dizzying rush.

'HELP ME,' his mind boomed, rattling her skull as he reached inside her, grasping the spark she'd been trying to extinguish for ten years. His fist closed around it and set it alight, conjuring with energy that flowed as if he were sucking the marrow from her bones.

Then the Aldar mask pressed against her thighs whispered, *Let me in,* and she didn't have the strength or will to stop it. Crimson fire flooded her brain. She tried to shut it out of her mind, but it was already too late.

The guns of the frigate boomed again, making the whole vessel heel over several degrees before it righted itself in a sucking rush of spume and waves. The sound drew Larch Hawkstone's eyes and he saw more balls strike and explode, but they hadn't found their range, because the gate of fire, the sorcery Vyre had wrought, still stood.

'C'mon, bring the damned thing down,' he snarled.

But his own vessel was surging towards the western shore, where the bulk of their quarry were. He turned to his Teshveld Borderers and ordered, 'To the longboat. We launch in two minutes.'

The troopship was boiling with activity, whistles shrilling and officers bellowing. The Bolgravian marines were in position while the sailors were readying the vessel to luff and come about. How Vyre's people had got themselves spread over the two shores, Hawkstone had no idea, but it was ideal: divide and conquer.

We'll get this done, give that blasted Ramkiseri prick his massacre, then go home laden with coin to drink away the memories. Just let me get Rosebud and Angrit safely out of it . . .

Jorl and Karil, the twin Bolgrav sorcerers with lank blond hair and a disdain for all lesser forms of life, were huddled together, manipulating the winds to fill the vessels' sails as they ploughed through the waves. Then another volley from the frigate's bombards reverberated through the bay, tearing up the eastern beach. There were fewer folk near the burning gate now, and Zorne's flagship was readying its own longboat.

Is it too much to hope that a stray ball takes Zorne in the back? he wondered.

But the western shore was looming in front of them and at the captain's signal, the sorcerer twins suddenly sucked the air from the sails and as the troopship came about hard, the longboats were already lowering, slapping into the waves. Hawkstone peered through the sea-spray and saw only women and children among the confusion of horses and wagons. It didn't look like anyone was set up to defend the beach.

Rosebud would be two by now, just a toddler. His only child, so far as he knew. *Krag it . . .* 'Move, you bastards,' he hollered. 'I want us on the shore before those damned Bolgravs!'

His Borderers poured into their boat and he settled into the prow. Rowers propelled them towards the shore, but in moments it became clear that the green-clad marines, trained to the oar, were ploughing ahead. Hawkstone's men were still sixty yards away when they were pouring ashore. As they were kneeling to aim their flintlocks there was still no sign of defence forming in the dunes above. Vyre's hapless travellers were all over the place and it was going to be a slaughter.

'Row, you feckers,' Hawkstone roared, '*row!*'

When Vidar saw the troopship luff and turn broadside, he feared bombards like Vyre was facing on the other beach, but instead, it discharged three longboats with practised efficiency, flintlocks slung over the shoulders of men in distinctive green uniforms: *Bolgrav marines* . . .

He'd come through the portal with his bearskin fury on the rise, but when he saw the panic rising among the travellers, he'd realised that what was needed here was *calm*. So he'd gathered in the hunters, knowing how much they loathed those hated uniforms.

He strode through the chaos of screeching children, panicky beasts and men who didn't know whether to stand or run, shouting to those with him to follow. 'Corbyn, Pick, Varte, all of you! You want to get hunted down like dogs, or you gonna fight?'

'I'll be takin' me chances,' Mat Varte grimaced. He turned and went sprinting off.

Any mix of folk included backsliders, he knew, but the rest were brandishing their weapons. 'Where's Vyre?' one shouted. 'Where's that kraggin' sorcerer when you need him?'

'He's comin' with the praxis to feck those marines any mo,' Vidar replied, 'but we must hold for him.'

Those with flintlocks were loading, tipping powder down the barrels, pounding in the balls and checking the flints. Those without guns were stringing bows and counting arrows. 'I c'n shoot faster with these anyway,' one remarked.

'True enough,' Vidar agreed. 'Now listen up: those marines will shoot maybe twice a minute if they're good. But they won't all shoot at once – they'll split into groups and rotate fire, meaning they'll volley every five or six seconds: that's the famous Bolgrav rolling volley. But they'll be on the beach, in the open and we'll be fighting from cover.'

'What, like cowards?' one of Rhamp's mercenaries jeered.

'No, like hunters,' Cal Foaley growled.

'Krag, yeah,' Corbyn spat, spittle flecking his beard.

'I feckin' hate Bolgies,' Jami Pick added.

Vidar slapped his shoulder. 'Then let's go!'

They fanned out into the dunes. Vidar spotted Elgus Rhamp standing with his armoured men and waved them forward. The knight saw and stared, then began herding his men into the dunes as well.

He hasn't got anywhere to run – he can't survive in the wild like us, so he's all in, too.

Across the bay, another volley of bombards resounded and the distant spot where Raythe stood was engulfed in flashes of flame. How many were left over there, he had no idea, but surely most were through by now. *Get over here, Raythe. Together, we've got a chance.*

Vyre's leggy daughter was still beside the portal, and women and children were still stumbling through. He could hear Varahana's voice above the clamour as she herded the newcomers to the rear. His heart thudded at the thought of what would happen to her especially, if their defence failed.

I won't let it.

He picked a spot for himself in the narrow strip of dunes between clumps of tussock and took aim. Jesco Duretto dropped to his side and did likewise, the Shadran smiling as if this were a soirée. Years fell like scales from Vidar's eyes and he remembered punctured, hacked and bloodied men lying in heaps, passionate patriots and cynical mercenaries alike, all ripped up by Bolgravian bombards and their infamous rolling volleys.

Feck, I hate this business, he thought as the second longboat spewed more marines, who came staggering through the surf to join the men from the first boat. *But I love it too. It's all I know.*

The beast inside him slavered in anticipation, the bearskin's burden, but this wasn't yet the maelstrom of blood and chaos that would bring out his darkest side. That would come later, when it came down to hand-to-hand combat.

'We hold!' he shouted to his unseen comrades. 'Make every shot count!'

Raythe saw the world through a scarlet haze. There was something lodged in his side that was sending knives of agony through him every time he moved. But he didn't have much longer to hold on.

Just twelve more people, then Kemara and I can go . . .

Raythe waved through the last few people, some old men who'd lain crouched in the grass, letting the women and children go first. There were four torn corpses around him, a man and his wife and two children who'd lost the lottery of death during the last cannonade.

Without the Westgate and Kemara to hold him up, he'd be down. He was screaming to the spirits, commanding them to churn the earth and swallow the smouldering balls before they exploded, but he wasn't always in time, and he could feel the link he'd plunged into Kemara, like a harpoon into a whale, was draining her to the core. She was faltering too, but he couldn't stop. If he did, he'd fail, and to fail here was to die.

The frigate was at the very edge of the shallows and now a longboat was ploughing through the surf, filled with Bolgrav marines in their green coats, long-barrelled guns strapped to their backs as they rowed.

'One more minute,' he pleaded to Kemara. 'Hold on!'

He feared she was too far gone, but she rallied, her face in a rictus of pain, almost demonic with her blazing eyes and bared teeth. From somewhere she drew on some deeper core and sent more energy.

He steadied, shouted, 'Come on,' at the last travellers waiting to pass through the portal – two old men carrying a blood-drenched third. 'Move!'

Once these last folk are gone, we have to go too . . . before I faint.

'Stay with me,' he shouted at Kemara. 'Just a moment longer –'

⟁

Kemara was at the tipping point, torn by need and fear. Raythe was white as a sheet and swaying, but his lips were pouring forth rune-words that opened up the earth, smothering cannonballs, while he kept the Westgate open. But the longboat was coming for them and the naval gunners had the range now. The next volley would almost certainly rip them apart . . .

Feck it, it's kill or die . . .

She opened her soul fully – not to Raythe Vyre, but to the mask, to *Buramanaka*, and his feral mind flooded hers, his smell and taste and urgency filling her mind in its rush to experience life again, and words learned years ago from Ionia burst from her lips.

'*Kaneska alla mizra!*' she shouted, spinning away to face the sea and extending her hands towards the dozen or so marines disgorging into the surf.

She felt Raythe recoil in shock – and then he leeched harder onto her as he shouted *Flux* in the rune-tongue – energy. His mind fused to hers like flame to powder, like blood and istariol, and their clasped hands crackled in an agonising current of power.

'*Cuzka lectruz a'nakish!*' she screamed in the ancient *Aldar* tongue.

'*Probas, aerius fulgur!*' Vyre shouted in Old Magnian, summoning the same power.

Two minds, one purpose: in sorcery it was called a *meld*, where two practitioners fused their powers, magnifying and multiplying their spells beyond their individual capabilities. Most weren't capable of doing it, and those who could usually only managed it with a few people in their entire career. It took months, even years, of training.

But somehow, she and Raythe managed straight off.

There was an appalling crack of power from the heavens, a concussion that shook their bones and stunned their senses. Instantly, a blinding flash of pure white light seared her vision, as if reality had split in two and spilled the light of heaven through the crack. That bolt of light stabbed from the skies into the water where the Bolgrav marines were wading ashore. She barely saw the result, just a crackling vision of silhouettes caught up in the rictus of a deadly dance, arms splayed, heads thrown back, water spraying about them as they leaped and fell.

She swayed from the rush, but more energy poured into her, sucked from all round her. She saw the three old men fall and felt the wounded one die. The flames of the portal went out and the grass around her feet withered.

But she and Vyre straightened, blinking in the aftermath, clung to the meld and roared out their conjoined commands, even as a distant voice aboard the frigate shrieked, *'Bombards, fire!'*

The closer the frigate got to the shore, the more intensely Toran Zorne felt the energies streaming through the burning edifice on the beach. Only around a hundred yards separated them now and he could make out a dark-cloaked figure clinging to the frame, supported by a red-headed woman . . .

It's Vyre . . . finally.

The longboat rode a wave to shore, the marines shipped oars and piled into the shallows, wading knee-deep in water as the skies swirled above, nature itself rebelling against the prolonged unleashing of sorcery. He could feel it like heat against his soul's skin: like a ringing inside his head.

It's a Westgate, he saw at last, realising that Vyre had greater proficiency than he'd been told. *He's moving his people across this bay – presumably there's no inland trail for their wagons.* It was impressive work. *No wonder he's eluded me so long.* It also raised the possibility that the Otravian might actually step through and escape him.

'Ready the next volley,' he told the captain beside him in the forecastle. 'Faster!'

I've hunted him too long. It's time to end this.

The captain bellowed his orders to the signalman, Trimble set the flags and the bombard crews worked feverishly, while Zorne focused on Vyre, amplifying his vision with the praxis so that he would see his quarry's demise.

A moment later, the *impossible* happened.

From a purple bruise in the sky burst a jagged bolt of pure light, smiting the shoreline and the wading marines. Zorne barely glimpsed the result, but he heard the cut-short shrieks as the water boiled, billowing steam.

He reeled, his composure shaken; when he could focus again, he saw blackened, smoking bodies floating in the waves through the haze of steam and the stink of ammonia and violets. Beside him the fat, be-whiskered captain was babbling in terror and Trimble, still chewing his moronic redleaf, just gaped.

Impossible, Zorne's brain offered. *That is impossible.*

His dazzled eyes sought Vyre and the redhead, but he could only make out their outlines. The fires of the Westgate had winked out and they were the only ones on the slope, holding hands with their outer arms raised, facing towards the ship.

They're going to do it again –

'BOMBARDS,' he shouted, 'FIRE!'

But before even one had belched its load, he felt that distinctive shift in the unseen that had heralded the previous blast and he knew he must move.

While all around him stood paralysed, he catapulted himself over the railing into space . . .

Then the ship behind him exploded and his back was pierced by dozens of knives of pain and something hammered into the back of his skull, blasting the world away.

Raythe wrenched his hand from Kemara's in horror, staring at the Bolgravian frigate – or what was left of it, a shattered hulk of burning timbers, subsiding with a sizzling hiss into the waves. Another powder keg blew up, and the poop deck, the last intact part of the ship, burst apart in an orange flash and more broken timbers rained down. Bodies floated amid the debris. His ears rang and his legs felt like jelly and the wound in his side was still leaking blood.

Beside him, Kemara had fainted, collapsing in a graceless swirl of skirts and hair. His eyes went from her emptied face to the wreckage and back again. Her chest rose and fell, her face ghost-white.

We performed a meld, but that wasn't the praxis she used. Somehow, she invoked the mizra *– but the meld still worked, better than any meld I've ever heard of.*

The sheer impossibility of it all stunned him.

A meld of praxis and mizra – surely that can't happen? And yet it did . . .

It was no wonder she'd told him to piss off when he offered to teach her the praxis. That door was already closed, and of course she couldn't tell him why without risking a witch-trial.

Staggering away, he dragged his thoughts back to the practical.

Two old men lay unconscious at his feet; the other was dead, his life snuffed out by the spells that had saved the rest. An eerie silence hung over the beach.

Then the distant rattle of flintlocks reached his ears. Across the bay, tiny smoke-shrouded figures were arrayed on the beach – *where his daughter was.* They'd landed the marines over there. The Westgate was closed and he was half a mile away, with no recourse but to prayers.

Zarelda saw the faint glint of the portal across the bay wink out and her mind screamed, *Father!*

But the crack of flintlocks resounded on the beach below her, a lead ball seared past and one of Rhamp's men sitting right beside her folded over with blood blooming on his chest. A third of the Bolgravian marines on the beach dropped to one knee to reload, swathed in smoke, while others stepped forward to aim the next volley.

Terror almost paralysed her, but she had to pull herself together. The gate was useless now, so she threw herself to the ground, even as another ball smacked into the frame where she'd been standing. Then, with a guttural cry of, *'Obvini – obvini!'* – which she guessed meant *attack* – the marines lumbered up the pebbled beach into the narrow strip of dunes, just as a third longboat hit the shore.

Then Vidar's voice rang out. *'Fire!'*

A ragged volley of flintlock balls and arrows punched into the Bolgravs and half a dozen of the imperials staggered and dropped. The Bolgravs immediately fired back, aiming into the dunes now, but even as they did, she saw Vidar's men rolling into hollows and behind rocks and the carefully coordinated volley splattered wastefully, as did the next as the Bolgrav marines sought half-glimpsed targets.

'Archers!' Elgus Rhamp shouted, and bowstrings sang, punching shafts into the Bolgravian formation, and suddenly the marines realised they were in trouble. Their officer staggered, an arrow in his chest, and now it looked like every one of the defenders' shafts and balls was hitting its target, carving through the imperial soldiers.

'Charge!' Sir Elgus bellowed, and his mercenaries rose and ran at full pelt, a ragged line of hunters led by Vidar and Jesco close behind. They slammed into the reeling marines with spears and swords and what followed was brutal. The Bolgravs were hacked down from all sides as their formation broke apart. Jesco moved like a dancer, spinning and lunging, while Elgus wielded his sword like a bludgeon, cleaving through limbs and all the while roaring savagely. One man tried to crawl away, but Tami leaped on his back and slit his throat, crowing shrilly.

Zarelda glanced back to the beach and saw the last longboat was being hauled around and relaunched, the men taking flight without joining the fray, leaving the marines on the beach to die. In a few more moments, it was all over and a brief cheer was raised, but it quickly subsided into relative silence, leaving just the moans of their own wounded, the crying of children and the braying of frightened beasts.

They'd held – they'd won.

'That makes it only marginally less horrible,' she whispered, but then she amended that assessment: this was far, far less horrible than losing would have been. She cast about and saw that Banno was whole, if white-faced, at the fringe of the cheering mercenaries, and she breathed thanks to Deo for sparing him.

Then she remembered her father and gazed back across the waves. *Dad?* she breathed. *Dad?*

Then a man emerged from the dunes and onto the beach and waved, and though he was only a dot, she knew it was him.

Zarelda fell to her knees in sheer relief.

PART TWO
Secret River

1

The luckiest prick in Shamaya

'Who's this one?' Raythe asked as he made his way from patient to patient. The casualties were lying under bloodstained blankets behind the dunes. Cognatus, on his shoulder in his favourite parrot shape, was unseen and unfelt. The familiar was unsettled, frightened by the power Kemara had manifested.

As am I ... Dear Gerda, she's a mizra-witch. But she was also their only real healer, and while he needed desperately to talk to her about what had happened, that had to wait.

The day after the battle, the expedition was still regrouping, hunting the horses and righting wagons and seeing to the wounded and dying. Kemara was in charge of medical matters, aided by Varahana's Sisters of Gerda.

She couldn't quite hide the flinch when she looked up and saw him. 'I don't know who he is. Someone fished him from the sea.'

'He's a Bolgrav?'

'Well, he's Imperial Navy,' Kemara replied. 'The navy pressgangs men from all nations. But he doesn't look Bolgravian, does he. His hair's too dark.'

'Is he the only surviving enemy?'

'He is now. He was washed all the way from the eastern beach after the tide changed. One of the marines on the beach survived a bit, but he died in the night.' She'd been awake since yesterday afternoon, Raythe knew. He'd helped her clamber across the river and around the cliffs, although they were both exhausted, but there'd been no chance for either of them to rest since.

The entire caravan had made it to Verdessa. The troopship had sailed away after the slaughter on the beach, no doubt fearing the same fate as the frigate, but it would reach the Verdessan garrison's docks at Rodonoi inside three days and Raythe had no doubt larger forces would be sent to intercept them. Tomorrow, regardless of the state of the wounded, they would have to move on.

'Do the best you can,' he told her. 'And when he wakes, assign a guard.'

'That won't be necessary – his back's been flayed good and proper. He won't be able to move on his own for weeks.'

Raythe winced in sympathy. 'Very well, I'll question him later. What of our own?'

'A couple of Rhamp's men were wounded, and two men and one child were hit by stray balls. There are two dozen others with minor injuries – cuts, burns and the like. And nine died.'

'I know,' Raythe replied, in a haunted voice. 'But we all knew the dangers, and we all joined this expedition anyway. You and I need to talk about magic.'

'When I'm done trying to save the people who placed their lives in your hands.'

He caught her shoulder. 'Do you still want your power cauterised?'

She met his gaze and for once she didn't shrug away his hand. 'I don't know,' she admitted. She bit her lip, then added, 'Whatever you've been told, the mizra is not *evil*. It's just different.'

That went against everything he'd learned – from Deist priestesses and Church sorcerers. *Consider the sources*, his parents might have said, cynics to their toes.

'Different how?' he asked, trying to sound non-judgemental.

'I don't know, because I've nothing to compare it to. It's, um . . . well, unruly, like an unbroken stallion.' She met his gaze, her defences down for once. 'It's addictive, and it's a death sentence, but when I use it—' She shuddered hungrily.

Her face changed and it was like watching a panther bare its teeth. But when he thought of what they'd done together, he couldn't condemn it. 'I'll keep your secret,' he told her, and for once elicited a grateful look from her.

'Thank you,' she whispered, and turned back to her work.

Still uneasy, Raythe went looking for his daughter.

He found Zar sitting on a driftwood trunk, and Banno Rhamp had his arm around her shoulder. They were so wrapped up in their conversation they didn't hear him.

'They've been giving me shit about it all day,' Banno was saying. 'I stuck a Bolgie in the side, but I couldn't make my arm swing again, even though he was helpless. Bohrne had to finish him off while I puked in the sea.'

Raythe's first taste of war had gone much the same way and he felt sorry for Banno, but they looked too intimate for his liking, so he coughed pointedly and they leaped up, blushing.

'M-Master Vyre,' Banno stammered.

'There're wagons needing repairs,' Raythe said. 'Go and make yourself useful.' He watched the young pair strain towards each other, clearly wishing to embrace but scared to, then Banno mumbled something and fled.

Zarelda put her hands on her hips. 'Just because he didn't kill people doesn't make him less of a man.'

'I never said so.' He went to his daughter and hugged her, holding her as close as his damaged side would allow. Kemara had stitched him up once she was certain she'd got the fragment of shrapnel out. 'Banno stayed when older men ran.' He stroked her hair, shuddering at the thought that she'd been shot at. 'So did my daughter. I'm very proud of her.'

He sensed her mood soften. 'I was so scared,' she admitted. 'But I kept the gate open.'

'I know, and that saved lives. If you hadn't, those last few folk to pass through would've been trapped in the spirit realm until it ate them up.'

He felt her shudder. 'Why can't the empire just let us go?' she asked sadly.

'If they did and word got around, others would follow. And they may have guessed the importance of Gospodoi's mission.' He thought on that. 'And there's another thing: someone warned me before we left Falcombe that a Ramkiseri agent was on my trail – a man named Zorne. He's said to be implacable.'

'Then I hope he was on the ship you destroyed,' Zar said. She, like everyone else, believed that he alone was responsible for the lightning strikes that had destroyed the frigate; there was now awestruck silence as he passed by.

'Me too.' But his thoughts were of Kemara. What the healer had done was illegal, but legalities didn't trouble him. It was theologically evil, too, and that didn't bother him either. But it was deadly dangerous, and that did scare him. After all, mizra had destroyed the world once.

But we blasted that frigate together. *I can't even separate her part in that from mine.*

If anyone got wind of what had happened, Kemara would be condemned, but that moment inside the meld told him that he *needed* her. If the empire found them again, she might be the difference between life and death.

He put these troubling thoughts aside and tousling his daughter's hair again, murmured, 'Remember your promise. Learn the runes, learn the praxis and keep that young man at arm's length, hmm.'

'Yes, Dad, but—'

'No buts. I've done my rounds and the only wagon that's not being readied for travel is ours. Let's get busy.'

Kemara watched Raythe until he was out of sight, then she exhaled and sagged. Another moment postponed, another few minutes purchased for her to somehow think this whole thing through.

Her patients were stable now, laid out beside fires on this desolate beach. All day, sheepish men who'd fled the impending carnage had been slinking back into camp, pretending they'd been chasing a run-away horse or some such, and had got back *just after* the Bolgravs went down.

'Hey, healer,' a rasping voice said, and she turned to find Osvard Rhamp leaning against her wagon. He pointed at his right arm, which was sporting a sloppily tied, blood-soaked bandage. 'See to it.'

She stiffened, then put aside her alarm. 'Certainly. We have cauterising knives in the fire, ready to use.'

Osvard's piggish face went a little slack. 'It's just a scratch.'

'Yes, but infection can kill a man more painfully than disembowelling. We can't risk that.'

He bunched his fist – then stiffened as Tami entered the tent.

'Osvard, stop being a prick,' she drawled, and evidently she derived authority from Elgus Rhamp, because Osvard lowered his gaze. But Tami wasn't done with him. 'I didn't see you on the beach, Osvard.'

The mercenary glowered. 'I was there.'

Tami lifted an eyebrow, remarkably confident for someone half his size. 'Really?'

'I have a salve you can take,' Kemara offered, to defuse the tension. She picked up a small clay pot with a wax seal. 'A light smear, twice a day.'

'Take it, Ossi,' Tami advised. 'I'll see you in camp.'

'You bet you will,' the man said sullenly, snatching the pot from Kemara and stalking off.

'He's a mean dog,' Tami sneered, 'but he responds well to a good lashing.' She pulled the curtain across the tent so the patients couldn't see them and dropped her voice. 'We ladies should look out for each other.'

Being alone in the small space with a former spy wasn't comfortable, but Tami seemed to be offering friendship – although that in itself felt suspicious. 'Do you have a medical complaint?'

'Not as such; I just don't want to get pregnant and I'm out of sour-nettle cream.'

'Come back tomorrow and I'll have a fresh batch boiled up for you,'

Kemara replied. She looked the other woman up and down, then asked, 'How did you end up with the Rhamps?'

'After the rebellion failed it was them or someone else just like them. I needed protection, and old Elgus was the best bet. He's decent to me, mostly. And I know he'd value a sorceress-healer in his camp.'

Oh, so this is recruitment. 'I'd prefer to stay clear of rivalries,' Kemara replied.

'Honey, those rivalries won't stay clear of you. Not now we know what you are.'

'Which is?'

'We saw, those who knew what to look for. You've been hiding your light, but you and Raythe were hand in hand on that beach, calling down the lightning. You're a praxis-sorcerer.'

She thinks it's praxis? That was a relief. 'It doesn't mean I want any greater role than I have.'

'It doesn't work like that. You're a player now and you'll have to pick a side.'

'Well it won't be Osvard's side, that's for sure.'

'Don't you worry about Osvard. You're too valuable now for Elgus to let him harm you – well, unless you chose Vyre's side when things get dirty.' Her eyes narrowed. 'You sleeping with him?'

Kemara snorted. 'I don't even like the man.'

'You'll come to: the only explanation for the power you generated to wreck that frigate is a meld, and that means you've got a real bond. You're going to end up joined at the hip, believe me.' She sighed wistfully. 'It's not so bad: he's got a certain charm and he's a survivor, so betting against him is no sure thing.'

She sounds a little too admiring, for Rhamp's lover. And how does she know so much about Vyre?

'Are you saying I should or shouldn't back him?' Kemara asked.

'I'm just saying that he'll want you on-side and he'll be persuasive. You'll need to look at what's real.' Tami stroked Kemara's cheek, presumptuously familiar. 'Pick the winning side, Healer.'

Then she was gone, leaving Kemara perplexed. *Did she just urge me to back Vyre, or betray him? Does she back Rhamp . . . or is she biding her time before she knifes him?*

In the shadows, Buramanaka cackled, enjoying the dilemma. She banished the mizra-spirit, too flustered to deal with it right then, and took a few moments to pull her own customary mask of self-sufficiency back over her face so she could deal with another round of dressings, poultices and blood. Bodies were seven-tenths liquid and the world was full of ways to spill it.

When she got to the imperial sailor, she found him awake, lying on his stomach with his head twisted so he could watch her. He had a plain face, flat and whiskery. She'd had to shave the back of his skull to get to the head wound that had almost killed him and his back was a mess from the burning splinters that had lacerated him, flaying his skin and laying the muscles bare – and then immersed in saltwater? No wonder he'd blacked out for a turn of the world. She'd cleansed and stitched his wounds and he'd live, but for now just existing had to be agony.

'You're awake,' she noted.

'Aye,' he mumbled, wincing and going rigid as he tried to roll onto his side.

'Be still,' she advised. 'I've got a paste on your skin to soothe it and stimulate regrowth.'

'Gerda on high,' he moaned, 'what happened?'

'When the ship's powder-kegs exploded, wooden splinters were blasted into your back and you were knocked out,' she told him. 'You ended up in the water, but you were face up and breathing, and somehow, you washed ashore before you drowned. You're the luckiest prick in Shamaya.'

He moaned, then managed a breathless chuckle. 'Never had it called that before.'

She snorted. 'You're lucky it didn't get ripped off. What's your name, sailor?'

'Moss Trimble.'

'That's a Pelarian name, but you don't look it.' He had olive skin and a face that belonged further east.

'My father was Pelarian, but my mother was Krodesh, from the Bolgravian steppes. I grew up in Pelaria, fought in the war, lost, ended up at sea.'

'Pressganged?'

He winced again, although he hadn't moved this time. 'Aye.'

It was the way he said it that convinced her. 'Must rankle, having to serve the Bolgies,' she said sympathetically.

'Aye.' He looked around, taking in the wagons and tents, then finishing back at her. 'I saw you,' he whispered. 'You and a man – you and he – the ship . . . *Holy Gerda*–'

'Hush,' Kemara said. 'That was all Lord Vyre. He's a praxis-mage. I was just standing there.'

If only that was true.

Trimble nodded, then muttered, 'What's going on? Me and the crew, we didn't even know why we were out here. Where are you people going?'

'Out of the empire. Want to come?'

He stared, blinked, and slowly nodded. 'Yeah, yeah, I really do.' He reached out and stroked her hair. 'I like red hair,' he breathed. 'Most beautiful thing there is.'

She forgave him the familiarity: for patients, healing was often one of the most intense things they'd ever gone through, matters of life and death, mortality and meaning. Men got emotional over it, and over her. She often had to remind herself of that, because to her, it was just work.

'You get yourself better, sailor. You've got a long road ahead before you're recovered.'

And so have I.

'All right,' Raythe shouted, 'roll the wagons.'

The call went down the line and one by one they began to move, the big team-drawn wagons and the little mule-carts and everything between. He waved to Zarelda, who was driving theirs, then trotted over to where Elgus Rhamp remained on foot, surrounded by most of his mercenaries.

'Sir Elgus, any questions?'

The knight reached up and scratched between Raythe's horse's eyes. 'No questions. We'll wait here half a day, then follow you once we know that the imperials haven't landed troops behind us.'

Raythe leaned forward. 'Don't let Osvard near Kemara Solus again. Warn him, the next time has consequences.'

'Can't blame him that time – the boy needed medical attention.'

'That's not what I've heard. Tell him.' Raythe glanced at Banno, went to speak and thought better of it. He saluted and cantered away.

Cal Foaley had found them a way forward – not a road, but open plains just half a mile inland. The land was stony and bleak, but it was flat; now he and the hunters were flanking the caravan. It promised to be a slow trek forward, but as yet there were no enemies in their path.

If we can head northwest fast enough, there's some chance we can evade whatever force the garrison sends after us, provided I can erase our trail quickly enough.

He made his way along the column, stopping at each wagon. Gravis Tavernier was unhappy – he was out of beer and grumbling about the barter economy that was growing in the caravan, undermining good coin. 'My girls are giving themselves away for food, then gobbling the take and cutting me out of my share,' he complained. 'You gotta fix it, Raythe.'

'Wouldn't it be a grand thing if they all repented, left whoring behind and found Deo.'

The brewer spat out a wad of redleaf. 'Gerda's tits, they better not!'

Raythe gave him a hard smile. 'If I hear they're being mistreated, I'll free them myself. Safe travels, Gravis.'

He moved on to Mater Varahana's wagon. One of the Sisters was driving while Varahana taught her little class, but as soon as she heard his greeting, the mater leaped up and walked towards him. 'Raythe, a word?' she called, adding, 'It's good to be moving again.'

'It is.' He smiled. 'How can I help, Mater?'

'It's about Kemara, of course,' Varahana replied, stroking the down on her scalp. 'I understand that she's reconsidering cauterising her powers?'

She could only have had that from Kemara herself. 'So I understand,' he confirmed.

'Then she'll get properly trained?'

Ah, of course, we're back to this . . . Admitting that Kemara was a mizra-witch was out of the question, but clearly Varahana had sensed something awry. 'I trust so.'

'But she helped you at the beach, didn't she?' the mater asked, training her perceptive gaze on him. 'I've seen sorcerers at war, Raythe – I've seen *you* fight – and you've never done anything as destructive as that before.'

'We melded,' he admitted.

He didn't need to explain more, for he saw several emotions flickering across Varahana's face, from shock to awe, via a flicker of jealousy. 'Are you really that close to her?'

He laughed. 'We can barely be civil to one another.'

'But I thought a meld required . . . ahem . . . *closeness*?'

'Not always. Sometimes a pairing can be very alike – if they meld it's usually only for a narrow band of spell-types – say, wielding fire, whereas opposite pairs fill in each other's gaps, and that's a lot rarer, but far more powerful.'

'And that's you and Kemara, I'm guessing.' Varahana surprised him by stroking his arm. 'I hope you and she find a way to work together. But if she wants to keep her powers, she has to knuckle down and train.'

'Absolutely. Although being this caravan's healer is a full-time task on its own.'

'My Sisters have been learning alongside her,' Varahana replied, 'and they will step up, if Kemara needs to spend more time with you.' She tilted her head into half-profile. 'Do you think I should shave again, or let my hair grow?'

'You're beautiful either way, Mater.'

'Darling man,' she purred, pecking his cheek. 'See you in camp tonight.'

She swayed back to her waiting class-on-wheels, while the children tittered and the Sisters frowned.

They probably think I'm corrupting her, Raythe mused, wondering if he was.

When he'd first met Varahana during Colfar's hopeless crusade, she'd been elegant, witty and charming, and out of reach, bonded to the Church, although refusing to buckle. She'd been an ideal friend when he'd so recently lost Mirella. They'd kept in touch since, enough that she had come to Teshveld when he did. Some nights, they'd been more than a little tempted.

But Mirella has that part of me . . .

Setting that aside, Varahana was right: he couldn't shirk dealing with Kemara and her magic. So he nudged his horse back down the column, seeking her cart. She had to deal with all manner of health complaints every morning, so she was invariably the last to leave camp.

Sure enough, she was right at the back and he didn't find her until late afternoon. Four of the most seriously ill patients were crammed onto the bed of her cart: three of theirs and the sailor, Trimble. He'd half-expected trouble over the man, but he was vocal in his dislike of the empire and the initial antagonism towards him had quickly dissipated.

The healer saw him coming and hurried off; when he called after her, she shouted, 'I need to pee,' which put paid to following her. So he joined the four wounded men, chatted to his people for a bit, then turned to the stranger.

'What's your name, sailor?'

His bland face was covered in a thick stubble now, and he chewed redleaf nervously. 'Trimble, Lord. Moss Trimble.'

Fear was the most common reaction to a known sorcerer, especially in the empire, so his unease was understandable. 'The name's Vyre. Raythe Vyre.'

'Milord.'

Raythe confirmed Kemara's report that he was a pressganged half-Pelarian – or at least, he reiterated it, rather than proved the tale. But when he asked, 'Tell me, was there a man aboard named Toran Zorne?' he saw Trimble flinch.

After a moment, the sailor said, 'Aye.' He looked around, as if checking to see if anyone was listening – they all were, of course – then added, 'Zorne ordered the captain round like he was a cabin boy.'

Of course, a Ramkiseri agent outranks even a naval captain, Raythe thought. 'What did he look like?'

Trimble chewed a few moments, then said, 'Dark hair, pale. Prissy about his appearance: had to be perfectly shaved, perfectly combed. Creepy, he was.'

'Odd. I'd pictured someone quite different,' Raythe remarked. *Strange, to be hunted by a man yet never know what he looks like.* 'So he died when the ship exploded?'

Trimble chewed some more, then said, 'Right by the captain, he was. Guess he's dead.'

'We found no other survivors except you – how did that happen?'

'I have no friggin' idea,' the sailor answered. 'Got thrown into the sea.' His eyes trailed to the returning Kemara Solus. 'Fine-looking woman, that. I like me a redhead.'

'That one's got sharp teeth and a sour tongue,' Raythe snorted. 'Best of luck with your wounds. I'm told you'll heal with time.'

'Hope so, milord, 'cause me back hurts like buggery.'

'I thought sailors liked a bit of buggery,' Kemara threw in, getting a general laugh. 'Lord Vyre, are you here for your headlice or the cock-pox?'

The four patients chuckled again and Raythe found himself colouring. 'Neither, Mistress Kemara. I have a wart that needs burning off and thought you could do it with your gaze. A word, please?'

She looked set to make some excuse, but instead muttered, 'Sure, let's get it over with,' and stalked away out of her patients' hearing. 'Well?' she asked as Raythe caught her up.

'I know you don't want to talk about this, but I need to understand. You say the mizra isn't evil and that you have it under control, but you and I might need that meld again. We can't leave it up to chance.'

She pulled a face. 'Meaning what?'

'We need to practise it.'

'You don't know what you're asking.'

'No, I don't, you're right – so enlighten me. Do you have a familiar – or is it a "demon", as the Church styles mizra-spirits? Did you really fail your tests? Have you actually been cauterised at all? Is *anything* you've told us about your past true?'

Kemara glowered up at him. 'Says the man who's never told me his tale.'

'Fine, let me rectify that right now. I was an Otravian noble, supporting the king. When the Mandarykes seized power, my wife defected and they tried to arrest me. I stole back my daughter and ran. We joined Colfar and I commanded one of his divisions – and that was a bloody disaster, as you know. I'm worth about a million argents to bounty-hunters, if you're lucky enough to meet one you can trust to share the reward.'

'So you're a freedom fighter in exile.'

'Call it that if you like. Otravia was a constitutional monarchy with an elected parliament; now we're an oppressed imperial province with a puppet government which rules by decree. Where once we were liberal and progressive, now we're turning citizens into serfs, burning books and hanging dissidents. I want my country and my life back, in that order.'

Her pugnacious face softened a little. 'Tell me that you'll not vanish with the istariol, if this mission succeeds.'

'You have my word . . . as a Vyre.'

'Your line were always called "the uncrowned princes of Otravia", weren't they? Your father was Premier.'

He balled his fists, not wanting to think of all he'd lost. 'Aye. The Mandarykes beheaded him for "corruption", then stole our property and lands for themselves.'

'And took your wife. You must really hate them. I bet you feel that the sacrifice of this whole caravan of people would be a small price to pay to bring them down?'

'I've certainly not forgiven them, but I'm a Vyre and an Otravian and whether you believe me or not, honour matters to me. I'll take my share and no more, and I'll give my blood for the people I'm travelling with – even Elgus, and that's more than he'd do for me.'

She harrumphed and fell silent, then said, 'All right. I'll take you at your word.'

That was a big, big concession for her, Raythe realised. 'Thank you, that means a lot.'

She pulled a face. 'Sure it does.'

'No, I mean it. That meld we shared–'

'Is all we'll ever share.'

He coloured. 'I presumed nothing more.' *Damn, but she's difficult.* 'But what of you? You used *mizra*. In any civilised place, or so-called, at least, you'd be on a bonfire.'

To her credit, she didn't splutter something stupid like 'I don't know what you mean' or 'You must be mistaken'. Instead she faced him and admitted, 'Yes, but I destroyed my own familiar, and that almost killed me. I swore I'd never use it again – not because the mizra is evil or wrong, because I don't think it is, but because it's too dangerous. The Church had invigilators on my trail. But back at the beach, I had no choice.'

'If you've got no familiar, what spirit did you channel when we melded at the beach?'

She hung her head. 'Something latched onto me in that Aldar rath. It followed me out.'

The dead Aldar . . . He stiffened, remembering the mask. *I knew I should have destroyed it.*

'Kemara, mizra almost destroyed our world. Tell me why I shouldn't be *petrified* of you.'

She glared at him. 'Isn't it simpler just to burn the witch and have done?'

'Of course not – quite apart from magical considerations, you're a valued member of this expedition.' He glanced about, seeing a few curious folk observing them, and dropped his voice, although no one was close enough to hear them. 'What we did was *impossible*. We melded two forms of *opposed* sorcery and instead of it imploding, it became greater than either of us. By rights we should both be dead, but instead we saved the entire caravan. Isn't that worth exploring?'

She looked up at him, her hard but handsome face creased with uncertainty. Finally she sagged and said, 'Fine. I was a trainee sorceress, a sworn novice in Ferrea. But my manifestation didn't go right. I chose the wrong familiar and when the matron tried to intervene, my new familiar lashed out through me and I almost killed her.'

'Holy Gerda,' Raythe breathed. 'What happened next?'

'She lived, but the Invigilators took me. I was locked up and tortured.'

'Surely they tried to help –?'

'What, actually put effort into a difficult case, when they've got so many *good girls* to work with?' she sneered. 'No, I was given to this *fecking sadist*, who had me for a week, then declared me irredeemably evil.'

'That's appalling.'

'Save it,' she snapped. 'Anyway, I was sentenced to death. But the night before I was scheduled to burn, a hole opened in the wall of my cell and a woman walked through, unlocked my manacles, threw me over her shoulder and hauled me down a tunnel of stars.'

'A mizra-sorceress?'

'Ionia, her name was. Turns out there's still some witches out there. We travelled for a year together, working as herbalists. She taught me the Aldar words and runes, trained me, looked after me – she was the closest person I ever had to a *real* mother.' She choked up for a moment, then took a deep breath and pressed on, 'But the Church caught her and she burned before my eyes while a crowd jeered at her. So I killed my own familiar, in case the witch-finders sensed it and caught me, then I ran. I've been drifting west for seven years. I'm here because this caravan is my last chance of a life.'

Holy Gerda, I really am harbouring a mizra-witch – and she slew her own familiar. That's unheard of.

'You say the mizra-demon latched onto you in the rath?' he asked.

She flinched, then said, 'Wait here.' She brought back something like a bowl wrapped in cloth from her cart. When she unwrapped it, he recognised the Aldar mask, a blood-red, horned visage of pure ferocity. 'I saw something like a ghost – of *Ionia* – and followed her to a chamber where this was buried.' She proffered it, adding, 'His name is Buramanaka.'

That was the name Varahana read on the sarcophagus. The mask was cold to the touch. *I resealed that chamber with earth-praxis and illusion, but she still found it. The mizra-demon must have reached out to her somehow.* 'Are you a danger to us, Kemara?' he asked.

'I don't *think* so,' she said. 'When Ionia and I were together we had complete control of our powers, but after she died, I was filled with anger and my familiar fed that rage – that's why I killed it. I could feel myself becoming everything the legends speak of – the destructive beast filled with wild magic. But I'm not that person any more, and Buramanaka is different. He's not feral – he's more like one of Deo's seraphim, austere and precise. His anger is cold, like justice.'

None of that sounded comforting, and Raythe had been taught that the mizra was malevolent and destructive, but when they had melded, he had felt only purpose and desperation. Despite the clear perils, the possibilities intrigued him.

What if the Church and the scholars have been wrong all along? What if generations of men and women have been persecuted for nothing more than being different? What if embracing that difference makes us complete?

'You've gone quiet,' Kemara noted, her voice flinty.

'Only because I'm a little overwhelmed.' *What if the mizra isn't the opposite of the praxis, but the thing that makes sorcery whole?* 'Do you see, we could change the way people think of the mizra, what if—?'

'Deo's Balls, Vyre,' she interrupted, 'to the world's eyes, you're a renegade and I'm a demon's bitch – that's not just what the empire thinks, but what every person in this caravan would believe. If I'm revealed, I'll face a lynch mob.'

That was almost certainly true. Raythe wasn't sure how even Jesco would react if he knew the whole truth. The fear of the mizra was pervasive, and everyone *knew* how the Aldar had fallen.

It would have been sensible to turn away, but there was such strength in her, and the thought that together, they stood on the threshold of a new understanding of sorcery, overrode more craven notions.

'You won't face a lynch mob,' he told her. 'We'll keep it to ourselves and explore it together.'

A little tension went out of her, but she still pulled a face. '*Explore?* What does that mean? Because that meld—' She shuddered. 'It was intimate – *too intimate*, like I could taste your spit and smell your thoughts. I guess that was the same for you?'

He nodded and started to speak, but she interrupted. 'I don't do intimacy, and I don't feel anything for you, so if it means anything more than holding your hand while conjuring, it's not happening.'

'Kemara, there's no sexual implication – more than that, there's plenty of evidence that sex gets in the way. Most meld-partners are the same gender – and yes, I know full well that doesn't preclude a sexual relationship, but most people aren't built that way. At the Academia, we were encouraged to pair up with as many others as possible. My best meld-partner was male, and not someone I particularly liked.'

'What happened to him?'

'He betrayed his country, executed my father and stole my wife.'

Her eyes went round. 'Holy Gerda.'

'Yes, Luc Mandaryke. It's a small world.' He fought down the bitter memories that always accompanied that name. 'What I'm proposing is a working relationship, that's all.'

She studied his face, then said, 'All right. Let's do it.'

In his relief, he went to hug her, then realised what he was about to do and stopped dead. 'Um . . . thank you, I appreciate it. We'll do amazing things together.'

She snorted derisively, but all she said was, 'Let's see.'

She's got more prickles than a porcupine, but I'm starting to realise why. 'See you tonight for dinner, then?'

She looked away, her handsome face in profile framed by coils of hair that gleamed like copper wire in the morning sunlight. She looked deathly tired, yet stronger than stone. His chivalric urges had him wanting to protect her, even though she'd probably break his jaw if he said so.

'Tonight, then,' she said, and stomped back to her waiting patients.

From his blanket, Trimble could see Vyre's fire, and his daughter, dancing round the flames like an imp, while Jesco Duretto played a fiddle. A skinny thing, this Zarelda, with a strutting manner like a nymph of the old tales. Her father was darker, a man who had a way with shadows.

But Trimble's mind wasn't really on them right now. He was watching the voluptuous redhead with the tough face who was labouring over a brazier, her face cast in firelight. *Kemara Solus*, he breathed, tasting her name.

'I do like me a redhead,' he murmured aloud.

One of the other wounded men looked up, an oldster named Rosset. 'What was that, fella?'

'Our healer-lady's a tasty piece,' Trimble replied. 'I'd like a piece of that.'

'Heh, heh. Got a sharp tongue on her, but I'd happily bury my face in that cleavage of hers,' Rosset chuckled. 'Minds me of a woman I knew back home, a sweet widow with a willing way.'

Trimble let the man ramble. The first few nights he'd felt threatened, very aware that he'd washed up among enemies, but most of these travellers were Pelarian and they'd quickly accepted him once they'd decided he wasn't an empire-lover. And their purpose intrigued him.

Istariol . . . They thought they could sneak out of the empire, mine a seam of blood-dust then return rich. The naïveté was laughable. *My empire will teach them the realities. Small people get nothing.*

On the evening of the fifth day since leaving the beach, the leaders gathered at Raythe's camp to confer. Elgus Rhamp's rearguard had rejoined them, reporting no sign of pursuit. The knight brought Banno, but sensibly left Osvard behind. Mater Varahana sat with Vidar, Tami was chatting to Jesco and Kemara, wary as ever, perched to one side.

Raythe carved a crude map into the gravel, saying as he drew, 'We're here, on the eastern Verdessa coast, and here's the imperial garrison at Rodonoi, about eighty miles west. We figure the imperial troopship will have reached them by now and we must assume cavalry will have been despatched yesterday. They'll average about forty miles a day, so in two to three days they'll be in our faces.'

'And where's your cartomancer's lake?' Elgus asked

Raythe touched a point in the mountains to the north, midway between their position and Rodonoi Fort. 'Here, in the foothills of the mountains, at the edge of the Iceheart. The empire don't know our destination, which is our big advantage. But they're four times faster than us, and that's theirs.'

'That's a damned big advantage,' Elgus growled.

'I know. Essentially, there's around twenty miles between the coast and the mountains for us to manoeuvre, and we're slower than them, so if they pick up our trail, all the praxis in the world won't stop them from finding us. The trail-obscuring spell can only do so much. Somehow we have to elude them. Any ideas?'

'Can we take them on?' young Banno asked.

'No.'

'But on the beach—'

'We got lucky,' Jesco interrupted. 'The lightning strike needed fortuitous weather; and the fact they had to attack from longboats played into our hands. This time we'll need to protect our wagons, which will force us to defend, and they'll be able to attack where and when they choose.'

'Can we evade them?' Varahana asked.

'If they sweep forward with a wide perimeter of scouts, that's damned unlikely,' Elgus said.

'Our hunters can pick 'em off one by one,' Vidar growled.

'They'll notice, Shaggy,' Tami drawled.

Raythe, turning over ideas in his mind, let the conversation falter, then said, 'I do have a plan. It's a gamble—'

'What isn't, with you?' Kemara observed.

'My gambles pay off,' he said, with more confidence than he felt. 'Listen, here's what I think we should do . . .'

Larch Hawkstone followed an imperial scout, a Ferrean mercenary, to the edge of the pines, and peered up at the hilltop where Vyre's people were supposedly holed up. To his right, the sea was pounding the coastal cliffs and the wind slashed in, straight off the snowy heights to the north. The air was bitter, even though the sun was about to rise.

'I've seen sentries,' the Ferrean murmured, 'and I've heard animals, too. They're up there.'

'Good,' Hawkstone murmured, as the scout signalled behind them and a few moments later, a man with blond hair and a lordly face joined them. Alexi Persekoi, the Rodonoi *komandir*, was followed by his arrogant-looking aides.

'They are trapped, yuz?' the Bolgravian komandir asked. His accent was aggravating, but they were the overlords, so Hawkstone concealed his distaste.

'They're on a headland and surrounded on the inland sides,' the scout confirmed. 'They've got nowhere to go but into the sea. And I swear they don't know we're here.'

Persekoi glanced at Hawkstone. 'This Vyre, he is unwary, think you?'

'They may believe they're clear of danger,' he answered, uneasily. Vyre hadn't seemed the unwary type, but perhaps they thought their victory at the bay had bought them their freedom?

'You believe this?' Persekoi asked. 'Your reputation you will stake, ney?'

I don't have a 'reputation', Hawkstone thought sourly. *And I didn't expect them to be this easy to find.* But around Bolgravian nobles, it was best to just shut up and let them do the thinking, so all he said was, 'Vyre is dangerous, but the fact remains, they're trapped, even if they do know we're coming.'

'Then we make silent advance,' Persekoi decided. 'No flintlock fire until we're among them.'

'And prisoners?' Hawkstone asked, thinking of Angrit and Rosebud. 'Children are blameless, and the women—'

'Children have value in southern flesh-markets,' Persekoi commented, avarice in his eyes. 'Young women also. Rest can die.' He turned to aides. 'Begin advance.'

Hawkstone rejoined his own men, wondering how to handle this. *Angrit's got to be up there, and our Rosebud. How do I get to them before these bastards do their worst?*

'Here they come,' Jesco whispered, crouched beside Raythe in the lee of a wagon.

Raythe peered through the gloom and saw a row of grey-clad men with long flintlocks break from the undergrowth below and start toiling up the steep, brush-covered slope. The sun was almost rising, lending enough light for visibility.

'Are we ready?' he asked.

'As we can be,' the Shadran murmured. 'Give me a half a minute.'

Crouching low, he scampered away, seeking the other men lurking in shadows with weapons primed and ready.

'*Cognatus, animus,*' Raythe whispered, and his familiar immersed itself in him. Cognatus loved these moments when he could unleash upon the natural world.

In the darkness to his right, Vidar was crouched, eyes glowing amber, teeth bared and breath coming in short rushes. Raythe worried again that Vidar might not be able to prise himself from the fray, but he needed him here.

'Gently, my friend,' he called. 'This is a fight we'll need to run from.'

The bearskin answered with a low growl.

For a moment, Raythe missed Kemara and the hideous strength she wielded, but they couldn't risk her falling into Bolgravian hands, and though she was deadly, she wasn't battle-trained.

This one's my fight, not hers . . .

He stepped to the fire, swept up a burning brand and raised it. '*Paratus nunc, praesemino igneous,*' he chanted, tracing *Ignus*, the rune of fire. Cognatus sucked at the bonfire, drawing some of that heat into himself, then exhaling it through the nebulum.

Below them, the dozens of firetraps they'd laid on the slopes burst into life, eliciting shouts of alarm as the flames roared through the brush. Then Jesco and his men opened up, a dozen flintlocks belching smoke, and the archers loosed shafts that ripped into the ranked soldiers. Bolgravian voices shouted in alarm as the pre-dawn burst into vivid chaos.

The sun kissed the slope and a lance of sunlight shot across the skies.

'*Paratus lumis,*' Raythe shouted, and felt the familiar's shriek of joy as the light poured over them. He shouted again, to curb the daemon's impatience. '*Expecto –*'

Wait . . .

A rosy glow lit the slopes as his comrades reloaded and fired again, then began to pull back. 'Go,' Jesco shouted to those around him, 'go, go, go –' and they fell back into the bare space around the embers of the bonfire where Raythe waited, his arms spread and shouting, '*Cognatus, ignus nunc!*'

His fingertips drew the rune and Cognatus roared, pouring flame from the nebulum to the material world, into the smouldering bonfire, which burst into life – then a dozen or more lit logs hurtled like rockets into the air and shot outwards over the top of the ringed wagons, trailing fire like comets. They slammed into the brush and exploded, sending jagged burning splinters ripping through the undergrowth like shrapnel.

'Easy does it, lads,' Larch Hawkstone muttered as he led his Borderers up the headland, through the thinning pines. 'Keep your heads down.' The defenders had not apparently noticed his contingent so far, concentrating their fire on the Bolgravians ahead. 'Let the Bolgies soak it up.'

As if in answer, fire flared on the headland above and suddenly musketry rattled over the crackling of a bunch of firetraps bursting alight.

Hawkstone shouted at his men to seek cover as alarm spread. He saw Komandir Persekoi floundering, momentarily stunned, but then emanating Bolgravian fury, he roared his men forward even as muzzle flashes lit the ring of wagons above and lead balls whistled down. Two men spun and fell and the rest dropped to one knee and fired blindly. Arrows flew too, silent and deadly, and Hawkstone hurled himself back into cover.

Vyre truly is the Pitlord Himself.

That thought caused him to consciously hang back – he'd never been a great one for that 'first into the breach' shit anyway, and certainly not on behalf of any kragging Bolgies.

Besides, where were the animal noises, or the screeching of women and children?

It's a kragging trap.

'Slow it down, boys, stay with me,' he ordered.

His Borderers looked scared, and willingly followed his lead in dropping to the ground, while the Bolgravians continued to labour upwards through the flame. As they advanced, sunlight burst through the eastern hills, lighting the headland and the sky in brilliant gold and casting the rest into shadow.

Let Persekoi and his bastards face whatever Vyre's got planned first.

His instincts were vindicated seconds later when the very air shook and the crown of the hill exploded into flame, sending burning tree trunks rocketing up then crashing down into the brush, igniting everything they touched. In seconds the entire slope was being devoured by the rapacious flames, with most of the Bolgravian troops trapped inside the maelstrom.

Hawkstone heard Persekoi screaming '*Obvini*—' in his guttural tongue, urging his men to attack, despite the chaos. *Madness.* And somewhere above, a beast roared like an enraged Pitfiend. He recognised that roar. *The bearskin is here.* The bearskin had been a guide on Gospodoi's mission, further proof of conspiracy. The Norgan, Vidar Vidarsson, now had a substantial price on his head too.

Maybe I can make a little money on him?

But right now, Hawkstone had no intention of walking into whatever Raythe Vyre had prepared, so while the Bolgravians advanced with all their famously blind courage, he called, 'Stay down,' and his Borderers did as he bade them.

Let the Bolgravs do it: it's their kraggin' empire, after all.

⬥

Raythe tore off his bandana and looked around. There wasn't much to see – the bonfire was a burnt-out ash-pit and those Bolgravians who had reached the summit were dead, cut down by his little group of defenders. It was time to go.

But even as he opened his mouth to holler the signal, half a dozen more Bolgravs burst through the cordon of wagons from the east flank, near the cliffs, led by a dashing young officer brandishing a sword in one hand and a pistol in the other. It could have been Raythe himself a decade ago. Behind him, his men raised flintlocks and took aim.

'You there,' the Bolgrav officer shouted in Magnian, 'surrender or die!'

A moment later, a looming shadow broke over them and an axe came slamming down on the hindmost soldier's skull, bursting it like a pumpkin. The Bolgravians spun round and in the instant the officer's eyes left Raythe, he darted right, throwing himself into a roll, just as the Bolgrav officer fired. The ball went whistling past his nose.

Vidar roared and his left paw raked the face off the nearest man, then his giant axe, wielded singlehanded, crunched into the ribcage of the next. As the Bolgravians recoiled, Jesco blurred in, a dagger punched into the eye of one man while his blade slashed the windpipe of a second, then he ducked a lunging bayonet and plunged his blade straight through the chest of the final trooper, so deeply the tip protruded out of his back.

The Bolgravian officer was suddenly alone. Jesco had already kicked his kill off his sword, and Vidar had turned towards the man, his eyes burning red.

Raythe felt sudden pity for the man. 'Just run,' he called.

The young Bolgrav hesitated . . . and Vidar growled.

'Leave him—' Raythe shouted, but too late. The bearskin leaped fully twenty feet forward to slam the axe into the officer's back, knocking him to the ground. The axe rose and fell, and again, a sickening succession of wet thuds, and Raythe's protests died in his throat. Vidar slavered over the butchered corpse, baring teeth and drooling as he reached for a severed arm.

This is what a bearskin is, Raythe remembered.

'Vidar,' Jesco shouted, grabbing the bearskin's wrist. 'No time, we've got to go.'

The berserker roared, barely comprehending, his face more beast than man – but Jesco pushed the axe down, leaned in and kissed Vidar's nose. 'Hey, wakey-wakey, big man.'

Vidar's face went from bestial to incredulous to *aware*, and suddenly he was himself again – and *utterly* outraged. '*You prick*,' he snarled, wiping his face. Then the backlash of the transformation hit him and he staggered away, his face clearing.

'One of these days,' he growled at the Shadran.

'Sorry, darling,' Jesco replied, 'but you're really not my type.'

'Stop flirting and run,' Raythe called, and sprinted towards the cliffs, a few hunters already ahead of them. Some were carrying bows with empty quivers, others long-barrelled guns, still smoking. They all shouldered their arms as they reached the cliff's edge.

The two days they'd been here hadn't just been spent on creating the illusion of a full camp. Rope-ladders had been readied to get them past the worst drops, and on the beach the two captured Bolgravian longboats awaited them.

The two dozen men who'd stayed behind to man the ambush were crowing as they launched. 'Bastards never knew what was going on,' Jesco laughed. 'Gerda's Tits, we're good.'

By the time the surviving Bolgravs managed to fight through the fires to the summit, Vyre and his men were two hundred yards from shore. By the time they were seen, that was three hundred and they were vanishing around the headland and letting the current sweep them along faster than a man could run.

Raythe pulled out his hipflask, filled with the last of his rye, and passed it down the line of rowers. 'Anyone hurt?'

A chorus of voices declared themselves fine.

'Not a feckin' scratch,' Jesco chuckled. 'Today is a good day to be alive.'

They made landfall unopposed at the mouth of a small river and sank the longboats in the outgoing tide before wading upstream to conceal their tracks. According to the cartomancer's map, this river would lead them all the way to the lake they sought.

The bulk of their expedition, led by Elgus Rhamp, were already two days ahead.

We had no chance of sneaking around the enemy if they thought that was what we were doing, Raythe reflected, so his plan had been to be *found* as swiftly as possible, so that the imperial forces would stop looking elsewhere. Being efficiently predictable, that was exactly what the Bolgravs had done.

And retreating back eastwards might even make them think we're running back home – with any luck, they'll pursue us that way and we'll have vanished into the mountains before they realise their mistake.

Today, as Jesco had said, was a good day.

But leaving Elgus Rhamp in charge had the potential to ruin all that, so he didn't relax. 'Come on, lads, let's get moving. Who knows what those clowns have been doing while we're gone.'

2

Retribution

Zar grunted in a most unladylike fashion, soaked with sweat as she slogged up the short climb, a heavy pack on her back weighing her down. She was dragging the reins of one of their horses, which was burdened with the canvas for the tent and a hundred other things from pegs to billies to food, and she was cursing it out rhythmically as she hauled the unwilling beast along.

'So you're a wagon-horse,' she growled. 'Think you're too good for baggage, eh? Well, get used to it!'

They'd left a dozen wagons at the ambush site to fool the Bolgravians, so everyone had to carry more. Their wagon was one of those they'd abandoned, and although she'd hated it – the lurching and jolting, the potholes and mud, and the incessant feeding and watering and rubbing down of the horses, it turned out that lugging your own bodyweight in gear was worse. The robust Teshveld village women seemed to manage all right, but she felt like an ant trying to carry a house.

Adefar flashed down from the skies, landed on the horse's head, then flitted away again.

'Thanks, and you're no feckin' help either,' she called after him, making people look at her funny, then make warding signs with their fingers. She was getting used to that, too.

She dragged herself to the top of the latest rise and looked around. Clouds of steam were rising from the line of beasts and people stretched ahead and behind. Only a few wagons remained; the rest of the essentials had been transferred to handcarts or loaded onto the carthorses, mules and their own backs. Even though the journey had already whittled down their possessions to the essentials, they still had to dump a lot more.

She fretted over her father and his friends, luring the empire to them so they could get away, frightened for him, just like during the rebellion, when at every parting she'd faced the terror that *this time* he wouldn't come back.

Jesco's with him, she told herself, *and he'd never let Dad die.*

They were following a moderate-sized river upstream through grey shingle and bare rock, and mostly the way was flat. They'd glimpsed herds of wild goats and heard wolves howling in the distance. The mountains, their skirts deeply forested, were now only a few miles ahead.

'Hey, Zar,' Kemara called. The red-haired healer was sitting beneath the willows lining the riverbank. Beside her, her mule, still hitched to her cart, was grazing. 'Thirsty?' She held out her water bottle.

'Sure,' Zar panted, flicking her horse's reins around a tree-stump then slumping down beside Kemara. She accepted the bottle and took a long, grateful swig. 'So, how's your praxis lessons going?'

Kemara's face twitched. 'Fine.'

'How come I never see your familiar around?' Zar asked. 'Adefar could play with him.'

'Raythe wants me to practise concealing it. And it's a loner like me, I guess.'

'What's its name?'

'Um, Bura,' she replied evasively, as if her familiar was too personal to be discussed.

'So, are you specialising in Mentius, Mundius or Proteus?' Zar asked, feeling shut out.

'A bit of each.'

Zar concealed her irritation behind another mouthful of water, then handed the flask back, wondering why, when magic was all she thought about – *well, apart from Banno* – Kemara didn't want to talk about it?

'Sorry to bother you,' she said, standing and tugging on her horse's reins. 'Hope you can get that broomstick out of your arse soon,' she added, as she stamped away.

'Sorry,' Kemara called after her. 'I've got something on my mind.'

'Whatever,' Zar tossed back, hauling on her *damned* horse's reins, as the trail rose before her.

Dear Gerda, let me get there soon . . .

Their destination was only a few miles onwards and a burst of energy took Zar ahead of the main body so she'd almost caught up with Elgus Rhamp's vanguard when she followed them out of the willows on the riverbank into a desolate scene: bleak, rocky slopes above a mist-wreathed lake. A lone stag saw them and thudded away.

She found Banno staring up at the wall of snow-covered hills that barred the way north. They'd been mostly obscured during the journey, but whenever glimpsed, they grew more forbidding.

'Deo on High, how do we cross these?' Banno wondered plaintively.

Zarelda had seen the maps. 'The lake's fed from the mountains on the far side. We find the inflow and follow it upstream to the istariol.'

'It's hard to believe there's anything north of here but ice.'

'Remember what Varahana says about istariol and the climate? A large motherlode heats the ground and creates fertility and life. If the cartomancer's readings are right, we'll find a place of richness.'

'They'd better be right,' Banno exclaimed. 'Otherwise we'll all die in there.'

'We'll make it,' she told him. 'Dad got me out of Otravia and the rebellion. He'll find a way.'

She thought of their headlong flight through Colfar's campsite as the Bolgravians rampaged in. *Dear Gerda, I don't want to go through that again.*

'Of course,' Banno agreed. 'He's a praxis-mage, I'm sure he can do anything.'

She smiled gratefully, wishing they were alone. But his father was near, and she could sense the contemptuous eyes of his brothers on them. Strange how different Rhamp's sons were.

'I guess I'd better make camp,' she told Banno. 'Your brothers don't like seeing us together.'

'I don't care what they think,' he retorted.

They shared a smile, but she was right: there was work to be done. She dragged her horse to a likely site, a patch of level ground beside the lake, then fought her canvas into place and hammered down the pegs. Around her, the rest of the caravan was doing likewise.

As usual, the camp divided up into three zones: Rhamp's thugs, Mater Varahana's Deists and the hunters and trappers. Her tent was near Varahana's camp but not in it, even though being on her own without her father or Jesco made her nervous. She'd slept the previous night with a dagger in her hand and must've woken at every sound.

Soon though, she'd coaxed a fire into being, and sizzled some vegetables in a tiny dab of fat winnowed from the rabbit she'd trapped a few days earlier. She wolfed down her sparse meal, then rolled up in her blanket, exhausted by the day's travel. Shutting out the sound of hymns and the raucous laughter from Rhamp's tents, she closed her eyes . . .

. . . and woke what felt like moments later to find her fire burned out, the camp in darkness and a dark silhouette crouching above her. As she went for her dagger they grabbed her wrist and clapped a palm over her mouth and a low male voice whispered, 'Quiet.'

'Let's do it now,' Osvard insisted. 'This is our chance.'

'No, we wait,' his father snapped, while Banno watched anxiously. It had been like this all evening, his elder brother chipping away, eager for blood.

It was always going to come to a head at some point; he'd seen it before. Elgus Rhamp liked to talk about his noble lineage, but he'd been screwed over so many times that he'd come to realise that he had to be the one to strike first. He didn't trust Vyre and he wanted the istariol for himself: it was simple as that.

But this journey had taken them far from their usual haunts and all the contacts and allies and patrons who usually protected them, giving them no haven if things went badly. They'd been forced to coexist with Vyre's people for far longer than anticipated and the strain was beginning to tell.

Immediately after Vyre's meeting at the tavern – was it really only two months ago? – Elgus had laid down the plan: 'Once it's found, we take control. Vyre dies, together with anyone who sides with him. Then we dig it up, all we can carry, and get the feck out.'

That was still the plan.

But what about Zar?

She was only sixteen, but Banno admired her peppy maturity and her adventurous zest, rare in girls, or at least any he'd met. They'd all been kept confined in preparation for marriage, silly hollyhocks with no life experience.

She's the first girl I've met who I like as person. I won't see her hurt.

But to break ranks was a huge thing, so he couldn't warn her, though he desperately wanted to. The dilemma was killing him. Trying to argue that they should keep their pledge to Raythe Vyre had earned him a fist in the belly from Osvard, and the contempt of Crowfoot and Bloody Thom – and Father had told him that if he blabbed to Zar, he was no son of his. So he'd pretended to toe the line, hoping things might resolve on their own.

But now they'd reached the cartomancer's lake and Osvard was demanding action. 'This is the place,' he was insisting. 'We don't need Vyre any more. That Mater is a scholar, she can find the blood-dust for us.'

'Aye,' Bloody Thom put in, 'and chances are Vyre and his lot are dead now anyway; or they're captured and blabbing to the imperials. We need to grab that istariol now, then get out.'

'Vyre's a sorcerer,' Crowfoot reminded them. 'His ambush might work. We can't count on him being dead.'

His cautious advice found an ally in Tami. The pinch-faced woman had been quiet, but now she said, 'Never bet against an Otravian sorcerer. You saw what he did to that frigate.'

Elgus frowned at his woman, while the rest chewed her words over. Tami seldom spoke against Elgus, but when she did, she was always proved right.

Banno knew he wouldn't listen, though, not this time. *Father will do this . . . I can't stop him. The best I can do is get Zarelda through it. But will she ever forgive me for not giving more warning?*

Elgus stroked his big grey beard, moving his mouth like he was sucking on a lemon: his thinking face. Finally, he spoke. 'Right, give me your vote. Crow?'

'We're going to do this sometime,' Crowfoot began. 'The closer we get to the blood-dust, the more prepared Vyre's going to be. I've seen a praxis-sorcerer in battle and it's not pretty, so we need to pick our moment carefully. If he returns safe from the ambush he'll still be wary; but if he finds nothing amiss here, he'll think we're with him and his guard will drop. That's the time to strike, not now.'

Elgus raised a hand to stifle an exasperated curse from Osvard. 'Thom?'

The swarthy veteran scowled thoughtfully. 'Strike now. Seize the daughter as a hostage. Slit a few throats – we know who. Then set up an ambush along the lakeside to catch Vyre and Vidarsson and that Shadran pansy, if they even survived the imperials. Sooner it's done, the sooner we can assert full control. The Mater will fall into line, and so will the rest of the hunters.'

'Yes,' Osvard said, thumping a fist into his palm, 'yes –'

Elgus fiddled with the ponytail knot in his beard, then turned to his woman. 'Tami?'

She smiled in that way that always made Banno feel that she had two games going at once. 'I could make a case either way, but we need to proceed carefully. I support my lord, Elgus, in whatever he decides.' Which was effectively not a vote at all.

'Pah!' Osvard snarled. 'Why ask a kragging woman? We have to strike now, like Thom says.'

'Banno?'

It was a risk, but he shook his head. 'I'm with Crow.'

'Another feckin' woman,' Osvard sneered, his eyes burning.

'Shut it,' Elgus growled. Then he ruminated some more, and nodded. 'Let's do it tonight.'

It was a still night, the first windless evening in what felt like months. Kemara jolted awake, roused from a lurid dream of a demon-masked Aldar lover licking her thighs.

There was a blurred shadow on the canvas of her tent, and footfalls rustled in the wet grass. She went rigid, her mind racing. Her four patients were in the next tent, but they were asleep. *Do I raise the alarm and precipitate whatever's happening, or do I try to steal away?*

Only one of those paths offered a chance of survival.

Maybe it's just a sentry? she hoped, but there shouldn't be any nearby. She eased herself from beneath the blanket, fumbling for the hilt of her dagger, conscious that it was the lesser of her weapons.

The air quivered at the mere thought: Buramanaka was awake, waiting.

The moment she spoke her summoning, though, whoever was out there would hear – even a whisper in this taut silence would sound like a shout. So all she did was slither sideways, eyes fixed on the gap between the canvas and the ground, where a couple of inches of foot and ankle were visible, in touching distance.

Then something pressed against canvas, a circular imprint an inch round – a flintlock muzzle, perfectly aligned with the middle of her bedroll. She heard the hammer click.

She writhed sideways and stabbed through the narrow opening, the dagger plunging into the man's boot as the night exploded in a roar, flame belching through the canvas and something ripping through her blankets, thudding into the ground beside her head.

The gunman gasped in pain and the dagger was ripped from her hand, so she hurled herself out of the tent flap into the night, twisting to see a man holding a smoking flintlock silhouetted against the planetary rings. Her patients called out fearfully, but he hobbled to her, gun raised to slam the heavy butt down on her skull.

'*Kaneska alla miz—*' she began, knowing she was already too late.

But then someone barrelled out of the dark and slammed into her attacker, hammering him to the ground. Ringlight flashed on a blade that plunged once, twice and again in a series of wet thuds, grunts and weak gasps. Then her rescuer rolled off the attacker and collapsed.

The stricken gunman made a shuddering attempt to claim one last breath before sagging and going still. The ringlight showed her Osvard Rhamp with a dagger buried in his heart.

The night came alive in bursts of frightened noises, interspersed with the rattle of flintlocks and the hiss of arrows and shrieks and cries of attackers and injured. But she had a more immediate concern. She crawled to the prostrate man who'd slain Osvard, and rolled him over.

It was Moss Trimble, the imperial navy man, breathing painfully. But his back was soaked in blood and as she gripped his arm, he slipped into unconsciousness.

'Shhh,' Banno hissed. 'Don't move.' His hand was over Zarelda's mouth, his body pressing her down, smothering her instinctive attempt to roll free. She twisted her neck, tried to read his face, but he was gazing towards a ring-lit glade where a cluster of men where advancing, weapons drawn. They came from the direction of Elgus Rhamp's tents.

Then he rolled off her, and murmured, 'Follow me – crawl.' He nudged her left, towards the lake, and they slithered through the dew-soaked tussock until he whispered, 'Down—'

They flattened themselves.

The Rhamp men reached her tent, where she'd been a few seconds before and for a moment they prodded at her blanket, puzzled to find it empty.

Then a sharp male voice rang out. 'Hold right there!'

They should have – they were caught cold – but the mercenaries thought themselves invincible; two men fired blindly into the dark, while the rest brandished weapons.

A trio of flintlocks blasted and arrows sleeted into the clearing, slamming into the small knot of men. Half went down at once, and the rest, crying out in frightened fury, reeled together, staring about them with stunned faces.

'Drop the weapons!' that voice called again and now Zar recognised Cal Foaley, the hunter.

Two fools still tried to charge, but arrows cut them down and this time the remaining half-dozen dropped to their knees and tossed their weapons away.

Zarelda thrust her fist into her own mouth to stifle her fear as torches flared. Banno clung to her, stunned, and unable to hide it. Though he'd come to protect her, he clearly hadn't expected such violence.

The torches lit the night in lurid smears of orange, painting the rough, grizzled features of some of the older hunters, taciturn men who seldom spoke. Foaley, tall and gaunt, a grey wolf of a man, was directing them. They stalked forward warily, disarming both living and dead, tossing their weapons into a pile.

Distant voices called from Rhamp's camp, asking what was happening, but no one answered. Zar saw villagers as well as hunters among the victors, and those with flintlocks or bows readied their weapons again. And among the victors she saw one woman: *Tami*. When Banno saw her, his eyes just about popped from his skull.

Then Tami pointed right at her. 'Banno Rhamp's over there, with the girl. Don't harm them.'

Two dozen heads turned their way and someone called, 'Stand up – real slow.'

Zarelda glanced at Banno, who was frozen in horror. She rose, but his eyes were fixed on the tangle of bodies and when she followed his gaze, she saw his younger brother Poel was among them, staring sightlessly at the rings of Shamaya overhead.

Then rough men stinking of wet fur and gunpowder hauled them apart, heavy hands clamping on her shoulders. One man drove a fist into Banno's belly and he jack-knifed and went down, dry-retching and choking.

'Hold,' Tami snapped. 'I said to leave them alone.'

'He's a Rhamp,' the hunter growled. 'He had it coming.'

'Not this one,' Tami said. 'He's the only decent one in the clan.' She hauled on Banno's shoulder, and he rose, gasping for air and eyeing the hunter who'd hit him vengefully.

'Banno,' Zarelda began, but he wasn't listening.

'What have you done?' he hissed in Tami's face.

'I've saved a lot of lives, including your father's,' the Pelarian woman murmured, waving the hunters back and leaning in to whisper, 'It's called deniability, lad. This was Osvard's initiative, and a few renegades he turned. Got it?'

Banno's eyes bulged. 'Why?'

'Because Osvard's a fool and your father's an even greater fool to listen to him. We need Vyre and we need unity.'

'But you spoke in favour of it!' Banno replied, his face bewildered.

'Did I?' the Pelarian woman asked. 'Elgus had already made up his mind. Arguing would only have set him against me and left me outside his tent when the plans were laid. It was time to let Osvard put his neck in a noose.' Tami shrugged callously. 'Come on. We've still got to get your father through this.' She strode away, calling out, 'Bring them. Let's go and settle things with Rhamp.'

A low growl ran through the hunters as they shouldered arms and stalked away, while the man who'd punched Banno snarled, 'Come on, boy, or I'll smack you again.'

Banno shoved him away and staggered to Poel's body, fell to his knees and began to cry. When Zar joined him, he drew her into an embrace and soaked her shoulder in tears.

After the initial flurry of shots and shouts of alarm, the camp fell quiet, feeding Sir Elgus Rhamp's fears. A third of his lads were out there, most of them Osvard's cronies. When he'd tried to assign Crowfoot to them, Osvard had stood up to him.

'Old Crow didn't argue for this,' Osvard had retorted. 'It ain't work for doubters.'

'Let him go,' Tami had said, then she'd murmured, 'I'll follow him.' As she did, she brushed his hand in a familiar way that got him thinking about her body. Disarmed and distracted, he'd nodded and they'd all disappeared into the darkness, shadows beneath the planetary rings.

In old myths, the ring was the wedding band of Kiiyan, the Aldar Goddess of Mercy. She'd been married to Saetus, the Tyrant of Heaven; when their adopted son rose to slay the old dragon, she'd married the son. The story came to mind now, because Tami was much closer to Osvard's age than his . . .

She's a good lay, true enough, but how does she feel about Osvard?

Though she'd saved him from betrayal more than once, Elgus had never fully trusted her. She gave sound advice and good head, but the bonds they shared were flimsy.

I should marry the bitch, tie her to me properly.

As minutes passed, his lads became edgier and he waved Crowfoot and Bloody Thom over. 'Osvard should be back with the girl by now. It's too damned quiet, too. Where's the uproar?'

'He's probably taking his time with the healer,' Thom smirked.

'He's unfocused,' Crowfoot opined. 'He needs discipline.'

That was true, though having it pointed out wasn't welcome. 'He needs to get back here so that we can move to the next phase,' Elgus growled, looking round and missing a face. 'Where's Banno?'

No one knew.

The boy's supposed to be here . . .

'I'll go and find out what's happening,' Thom offered.

'Don't go alone,' Crowfoot advised. They were opposites in many ways, but they'd always looked out for each other.

But even as Bloody Thom was selecting his men, people emerged from the gloom: ranks of hunters, and villagers too, mostly men, and all of them were armed. They formed a cordon at the edge of the firelight. Cal Foaley led them, with the robed Mater Varahana, who called Elgus' name in a clear, austere voice.

What in the Pit?

A new explanation for the unnatural quiet after those shots became apparent – especially when a pair of hunters dumped a body unceremoniously at the edge of the firelight. When Elgus saw the lifeless face, it was a punch to the throat.

Ossi . . .

Then another man strode forward and dropped Poel beside his dead brother and it felt like the marrow had been sucked from his bones.

My sons . . .

Another dozen men were hauled forth, all roped up, and Foaley's men shoved them to their knees. Elgus could guess the rest: they'd been ambushed, and these were the survivors. He pictured those he couldn't see: a dozen or so of the youngest hotheads. Half his next generation of fighting men, wiped out in a few minutes. But right now, that was as nothing to the sudden, crippling blast of loss that almost flattened him.

My sons, two of my sons . . .

It was all he could do just to remain standing, looking up at the treacherous band of silver in the skies.

'Who did this?' Bloody Thom roared, striding forward, heedless of the flintlocks and arrows that instantly aligned on his chest and face.

'They did it to themselves,' Mater Varahana replied, unflinching in the face of the big warrior. 'If a man transgresses, let Deo's wrath fall upon him. Osvard attacked Kemara Solus – again. She was protected by one of her patients and Osvard died in the struggle.'

The bitch led him on, Elgus wanted to rail, even though he knew that wasn't true. Osvard had fixed his eye on her and he'd never taken the word 'no' on any matter.

But Poel was a good lad, my shining light . . .

He was aware that those behind him – forty men, experienced in butchery – were waiting on his word, even though they were staring down flintlocks and arrows. One word, and half the men here would die.

Hot, bloody vengeance, or a quick death . . .

It was so very tempting to rise up with a bloodthirsty roar and show these stinking pelters and peasants how a real man fought. He'd lose a few, but they'd prevail and then he'd make that damned priestess beg, and as for the men who killed his sons —

Krag, let's do it —

'Hold!' a sharp female voice rapped out.

Tami. He stared at her as suspicions crystallised. *What are you doing out there, woman? Why didn't you warn my lads what was happening?*

'Elgus,' Tami called, interposing herself between Bloody Thom and Varahana. Her manner was cocky and commanding. 'I'm sorry for your losses – and I am sure that *if you'd known* of this foolish attack by your rebellious son, you would have prevented it.'

Only then did it dawn on him that she was offering him a lifeline, a way of backing out of this lethal situation without losing all respect – and giving him a chance to strike properly later, instead of throwing his lads onto the guns and shafts of a prepared adversary.

But the lads know this came from me.

He'd be challenged. Bloody Thom might think he'd lost his balls over this. But Crowfoot would still be loyal. He wavered, then decided: *Take the loss, get to the bottom of this, then strike again when I'm ready.*

'Osvard was always a wild one,' he conceded. 'Never knew how to take refusal. And Poel followed him round like a pup since they were kids. Didn't know any better.'

Dear Gerda, I've lost two sons in one bloody night. He looked around. 'Where's Banno?'

There was an intake of breath, then his middle son – *his only remaining son* – stepped from the shadows. Vyre's girl was lurking near. 'I'm here, Pa.'

By the Pit, did the boy betray us over that girl?

His gaze crawled from Tami to Banno and back again. Had either of them broken the faith – or was it neither? Was there another traitor, or had Foaley just been too wary and Osvard walked into a trap?

'C'mere, boy,' he called brusquely. 'Banno, here!'

He watched Banno exchange looks with the girl, then tentatively walk across the clearing, past Bloody Thom, whose gaze followed him evilly. 'Father?'

'Where were you?' Elgus murmured, seething at the possibilities. 'Did you warn them?'

Banno's face was aghast. '*No!*'

He never did learn how to lie, Elgus mused, while his lads watched and waited, still wondering if they were going to be pitched into a bloodbath. But Banno hadn't been in camp, so at the very least, he'd gone to warn Vyre's wretched daughter. Thom would kill him for that, and so would most of his lads.

But he was now his only son: his sole legacy. *I have to protect him.*

He leaned in and muttered, 'You were shitting in the woods, hear me? You were taking a dump when this went down. Hear me?'

Banno nodded. 'Uh, I was out in the trees,' he said, loud enough to be heard. 'Had the shits.'

Someone guffawed but the rest listened stonily, making up their own minds.

Elgus pointedly embraced Banno, calling out, 'Only son I got now. Boy loved his brothers, wouldn't have ever wanted 'em harmed.'

His lads hesitated, then murmured agreement. They all had questions, but Elgus ran a military force, not a bloody debating society: they knew to shut up and follow the leader.

'Tami,' he called. 'Come on over. Tell me what happened to my boys.'

Everyone turned to face her and she squirmed. *If she stays out there, she's guilty. If she comes in here, she still might be – and I'm going to find out, the hard way.*

Her expression told him that she knew that too, but she wasn't short of guts, that one. She strutted past Thom and came right up to him. 'I'll tell you what I saw.'

'Aye,' he growled, and picked the nearest capable man. 'Morro, take a detail and fetch the bodies of those foolish enough to get caught up in this. Anyone harmed by my lads can claim compensation. Crow, Thom, Banno – get yourselves to my tent. We need to talk.'

'Sir Elgus,' Mater Varahana called out, 'would you like me to prepare the bodies for burial?'

The nerve of the bald bitch. I've half a mind to –

But he exhaled and let the thought go for now. Adding Varahana's name to his death list, he called, 'Mater, I would indeed be grateful.'

With that, he went back to his pavilion. As they entered, Crowfoot and Thom wordlessly grabbed Tami's arms and Crowfoot wrapped his hand round her mouth to silence her. Banno's eyes went wide.

Too squeamish, my lad. But he's got to step up now.

'Secure the perimeter and keep everyone close,' he told his lieutenants. 'No one rushes off to try and get even – they'll be expecting that. When we take them down, we do it on my say-so, in my time.' He gestured to the central pole. 'Tie my bitch to the pole.'

She struggled until a fist to the belly made her fold, then they tied her and gagged her so she couldn't rouse the camp and bring Varahana's folk running. Elgus waited until she was secure, then grabbed her by the hair and jerked her face up. 'Did you warn them?' he snarled.

She shook her head, eyes pleading.

'Did you warn them?' he repeated, balling his fist. 'Someone did.'

Again, she jerked her head side to side.

Liar.

He broke her nose with one brutal blow, sending blood spraying, then running down her face as she sagged, her head rolling groggily. 'You murdered my sons,' he accused. He took a step back, then smashed his steel-capped boot into her ribs, hearing bone shatter. She reeled, choking into the gag, eyes bulging, tears streaming, wheezing for breath through the bloody gag.

'Father,' Banno blurted, his face white.

He whirled on the boy. 'What did you see, boy?'

Banno's eyes shot to Crowfoot and Thom as he remembered the pretence of knowing nothing.

'I-I-I must've gone the wrong way in the woods,' he stammered. 'I got to the edge of a clearing . . . Poel and the others were in the open when a bunch of hunters – dear Gerda, they surrounded them, challenged them – but our lads thought they could take them. They attacked–'

The arrogance of Osvard and his cronies . . . Elgus squeezed his temples to fight the blazing headache rising behind his eyes. Crowfoot was staring at Banno with hawk eyes, and Bloody Thom was fulminating towards bearskin rage.

Elgus spoke before either lost control.

'Was Tami with them?' he demanded.

Banno's eyes went to the battered woman kneeling in the mud with blood streaming down her face and Elgus thought: *He loved his brothers. I can trust this. She lives or dies on his word.*

'No,' Banno said, shaking his head, his voice breaking, 'I didn't see her there.'

Elgus exhaled and exchanged a taut, pregnant look with Crowfoot and Bloody Thom.

'It doesn't mean it wasn't her who tipped them off,' Crowfoot noted. 'She's supposed to be *our* insider – she said she could twist Vyre round her fingers. She should have known – she should've warned us.'

'We should kill the kragging bitch,' Thom agreed.

'I don't think anyone tipped them off,' Banno replied, his voice finding firmness. 'Foaley and Varahana aren't stupid – and Vyre probably saw it all coming with his praxis-magic.'

That's plausible, Elgus supposed, watching pitilessly as Tami wheezed in bloody gusts.

'What about Osvard, then?' Crowfoot asked Banno. 'You said you saw Poel, but not Ossi?'

'I didn't see him,' Banno said, 'but Varahana spoke truly: he went at Kemara, and got himself killed.'

'Who did him?' Thom growled.

'The navy man, Trimble,' Banno replied. 'That's what I heard.'

Trimble. Elgus added that name to his death-list. Drawing on all his hard-won experience, he forced his rage down. Some captains were flashes in the pan, but he'd always loaded his weapons carefully so that when they discharged, they struck home.

'Crow, Thom,' he said finally, 'do the rounds, make sure all's in order and the bodies are being treated with dignity. Banno, you stay here with me.'

The two veterans frowned, but they did as asked, leaving him alone with his son and the battered prisoner. Elgus went to Tami and removed her bloody gag, so she could breathe a little easier. Her eyes were big and frightened, but she didn't plead, just panted, wet and rasping.

What use is she now? Elgus wondered. *I'll never trust her again.*

'Well?' he asked. 'What shall I do with you?'

She went to speak, but he shut her mouth with his hand.

'I don't want to hear your lies,' he told her, reaching for his leather-wrapped cosh, which he handed to Banno. 'Kill her, boy. Beat her to death.'

Banno hesitated. 'Father?'

'I said kill her, you blasted weakling – kill her!'

'He'll do no such thing,' a new voice crackled.

He spun, outraged, to see Kemara Solus at the flap of the tent, and behind her, Mater Varahana stood with the two guards who should've prevented the interruption. But they were plainly terrified, because blue lightning was dancing on the healer's fingertips, the air was sizzling and her eyes were lit with pale, feral light.

'Holy Gerda,' Elgus breathed, going stock-still.

'Tami didn't warn anyone of anything,' Varahana stated in a lordly voice. 'We've been alert to treachery from the get-go – but I'm willing to give you the benefit of the doubt over whether Osvard was acting under your orders.'

He bunched a fist, finding courage in his rage. Sorcery was a clumsy weapon in close combat – it was too slow. That's why most sorcerers did their work from behind phalanxes of infantry. 'If I say the word, you won't get out of here alive,' he snarled.

'Neither will you,' Kemara replied, her face hard and that unearthly light gleaming brighter. 'Shall we?'

He decided she meant it and slowly withdrew his hand from his sword hilt. 'Now what?' he rasped.

'We all take ten paces back and a deep breath,' Varahana said. 'We did what we had to, to protect ourselves; you didn't know what Osvard planned, and there's an end to it. Oh, and a runner has arrived – Vyre's party defeated the imperial force. They'll be here soon.'

Shit.

But realising that the game was up, he feigned relief, and judging by the healer's control of magic – he'd not realised she was so advanced – taking her on might well have been suicidal.

'I really didn't know what Osvard intended,' he lied. 'There'll be no further problems.'

Tami will tell them the truth if I free her, but they likely know that anyway. The real issue is whether they believe I'm repentant and won't try again. Neither Varahana or Kemara were fools, but they wished to preserve the peace. They'd want to believe he'd changed his mind.

'I misunderstood Tami's role in this matter,' he said, as if won over.

He bent over her and stroked her cheek as if regretful. 'From now on, we're behind Vyre all the way.'

With knives sharpened and drawn.

Varahana said nothing, probably worried that rejecting his words would provoke violence.

Elgus turned to his son. 'Banno, cut Tami free.'

His son obeyed, with considerably more alacrity than he had the instruction to kill her. Not only that, but he put his shoulder under Tami's arm and helped her from the tent. Varahana followed, and Kemara backed out last.

'You learn fast,' Elgus said. 'Or else you're only pretending to be a novice sorcerer?'

'That's for me to know and you to guess. If I were you, I'd be putting aside any remaining ambitions to cheat us, Sir Elgus. We're only going to succeed if we work together.'

'Or else?'

She slammed a bolt of energy into his armour tree and the wood split in a blinding flash, sending sparks flying and leaving the timber blackened. The spare greaves that were hanging from it fell, twisted and glowing orange.

Deo on high . . .

'There is no "or else",' she rasped, then she spun and was gone.

He let out his breath slowly, trembling with fear and rage, and wondering if this was the beginning of his end.

Raythe, Jesco and Vidar led their band into the camp, looking round them curiously as they were met by Cal Foaley. A runner had intercepted them downstream, so they knew what had transpired at the camp, or a version of it, anyway.

'What's happening?' Raythe asked.

Foaley, who was considerably younger than his grey hair and weathered features suggested, gestured towards Varahana's tent. 'The healer is tending Tami, Varahana's blessing the bodies and Rhamp's men are digging holes.'

'How's Elgus taking this?'

'He hasn't come out of his tent.'

Raythe frowned. 'Best I go pay my respects.'

'Is that wise?' Vidar asked.

'Probably not, but we need to normalise things again.' He shook Foaley's hand and said, 'Well done, Cal. You're on bonuses when we get some money out of this venture.'

'I'll take that, milord,' the rangy hunter said. 'What's double nothing anyway?' He smirked at his own humour and sauntered off.

The camp remained quiet, despite his return. The wives and children of the hunters and villagers were being kept a long way from Rhamp's people; there were armed men stalking back and forth either side of a hundred-foot strip of no-man's-land. As soon as Raythe and Jesco set out across it, a bunch of Rhamp's men gathered behind Bloody Thom and came to meet them.

'You've got a bloody nerve coming here,' the big mercenary snarled.

'I think it's more important that we talk right now, rather than beat our chests – don't you?' Raythe replied. 'Enough lives have been lost.'

Bloody Thom paused, then growled, 'Wait here,' and headed for Rhamp's pavilion.

After a few minutes of silent staring from the other mercenaries while Jesco blithely whistled a jig, Bloody Thom returned with Sir Elgus. The big knight looked sunken and grey, with bloodshot eyes and a haunted air.

'You made it back,' he said glumly.

'Aye. The plan worked perfectly, we bloodied the Bolgravs' noses and with luck they still don't know which way we went. But we need to press on, just in case. The river carrying the istariol traces runs into the north edge of this lake, according to the cartomancer's journal. The real hunt begins now.'

The Pelarian knight listened in silence, then mumbled, 'You probably think I tried to work you over.'

273

'It crossed my mind.' Raythe held up his hand to cut off Elgus' next words. 'But I expect it was just Osvard and his cronies. I'm sorry for your loss, but he overstepped once too often.'

They studied each other in silence, then Elgus asked, 'So you'll still work with me?'

'Of course. Must the sins of the son be visited upon the father? Listen Elgus, we're just a group of refugees, walking off the map's edge. We don't know what we're going to face, but to survive we *must* work together. Osvard didn't understand that, but I'm sure you do.'

Actually I'm not sure of any such thing, but I still don't believe you're irredeemable.

They engaged in another 'you blink first' contest, then Sir Elgus growled, 'You're in charge, Lord Vyre. We'll play our part. Now if you don't mind, I have two sons to bury.'

Kemara was dabbing at Tami's face with a wet cloth when the Pelarian woman stirred and opened her eyes. She'd been sedated and now she woke in stages, blinking dimly before seeing Kemara. Her eyes flickered about, taking in the healing tent and the other patients in their bedrolls.

'Wor'appen'd?' she wheezed.

'We got you out,' Kemara said. 'I've straightened your nose and strapped your ribs.'

'I think I remember . . . your eyes went funny.' She grabbed Kemara's hand. 'Thank you.'

'We owed you – but you were stupid to go back into his camp afterwards.'

'Thought I could brazen it out,' Tami croaked. 'You're right . . . kraggin' stupid.' She fluttered her eyelids weakly. 'But you came for me. My heroine.'

Kemara extricated her hand, giving her a forbidding look. 'Shut up and hold still.'

She finished cleaning up the battered woman. 'I suppose I'd better find a new camp,' Tami said when they were done. 'Raythe's, I think.' She gave Kemara a sly wink. 'He and I go back.'

Like I care. 'That's up to Lord Vyre. Now, if you'll excuse me?'

She left Tami to tend her other patients. One of the four had developed pneumonia and his lungs were clogging up, but two were nearly healed. And then there was Trimble, her rescuer.

I'm grateful, but he makes me uneasy, Kemara thought as she knelt beside his pallet. There was a troubling intensity to his gaze, and she wished he'd leave her hair alone. She'd taken to tying it up to keep it from his reach. *But when Osvard came, it was him who saved me. He's entitled to a few liberties.*

So she put on a warm smile as she asked, 'How's my best patient today?'

'Pretty damn sore,' the sailor replied, grimacing.

'Roll onto your front,' she told him, helping him twist onto his belly. She peeled off the bandages while he groaned at each tear. His back was a mess of weeping wounds, but they weren't infected and they'd been scabbing over nicely, until he'd torn the stitches open in the struggle with Osvard Rhamp.

'This is going to hurt,' she told him, reaching for her needle and thread.

It did, too, she could tell, but he was stolid, too proud to vent more than the occasional involuntary hiss. He had a neat, compact body and, unusually for a seaman, there were no tattoos. And though he spoke like a sailor, he'd clearly been educated; she sensed deeper layers, and she found herself just a little intrigued about what they might be.

When she was done, she rubbed in some cleansing lotions and he groaned with a mix of pleasure and pain. 'You got good hands,' he sighed. 'Best I've felt, ma'am.'

'It's Kemara.'

'I know that,' he said, looking up with one eye, 'but I'm not sure what's proper to call a Novate?'

'I've only taken preliminary vows. Gerda and I are still working each other out.'

'You'd be wasted in the Church. And you can call me Moss.' He tried a smile, which she frowned down.

'Stay put, as much as you can,' she told her. 'You pull those stitches again and you're on your own. Anything else you need before we load you in the wagon again?'

He gazed up at her and said, 'I ain't been able to shave since . . . the ship. The Bolgravs liked their sailors clean-shaven – some stupid regulation. So what do you reckon – shave or no?'

She studied his stubbled face. The thickening beard gave his features a warmth they might not otherwise have, so she said, 'Keep the whiskers. It's going to be cold where we're going.'

As she rose, he caught her ponytail. 'I like your hair up. It catches the light different, like that. Like frozen sunlight.' Then he let go, before she could object.

She'd been propositioned on a nightly basis at Gravis' tavern, but it'd been a long time since someone had thought her worth courting. It was mildly flattering.

So she didn't hit him.

Raythe strode to the edge of the lake and called, 'Well?'

Mater Varahana, knee-deep in the freezing waters, was staring at a glass vial she was holding up to the light. It was a bleak day with a bitter wind and the sun was buried in thick cloud.

The caravan had moved to the north side of the lake, beneath the mountains. This was the only river that ran into the lake, so following it upstream should be their path. But Raythe needed to be sure, so they'd taken samples, expecting it to be a formality.

'There's still nothing,' the Mater replied, her voice disappointed.

'Kragga,' Raythe fumed. *Where in the flaming Pit is the istariol? That sample the cartomancer had was almost orange, so it should be easily spotted – so where is it?*

This side of the lake lay in the shadow of towering peaks locked in snow and cloud. Mist hung over the lake. It had a dull, lifeless sheen and looked about to freeze over, despite it being late summer. The glacier in the next bay was barely dissolving into the water. The only sounds were the whispering winds and the lowing of the remaining animals.

If we can't find a way forward, we're screwed.

'Are you sure?' he called.

'Yes, I'm sure,' Varahana replied, in a testy voice.

On the shore, Jesco, Vidar, Kemara and Sir Elgus watched with worried faces. The knight was standing well apart from the others. A further clump of onlookers gathered along the shoreline, wondering if they'd come all this way for nothing. Perhaps they had.

'Raythe?' Varahana called.

He turned hopefully. 'What is it – have you found something?'

'No. I just want to know if I can get out of the water now, before my fanny ices over?'

'Yes, of course . . . Damn!'

He stamped away, through the shallow river and onto the far shore, feeling his toes go numb through his soaking boots, but he couldn't face all those accusatory faces just now. He needed to be alone, to think.

The stony shore took him round the headland to the next bay, where a daunting wall of rock and ice blocked the way forward: the glacier they'd found earlier, a crumbling snake of ice many times his height and a hundred yards or more wide winding out of the mountains. It must've been the main river feeding this lake, before the Mizra Wars and the onset of the Ice Age. Now, according to the books he'd read as a student, it crawled forward a few feet every year.

Perhaps I read the journal wrongly – maybe there's another river flowing in somewhere west of here? Or maybe it's the wrong kragging lake altogether? Vidar says it's the right one, but perhaps he's remembering wrong?

Finding his way around the face of the glacier was easy enough. He found himself splashing through the shallows where the ice slowly melted, trudging over rivulets full of mossy stones, and the remains of ancient branches that had been caught up in the flow before the river froze. He passed on . . .

. . . and then stopped and walked back, staring at the dirty residue in one such rivulet.

A minute later, he was back at the small headland, screeching at the top of his voice across the river to Varahana and the others, '*I'VE FOUND IT!*' He couldn't stop himself jumping with excitement as he screamed again, '*I'VE FOUND IT!*'

3

Ice river

It took them a day to build a ramp from the base of the glacier to the top so they could haul up the remaining carts and the beasts. Raythe had feared the way would be impossible, but Cal Foaley had scouted and returned, reporting that it was in fact a surprisingly easy path to negotiate.

'Water freezes level when it can,' Foaley said. 'The movement of the glacier's broken it up in parts, but the surface has been snowed on repeatedly for centuries. It's traversable.' He laughed. 'I'm beginning to believe.'

'Only beginning? Then why'd you leave Teshveld in the first place?'

'It seemed a better idea than strangling slowly in the empire. Really, I just wanted to breathe free air.'

Unbelievable – but I guess if you've got nothing to start with, you've nothing to lose. Raythe clapped his shoulder and said, 'I'm starting to believe too. Did you find anywhere to camp?'

'We'll have to camp on the ice,' Foaley said, 'but you can build fires against the banks on the leeward side. The ice looks solid right to the bottom. I wonder how old it is?'

'I imagine it was a river up until the Mizra Wars and the forming of the Iceheart. When it froze, the traces of istariol froze too. We follow the glacier north, we'll find the istariol.'

'This trek's getting harder and harder.'

'If it was easy, it would've been found by now. I wonder how far the glacier goes?'

'I went about five miles in and it still went on and on,' Foaley replied.

'Judging by the size of the canyon, it used to be a long, wide river. I'd say the old headwaters are a ways north, somewhere in the Iceheart.' He met Raythe's gaze. 'Even snow-deer don't live up there. There'll be nothing – no vegetation, no forage, and nothing to hunt.'

'I know. But concentrations of istariol create their own climate zones. Sorcerers have found hundreds of square miles of lush, fertile ground well above the ice fields. Any luck, there'll even be creatures you've never hunted before.'

Foaley's face lit up. 'Now you're talking.'

'While you were scouting, Vidar's had the others scouring the land for whatever game we can, and we've even got some folk fishing – the lake's well-stocked. We'll smoke whatever we find tonight, so that it's preserved for the journey. I'm hopeful we'll have two weeks' food. I know that's not a lot, but that glacier can't go on for ever.'

'It doesn't have to; we'll not make more than three or four miles a day on the ice. Raythe, you realise that might mean that after only twenty miles, we'll pass the point of no return?'

'Aye. Ideally, we'd camp here and send a smaller team to locate the istariol before we risk anyone else – but the empire might be right behind us, so we don't have that luxury.'

Foaley considered, then nodded. 'Aye, we can only go on . . . But what if we reach the point of no return before we find the istariol?'

'We'll decide that when we get there,' Raythe replied grimly.

He thanked Foaley, then headed back to his own increasingly crowded camp – Tami was now a fixture as well as Kemara and who-ever she was tending. Tonight that was a trapper named Veet Brayda, who'd been wounded at the beach, then developed pneumonia, and the sailor, Trimble, whose back was still a mess. There was always a con-stant stream of people with minor and not so minor complaints too.

Raythe found himself beside the Pelarian sailor as they ate. 'So you're going to make us rich,' Trimble observed.

'We hope so. What would you do with a bit of wealth, Master Trimble?'

'I'd find me a good woman and settle down.' He glanced at Kemara. 'A nice Ferrean girl, I reckon.'

'Kemara's a sorceress. I would counsel you to look elsewhere.'

'Not sure I can, milord.'

Patients and healers, a dance old as time, Raythe thought. *Idiot.*

Kemara spooned the sedative into Veet Brayda's mouth and listened to his thin, liquid breathing. His pneumonia was getting worse and the slow crawl along the glacier in this frigid air was likely going to kill him, but he couldn't be left behind.

'He going to make it?' Moss Trimble asked. He was lying on his front, the bandages on his back newly changed. The skin was healing well, though: better than she'd thought it could. He was made of resilient stuff.

'I hope so,' she replied, wiping Brayda's mouth, 'but there's not much more I can do.'

She had only the two patients in her cart now. Tami was sheltering in Raythe's camp – and clearly angling to move closer still to the Otravian noble – while her other patients had returned to their own families. There'd been an outbreak of pregnancy and three of the children had frostbite from some stupid escapade on the ice, but none of them needed to sleep in her camp.

She'd set her tent a little away from the others, for privacy, and so that Veet didn't disturb them with his coughing fits, which gave her just Trimble for real company. But that was fine: he was interesting.

They'd just finished eating when Trimble said, 'I'm told you went into Rhamp's tent and faced him down?'

Kemara pulled a face. 'What of it?'

'You said it was just Vyre who made my ship burn?'

'It's not something I like to talk about.'

'Tami said you're new to it?'

She considered lying, then admitted, 'Not really, Moss. I went to an

Arcanus Academia when I was younger, but I didn't do well. So I left. I don't really use it any more. The empire doesn't like untrained sorcerers.'

And they really, really, REALLY don't like mizra-witches.

'Can you use it to help this poor mutt?' Moss asked, looking at Veet.

'I'm doing what I can. Protean sorcery includes healing, but I never got the training I'd need for such tasks.' *And the mizra isn't conducive to healing,* she thought bitterly. *It's best at wrecking things . . .*

She stared out at the rest of the camp, strung out over several hundred yards. The villagers and hunters were mingling freely now, but Rhamp's mercenaries were still apart, with a fifty-foot space between that few crossed. The mood was as cold as the air.

She wondered if the rift in the expedition would heal, or fester? She remembered how Sir Elgus had been in the tent: torn between the need for vengeance and an acceptance of how badly he'd erred. His force was weakened now, too. Surely he couldn't risk any further power-plays?

But I feel no safer, even with Osvard dead.

She rose, told Trimble to get some sleep and headed for her own blanket.

'It's going to be a damned cold night,' Trimble replied, then he winked. 'Two bodies are warmer than one.'

'Piss off,' she chuckled. But she was still smiling as she wrapped herself up and closed her eyes.

It was hard to know where the mask ended, even whilst he wore it. Toran Zorne had been a lot of men and to him, personalities were things you donned, then put aside. He hadn't known Moss Trimble, but he habitually soaked up impressions of those around him, so when he was pulled from the sea, scarcely believing he was still alive, he'd latched onto Trimble's persona to conceal his own.

His first task had been to eliminate anyone who knew him, so that first night, despite the agony of his lacerated back, he'd crawled to the next pallet and smothered the other imperial man Vyre's people had rescued.

After that, his focus was to construct this new identity, partly himself, to explain his racial stamp, and partly Moss Trimble, an earthy being with crude desires, or so he deemed. He'd stolen the redleaf from the sailor he'd murdered and chewed it to discolour his own teeth, because Trimble was an addict. He'd also been a man who lusted after redheads, but who concealed his predatory nature with a gruff kind of charm.

I've infiltrated rebels and spy rings. I've walked with kings and priests, beggars and thieves. I am a chameleon.

But right now, he was alone, and his empire was far away. He had to tread very carefully.

Once the healer's breathing became regular, he whispered: '*Animus Ruschto,*' and his familiar entered him. Ruschto had been hiding, but tonight Zorne needed the praxis.

'*Consano, corpus caecus,*' he murmured, commanding the spirit to resume healing his back. The praxis was all about restoring the natural order and the spell formed easily. A tingling sensation suffused his skin, repairing it. He'd seldom been able to do this since his rescue, making the journey a torment, but a gradual recovery was more plausible than some miraculous cure.

As he repaired, he watched Kemara's sleeping face, red hair a tangled frame for her sharp, lived-in face: a woman of substance and secrets. Trimble would've wanted to possess her, but Zorne didn't care either way. Other people stank – he'd never enjoyed being close to them. He had always hated their breath, their odours, their secretions. His parents had never been able to understand why their child bawled when hugged, why he was so cold and distant from such an early age. So they'd beaten him, which had driven the wedge deeper.

It's no wonder I'm always alone.

That was fine, he liked his own company. Loneliness didn't factor into the equation.

Before he slept there was one more task to perform. He whispered the spell and carved the rune-shapes he needed, a blend of flux and anchor, to create a psychic beacon attuned to the imperial sigils. Any listening imperial sorcerers would sense it and know where to look, but no one else would be aware.

He didn't kid himself, though: it was highly unlikely that any imperial sorcerer was close enough to detect it. More likely, he was trapped with these doomed heathens as they walked off the edge of the world.

'Abeo,' he whispered, the spell ended and Ruschto faded back into hiding. A feeling of warm numbness suffused his back and he felt a pleasant weariness that lulled him.

Vyre will lead me to the istariol and I'll bring the empire down on him. Then I'll claim Vyre's bounty and never have to work again.

Except he would, of course. The hunt and the kill were all he knew. Life was for fulfilling one's passions, and finding people was his.

The hunt and the kill.

Waves crashed against the coast, whipped up by the winds churning the smoke rising from the headland, where Vyre's trap had closed on the Bolgravian pursuers. Larch Hawkstone lurked near the Bolgrav komandir and his aides, waiting to be noticed.

Vyre's gone and my lads want to go home . . .

Finally, Alexi Persekoi waved Hawkstone in. The komandir didn't look so certain any more, and he'd been snapping at his aides, his anxiety clear. 'Yuz, Kapitan?'

'Komandir,' Hawkstone greeted, saluting.

Persekoi wrinkled his nose at Hawkstone's stained leathers, a sharp contrast to the immaculate stiff grey coats and golden braids of the Bolgravs. 'What you want?'

'I respectfully request clarification of my orders. I was assigned by my Governor to Under-Komizar Zorne, who is now deceased. We are ready to stand down and return home, sir.'

Persekoi's handsome face turned ugly. 'Pelarians, always backsliding. This is why you is conquered people. Answer is *ney*. You is assigned to Bolgrav military. Now you report me.'

'But—'

'Obey, or face charges, Kapitan Hawkstone. Your choice.'

The Pit take him. Hawkstone saluted again. 'Understood, sir,' he said through gritted teeth, and walking away under the contemptuous gaze of Persekoi's aides, thought, *The Pit take them too.*

He found Simolon and the other lads beside a river below the headland where the recent humiliation had unfolded. Nearby, a Bolgravian mater was chanting prayers over the graves of her countrymen.

Vyre's people had vanished into the mists. Persekoi's scouts had gone in all directions, concentrating on the east, where timbers from Vyre's longboats had been found. But the two sorcerer twins insisted they'd detected a sorcerous beacon north of here, and that was where Persekoi now purposed to go.

What's Vyre up to? There's nothing up there but the Iceheart.

'What's happening, Larch?' Simolon asked, as the lads pressed around. 'Can we go home?'

'Persekoi says "ney", the prick. We're to go north with the Bolgies.'

A burst of profanity greeted the announcement. Many had families back in Teshveld and in truth, few of them gave a shit whether Vyre was caught or not.

'I know,' Hawkstone agreed, 'but Persekoi is the law here.'

'I hope Vyre's lot get away,' one of his scouts, Trenchard, mumbled.

'I don't,' Hawkstone lied, for appearance's sake. 'Vyre's a rebel and a renegade and he's screwed us twice now. Let's take the bastard's head.'

And get my woman and daughter back.

'Yeah,' the rest mumbled, and the abashed Trenchard joined in. That resolved, Hawkstone got them working, readying for the journey inland.

'Boss,' Simolon said, once everyone else was busy, 'how do the Bolgies know where Vyre's gone?'

'A praxis-sign, apparently. Something the Bolgie sorcerers have detected.'

'Why would Vyre leave a trail?'

'Who knows? It's all bat-poo to me.'

Inside an hour they were underway, marching amid a stream of fresh Bolgravian infantry Persekoi had brought in from the garrison at Rodonoi, emptying his barracks in a bid to restore his reputation. The four sorcerers – the twins had been joined by two ancients – were currently surveying the desolate coast with confused disdain, as if they couldn't believe all their years of learning and magic had brought them here.

But when the two newcomers turned their heads, he felt a chill: both had white, empty orbs for eyes. *Izuvei*, he realised: the Mutilated, sorcerers who burned out their own eyes to better see the spirits, or deafened themselves to better hear the nebulum, and other such masochistic horrors.

Their blank stares transfixed him momentarily, then they nudged their mounts and cantered away, leaving him and his men shivering in their wake.

'The blind leading the blind,' Simolon jested nervously.

'Those worms killed my brothers,' Trenchard growled. 'Pelas govo a nagrei.'

Pelaria will rise again.

'Stow the rebel talk, lads,' Hawkstone growled. 'As long as they lead us to Vyre, that's all that matters.'

With that, they shouldered arms and headed upstream.

⟁

The journey up the glacier began in a series of staggering vistas, every bend revealing a new peak of crystalline ice gleaming beneath starkly azure skies. The weather held, a small miracle that might be their salvation, but the air was bitter, burning bare skin numb. For some, the cold settled in their lungs, strangling their breath.

We're going to lose people, Raythe worried.

They had to move slowly, the first walkers testing each footfall, and they travelled in almost complete silence. An avalanche could destroy them, blocking the way forward – or back. Even the animals sensed the danger, muting their normal calls. They had very few wagons left; most had been broken up for fuel, leaving only those truly deemed essential to be hauled along the river of ice. The first day they managed only four miles; the second just two, thanks to a sharp ascent up an old gorge and a steep slope full of broken ice.

Beyond that, however, the way became smoother and they'd made another eight miles by mid-afternoon on the third day, when Raythe, moving up the column to the vanguard, found a bottleneck where the ice had given way and a wagon had fallen through. The two horses, both with broken legs, had been killed to silence their agonised cries. The wreckage was twenty feet down.

'Whose wagon?' Raythe asked.

'Gravis Tavernier,' Elgus Rhamp growled, appearing at Raythe's side and putting a hand on his reins. The tension between Rhamp's people and the rest was still palpable and this was the first time they'd spoken since the morning Osvard and Poel had been buried. It was mostly his people here, staring down at the shattered barrels. Gravis, shaking like a leaf, was being hauled out. 'His was the largest and heaviest – there must've been a weak point in the ice.'

'I thought he was out of stock and rolling empty.'

'He's got yeasts and wheat and whatever else he needs for a new batch when we arrive.' The knight spat on the ice. 'Or he did have. Gonna be a long time between drinks, for real.'

'It'll be worth it,' Raythe told him. 'The istariol will repay us a thousand-fold.'

The Pelarian hung his head. 'This expedition is going to kill us all, Vyre.'

A nervous murmur ran through those listening and Raythe pushed aside his annoyance. Expressing fear in front of everyone was about the worst thing a leader could do right now.

'It's going to be the making of us, Elgus,' he said loudly, before adding in a whisper, 'Keep your doubts to yourself, man.' He turned to those working to recover the wagon. 'Pull the gear from the wagon and share it about. Keep the noise down – and take care.' He swung himself from the saddle. 'I'll give you a hand.'

It was a small thing, but seeing him mucking in galvanised the rest. Villagers, hunters and mercenaries alike formed a human chain to rescue what could be salvaged; somehow the shared work felt like a gentle balm after the raw tension of the past few days. When it was done, Raythe roped himself up to the men above and climbed down into the icy hole. He quietly summoned his familiar, then extended his senses down into the ice. As he'd hoped, there was a streak of dirty orange running through the lower reaches of the glacier: frozen istariol. It wasn't enough to warrant digging out, but it was a sure sign that they were on the right track.

He climbed out and asked for quiet and space, then traced the rune *Isa*, for ice, and instructed Cognatus. Together they sealed over the hole, burying the dead horses and the smashed wagon again. Raythe wondered how many centuries it would take for the wreckage to reach the sea.

The awe in the watching faces as the ice slithered in from the sides and filled the hole was also a kind of binding: a reminder of his powers, and that they weren't entirely at nature's mercy. Even Rhamp's mercenaries looked suitably intimidated by the spell-work.

'He's keeping the skies clear for us,' he heard the blacksmith's wife tell her children.

'No, I'm not,' he replied. 'Deo and Gerda are doing that.' He looked around the circle of faces. 'Hold the course,' he told them. 'Keep believing.'

To his surprise he found himself shaking hands as he worked his way back to his horse.

Elgus muttered, 'I left the empire to escape bloody politicians.'

'People means politics, Elgus,' Raythe replied. 'You know that.' He offered his hand and heard everyone murmur appreciatively at this little symbol of reconciliation. 'We're in this together, Elgus: to the end.'

The knight clearly felt cornered, but he clasped Raythe's hand and murmured, 'To the end.'

That done, Raythe rode back down the column, warning each group he passed to beware of the weak point. He knew all their names now and found himself worrying about them all – this man's health, or that woman's bad ankle, and all the swarming children. As he rode, he pulled a wry face, realising that what he'd said to Sir Elgus had been more or less sincere.

We're in this together, to the end. Although death was also an ending.

These people had become significant to him. They'd placed their lives in his hands and that wasn't easy to put aside. When they set out, he'd regarded them as merely *necessary* – now he regarded many with respect, even affection. They'd come through a lot with him. *They mattered.*

A new weight had settled on his shoulders, one he hadn't wanted or expected: *responsibility.*

With that in mind he set off back down the column, Jesco trotting along behind, looking for the rearguard. He counted off families as he passed them; the Borgers, the Woodburns, the Geldermarks and Tolleys . . .

But no Kemara Solus, who'd been with the Tolleys in the morning.

'The healer's behind us, trying to cure Veet Brayda,' Sim Tolley told him. 'We offered to wait with her, but she said the rearguard weren't far behind, so she'd be fine.'

Sunset was imminent, the advance guard was miles ahead now and the main body of the caravan would be preparing camp. Raythe began to worry, so he summoned Cognatus and used *Aspectu*, the rune of farsight, to seek her. But in this lifeless place, other spirits were few and Cognatus found none to link to. So he sent the familiar onwards as a bird, then turned to Jesco.

'She's behind us somewhere, on her own. We need to find her.'

The Shadran was scanning the skies anxiously. 'Then let's hurry – your run of lucky weather's ending, my friend. There'll be a blizzard tonight.

'Now which way?' Banno asked.

'I don't know,' Zarelda admitted. 'We need to wait for Father.'

A trick of the scouting rosters had seen them posted to the same patrol for once. The six of them, led by Vidar, had reached a confluence of sorts; they were currently resting on a rocky ledge with a view beyond the canyon. The glacier was still there, but intriguingly, there was a frozen lake before them. Zar wondered if it was possible that it, not the upper slopes of the mountains, could be the source of the istariol.

She narrowed her eyes, squinting against the gathering gloom. The setting sun piercing the clouds lit the misty haze hanging over the far shore a mile or more away. 'There might even be trees over there,' she commented.

'If there are, they're probably dead,' Banno replied. 'We're at least twenty miles into the Iceheart.'

'This is just the edge,' she replied. 'The true Iceheart is a desert of ice. But you're right, if there are trees this far north, they're dead ones, preserved by the cold since the Mizra Wars.'

They were all heavily wrapped up, with their faces well greased to protect from chapping. But the day's trek had kept Zar warm, as did being with Banno, even if he was subdued, still stricken by his brothers' deaths.

They weren't worthy of his grief, she thought, but didn't say: after all, she'd only ever seen them at their worst.

Vidar had been chatting to the other three scouts, but he joined Zar and Banno and asked, 'Can you can get to the far side of the lake before you lose the light?'

'What, you mean unchaperoned?' Zar teased, while Banno looked up hopefully.

'None of my business,' Vidar snorted. 'But the sooner we know what's over there, the less time we waste. I'm sending Ando and Norrin up the glacier a way, to see if they can spot anything helpful. Meanwhile I'll take Tasker back and find Raythe. There's no one out here; you two will be fine so long as you're careful.'

'We will be,' Banno said earnestly.

Excited by this show of trust in them, Zar and Banno clambered over the broken ice where the glacier met the lake to the flat surface beyond. From there it was an easy trot over the ice, heading for the northern side. They hit the shore without mishap and went straight from pure ice to gravel covered in old snow. The light was failing, but they could see that they'd emerged onto a plateau. Then they came upon a tree, rimed and blackened, and then many more, the edge of a forest. They weren't pines, but some more exotic lowland species. The stark bare branches were caked in ice.

'Every tree is dead,' Banno panted. 'It's like we said.'

Unconsciously, they moved closer together as light faded and the mist crept closer. Zar called Adefar into herself, feeling her senses expand as they hurried around the increasingly swampy shore, seeking a place to camp.

'I've got a strange feeling,' she told Banno, in an involuntary whisper. 'It's like we're not alone . . .'

'Damn the thing,' Kemara swore, slamming her fist against her broken cart.

Veet Brayda was dying, but she couldn't stop trying to save him, so she'd stayed behind when the Tolleys moved on, just her and Moss Trimble and poor Veet, and Beca of course. They weren't the last in line, though: Vidar had positioned scouts at the rear and they shouldn't be far behind her. Even so, she was really wishing she hadn't sent Sim

Tolley on. Veet kept coughing up blood and she'd had to stop repeatedly to drain his lungs. Trimble's back was still too painful for him to be any help, so he mostly slept.

Then the axle broke, her cart collapsed and the spokes of one wheel snapped, throwing her off and tossing around her two patients, who'd been lying side by side in the back, sending Veet into another coughing fit. Trimble's stitches broke open yet again, but she still had to get the sailor to help her with Veet. All the while Beca, trapped in a crooked harness, brayed at them in fury.

She managed to free Beca, then lifted the cart enough for Moss to slide a box beneath to prop it up. Then they stared at the cart and wondered what to do next.

'I can't leave anything behind,' she told Moss. 'These are the caravan's entire medical supplies.'

'They shouldn't have let you fall behind,' he noted.

'But they did,' she grumbled, 'and really, it's my own fault. I'm the one who sent Tolley on his way.'

'He should've stayed regardless,' Trimble growled, in a way that gave her pause. He'd been nothing but cheerily affable so far, but right now there was something dangerous in his face. But then he shrugged and was himself again. 'They'll miss us, for sure. Probably think you stopped off for a romantic evening with your favourite patient.'

'Piss off,' she laughed, relieved to be back on familiar ground. 'I don't fancy Veet at all.' She looked up at the darkening skies. For the first time in days the sky had an air of menace. 'We can't fix this and it's too late in the day anyway. There're scouts behind us. Let's make camp, feed them when they arrive and deal with it in the morning.'

Moss gazed up at the churning clouds, nodded, and said, 'Aye, but it's going to be a bad night, I'm thinking.'

Kemara had to do most of the work herself, but Moss pitched in as best he could, seeing to Veet's comfort while she hauled the gear from the cart and pushed it all against the leeward wall, then pitched the tent. She picketed Beca and fed her some grain, before hauling her small stack of firewood into a crevice where she could build a fire.

But when she came to the tapers, they were soaked – they'd fallen in the snow when the cart tipped – and with that discovery came the first whistle of the winds howling down the gorge and whipping at the tent. In seconds the pegs had been ripped out; a moment later the sheltering cover had been torn away and sent flying. She shrieked after it as despair settled in her stomach.

They'll find our bodies in the morning, she thought with a shudder, then chided herself. 'Come on, Moss – let's pile everything against this wall. We'll shelter in here.'

They lugged everything crucial up against the mouth of the narrow crevice, building a low wall of boxes packed with snow to hold together, while Beca bleated anxiously. She could see more of Trimble's wounds had opened again, the bloody marks soaking through his shirt as he laboured beside her, shoulder to shoulder and hip to hip.

'Rest now,' she told him. 'I'll light the fire, then see to your back.'

He looked at her, and then the ruined tapers. 'Do you have others?'

'No. I'm going to have to use the praxis . . . You all right with that?'

He tensed up, but said, 'Do what you must.' Then he winked. 'It'll be cosy.'

Oh Deo, am I going to be fighting him off tonight? Her stomach clenched, the reflex of years spent pushing people away, even though Moss seemed decent enough. But she had walls inside her he'd never have suspected.

'Stay back,' she warned. 'I need to concentrate.' *Mostly, I need you to back off.*

His eyes narrowed slightly, but his annoyance was momentary. 'I've not seen magic up close.'

'It's not a sideshow,' she snapped. 'Keep Beca calm. I'll be linking to a familiar spirit, then using words and signs to instruct it. It only takes a few moments and fire is easy. Just don't distract me.'

She turned from him and spoke the forbidden words just loud

enough to reach spectral ears – that meant Moss would hear them too, but he wouldn't know that it wasn't Old Magnian she used. *'Kaneska alla mizra.'*

Buramanaka touched her mind, a hot caress that conveyed hungry eagerness.

'Cuzka inim kasai,' she instructed, while tracing the Aldar rune.

The fire burst into life and the familiar danced in the flames, causing the smoke to swirl into the shape of his masked visage. Behind her, Moss sucked in his breath and she hurriedly called out, *'Saru–'* in dismissal, and when Buramanaka resisted, *'Ima saru!'*

The flames all but went out as the spirit was sucked into the nebulum and vanished.

She spun to find Moss Trimble holding her knife.

For a moment she feared for her life, but even as she found her tongue, a voice called, *'Kemara?'*

She didn't take her eyes off Trimble, who looked at her and then the fire. 'I thought I saw–' he began.

He saw the face of Buramanaka in the smoke. Damn it!

'It was nothing,' she assured him, pulling the knife from his unresisting hand and placing it beside her cooking implements again. 'Someone's here,' she told him.

Trimble's face closed right up as the voice outside their little niche called again. *'KEMARA?'*

'In here,' she shouted, recognising Raythe's voice as the Otravian appeared at the mouth of the small crevice, holding a horse's reins. Jesco Duretto was behind him as usual, his serenely handsome face taking in her and Moss with a knowing smile that set her teeth on edge.

Bloody men – the first thing they think of when a woman's alone is that she's available.

'Lord Vyre, fancy being pleased to see you,' she drawled. 'Our cart broke an axle and a wheel.'

'I saw,' Vyre replied. He tossed Jesco his reins and the Shadran set about securing their mounts beside Beca, then dragging the broken cart to the mouth of the crevice. Raythe edged in and checked on the unconscious Veet Brayda, then asked, 'Have you seen the scouts? Mytcha and Rabb Colston were at the rear today and I've not passed them yet.'

'I've not seen them,' she replied, coming to her feet. Trimble struggled up beside her. He looked somewhat flustered, and no more pleased to see Vyre than she was. 'I was the last in the line when the cart tipped.'

'Then we have a problem.' Vyre gestured to the outside. 'Come and see.'

He led them out into sleet and swirling snow and around the next bend, just a dozen yards onwards. From there they could see the gorge widening into a small, steep-sided valley – and the orange flickers just visible through the swirling snow suggested at least a dozen bonfires burning at the far end.

'Are you sure there were no wagons behind us?' Kemara asked, while Moss just stared, his face a mask.

'None,' Raythe said. 'You're the last, and the scouts haven't reported in. I'm afraid that those must be imperial men, and that Mytcha and Rabb Colston have been taken or killed.'

His words felt like a crushing stone placed on her chest, which was just one of the many ghastly ways that mizra-witches were made to suffer. More and more weight was added until they suffocated.

No one ever escapes the empire.

4

Ice on fire

Toran Zorne stared down at the bonfires as the storm winds battered at him and the three fugitives, wondering what to do. Fate had delivered him Raythe Vyre, after so many months of futile pursuit – but he had no weapon, and Jesco Duretto was here too.

And Kemara Solus is a mizra-witch . . .

That shock paralysed him more than anything else. Vyre was just another mission, set him by his Ramkiseri overlords and their friends, the Mandaryke family. Just another bounty.

But she's *a mizra-witch . . .*

The moment he'd heard her spell-words and realised she was conjuring *mizra*, he'd been terrified that the demon she'd conjured would recognise what he was. He'd been moments from plunging the dagger into her back when she turned and saw the blade, and then Vyre had shouted and he realised that the Otravian had to be another of them – another witch, another servant of the Pit. Kemara's humanity, her healing skills, her earthy humour and stubborn kindness, were as much a mask as his. This was a den of vipers, a cabal of devils, and his life hung in the balance.

Faced with that, he'd retreated back into the Trimble identity. *I've killed other sorcerers before,* he reminded himself. *I've killed Shadran blademasters too. I'll take them all – when the time is right.* Attempting anything right now would be suicidal, and in any case, no one truly knew what a mizra-witch could do.

It's said that one witch is more powerful than a dozen sorcerers, because their familiars have had centuries longer to accumulate power.

But his task – *infiltrate and strike* – hadn't changed, and now his allies were close. Tomorrow morning might bring this all to an end. New plans formed in his mind as they returned to the crevice and huddled together beside the witch's fire. Smoke chimneyed upwards in swirls and though the wind howled down the ravine, it only brushed their shelter.

Jesco set about repairing the cart's axle; shortening it enough so that the wheels still rolled independently, then replacing the broken spokes. It wouldn't be as robust as before, but they'd be able to move it come dawn. Kemara cooked, while Raythe and Zorne prepared bedrolls.

'I can take first watch,' Zorne offered, seeking opportunity.

'No need,' Jesco replied, from the mouth of the crevice. 'You're injured, and I'm used to sleepless nights.'

He knew better than to argue, especially when Kemara said, 'Let me look at your back. I'm sure Lord Vyre can cook.' She and Vyre swapped places and Zorne let Kemara pull off his bloodied shirt, wincing as more scabs broke. 'I feel like I'm going to be repairing these damned stitches for the rest of my life,' she remarked.

'You're that desperate to keep me around?' he quipped.

'Krag off,' she snorted, and she got to work, pulling out the broken threads, gently massaging in a lotion to prevent new infection, then getting to work with her needles.

All the while Zorne could feel Jesco Duretto studying his bare torso, but he didn't let the gaze of the man – an unashamed pervert – unsettle him. He'd played that role before, too: sometimes there was no other way to get close to the target.

Jesco winked, then chuckled as 'Trimble' flipped a finger in response.

'So, Lord Vyre,' Kemara said, kneeling behind him. 'What do we do about those Bolgravs?'

Vyre glanced up. 'I have a few ideas.' He leaned over and whispered in her ear.

Whatever he said, Kemara looked shocked. 'Is that even possible?'

'With the power we can generate,' Vyre replied, 'anything's possible.'

Those words confirmed all Zorne's suspicions. *They're both mizrawitches . . . and they must be stopped.*

⊕

The two scouts should have been dead already. Larch Hawkstone's Borderers had been scouting ahead of the main Bolgrav forces, presumably following Vyre's people up the glacier, although they'd seen little sign that anyone had passed this way. Persekoi told him that Vyre was concealing their tracks with sorcery, an uneasy thought.

Given that, Hawkstone's group hadn't pushed too hard to catch up, but by late afternoon they reached a wider section of the canyon, where they'd surprised two of Vyre's scouts. An arrow to the back took one down and they'd surrounded the other before he could run.

Hawkstone knew them both: Mytcha and Rabb Colston, farmers from Teshveld who'd vanished with the rest of Vyre's people. They'd pulled the arrow out of Mytcha's back – it hadn't hit anything critical – then handed them over to the Bolgravs, even though they were just two ordinary lads caught up in someone else's schemes.

But Persekoi gave the Colston brothers to the Izuvei sorcerers, and that's when things got bad.

First the sorcerers, an old man and a woman who might have been his sister, lit a bonfire, then they carved a huge hexagon into the ice and after stripping the Colstons and inking them with runes, strapped them to two wooden cross-beams set in the middle.

Most of the Bolgravian soldiers found other things to do rather than watch, and after a few minutes, so did his own men, but Hawkstone was morbidly fascinated.

Know your enemy, he told himself. *Learn their ways.*

The blind sorcerers took up position on either side of the scouts and began carving more symbols on the air while chanting, calling their familiars to them; that much Hawkstone could follow. He watched as they drew energy from the bonfire into themselves and reshaped it until shifting faces with leering eyes appeared in the flames – then the firelight flowed like liquid into the carved hexagon, lighting it up some-how without melting the ice.

Mytcha and Rabb tried to scream, but they'd been well-gagged: this was avalanche country, after all. They strained at their bonds while the blind sorcerers chanted, gesticulating in graceful patterns.

Then the real horror began.

The surface of the glacier within the hexagon became a sea of blue-white hands and arms that rose and crawled towards the two men, first seizing their legs, then slithering up their limbs. Their eyes bulged, their mouths worked behind the tight gags, they fought the bindings until they bled, but the ice slowly engulfed them, overwhelming thighs, hips, waists and chests, making their body temperature plummet.

Finally, only their heads were free – and still they twisted and writhed, when they should have been dead: something in the sorcery was preserving the spark of life, but it wasn't sparing them the harm or the pain. Beneath the ice, their skin peeled, revealing muscles and ten-dons that strained and stretched and tore in spurts of gore.

They *should* have been dead. If he'd dared, Hawkstone would have killed them himself, out of mercy, but all the gold in Shamaya wouldn't have induced him to interrupt these two horrific practitioners.

'This is power that wins empire,' Komandir Alexi Persekoi remarked, joining him, his voice slurred. The flask in his hand stank of very strong liquor.

'Aye,' Hawkstone croaked.

'When they are done, they will know these two insides outed, yuz,' Persekoi went on, his voice shaky despite the boastful tones. 'No man can withstand. This is *true* power.'

It's a kragging travesty, Hawkstone thought.

'One day, all world will be empire,' Persekoi went on. 'One race under Deo and emperor.'

The Izuvei sorceress snarled something in a guttural voice and Mytcha and Rabb Colston fell apart like slowly shattering vases of pink and scarlet.

Hawkstone turned and vomited. Persekoi slurped from the flask, carefully not looking at the remains of the two men. Then boots approached and Hawkstone turned to see the two blind sorcerers standing before them.

'The man Vyre is seeking istariol,' the woman said, her voice like rustling parchment. 'A motherlode, somewhere upstream.'

Hawkstone felt his eyes bulge, but he remained still and silent, lest this terrible pair decide that saying this in his presence was an error that would require rectifying.

Istariol. Sweet Gerda, so that's what this is all about?

It made sense now: Gospodoi's mission, his death at Vyre's hut and the subsequent disappearance of half the district. Istariol, the powder worth more than gold, had lured the folk of Teshveld all the way here: a dream of the impossible. Almost, he wished he were with them.

Then he looked at the two piles of icy pink sludge that had been two decent but stupid men. *Fact is, they're doomed. Vyre doesn't stand a chance.*

'Come to my tent,' Persekoi told the two sorcerers. 'Tell me all.' Then he remembered Hawkstone. 'You heard nothing, Kapitan. *Nothing*. Yuz?'

'Aye, yuz, whatever,' Hawkstone babbled, backing away under the blind gaze of the sorcerers. 'Nothing at all.'

'Good. Rejoin your men. Be ready to move swift tomorrow.'

It was one of the happiest evenings of Zarelda's life since she and her father fled Otravia. She and Banno made camp alone, chatting and cooking together as if already married. It felt wonderfully natural.

Clouds boiled around the peaks from which they'd emerged, engulfing the mountain, but the wind was gentle here. The air had a strange warmth to it, and a faintly unpleasant smell that reminded her of rotten eggs. Stars gleamed through the ragged clouds and the planetary rings glowed like a blade. It was eerie but beautiful.

'Hey, this isn't bad,' she commented, as they devoured a stew made of dried meat and vegetables; she'd contrived to add some taste by adding mushrooms she'd found. At least, she hoped they were mushrooms. 'Best meal since Teshveld, I reckon.'

'Uh-huh,' Banno replied distractedly, staring up. 'I hope everyone's all right. There's a storm hitting the mountains.'

They watched the distant lightning flashes while huddling together for warmth, until she drew her blanket around his and leaned into him. Inhaling his scent didn't feel awkward – in fact, since agreeing to stay chaste, these little intimacies had become easier, because they knew where the boundaries were.

They cuddled as the fire burned low, Adefar asleep unseen beside them, and discussed what life might bring. 'I want a real life, not as an exile,' Zar said. 'I was twelve when we lost our home.'

'Do you remember it?'

'Of course. We lived in a manor house in the country, outside Perasdyne. My bedroom was bigger than Gravis' taproom and I had everything I could ever have thought of wanting.'

'Sounds wonderful. I shared a room with Poel in a draughty old castle. We were always cold, even in summer. But when I think of fat Bolgravs living there, I get so *angry* – that's why we have to keep fighting.'

'Sure, but we don't have to stop living,' she replied, twisting to look at him and she leaned in for one of his delicious warm kisses.

Then something in the darkness made a clicking noise, that was answered on the opposite side. They froze.

'There's something out there,' she whispered.

When they looked round, she saw the firelight glint briefly on a small disc of light – something like an eye.

They disentangled and Banno added two branches to the fire, keeping one end clear so that they could be used as torches. Once they'd caught, he murmured, 'On my word, we stand and wave these branches.'

Soft footfalls crunched on the frosty ground behind them and Zar tensed, her heart thudding. '*Adefar, praesemino,*' she whispered, and the familiar flowed into her.

'*Klark-klik-klik,*' came that sound again. '*Klark-klik-klark.*' The footfalls sounded closer.

'Now!'

They grabbed the branches, spun and stood, gasping in shock, as big, strangely shaped creatures recoiled from the flames.

It took them both a minute to realise the creatures were huge birds, towering creatures that were double Zar's height, with long necks and eagle-like beaks that were large enough to rip their heads off. There were five in all, two before her, one in front of Banno and two others circling in hungrily, stepping daintily through the snowdrifts, heads bobbing. They had thick body feathers, gaudily coloured in greens and browns and snatches of red, and their beady eyes gleamed. Each walked on giant three-clawed talons, big enough to wrap around her waist.

Then the largest emitted a menacing warble and the closest one lunged – then shrieked and leaped away as Zar instinctively interposed her burning brand and in her fear channelled praxis-energy, so that the brand flared up and the fire almost caught the giant bird's head. It screeched piercingly, dancing backwards, and its fellows all recoiled too, squealing in fury.

'It worked – they don't like the fire, so keep it up,' Banno urged.

Another burst of flames sent the birds skittering back again, but they didn't go too far and moments later were again circling menacingly.

She needed to do more. '*Adefar, accendo nunc!*' she called, drawing Ignus, the rune of fire, making flames belch and swirl around them. The giant birds shrieked and leaped back – then they all abruptly turned and fled into the darkness.

Banno put a hand on her shoulder. 'Deo Above, what are they?'

She shook her head mutely, staring into the dark, fearing they'd all come rushing back at once, but minutes passed and the only sound was the lapping of the narrow band of melted water on the stony shore. 'I think they've gone,' she whispered, releasing Adefar before he became drained. 'That beak was big enough to break a thigh-bone,' she marvelled. 'And those claws! Gerda on High!'

Banno added more branches to the fire, keeping his sword close to hand. 'I've never heard of such things,' he exclaimed. 'They looked like something from the Pit.'

'I think I've seen pictures of them,' Zar said excitedly. 'Those sort of birds lived in the Aldar times.' Then it struck her. 'If they live here, they must prey on something other than people. I told you the air felt warmer.'

Banno clutched her arm. 'The istariol must be here!'

After that, it was impossible to close their eyes, but Zar and Banno tried, huddling together, taking turns at staying awake. It was lovely snuggling beneath the crook of his arm, resting her head on his lap, but she was too excited to sleep. They'd come so far, found paths no one had taken in hundreds of years and actually escaped the empire – and this must be the place they sought.

Father isn't insane after all. Who knew?

Finally, light seeped back into the eastern skies and the distant storm clouds broke up, giving way to a crystal-clear morning. They wolfed down the remainder of their rations, gazing back across the frozen lake.

'We need to get back and tell them what we've found,' Zar said excitedly.

'Let's look around first,' Banno replied. He studied the churned mud outside their campsite and whistled. 'Look at these.' He showed her the taloned footmarks of the giant birds. 'I wonder what they taste like?'

'Chicken, maybe? With the biggest drumsticks ever known.'

'And look!' Banno plucked a green and orange feather from the frosted ground. It was more than a foot long. 'I think that's a tail feather – wait until we show everyone.'

There was an entirely different feel to these dead woods in daylight. The wind was shifting to the northwest, wafting warmer, pungent air into their faces. The ground wasn't the dreary grey they'd expected but was streaked in green moss. They followed a watercourse upstream, exploring deeper into the woods, and though they saw no more giant birds, they heard distant, piercing cries like herons, and the creaking of what might have been a toad.

When Zarelda went to cross the stream, she cried out – the water was warm, with tendrils of vapour rising from the surface.

'Feel it,' she told Banno. 'The water's giving off steam.'

A few paces on they found a pool where bubbles were coming through from the shingle bed. It was much hotter, too, and Zar was half-inclined to strip and hurl herself in: it had been so long – a lifetime ago – since she'd bathed in hot water; she felt like she'd never be able to scrub all the grime from her skin.

Then Banno put his hand on her shoulder and pointed into the woods beyond the pool and all inclination to relax evaporated. There was a wooden arch like a gateway straddling the stream and every inch of it was festooned with stylised demonic faces with big leering eyes and protruding tongues. The bases were carved into the shapes of men, each face fiercer than the one below, culminating in a big reptilian beast at the top of the arch snarling down at them. It was frosted in moss and grime and it looked as old as the dead trees around it.

To Zarelda, it was a sombre reminder that people had once lived here, an ancient race long lost to time.

They're dead and gone, she mused. *Is that what'll happen to us?*

'Here they come,' Raythe muttered unnecessarily.

He'd made what preparations he could make: a summoning circle was etched into the ice with runes and signs to instruct Cognatus, who lurked nearby in the nebulum, ready to enter him at a moment's notice.

But the task before them was practically impossible.

It would do no good simply to block the glacier path: he had to destroy their pursuers so thoroughly that no one would ever be able to return to the garrison at Rodonoi and tell them to send more men. That meant he had to strike when the entire enemy force, perhaps as many as five hundred men, were bunched together. The long valley to the south was too flat for the avalanches that were his best hope; he needed to get them beneath cliffs.

As soon as the storm had cleared, some time before dawn, he'd taken his tiny group half a mile back along the glacier, where he'd seen a natural stone ledge at the north end of a narrow, steep-sided gully. It was better, though still not ideal, for the space below might be too small for all the Bolgravian soldiers, but it would have to do.

Kemara, standing beside him with a pistol in her right hand, was clearly just as scared of her own power as of the enemy. He couldn't quite believe they were going to risk another meld, but he didn't see any other choice. Jesco was above him, perched halfway up the cliff, readying his flintlock, but sorcery would be their prime weapon; Jesco was here to ensure no one took advantage of those moments when the sorcerers would be most vulnerable.

Moss Trimble had been sent back with Kemara's cart. His injuries meant fighting was almost impossible; and in any case, someone had to report to the others if they didn't return. And Raythe didn't know the man: pressganged or not, he'd been an imperial sailor until the last couple of weeks.

Trimble and Kemara had looked pretty cosy when he and Jesco has arrived last night, which gave him an odd twinge. The healer could be infuriating, but there was something compelling about her, and seeing Trimble sniffing around her provoked unexpected anger.

I can't have her distracted from mastering her powers, he told himself. *That's all it is.*

He glanced at her hard-set face as she murmured her own preparatory spells and wondered if she really could control the powers she drew on. Legends of the Mizra Wars spoke of vast explosions of darkness that ate all life, devouring the Aldar and all their works. The healer didn't look like she'd be much of a match for forces like that. But it was too late for second thoughts, for Jesco had spotted the enemy.

'Scouts coming,' he called from above, pulling Raythe back to the here and now.

Six men had emerged at the far end of the gully below, clad in furs and armed with flintlocks. The Bolgravs tended to use local scouts, but even if they were Pelarian, they could afford no mercy.

Raythe looked at Kemara. 'Are you ready for this?'

She gave him a hard stare. 'Are you?' From beneath her cloak she drew the scarlet mask, all teeth and horns and cavernous eyes.

The way it clung to her face, needing no strings, made his hackles rise, but he steeled himself to that sinister presence, stepped into the circle he'd inscribed and called out, '*Cognatus, animus.*' His familiar flooded into him, tingling his nerve endings. '*Praesemino . . . tutela nunc,*' he added, and lines of light ignited in the ice at his feet.

Beside him, Kemara's lips moved, her hands tracing arcane patterns. Her own familiar flowed inside her in a shadowy ripple and her eyes flashed deep crimson.

Then Jesco's flintlock *cracked*, the sound reverberating through the icy canyon, and two hundred yards away, one of the scouts dropped, clutching his chest, while the other five sought cover in the snowdrifts. Shards of ice, shaken free by the gun's report, tumbled down the cliffs on either side.

Three flashes came from down the valley, puffs of smoke erupted and moments later flintlock balls whistled past. Kemara flinched, but Raythe barely noticed: the battlefields of Otravia and Pelaria had taught him to ignore what he couldn't control. '*Cognatus: paratus,*' he snapped, '*sonus magna.*' He gestured to the cliffs above the gully—

—which triggered a massive *boom!* that resounded through the canyon, sending up clouds of snow-dust and shards of ice into the air. Raythe looked around anxiously, fearful the sound might have set off something too near their position, but despite some small falls, it all held. For a full minute the rocks and ice kept sliding down, until the canyon below was partially blocked by sliding snow. He nodded in satisfaction, his purpose fulfilled: the enemy would be forced to bunch together to advance up the middle of the glacier. Moments later the scouts scurried into the distant narrows and vanished, leaving their fallen comrade behind.

'*Cognatus, opperio,*' he said, bidding the familiar wait, then called, 'You all right, Jes?'

'For now,' the Shadran replied. 'Some of those ice-falls got a little close.'

'Kemara?'

'Ready,' she answered. Eerily, the lips of her blood-red mask moved when she spoke.

He didn't like it, but if it helped, he could put up with it. 'Good. Prepare.'

He'd hoped they'd get twenty minutes, but they got only ten before grey-coated Bolgravian soldiers began filing into the canyon and forming up in skirmish lines. Then four horses rumbled in, towing a bombard, and he began to get profoundly nervous. Then came another and the two cannons were hastily unloaded and readied. A contingent of officers arrived and the assault went from pending to imminent.

The nebulum around Kemara was heavy with the presence of her mizra-spirit and Cognatus was simmering with energy inside him, although he felt his familiar quail at that unseen but baleful presence. Gritting his teeth, he told Kemara, 'In ten seconds.'

Those moments vanished in a string of commands, then their minds touched – and *ignited.*

Toran Zorne hadn't gone far.

Thanks to his own spell-work, his flayed back was far better healed than the mizra-witch realised; he'd used a veneer of scarring and bleeding to hide his sorcery-aided recovery. At need, he could run and even fight. Instead of obeying Vyre's command, he drove the cart around the next bend and abandoned it, leaving Veet Brayda asleep but taking the man's flintlock and powder.

My people will overrun Vyre's position, we'll seize control of the caravan and make them reveal where to find the istariol, he thought, finding a vantage behind where Vyre and his cronies were making their stand, just as shots rang out in the ravine. Jesco Duretto was lying on a ledge, exchanging fire with unseen attackers further down the canyon. The two sorcerers – *no, witches* – were on the glacier surface. He could see the ice glowing from protective spells and feel the pressure building in the nebulum.

He crouched behind a boulder a hundred yards away and sighted along the barrel at Vyre's back. It was the closest he could get, but it was still a chancy shot.

If I shoot when others do, I might be able to conceal my attack.

He thumbed the hammer back and took a breath – then came a deep booming sound and as something snapped overhead, he instinctively glanced up and saw a shard of ice break away. He hurled himself aside an instant before it speared the surface of the glacier just where he'd been. He kept rolling, showered in broken ice, as more crashed about him.

By the time he'd ascertained that the cliffs weren't about to collapse on him, the situation had changed: the Bolgravians were no longer shooting and Vyre and Kemara were walking around, which would make aiming problematic.

He was forced to wait again.

Ten minutes passed before Vyre and Kemara returned to their positions. Jesco settled over his gun. From the distance came the calls of Bolgravian officers, muffled by the falling snow.

He settled down to take aim once more.

Simolon leaned into Hawkstone and muttered, 'Here, Captain, are those Bolgies mad?'

'They're Bolgies,' Hawkstone replied. 'They think even nature won't dare touch 'em.'

The Borderers huddled in the lee of a cluster of boulders near the entrance to the ravine, watching the Bolgravs ready the bombards. Given that the light rattle of the flintlocks had been enough to trigger slips on either cliff, Deo only knew what a cannonade would do. But the big boom that had brought down the snow suggested that it wasn't just soldiers they faced here: Vyre was up there somewhere.

And he's forced us to advance in a narrow column, Hawkstone noted. *Even if all he's got up there is a company of men with flintlocks, we're going to have a rough time of it.*

So he called his lads in, telling them, 'Heads down, boys. And if they trigger an avalanche, stay here in the middle.'

Another string of orders rang out around the bombards as a group of horsemen trotted from the narrows, including the four sorcerers. An angry exchange took place, then the gun-crews were stood down. Persekoi, flushed and furious, bawled out his gunnery captain before rounding on his aides and snarling out orders.

'I guess even they can see sense sometimes,' Hawkstone murmured to Simolon.

In a few minutes, sixty-odd infantry men were marched to the fore: enough to make Vyre reveal his hand, but not too many to lose if things went badly. Bayonets were fixed and they advanced up the slope.

'How many d'you reckon'll make it back?' Simolon whispered.

'Too many,' Hawkstone muttered, which worked, no matter the result. Simolon grinned.

As the footmen climbed the slippery slope towards Vyre's position, the four Bolgravian sorcerers arrived, dismounted and formed a loose line. They raised staves above their heads, chanting and carving symbols of light in the air. Around them, little whirlwinds began to dance and shadows shifted under their feet. Hawkstone's arms pricked into goose-bumps as the temperature suddenly dropped.

'How do those blind bastards always know which way to face?' Simolon muttered.

'They can probably hear you from there,' Hawkstone replied. 'And they can see inside you – so shut it.'

He turned to watch the imperial soldiers reach the sharp slope at the top of the valley, just below Vyre's position. There'd been no more firing during their advance, making Hawkstone wonder if they'd run.

Either they've gone, or they've got something up their sleeves. He ducked his head and prayed to Deo that Persekoi wouldn't send them in next.

Kemara had a moment's doubt, wondering if this was the last thing she would ever do, but the mask on her face felt like armour and the mizra was like dancing on a volcano, so when Raythe Vyre said, 'Now—' she was ready.

'*Kaneska alla mizra,*' she snapped, the darkness boiled and Buramanaka snarled. '*Shiku shita kori,*' she added, sending the ravenous spirit's awareness beneath the surface of the glacier, seeking the rock below—

—and the istariol Raythe had noticed earlier, a core of blood-dust running from its source to the sea.

I hope the kragging Bolgies don't know about it, she worried as the footmen below halted, unshouldered their guns and took aim. She and Raythe were in the open, gazing down their barrels.

Dear Gerda, protect us . . .

As the Otravian directed his praxis-spirit, she called to Buramanaka, '*Kaneska, shiku istari.*' Her awareness followed her familiar down through the ice to where the precious red powder ran like a thread through the very bottom of the ice current. The mizra-spirit latched onto it and she sensed glee.

A flintlock fired, Jesco Duretto getting his retaliation in first, and she heard a sharp cry of pain below. Someone barked an order and Raythe's voice snapped, '*Now.*'

'*Kaneska, moyasu istari ima,*' she commanded, as Vyre said the same in Old Magnian: *Burn the istariol now.*

And an instant later the entire section of ice before them, two hundred yards of dirty white glacier, was lit from below by a scarlet flash, streaking the faces of the Bolgravian soldiers and causing them to look down in sudden fright. A few instinctively pulled their triggers, flint-locks belched smoke and fire and lead balls whistled around her.

Then the entire section of glacier below exploded, throwing great chunks of ice and fountains of suddenly liquefied scalding water into the sky. The soldiers barely had time to shriek in terror before the surface bulged and broke, engulfing them in ice and churning water. Then those behind them went down as the meltwater surged down the slope, billowing clouds of super-heated steam. A pile of boulders in the middle held firm, an islet where a few men managed to cling on, but the bombards plunged into the maelstrom and were gone, along with riders and footmen.

But at the far end, she could see four figures still standing, each atop a pillar of ice that had somehow resisted the burst of energy.

Then Vyre shouted, '*Lagus, impetus*—' and drew her deeper into the meld and suddenly, all she could feel was *him*: his smell, his taste, his energy, his will. It was like being thrust into his arms naked, but *far* more. She could read his intent and blending her will to his, shouted, '*Mizu suishin suru*—' impelling the water ever faster.

She could see them – Buramanaka and Cognatus, like angels of dark and light, hostile but yoked together. Something that was greater than either of them coursed through them and her whole body arched in pain-pleasure. Her feet left the ground, her mouth venting a howl of ecstatic agony; beside her, Vyre was doing the same and she felt all he did, all that exquisite torment.

A moment later, the mountains of ice still piled on the cliffs on either side, plus everything that had already fallen into the ravine, boiled together into a torrent, bursting against the four pillars of ice and smashing two of them down and she sensed two of the figures spinning away into the flood.

But the remaining two were resilient as granite, and she could have sworn she saw blind milky orbs that pierced her to the bone. She struck as they did and their powers met in the middle like giant glass hammers that shattered upon each other, and the concussion hurled her

311

and Vyre backwards, sending them tumbling across the surface of the glacier. She fetched up in a snowdrift, battered and dazed.

Then someone loomed over her and despite her dizziness, she recognised a gun: she snapped a shriek that Buramanaka turned into a command and the shape was battered away.

Raythe had been ripped from her senses, Buramanaka was howling through her and the pit of inner darkness around which she danced suddenly tilted towards her.

And this *is how we lose control*, she realised as she tried to rise to fight. *This is how the mizra takes us.* The world spun again and she began to fall–

But someone grabbed her arm, the world steadied and Raythe's psyche anchored her once again to the here and now. Her feet planted, she shouted, '*Kaneska yameru*,' and slammed the door in Buramanaka's face.

Instantly, the mizra-spirit was gone and she was back. She ripped the mask from her face and stared up at Vyre, her skin flushed, her body burning up and soaked with perspiration. She had an impulsive desire to *bite* him, to *crush* him, to burrow into him and never emerge –

. . . then she remembered herself and shoved him away.

'Are you all right?' Raythe panted, as her hyper-awareness of him receded. His brow beaded in sweat and his hands were shaking. 'Kemara? Talk to me.'

'I'm fine,' she snapped, angry to have been the one who failed. 'I'm sorry, I couldn't hold it. What happened?'

He steadied her, then helped her stand and pointed down the valley.

Below their perch, she could see the gully was now bare of ice: the liquefied glacier had swept almost everything away, including all four of the icy pillars where the imperial sorcerers had made their stand. Bodies dotted the ground, but a dozen men were clinging to a small pile of boulders at the far end. The remains of the bombards were piled against the bottom rock, smashed beyond repair.

She stared, then mumbled, 'Well done, I suppose. I'm sorry I wasn't more help.'

Raythe gave her a puzzled look. 'Kemara, that was *mostly* you.'

'What?'

'You were like riding a runaway bull – I just clung on and occasionally tugged on the horns to steer you.'

She stared, trying to take that in.

Someone groaned behind her and she turned. To her surprise, Moss Trimble was lying on his back, winded and gasping. Beside him lay a flintlock, the long barrel twisted at right angles.

Jesco slithered down from his perch and stalked towards the sailor. 'What are *you* doing here?'

'Came back,' Moss panted. 'Shamed to be runnin'.' He sat up, grimacing at the movement. His back was streaked with blood again.

I nearly killed Moss, but Raythe dragged me back from the precipice, she realised, appalled at what she might have done. 'Moss, I couldn't see straight – I didn't know it was you.'

He gave her an unsteady look, but nodded. 'Heat of battle. I had no business being there.'

'But you came back to help,' she said, conscious of the others watching. 'Thank you for that.'

He was willing to risk himself for me.

Only Ionia had ever risked death for her, so Moss's act threw her into a swirl of gratitude and confusion. Then she recalled the way Raythe Vyre had taken over her senses during the meld and felt overloaded with *otherness*, as if she were a silent party in her own body, a secondary presence that might be ousted at any moment. Scared by the sensation, she stammered, 'Sorry, sorry, sorry,' and stumbled away.

The three men were all staring at her, but she regained her self-possession and focused on Trimble, who looked confused, as well he might. 'It's all right, Moss. I'll be okay in a moment.'

She wasn't, though – all the stored-up terror of standing in full view of the guns, the lead balls pinging around her that but for sheer luck could have buried themselves in her, and most of all, the glorious potency that had plunged through her, impaled her and ridden her to rack and ruin. It all combined to make her legs go weak, so she dropped to her knees, hugging herself and shaking.

That first time at the beach was just scratching the surface. This time, I almost lost it all.

'Hey,' Raythe said gently, reaching down to pull her up, 'you got through.'

She knew he was trying to be nice, but she just couldn't stand his presence right then. She snarled, 'Don't kragging touch me. Keep your blasted chivalry to yourself.'

Raythe straightened, his face hardening. 'You need to improve your control,' he snapped.

That, unfortunately, was true. 'I'll do it,' she blurted, jerking her gaze away. *I have to.*

Raythe looked doubtful, but Moss Trimble said with quiet sincerity, 'I believe in you.'

It was a small thing, but it gave her the strength to go on.

Toran Zorne walked to the edge of the stony lip that now marked the end of the glacier. The small canyon below, only minutes ago filled with ice, was now scoured stone. A few dozen scouts were all that remained of the Bolgravian force. *Deo on High, am I on my own?*

When Vyre joined him, it took considerable strength not to flinch from him. 'Trimble, I told you to go back to the caravan,' the Otravian said tersely.

'I couldn't leave –'

'You'll do as you're told in future. If that had gone wrong, no one would have known what happened, or got any warning. I thought naval men could take orders?'

Zorne hung his head, his Trimble mask now fully in place. 'Sorry, milord.' Pointing down the ravine, he asked, 'So is the whole glacier gone?'

'I doubt it,' Vyre replied. 'I only sensed the effect for a few hundred yards, a mile at most.'

A mile . . . they melted a mile of glacier. That's unheard of.

'What will you do now?' he asked. 'Kill the rest?'

'That's not so easy. There's still dozens of them out there and I can't repeat that trick. The best I can hope for is that they're dissuaded from following and don't make it home.'

That could happen, Zorne worried, *but my empire never gives up. Someone will come. In the meantime, I must lay low.* The thought of having to cosy up to these snakes any longer was horrifying, but he steeled himself for the task. *I'm a trained agent of the Ramkiseri,* he reminded himself. *I can endure anything.*

'What did you do?' he asked, seeking reassurance that Vyre didn't completely overmatch him.

'I used the istariol traces in the glacier to melt it,' Vyre replied. 'Well, I say "I" but it was mostly Kemara.' He glanced sideways at Zorne. 'You should stay away from her. She needs all her concentration to master her powers.'

Zorne pretended to contemplate his words in the way he imagined Trimble would have. *I see him as a loyal man, quietly reassuring to those around him.* 'Perhaps my friendship will anchor her?' he suggested, pleased at the seafaring terminology in his response.

Vyre sniffed, 'It's your life,' and stalked away.

Is he jealous? Zorne wondered. Relationships were a mystery, but perhaps Vyre desired the witch? They were of a kind, even if they often argued.

Perhaps that's something I can exploit?

He found himself gazing at Kemara and when she saw, he tried a smile – and she responded in kind. Perhaps she was softening? *I'll be her blind spot – and then the dagger in her heart.*

PART THREE
Ancient and Always

Poumahi

'It's a poumahi,' Mater Varahana announced, examining the carved arch over the steaming river. 'It's an Aldar word – it's got two meanings. In this case, it signifies a kind of totem, like those the Krodesh use to mark their territory.'

Raythe, Vidar, Kemara and Elgus studied the relic. 'What's the other meaning?' Raythe asked.

'Ghost-watcher.'

That wiped the smile from Jesco's face.

It had taken Raythe three days to catch up with the expedition and move everyone off the glacier and across the frozen lake into the dead forest. He prayed the survivors crawling home didn't make it, but had to admit that bloody-minded persistence was a defining characteristic of the Bolgravian Empire.

The brief spell of fine weather had given way to fog and low cloud which rendered the world a grey blur. But they'd been hearing bird-life, and some had even glimpsed the giant birds that had attacked Zar and Banno; in the daylight they looked to be flightless.

'Whoever left it here is as dead as this forest,' Elgus Rhamp said. 'Let's use it for firewood.'

'No,' Raythe replied, 'there's plenty of dead wood without destroying such an ancient artefact. Pass the word down the column: no one touches these things. Vidar, have the scouts returned?'

'Foaley got back in an hour ago,' the Norgan ranger replied. 'He says there're no trails, but the undergrowth died away a long time ago, so it'll be easy to pick our path. He found three more of these poles with faces, by the way.'

'Perhaps they mark a trail?' Raythe suggested. 'Regardless, we'll follow the river as best we can. I've found istariol traces in it: the motherlode's upstream and it can't be far.'

They reacted with subdued excitement: they could almost *taste* success, three months after leaving Teshveld and the empire behind.

'We're a hundred miles north of Verdessa and the last imperial outpost,' he reminded them. 'There's no one out here and anything we find is ours. We just need to keep together now.'

'For a change,' Kemara put in.

'Aye,' Vidar agreed, 'everyone must keep in sight of another wagon. We'll travel as fast as our slowest wagon.'

There was a chorus of agreement and Raythe added, 'And if we find *anything* odd, I want to see it. I'll be with the vanguard today – I need to ensure the river is still carrying istariol. We don't want to bypass the place we need through carelessness.' He watched them process that. 'Any questions? Then let's get underway.'

'Can you feel it?' Kemara murmured to Beca, stroking the mule's mane to encourage her as she tugged the cart up out of another dip, following the wheel ruts left by Relf Turner's wagon. 'It's getting warmer and drier.' She scratched between the mule's ears. 'You'll appreciate that, won't you, girl?'

They'd spent the day slowly crawling through the murky forest, but now they'd started climbing and the forest was coming to life around them. The riverbanks rose several feet above the surface and the water was running faster, but despite the ascent, the air was no colder.

'Are you talking to your mule?' a merry voice asked and Zarelda appeared from the mist.

'Of course,' Kemara chuckled. 'Beca won't go anywhere without being asked nicely.'

Zarelda glanced at Moss in the driver's seat, wrapped in blankets. He waved, but she ignored him.

'He's an imperial,' the girl muttered. 'Watch out for him.'

'He was pressganged,' Kemara replied, 'and right now I'm grateful he's recovered enough to drive, because Regan Morfitt's going to give birth any day now and I can't drive and midwife at once.'

'Even so,' Zar muttered. 'How's poor old Veet?'

'No better,' Kemara sighed. 'His lungs are just about gone and nothing I try is working.'

A fully trained healer-sorcerer would know a way, she thought bitterly, but she was insufficient to the task and Vyre knew little more.

She put that aside with an effort, and asked, 'How're your praxis lessons going?'

'Dad's too busy for me,' Zar grumbled, 'but I can reach it easier and easier. What about you?'

Kemara frowned. 'I'm too busy too.'

Clearly Vyre had kept his promise not to tell anyone about her mizra 'problem', so she wasn't about to. She could just imagine the conversation. 'Oh, by the way, I'm a witch and by rights should be burned alive' wasn't a great opening line.

'I don't know how you can think about other things,' Zar exclaimed. 'Magic's more important than *anything*.'

'No,' she replied, 'my patients are.'

Just then, Veet Brayda coughed weakly, then fell silent.

'One day, I'm going to find a spell that fixes pneumonia,' Zar declared, then added, 'Best get on. Vidar has us running perimeter patrols and I've got this flank.' She waved and trotted away.

'Bright girl,' Moss commented.

'She is,' Kemara replied. 'How's your back holding up?'

'I'm getting by,' Moss answered laconically, 'but I don't think Veet's breathing.'

Oh krag . . . Kemara walked back as Moss reined in, peered into the cart and flinched. Veet was lying open-eyed, blood drying on one corner of his mouth. She reached in to feel his pulse, then let out a heavy breath. 'Aye, he's gone.'

'Do we bury him here?'

'No, we'll wait until we camp tonight. Least we can do is give those who knew him a chance to say farewell.'

Moss made the Sign of Gerda and she closed Veet's eyes and covered him, thinking, *How many have died on the road, so far? Eighteen? Twenty? And the worst is probably yet to come.* 'Deo take his soul,' she murmured.

'Aye,' Moss said, then he clicked his tongue and Beca heaved the cart into motion again.

'That damned beast obeys you better than me,' she grumbled.

'It's my charm,' the Pelarian sailor replied. 'And my gentle touch.'

She rolled her eyes at him and snorted, but found herself concealing a smile as she walked back to her place beside Beca. It'd been a long time since a man had made her smile, but Moss could. He was steadily clearing her hurdles, though he still had a way to go.

Then she heard an agonised wail from the Morfitts' wagon, just ahead.

Oh Gerda, she groaned. She went for her birthing gear, thinking that while Veet's death was sad, life kept on begetting life.

Hunger woke Zarelda on a frigid morning where the steaming breath of men and beasts hung over the camp like ground mist. But after the austerity of the trek up the glacier, hope now sustained them too.

Today, we're going hunting.

Her father was already awake, as always, discussing the food supplies with Jesco and Vidar. She gave them a vague wave and went to pee, squatting over the trench beside a village girl who might as well have been a different species entirely, dressed neatly as she was in her cotton dress and ribbons.

'Good luck today,' the girl breathed. She was probably Zar's age, but pale and sheltered, barely touched by the hardships of the road: a hollyhock, the sort of girl Zar normally despised. But looking more closely, she saw the girl's hands were chafed from hard work, and there was no spare fat on her. She too was pulling her weight, just in a different way.

'Thanks,' Zarelda replied. 'Um–?'

'Sheena Grigg,' the girl answered. 'Is it true the birds out there are ten foot tall?'

'At least – and really dangerous, with huge beaks and claws. But we know what we're doing.' She struck a manly pose. 'We'll catch plenty, enough to feed the whole caravan.'

Sheena gazed admiringly, but without envy. 'I'm learning to cook, to be the best wife a man could want.'

Well, it's an ambition, Zarelda thought. They finished peeing and Zar hurried back to camp, thankful that her own horizons were wider.

I'm lucky, she reflected. *There was no guarantee I'd become a sorcerer.* But even if she hadn't, she couldn't ever have seen herself as a typical wife, and even less so out here. *I'm going to be like Tami, wild and free.*

'Be careful,' her father told her, as they wolfed down their meagre breakfast. 'These flightless birds sound dangerous.' Then he grinned. 'I wish I was coming too.'

Instead, he'd be spending the day seeking istariol traces in the river. That was vital, of course, but for once she felt like she had the more important role. The caravan's provisions were almost gone and starvation was a real and present threat.

'I'll save you a tail feather,' she smirked as she got ready. 'You can wear it in your hat.'

'Sure,' her father said, giving her a hug. 'Take care, don't get hurt, follow instructions and–'

'I'll be fine,' she told him, scampering off; after all, she now knew more about hunting than he did. Collecting her bow and arrows and the torch she'd prepared the previous night, she set out to meet Banno, feeling intrepid and not a little nervous.

The hunters were gathering, exchanging greetings, and Zarelda felt proud to be the only woman in the group. She'd gained a reputation as an excellent archer, as well as being stealthy and possessing good bush-sense.

A crowd had gathered to see the two-dozen-strong hunting party off, so Cal Foaley drew them into a circle. 'I won't brief you here, with half the camp listening in. Give 'em a wave, then follow me out.' Then he led them into the woods, to cheers that quickly faded.

'Sleep well?' Zar asked Banno.

'Would've slept better with you beside me,' he whispered, and they shared a smile, remembering the night alone by the lake. Even the frightening encounter with the giant birds now felt romantic.

Maybe next time we won't hold back, she mused, feeling a little hot and bothered, but in a pleasant way, buoyed along by a giddy sense of possibility.

They reached a clearing, where Foaley gathered them in. 'Right then, listen up. Gan Corbyn's found a flock of the beasties – Mater Varahana says they're called phorus birds, if you like proper names – in a glade west of here. So we're going to split up: some will head for the river and set up snares and archery stations at the crossing. That's the anvil. The rest are with me and we'll form the hammer. We'll drive the flock into a trap and with luck net the lot – that's about forty birds.'

A few men vented low whistles and one asked, 'Are they really twice a man's height?'

'Zar and I have seen 'em,' Banno replied. 'They've got claws like daggers and beaks that could crack a skull.'

Some looked disbelieving, but Gan Corbyn backed him. 'I seen 'em too, just an hour ago.'

Having a full adult verify the tale made it real, apparently, because the hunters all nodded, which made Zar quietly fume.

Foaley gestured for silence. 'These aren't cattle we're hunting, but predators in their own right. Varahana says the old records spoke of these creatures hunting in packs and being able to run like deer. Respect them.'

'Don't get close,' Gan Corbyn added. 'It's arrows and spears, and fire-brands to drive 'em before us.'

'I can light the torches without needing a fire,' Zarelda put in, earning some uneasy glances.

'Good,' Foaley said shortly, 'that'll reduce the chances of them detecting us before we're ready to drive them. Beaters, step to my left: you'll be with me. Trappers and archers to my right; you'll remain here with Gan. Now, any questions before we go?'

Everyone signed readiness and off they went. Zar stayed close to Banno as they began their circuitous trek through the forest, seeking the right point from which to drive the flock towards the river.

A few minutes in, a hunter named Goskyll jogged in beside Banno. 'So,' he puffed, 'one of the mighty Rhamps is actually doin' something useful, eh? About time.'

'Banno's been scouting and hunting all along,' Zarelda retorted, 'as you bloody well know.'

'Aye, but he's the only one, ain't he?' Goskyll replied. 'Rest just piss around in camp, causing trouble.'

'We're fighting men, not hunters,' said Banno equitably.

'Fighting men? More like farting men, stinking the camp out.'

'If you've got nothing to say, you can krag off,' Zarelda told Goskyll. 'You think you're better than them, fine; but Banno's one of us.'

Goskyll's belligerent face twisted into scorn. 'So the Rhamp lets his woman do his talking, does he?'

'Zar's not my woman—' Banno went to say, his earnest face turning angry.

'Nah, 'course she's not,' Goskyll jeered. 'Can't be, when you're not even a man.'

'You shut your mouth,' Zarelda warned, as Banno put his hand to his hilt.

Seeing that, Goskyll fondled his own weapon. 'You in for a beating, Rhamp?'

'Just piss off,' Banno replied, sounding boyish before the full-grown hunter.

Goskyll might be older, but to Zar, he reeked of belligerent stupidity, the sort who couldn't keep more than one idea in his head at a time.

'Just leave us alone,' she warned, 'or I'll tell my father—'

Goskyll wrinkled his nose, but he also appeared to take on board the reminder of who she was. 'Oh, you going to whine from behind the skirts of 'is Lordship now, Princess? Pampered brats deserve each other.' He spat at Banno's feet, but contented himself with sneering, 'You're not wanted out here, Rhamp, and nor are your father's thugs. Watch your back.'

Banno looked angry, but Zarelda knew he didn't have the streak of violence this man showed, so she was relieved when, after a tense few moments, he removed his hand from his sword. No doubt to Goskyll it looked like cowardice, but not to her.

'Anytime you want a real man, you come find me,' the hunter leered at her. 'I'll give you a proper seeing to.' With that he swaggered away.

She grabbed Banno's arm and feeling him shaking, hugged him, to hold him in place. Goskyll would tear him apart, but she didn't think less of him for that. The miasma of violence that hung round men like Goskyll made her feel ill. 'Forget him,' she urged. 'You're more of a man than he'll ever be.'

'I'll get stronger, I'll practise my sword-drill—'

'I don't care. What's important is that you don't ever turn out like that pig. He's more of an animal than anything he hunts.' She kissed his cheek and held him until his tension dissipated.

Eventually Banno calmed, but she could still sense his shame. She wondered what it must be like for him, to be the sensitive one in a violent, brutal camp like his.

'Where was he when we first found these birds, anyway?' she said, putting energy into her voice. 'Let's go hunting and show them all.'

The journey proceeded without further incident through an increasingly *living* forest that nevertheless had a sinister sense of abandonment and decay. Mist soaked up any noise and conversation drained away, silenced by the eerie landscape.

About half an hour after leaving the trappers behind, they reached a small clearing at the foot of a low hill, where Gan Corbyn's son Tasker was waiting to monitor the flock of phorus birds. He reported that they'd unearthed a warren of cat-sized rodents and were feeding ruthlessly.

'You should see them move,' Tasker Corbyn enthused. 'They swarmed over these huge rats an' just *slaughtered* them – they're digging up the last few nests, just over that rise.'

Zarelda strained her ears, fancying she could hear their calls.

'Then the smell of their feeding should mask our approach,' Foaley said. 'Thanks to Zarelda and Banno we know they don't like fire, so let's make sure they fear us.' He ran through the details again: they would light their torches and fan out in a horseshoe formation, then drive the flock towards the river crossing. 'It should take us about twenty minutes to get them where we want them, so long as we keep it tight. Close up as you go and don't flinch if they rush you. We don't want them panicking, just scared enough to back off.'

There's only a dozen of us and more than forty birds, Zarelda worried, remembering those giant, mad-eyed creatures with their terrifying beaks. *If they just turn and charge us, we'll get mowed down.* She fancied everyone was thinking the same, but they were out of meat and desperate. Voicing such fears wouldn't help.

'Zarelda,' Foaley commanded, 'light us up.'

She'd never produced a spell on demand for anyone but her father, but Adefar came at her call, giving her the confidence to conjure flame and light the men's torches from the palm of her hand. They all looked impressed, though some, like Goskyll, were still undressing her with their eyes, making her seethe inside.

'Right,' said Foaley, 'we've got about an hour of flame, so let's get moving.' They fanned out, Zar and Banno going left, and once Foaley signed them forwards, they moved into the trees, losing sight of all but those immediately to the left and right, who were just dark silhouettes trailing orange flames. Zar had Banno to her left and Goskyll on her right, which she didn't like at all, but she concentrated on picking her way forward down the slope into a thicket, where she heard the phorus birds straight ahead.

They reached a patch of torn-up earth, the scars of the birds' claws like wounds in the soil. The dog-sized rats Tasker had described were lying everywhere, limbs torn from bodies, their abdomens ripped open and the insides devoured. The air stank of blood and foulness, making Zar's stomach churn.

Torches closed in on either side, forming a cordon as they advanced, and she heard scrabbling claws, squabbling birds and the shrieking of cornered rats. Then from somewhere to her right, Cal Foaley began to sing a hymn to Gerda and they all took it up.

'With the strength of She who died for us, I march to victory,
Ever with my head held high, cross land and o'er sea,
Through cannon's fire and flames of war, onwards and ever free,
Gerda my strength, my light; I pledge my soul to Thee!'

The phorus flock fell silent, then some started emitting querulous calls. Lifted by the song, she raised her torch higher and started singing the second verse as they closed in. Through the ghostly trees a dark shape bobbed out of the gloom, cawing like a crow, twice her height with big eyes gleaming.

'Gerda my strength, my light; I pledge my soul to Thee!'

The phorus bird glared at her, raked the turf and shrieked, but she thrust out the flaming brand and it darted backwards, jabbing at her with its beak but not daring to come fully into striking range.

She took another step forward as they belted out the third verse and chorus and more phorus birds appeared. She had four birds before her now, giving ground step by step, but they were barely retreating, almost daring her to come in range of their lunging beaks. But her fellow beaters loomed out of the mist, closing off every direction except the river.

She faced fully a dozen of them, grouping around one giant male with vivid feathers of emerald and orange and looking ready to charge – until a flintlock cracked and the male staggered, a bloody hole in its breast. As it fell, the rest of the flock recoiled, snapping and hooting but giving ground, flustered and unnerved, as much by the gun's sound as the sudden death.

As one, the hunters strode forward.

'Be thou with me every step, upon the path of life
Through the tender year of youth, in vigour and in wealth,
Strengthen my soul as body fails and keep me true in faith,
Gerda my strength, my light; I pledge my soul to Thee!'

For one terrifying moment it looked like the phorus birds were rallying, but a second shot into the air broke their nerve and they began to fall over themselves to retreat. With mastery established, the game changed from confrontation to herding. The birds fell back with growing urgency, seeking to outflank the beaters and their frightening fire-brands.

The hymn ended and they began to jog forward. Zarelda lost track of time as they ate up the ground and before she knew it, they were on muddy ground and she could hear the music of the river ahead.

The ground dropped towards the very bend they'd targeted and she heard Banno whooping. Goskyll reappeared on her right, hollering and waving his torch at the dozen or more phorus birds before them. He threw a look at her, shouting, 'Watch me –'

Then he yelped as the birds turned at bay as if sensing the trap ahead. One bird loomed over him and he thrust the torch into its face –

– and as if in slow motion, another bird darted in and raked open his belly with a taloned foot.

Goskyll shrieked and fell to his knees and the first bird's massive beak hammered down, caving in his skull. He flopped bonelessly to the ground and the bird tore into his back, then looked up.

Straight at Zar.

She barely had time to think: the murderous bird was screaming and charging, its fellows behind it, straight at the only thing between them and freedom: *her.*

Instinctively, she shrieked, '*Ignus!*' and the torch in her hand redoubled in intensity, but the phorus birds kept coming, blood-crazed now and blind to sense. She realised at the last instant that they were going to go through her regardless and she'd end up like Goskyll or the rodents, just bloody rags of flesh.

'*Adefar*,' she bellowed, '*flamma omnia!*'

It was the same spell, but at its most extreme: heat boiled through her and then streamed up the torch, charring the wood to ash and setting alight the very air before her. It was agony and ecstasy, blazing her vision to scarlet and shadow.

It lasted just a moment, draining her like an emptying cup, and then she pitched forwards, landing on her knees at the feet of the onrushing flock.

But the lead bird was screaming as its plumage ignited and the rest recoiled, driven back by the heat and the dancing flames swirling in the air before them. As their leader croaked and collapsed, they whirled and stormed away in terror. Then Banno was shouting her name and sprinting in and a moment later bowstrings were singing and a ragged volley of shots tore through the air.

It was the last sound Zar heard as she fainted away.

Zarelda woke to the scent of cooking meat and the babble of voices. She was under a cloak – Banno's; she recognised the warm, earthy smell – and comfortably close to a blazing fire. Above it, the entire torso of a phorus bird was being roasted.

She sat up, feeling dizzy, then looked around. It was evening and the hunters who'd set up camp near the river were laughing and boasting about the catch.

'Hey,' Banno said, offering her a flask, 'for the heroine of the hour.' Around him, the men stopped and burst into applause.

She smiled wanly, and put her lips to the flask.

It was just water, cold and clean, and she perked up after guzzling it, remembering that panicked moment when she'd done everything her father had warned her not to do, overextending beyond her established capabilities. It hadn't been heroic.

I could just as easily have torched myself.

But it did feel good to be the hero.

Foaley was explaining to those who'd missed the action that when the flock had sensed the closing trap, they'd tried to break out. 'When Goskyll went down, we almost lost them. Zarelda cut off their final bid for freedom.' He looked at her. 'If you hadn't, they'd have all escaped.'

And you'd be dead, Banno's eyes added. 'I should have been closer,' he murmured. 'I'm sorry.'

'Stop apologising,' she snapped. 'We were lucky they came at me – if it had been someone else, they'd have got away.'

'Aye,' Foaley said, 'you did us proud, lass. You did your father proud.'

He'll probably bawl me out for an idiot, she thought, but no one here needed to know that, and she decided she didn't need to tell them. 'Is Goskyll . . .?'

Foaley flinched. 'Aye. We buried him while ye slept, lass. I'll show you the grave when you're up and about.'

She nodded. Although the man had been a creep, he'd not deserved to die like that. But life was random and cruel. 'I'd like that,' she said quietly.

Then Norrin Harper struck up a melody and a few hidden flasks of carefully preserved alcohol came out.

And Banno gave her some gaudy tail feathers as trophies.

'One's for Dad,' she laughed, 'to remind him who's boss.'

2

Bathing hole

'This'll do for a camp,' Raythe told Foaley, looking at the flat, dry ground, and their small party of scouts called a halt. It was late afternoon, and ideal.

He'd divided his time between successfully testing for istariol in the river and following the scouts as they traversed the eerie, mist-shrouded woods. They'd glimpsed more of the huge birds, the Killerbeaks, as they were calling them. They hadn't needed to hunt; yesterday's haul had been more than sufficient and even now the best of the cooks were trying different ways of preserving the excess meat. Raythe was still glowing, knowing Zar's fire-spells had saved the day, although he wasn't quite so happy that she'd been in such danger.

He sent Jesco back to guide in the main body of the caravan, then joined the other scouts in readying the campsite for their arrival. Working alongside his people always brought a reward, in lifting their spirits. A leader needed to be seen to serve, he knew well by now.

Not long after, the main body arrived, cooking fires flared up and people busied themselves with the myriad tasks of the day. Only Norrin wasn't labouring, instead playing his harp beside the central fire, but no one minded when he entertained them so well.

There was an extra concern today: many of the women were gathering around Kemara's cart, where Regan Morfitt was in her second day of labour. There had been four new births on the road already, but one of the older men had died of heart failure as well. *Life and death, the eternal cycle.*

'Hoi, Raythe!' a gruff voice called, and he turned to see Vidar trotting in on his brown mare.

'Just the man,' Raythe replied, striding to meet him. 'What lies ahead?'

'Grassland rising in a long slope to a plateau,' the bearskin replied, swinging from the saddle and handing the reins to an eager boy. 'But we lose the river, somewhat. About three miles upstream, the banks become a gorge with no room on either bank for passage. But we can follow it from the top of the cliffs. And there's more of those carved poles, mostly fallen and rotting. Whoever left them is long gone.'

By Vidar's standards, it was a massive speech. 'Any sign of game?' Raythe asked.

'Plenty: Killerbeaks, and smaller walking birds too, less aggressive, but they can run like the wind. Ain't seen a thing that goes on four legs yet, mind.'

'Sounds like they'll be a tricky to hunt,' Raythe smiled.

'Can't outrun a lead ball,' Vidar drawled, patting his flintlock. 'I caught a glimpse of the northern horizon, too. We're heading into mountains again – there's a whole blasted wall of 'em, right at the edge of sight.'

'It's warm as southern Pelaria here. The istariol won't be far away now.'

'Gerda be praised. It's already going to be a fair hike to get the stuff back to civilisation. If we faced another mountain trek, I'd say it couldn't be done.'

'But it can.' Raythe slapped his shoulder. 'Good work, Vidar. Get some food and rest – if you can: the camp's lively tonight. Everyone can sense that we're nearly there.' He looked around. 'Have you seen Zar?'

'Nope. Try the river: she had that flank this afternoon.'

Raythe went searching, and found his daughter sitting alone on the riverbank, her hair wet but her clothes mostly dry. 'Been swimming?' he asked as he sat, putting an arm around her shoulder. 'Bloody lazy scouts.'

'Huh!' she retorted. 'We work harder than anyone. I must've walked thrice the distance you did today – and you had a horse.' She pointed across the misty river. 'There's a spot on the far bank down there where the water's like a warm bath. It was *heaven*.'

'Glad you found it – I might have to have a soak myself,' he said, tousling her hair. 'I'm sorry I'm away all the time. How are you?'

'Practising hard.' She flashed through some rune-patterns with her fingers. 'Adefar and I have all the basic spells down pat. He's obedient as a cherub, too. We just need to learn more spells.'

'As soon as we can set down our loads a while, I promise.'

'Sure you will,' she grumbled.

'No, I really do promise, it'll be my first priority.'

She looked up at him. 'Is Kemara practising? She won't tell me – and people are talking.'

'She's managing,' he lied. Kemara's mizra wasn't his secret to reveal, he decided, so he turned his mind to something just as awkward. 'What about you and Banno? Are you, um . . . being careful?' When she hesitated, he added, 'I'm family, I have a right to know.'

She squirmed and went scarlet. 'Dad, we're being very proper. I'm still . . . you know . . . virginal.'

'Oh!' He'd assumed his admonishments to put the praxis ahead of love would be ignored.

She gave him a forbidding look and pointedly asked, 'How about you, Dad? Seeing anyone?'

'Me? None of your business!'

'Why, am I not family?'

'Touché,' he snorted. 'No, no one.'

'Not Tami?'

'Definitely not Tami.'

She pursed her lips, then said, 'You should court Kemara. I don't like that creepy sailor she's always with. He should be travelling on his own by now. His back looks repaired enough to me.'

'Kemara? I don't think so.'

'Why not? You work with her on her sorcery. You can meld together and that's got to mean something.'

'She's a grumpy cow who thinks I'm a charlatan. And she's not my type.'

'Why, what type's that?' she asked cheekily.

'Women like your mother,' he replied, to shut the conversation down.

Unfortunately, it didn't work. 'Do you think Mother's all right?' Zar asked wistfully.

'No, I think she's probably pretty damned miserable, but at least she has the compensation of a vast marble palace, servants to do everything for her and inexhaustible wealth to comfort her,' he snarked, then he remembered who he was ranting to. 'Ah, sorry. And thank you for waiting.'

'Huh. If it were up to me . . . But Banno's more worried about propriety than I am.'

'Really?'

'Yes – he's petrified of you, for a start. The mysterious praxis-sorcerer. And I think he really, really wants to do the right thing by the Church. He's quite serious about that.' She gave him a tart look. 'If all boys are like him, I'll be a spinster yet. Won't that make you happy?'

'Ecstatic,' he told her, with a wink. 'Get yourself back to camp. I think I'll have that swim.'

Toran Zorne decided that the evening was a write-off in terms of inveigling his way further beneath Kemara Solus' skin. Her little cart was the centre of a gathering of women right now, all helping, advising, cooking or just nosing around, while the slow-moving crisis of Regan Morfitt's prolonged labour unfolded.

'The joys of a healer's lot,' Kemara told him. 'You can drive tomorrow – I'll be asleep in the cart.'

'Of course,' he said. 'But I'll get no sleep tonight unless I get away from all this – and I don't think your friends want a man here anyway. I'll rest elsewhere.'

So he took his bedroll away from camp to a spot with a good vantage over the comings and goings to the river. It was quiet just now, so he took his time, gnawing on a strip of cured phorus meat – the taste and texture reminded him of wild turkey – while laying out his things. It was late afternoon, daylight still, but after ascertaining that he was alone, he went to work.

First, he traced a symbol using a burning stick, drew on the praxis and muttered, '*Animus, Ruschto.*' He felt his familiar crawl into his senses. '*Praesemino pharos, intimus Jorl et Karil,*' he then added, constructing a beacon that only the twin sorcerers Jorl and Karil, who were hopefully among the pursuers, could sense. When it was ready, he gathered the energy, traced the rune of fire and said, '*Incipere, nunc.*'

Ruschto fed the spell and the sending pulsed out through the nebulum.

He'd been doing this for days, ever since the destruction of the imperial column in the glacier. Four pillars of ice had resisted Vyre's flood, but he didn't know who the other sorcerers were. Ominously, all four had eventually been swept away, so Jorl and Karil might well be dead.

A sending like this was inhibited by distance, and the mountains provided another barrier, so Jorl or Karil would have to be alive and have reached the lake where the glacier met the istariol-bearing river for them to receive it. The odds felt remote.

But the nebulum chimed and a curious voice said, '*Zorne?*'

His heart thudded so hard, he almost lost the link. '*Jorl?*'

In moments, he knew everything: Komandir Persekoi had rallied his men and was just days behind. Losses had been minimised by two Izu-vei sorcerers: four hundred men still followed Persekoi, although they'd lost most of their gunpowder, both bombards and almost every horse. But they were even now traversing the frozen lake, having found the caravan's trail.

Jorl bade him wait while he consulted, then returned to say, 'Persekoi bids you delay them – kill this man Vyre to create a disruption. We'll be upon them the day after tomorrow.'

Zorne grimaced. Too often, his missions went this way: a superior who didn't understand the real situation would force him into an unwise action, usually for their own glory. 'Vyre is too important,' he argued. 'He may be the only one among them who can find the istariol.'

'Lord Persekoi says that the Izuvei can find the istariol. Fulfil your mission and eliminate Vyre: that will throw them into confusion, and we will fall upon them from the rear.'

Zorne fumed silently, but he knew he'd do as he always did and put his faith in the system.

'Those above us see the bigger picture, so place your trust in their judgement,' he'd been told again and again. So he tried to see it from Persekoi's point of view.

Vyre is the only one in this column who can threaten his forces. Eliminate him, and the rest will fall apart. This foolish expedition will end in slavery and death, as it deserves to.

My role, as always, is to obey.

'I understand,' he intoned.

'Excellent,' Jorl replied, and repeated, 'Kill Vyre, delay the caravan. Those are your orders.'

The connection was broken before he could reply.

Once he'd got over his annoyance, he considered the news that Persekoi had two Izuvei sorcerers with him. *Intriguing.* He had once contemplated cauterising his normal senses to enhance the mastery of his magical senses himself, but his Ramkiseri masters had had other plans for him.

'You are cauterised of emotion already, Zorne. You have no empathy. That is a far greater gift, for it makes you relentless and allows you to disappear into your task. It frees you from doubt and regret. Keep your physical senses and hone yourself into a blade.'

He's spent his life doing exactly that.

'*Ruschto, abeo,*' he sighed, and the familiar drained from his senses. He sat back on his haunches and took heart that his empire was still with him.

His orders troubled him, but he'd obey, of course. A single dagger was all he'd need – in any case, 'Trimble' had no other weapon – so he slipped it under his belt, then drifted to the edge of the campsite, as if just stretching his legs. Presently, he saw Vyre's daughter head for the river, and twenty minutes later Raythe Vyre himself took the same path. Zorne followed warily, ghosting through the mist that clung to the river, through thick bush dotted with mud-pools belching noxious gases, taking his time to get the lie of the land.

Then he heard footsteps and darted behind a tree just before Zarelda Vyre returned, her hair wet. She passed within feet of him and he almost seized her to use against her father – but a male voice greeted her and he watched Banno Rhamp kiss her chastely.

Zorne let them depart unharmed, for now Raythe Vyre was alone.

Moving into the shroud of mist that clung to the willows on the riverbanks, he closed in on his prey. '*Ruschto, animus,*' he whispered, and his familiar returned, sharpening his sight and senses. He inhaled a calming breath of damp loamy air, laced by the noisome fumes of a bubbling mud-pool. Every sense was jangling. Then he found Vyre's clothes hanging from a low branch and glimpsed the man's head and bare shoulders wreathed in steam in the river, forty yards away in a pool beneath the far bank.

There must be an underwater thermal. Dear Gerda, to be clean again –

He settled behind a bush, ready to rise and pounce, blade in hand, as Vyre left the water. The Otravian would die before he could summon his familiar, let alone reach his weapons.

But then a sharp point touched the back of his neck and he went rigid, mastering the reflex to flinch.

'Such discipline, for a simple sailor,' a woman snickered. 'If that's really what you are?'

Tami. He cursed himself, realising he'd been too focused on his prey and forgotten his own safety. An elementary error – and possibly a fatal one.

The Pelarian woman plucked his dagger from his belt, but the blade against his neck didn't waver. 'Now why would you be sneaking around the boss?' she drawled. 'Unless you just like watching men bathe?'

He could picture her stance as clearly as if he were standing to one side watching them both: her dagger was in her right hand, and his now in her left – swords were too slow for close-quarter work. He knew her build: smaller than him, lean and wiry, but he didn't underestimate her. Her reflexes were primed; anything untoward and she'd ram her blade into the place where his spine met the skull, instantly severing the cord, then it'd plunge into his brain. He'd be dead before he hit the ground.

How fast were those reflexes? *Very*, he decided. But she was a loner, so it was just him and her – aside from Vyre, of course. And Ramkiseri training covered just this sort of situation. He knew the moves he'd need when the chance arose.

That came sooner than he'd dared hope: someone shouted, 'Raythe!' from upstream; he didn't hesitate, banking on her attention wavering, if just for an instant . . .

He spun and ducked and instead of killing him, Tami's knife slashed the back of his scalp, but his elbow slammed into her throat, choking off her cry. Her eyes bulged but she pulled back her left arm, holding his dagger – but he tangled her legs, twisted and bore her down, a moment before she slammed his own blade into his side. They crashed into the mud, his sight red, in agony, but he was on top.

Tami tried to stab again, but he ignored the pain and rolled onto her left arm, pinning it, then caught her right arm and held it, finding himself face to face with her. As her tortured throat sought air he bit her, clamping his teeth over her windpipe and squeezing, tasting blood and choking her cry. She weakened quickly and he used that to change his grip on her right wrist and twist, snapping it.

Convulsing, she dropped her blade, which he snatched up. Then he unclamped his teeth, licked away her blood and looked down into her eyes, into her soul.

Tami made a pleading sound, a helpless, gagging that jolted through him like a bolt of adrenalin. The elation of the hunt filled him, that moment when the prey succumbs. His whole body pumped with energy, even arousal.

Then he drove his blade down into her breast, through the ribs and into her heart, and watched enthralled as she died, kissing her so that he inhaled her last breath, basking in the moment of ultimate victory, when one became predator and the other, merely prey.

This is why I'm alive. This is why I love my work.

A moment later the pain hit him from the stab wound to his side and the cut on the back of his head. The latter was more of an annoyance, but the former was soaking his shirt, even though, numbed by adrenalin and triumph, he could scarcely feel it.

'Is someone there?' Raythe Vyre called from the far side of the stream.

Zorne rolled aside and peered carefully through the bush to see Vyre standing in waist-deep water, looking his way. A moment later, he felt the thrum in the nebulum that told him that the sorcerer was summoning his praxis-familiar.

Then that voice came again from upstream, calling Vyre's name. 'Raythe? Damn this fog!'

It's the Shadran, Zorne realised as his ardour cooled. If he'd had a flintlock or pistol, he might still have chanced it, but there was only cold steel and Vyre was wary now, and Jesco was getting closer.

'I'm here,' Vyre called to Jesco.

Zorne hurriedly wiped and sheathed his dagger, put Tami's back in her sheath, then scooped her up. She was sparrow-light, even in death, and it took only a moment to haul her to the bubbling mud-pool and push her down. Her empty face still made him shiver hungrily, even as it sank beneath the surface.

By the time Vyre and Jesco met, he was gone.

He spent the rest of the evening using the praxis to seal over his two wounds, then returned to the river, further downstream, to wash the blood away. By then, his post-kill flush had ebbed, leaving a profound sense of contentment, despite the ultimate failure to take down Vyre.

Tami came and went as she willed, so they won't be immediately alarmed if she's missing. And there'll be other chances. If it takes longer than Persekoi likes, well, damn him. Who is he to command a Ramkiseri under-komizar?

As he returned to the main camp, he recognised traditional birthing songs; presumably the celebrations were for the Morfitt woman, who must have finally delivered her brat. He should join them, but his wounds were too fresh, the blood-loss still debilitating, and a healer like Kemara would instantly recognise them as knife wounds.

I'd have to kill her too.

Much as the thought excited him, it was too soon.

Taking her life is a meal to savour, not one to devour recklessly.

3

Over the ravine

Raythe woke early from a nightmare of being stalked through misty forest; weirdly, the morning was just like his dreamscape. But they were well into the Iceheart now and he was now certain the istariol was near. That galvanised him into action.

He wasn't the only one; perhaps it was the eerie nature of the mist-bound river, or the poumahi poles they kept finding, the darkly demonic faces, lascivious tongues and leering eyes seeming to watch the travellers as they passed. Restless unease and a sense of urgency filled the camp. So despite hangovers from celebrating the birth of Tyl and Regan Morfitt's baby son, everyone was up and about, also eager to get moving.

They breakfasted, packed and loaded up without needing to be chivvied along. Boisterous children ran about, herding the remaining cattle under the direction of Gan Corbyn. Everyone was ready to move – except Tami, whose little pup-tent remained untouched.

Raythe strolled over and nudged the flap. 'Hey, Tami, you in?' No one answered and he poked his head in, but she wasn't there and her pack lay untouched. *Odd* . . .

'Have you seen Tami?' he called to Zar, who was pulling on her own pack.

'Nope.'

It was possible last night's celebration had turned amorous for her, but even so, she should've been back by now. 'Zar, could you please pack up her gear? She's not back and I need to coordinate the vanguard.'

His daughter gave him an offhand salute, while he peered around, expecting at any moment to see his former lover sauntering back, that crooked grin on her face, but she failed to materialise, and duty called.

'See you later,' he told his daughter, then he mounted up, collected Jesco and went looking for Vidar.

They found the bearskin briefing the scouts. 'You still wanting us patrolling our back trail?' Vidar asked, as he came to meet him.

'Fair question. What do you reckon?'

'If we were the military, there'd be no question. But the lads are tired, they're certain no one's back there – and these poumahi give them the creeps.' The Pelarian chuckled. 'You should hear these kids whine.'

'That settles it then – send 'em out,' Jesco put in. 'Can't have the poor darlings going soft.'

Raythe laughed. 'Fair enough – full perimeter cover: back, front and both flanks. I don't think there's anyone here, but let's keep our discipline.'

'Aye,' Vidar agreed. 'Finding the istariol might be the easiest part. The empire's bound to send more men as soon as they realise what's happening, so best we maintain a war footing.'

'If you can see to that, I'll travel alongside the gorge again. Maybe today I can follow the istariol to its source.' He turned to go, then asked, 'Have you seen Tami?'

'No, but I seldom do.'

'She does come and go,' Raythe agreed. 'But she usually tells me what she's up to.' He frowned, then put the matter aside. 'She'll show up. She always does.'

Vidar looked around. 'Hey, these are new lands. What're we going to call them?'

'I've not given it a thought.'

Jesco grinned. 'That settles it then: I dub them Jesland.'

'Ha! I don't think so,' Raythe laughed, then suggested, 'Zareldia? Or would it go to her head?'

'Undoubtedly.'

'Then let's hold off. Anyway, we're not planning to stay, so who cares?'

By midmorning, they were ascending into uplands, still loosely following the river, which was confined in a deep gorge, pouring through twisting rapids and pounding over waterfalls. Twice Raythe clambered down the cliffs to test the churning water, and both times it still contained istariol.

But at midday, Raythe and Vidar reached a cliff-top and stood there flummoxed, for a hundred yards below, the river emerged from the earth in a great torrent that sent clouds of spray a hundred feet into the air. They had found the headwaters.

'Is this it?' Vidar asked.

Raythe winced, not wanting to even contemplate the difficulties of mining such a site. 'It appears so,' he admitted. 'I'll need to climb down and do another test.'

Dear Gerda, we couldn't even send a boat into those caves, not with waters that swift.

Then a voice called out, 'Raythe, is that you?' and Cal Foaley rode out of the mist. 'There you are. Come and see what I've found.'

'Unless it's a way down into those caves, I don't want to know.'

'Yeah, you really do.'

They followed the hunter up a short rise, walking right out of the fogbank that gripped the lower slopes and stepping into unexpectedly cool, clear sunshine. The vista made him stop and stare.

They were at the southern end of a high plain several miles in length. The hills that closed in on either side were clear of snow, and brilliant blue skies stretched away to the far north, where distant ranges glittered white. It was a breath-taking panorama, enough to make the heart soar – even without the hill at the north end of the plain, some three miles away. It wasn't tall, but the colour suggested it was almost bare of vegetation. Even at this distance they could see it rose in tiers, at least three concentric circles, which couldn't possibly be natural.

'What is it?' Raythe asked.

Foaley grinned. 'It's some kind of old-time fort. Each of those rings has a fence of wooden staves, twice the height of a man. It's mostly broken down, but it offers shelter and I reckon it could even be fortified again, given time.'

'I suppose, but the istariol's down there,' Raythe told him, pointing at the ground.

'I don't think so.' Foaley gave him a broken-toothed grin. 'I ain't showed you the best bit yet. That outflow down below? That ain't the river's source. There's another canyon on the other side of that hill-fort where two rivers meet, right before they plunge underground, presumably emerging down below us. And I ain't got the words to describe what's on the other side of that canyon, so best you just come and see.'

Jesco pulled a face. 'I hate mysteries. Just tell me.'

'You just hate waiting,' Raythe retorted. 'Vidar, send a runner to fetch Mater Varahana and Rhamp, then we'll all press on and see this marvellous sight Cal's promised us.'

They waited twenty minutes, studying the distant hill-fort and probing Foaley for more information, but he remained tight-lipped. Finally, when Mater Varahana trotted up on a borrowed mount, uncomfortably silent alongside Rhamp on his warhorse, they set off, eager to see what lay ahead. The wind rose as they went, blowing cold in their faces as they crossed the small plain, until they found themselves before another of the poumahi arched gates. This one was sun-bleached to a desiccated silvery-grey, as were the wooden posts that wound in layers about the hill. Within, they saw tumbledown huts, a few intact but most lying open and engulfed by vines and brush. Nesting birds, thankfully the small, winged variety, rose angrily, squawking at the intrusion. The hill fort had clearly been abandoned long ago.

'Mater Varahana, what do you think?' Raythe asked the priestess.

'This must have been a village of a tribe that served the Aldar,' she replied. 'It's too primitive to be an abandoned Aldar rath. They must've died in the Mizra Wars, like their masters.' She slid from her horse's back, wincing as she rubbed her bottom, and gazed about. 'There were many human tribes under the Aldar tyranny, but they all perished when the Mizra Wars precipitated the Ice Age. This is an incredible find.'

Foaley chuckled. 'With respect, Mater, you ain't seen nothing yet. Come with me.'

Instead of taking them up into the hill-fort, he led them around the hill. The perimeter fence was surprisingly intact, given the enormous passage of time, and they wondered aloud if this tribe had managed somehow to hang on for a while after the Ice Age began. Then they reached a vantage point looking north, and all words died in their mouths.

As Foaley had reported, the plain ended in another massive canyon behind the hill-fort. Beneath a clearly manmade platform of stone, two rivers converged from the northeast and northwest, meeting in a swirling maelstrom that plunged beneath the ground, almost certainly forming the same river they'd followed upstream to get here. But even that mighty sight was as nothing to what lay across the ravine.

Two hundred yards across that gulf rose a mountain, its lower slopes covered in stone buildings many times higher than even the tallest spires of Reka-Dovoi, the Bolgravian capital. It wasn't just the height that made their eyes widen, but their alien beauty: curves and spirals, strange angles and spindle towers apparently wrought of copper and glass. The lower reaches were tangled up with lush vines that caressed the buildings, prised them open, devoured them and buried their bones.

But the upper levels were clear of the reclaiming tendrils of nature – because, but for massive chains at each point of the compass, the upper reaches, crested by the walls and towers of a mighty fortress like the crown on a tyrant's head, *floated* several hundred yards above the city.

A floating rock tethered to the earth: a throne from which an Aldar emperor might rule.

'Holy Gerda,' Mater Varahana croaked. 'Deo on High.'

'It's the rath of the last Aldar King,' Jesco blurted. 'It's Rath Argentium, the castle of Vashtariel himself.'

Jesco may actually be right, Raythe thought wildly, then, *There's no need to test which of those rivers is carrying the istariol: it comes from right over there.*

For a long while, they stood there, speechless, just staring.

'Look at it,' Raythe said, eventually. 'We couldn't have asked for more. We won't need to make camp: we've got a ready-made city to live in, and there'll be already established mines. This is the answer to all our prayers.'

Kemara's cart rolled to a halt in the midst of a celebrating camp. Norrin and Jesco were making music, and those not cooking or putting up tents were clapping their hands and singing along. Mater Varahana was leading her flock in prayer, and everyone was bringing out what little special food they'd hoarded for this moment.

She was last to arrive, as usual; she'd been treating one of Rhamp's men, who'd slipped beside the river and broken a leg. Moss Trimble was in his now customary place in the driver's seat while she rode with the mercenary, a veteran named Miki Brond. He was in severe pain, every bump on the way racking him, so she'd used a lot of her sedating herbs on him.

'What's going on here?' she wondered.

The new camp was in front of a strange hill ringed with ancient wooden palisades and a lot of the poumahi carvings. It looked very like a primitive fort. She chose a campsite beside Lynd Borger, the burly blacksmith, and called 'What's happened? Have we found the istariol?'

'Aye, praise Gerda! On t'other side of the hill. Vyre's been sending for you. He'll be round there.' Then he shook his head and added, 'You won't believe yer eyes, Healer.'

She glanced at Moss. 'Can you see to Miki?' Her new patient was fully unconscious now, his leg splinted and bound.

347

Borger peered into the cart and grunted in amused sympathy. 'What'd that fool do to hisself?'

'Tried to dance a hornpipe on a slippery rock,' Moss remarked, gazing about.

'Let me help you get him to ground, then you two go and see,' Borger offered. 'T'is only fair, the rest of us's already seen it. You'll find half the camp round there; if you see my wife, tell 'er the meal wants cooking.'

After getting the mercenary into a bedroll and unpacking the basics, now a well-practised routine, Kemara and Trimble walked around the hill, studying it curiously – but when they rounded the final outcropping and saw the ravine, and the ancient and alien city on the far side, they both stopped dead and stared.

After a moment, Kemara realised that Moss had taken her hand and she'd not even noticed. Nor did she pull away, because she needed someone to hold onto as she took in the towers and spires glinting in the afternoon sun, the thunder of the confluence and the massive, jaw-dropping sight of a whole mountain-top floating above it all, bound by chains with links as big as houses.

'*Shansa mor*,' she blurted. 'It can't be real.'

'It's the city of Vashtariel,' a boy shrieked, as he tore past. 'I'm King of the Aldar! Rrrr!'

Kemara looked at Moss' face, caught in a rare moment of stunned openness. Horror warred with wonder, as if his world couldn't encompass such a place.

That was fine – neither could hers. But her heart was thumping and she wanted to see it all, to stand at the summit of the highest tower, right now.

But it was over there, and she was here – and she was holding hands with a man and she didn't *do* that. Firmly, she withdrew her fingers and took a deep breath to steady herself.

A young girl edged up shyly. 'Mistress Kemara,' she said in a worshipful, scared voice, 'Lord Vyre wishes you to join him at the edge.' She looked at Kemara and then Moss and giggled, spun and fled.

Kemara had to suppress an urge to dance. 'Come on, then, let's find out what's happening,' she said, and made her way, Moss close at her heels, through the amazed travellers, her eyes so fixed on the mountain of buildings opposite that she twice stumbled for not placing her feet securely. At the edge she found a ledge, fenced from the drop by still-intact wooden stakes. Vyre was standing on an elevated mound above and behind the ledge, with Elgus Rhamp, Jesco Duretto, Mater Varahana, Cal Foaley and Vidar Vidarsson already there. She climbed up, Moss with her.

'This is a leaders' meeting,' Raythe told her, frowning.

'I trust Moss.'

'Doesn't matter.' He fixed Moss with his cool gaze and added, 'She won't be long.'

The sailor's face went stony, but he tugged his forelock and said, 'Milord,' and went back down.

'This isn't the bloody empire,' Kemara snapped.

'It's nothing personal,' Raythe replied, 'but this group was selected for specific skills and influence. If he has something we need, I'll invite him myself.'

'He seems a solid man,' Sir Elgus commented. 'Don't wait for Banno – I've got him in charge of setting up camp on the south side. He's got your daughter helping him. Quite the team, those two.' He snorted in amusement when Raythe frowned, then asked, 'Where's Tami?'

'Haven't seen her all day,' Jesco put in. 'Not since the celebration of the Morfitts' baby.'

'She's a law unto herself,' Varahana said. 'Perhaps she's off looking for a way across?'

'Speaking of which,' Raythe said, making a grand gesture, 'behold.' He pointed away to the west.

They all squinted in the same direction and their elevated position revealed a thin arch catching the light of the afternoon sun and gleaming like the planetary rings.

'Dear Gerda,' Kemara breathed, 'is that a *bridge*?'

'We think so,' Raythe said, 'but it's too late today to find out. Tomorrow, I'll go there myself.' They all started to talk and he raised his hand. 'Remember, this place is centuries old: if it is a bridge, it mightn't be fully intact – or it might collapse the moment we step onto it.'

'The Aldar built to last,' Varahana replied, with an almost maternal pride.

'They didn't last themselves, though, did they?' Kemara noted, more to burst Raythe's bubble than in genuine pessimism. In truth, she felt utterly exhilarated. After all she'd been through, this impossible dream might be about to come true.

'You're right,' Raythe replied, 'but I think we're all glad they're gone: who'd want a mizra-wielding witch-queen in our path, after all?' he added, fixing her with a 'let's play nicely' look.

Oh, to be a mizra-wielding witch-queen, she thought.

'For now, we'll camp where we are,' Vyre went on, 'and tomorrow we'll investigate the bridge. And everyone? Congratulations! We've been through a lot, but we've arrived.'

He made a point of shaking hands with them all, leaving Kemara to last and murmuring, 'A word before you go.'

While she waited, she gazed at the extraordinary vista, wondering how many people once dwelt there. Did they see the end coming? Did they all perish at once, or slowly die out? Were their bodies still lying there, old bones locked in the past? What ghosts stalked the ruins?

Momentarily, she opened up to Buramanaka, and was stricken by a wave of grief and fury that was so devastating that she shut the link back down instantly. But it was enough to confirm that this was indeed Rath Argentium, the legendary centre of Aldar power.

Finally, they were alone, though Moss still waited below, out of earshot.

'Kemara,' Vyre said, 'now we're here, you and I have to start practising that meld, as agreed. We've not managed a single session' – he held up a placatory hand to cut off her retort – 'and that's as much my fault as yours. But we're here now, and it's a priority.'

It was fair. 'Of course,' she conceded.

'Do you have your familiar under control?'

The honest answer was that she wasn't sure. Her first mizra familiar had been a challenge, but Buramanaka was another thing altogether, a prince of his kind. But she didn't want to admit her fears. 'I'm not going to go mad and kill us all, though some days it's tempting.'

Raythe gave her a 'don't joke about it' look. 'I'm trusting in that meld we shared. I firmly believe we're going to need that kind of power again when we re-emerge into the world.'

'So while I'm useful to you, you'll suspend judgement? Am I supposed to feel grateful?'

'That's entirely up to you. But it's a *secret*, you hear? You guard it with your life. Not even Zarelda can know.' He glanced down at the waiting Moss Trimble. 'And no pillow-talk.'

'There's nothing—' She coloured. 'That's none of your business.'

'It's not even Mater Varahana's business – you're still a Novate, remember.'

'I think we both know I'll never take full vows: I can hardly become a full Sister now, can I?'

'Then you should formalise that,' Raythe told her.

He was right again, damn him. 'I guess I should.' Her days of needing Church shelter were over anyway. Everyone knew her as a sorceress now.

'I'm sure Varahana will understand,' he said in a surprisingly conciliatory voice. 'Come, let's get back round to the camp, so I can address everyone and tell them what's what.'

Banno and Zar were just about the last to see this fabled sight across the canyon. His father had left him in charge of the Rhamp camping site and the tasks were endless – siting the tents and feed-troughs, setting out cooking fires and ablution trenches and myriad lesser decisions – and all the while he had to listen to everyone else marvelling at what they'd seen. Zar helped him, but it still took *for ever*.

Finally, though, his father returned and took pity on him. 'Off you go, lad,' he said with gruff good humour, waving for his chief henchmen, Crowfoot and Bloody Thom, to join him for another conference. 'Take Vyre's daughter and go and see it for yourself.'

Banno did wonder what they were talking about this time; despite all the assurances and public peace-making, he still worried that they'd try something once the istariol was found. *Don't make me choose sides, Father*, he prayed, as they set off.

They'd barely gone a hundred yards when they ran into Raythe Vyre himself – who told Zar to turn round. 'It's night time. The city will still be there tomorrow.'

'But Dad, we're the only ones who haven't seen it,' she complained.

'But it'll be dark in an hour and I'm speaking shortly.'

Her face fell and Banno felt compelled to speak up. 'Lord Vyre –'

'Raythe,' the Otravian corrected, perhaps a sign of acceptance.

'Sir,' Banno resumed, not pushing his luck, 'we've been hearing all afternoon how incredible it is – but we're the only ones who haven't seen it. Please, we'll run all the way there and back. Father says it's not far.'

Raythe frowned, but after a moment, he said, 'Fair enough, but hurry back: I'd hate you to miss one of my famous speeches.'

Zarelda punched her father's arm. 'Thanks, old man.' She grinned and scampered off.

Banno shared a smile with Raythe: the first time. It felt like another step in the right direction – then he went after her, caught up and they carried on hand in hand.

As they rounded the base of the hill, they passed Kemara Solus and Moss Trimble, in intent conversation – then they came in sight of the canyon and with a gasp, both stopped dead. The setting sun gleamed on the ruins, glinting off verdigris-streaked bronze amid the vines swallowing the lower reaches. But it was the mighty rock chained above the city, and the castle atop it all, that caught and held their gaze.

'It's like we've fallen into a legend,' Zar breathed.

'Rath Argentium,' Banno whispered, wanting to remember this

sight for ever. 'I always loved the tale of Gerda and the Aldar King. But how can a whole mountain peak float like that?'

'It's to do with the way istariol reacts to the nebulum when it's activated,' Zarelda answered.

'What's nebulum?' he asked, feeling inadequate.

'It's the energy field that life generates – spirits dwell in it and sorcerers use it for energy.' She pointed to the giant floating peak, which was at least five hundred yards across. 'That contains enough activated istariol to bear its own weight – without those chains, I bet it'd just float away.'

'What's underneath?'

'The hole it left, I suppose. Dad says this can happen naturally – usually the breakaway rock only goes up a few dozen feet. It was what made istariol easy to find, back then. Now the imperial mines have to go really deep.'

'How come you know so much?'

'Reading, listening.' She grinned shyly. 'I'm a sponge, I just soak it all up.'

They turned to each other and kissed impulsively, a light peck that turned hungry, and for a few moments they even forgot the wondrous vista, losing themselves to touch and taste.

Then Zar pulled away and grinned. 'We'd better get back before Father sends Jesco and Vidar to find us.'

They ambled back, holding hands, and Banno realised that he was completely happy. *We've arrived and I really, really think what Zar and I have is growing into something special.* He felt as if he could do no wrong.

Then something away to the east caught his eye: a wisp of vapours rising from behind the hills and climbing against the clouds. 'See that?' he said, puzzled. 'Those dark patches against the low clouds? Could it be *smoke*?'

Zar frowned. 'Perhaps it's Tami – her cooking fire?' The former spy was still missing, and they all presumed – or hoped – that she was scouting the wider region.

'To make a plume that large? No, that's too much smoke for one person's fire – and Tami's like a ghost.' Banno stared. 'You know, if it *is* a cooking fire, it would be a big camp.

They looked at each other wide-eyed when he realised what he'd just suggested.

Other people out here?

'Perhaps it's a grass fire, from lightning strikes or something?' Zar suggested. 'It's summer – even though it's cold – and these upland plains are quite dry.'

'More likely,' he agreed, then a darker thought hit him and he blurted, 'What if it's the imperial force? They might have survived and followed us, but somehow ended up over there?'

'Gerda, I hope not,' Zar breathed.

The plume was dissipating in the upper air, but a distinct trail was still wafting upwards. 'I reckon it's about two miles away,' Banno said. 'We should send a patrol up that hill – I mean, maybe it's just a grass fire, but if it's not . . . ?'

'We need to tell my father,' Zarelda said, and took to her heels. He threw up his hands, then pelted after her. They tore around the base of the hill, and into the camp, just as her father was preparing to address the travellers.

Someone had hauled a wagon into the central space and Raythe was climbing up. He looked surprised when spontaneous cheers burst out; after a moment he waved at them like a candidate for village council. It took some time for the boisterous crowd to fall silent.

Banno pulled Zar through the throng, wanting to get close so they could tell Raythe what they'd seen as soon as he was done speaking. As they found a space and caught their breath, he reached again for Zar's hand.

'Friends, friends,' Raythe began, 'we've –'

A shot rang out and hooves thundered as Rix Morro and Tasker Corbyn galloped into the camp, smoke trailing from Tasker's flintlock.

'Alarum!' young Morro was shouting, *'Alarum!'*

A ripple ran through the crowd, as Tasker reared his mount and shouted, 'It's the imperials – they're only a couple of hours behind us–'

One of Gravis' tavern girls screamed and pandemonium broke out, men bellowing, children squealing and everyone shoving this way and that. Then another shot rang out and Jesco Duretto called out, 'Stand still, you bloody idiots – there's nowhere to run to, anyway.'

That momentarily stilled everyone, then Raythe called out, '*Hold*–' and the cry was taken up by Elgus Rhamp and Mater Varahana. '*Listen to me!*' Once he had everyone's attention, Raythe pointed to the hill-fort above them. 'So they found us: in a place we can *defend*.'

'Aye,' Elgus thundered, 'and we'll make the bastards wish they'd lost us–'

That lifted them, but Banno could taste the fear in the air.

Everyone knew the Bolgravian Empire never gave up.

'Listen up,' Raythe shouted, as the travellers huddled closer. 'I want everyone and everything we possess inside that hill-fort. Mater Varahana, you'll take charge of the withdrawal and deployment of wagons and tents. Sir Elgus will set the defences. Mistress Kemara will set up her field hospital inside the second tier. Master Foaley, send out scouts.' He clapped his hands. 'By Gerda, we've travelled three months and five hundred miles and we'll not be beaten now!'

To emphasise his words, he conjured light around his hand and everyone cheered as if he'd just hurled lightning at the Bolgravs and they were already running.

'Lord Vyre destroyed the frigate,' people babbled, clinging to hope. 'He'll save us all.'

'Now go,' Raythe shouted, 'and let's defend this place like we would a fortress.'

'Gerda is with us,' Mater Varahana clarioned, and her cry was quickly taken up as everyone burst into purposeful movement. The civilians went for the wagons, while the fighting men crowded in around Sir Elgus.

Banno let go of Zar's hand, saying, 'I have to join Pa.' Then he seized her and kissed her hard, not caring who saw. He tried not to think that it might be their last kiss.

'What about that smoke we saw?' she panted as they pulled apart.

'We've got bigger problems than that,' he told her. 'If it is a grass fire and it burns this way, let's hope it takes the imperials and not us. Go to your father. He'll protect you.'

But Zar didn't let go; instead, her face lit up. 'That's it,' she exclaimed, 'the fire – a sorcerer could *make* it come this way – Father and I – we could do that.'

Larch Hawkstone trudged across the grassland, eyeing the hill-fort uneasily. His fourteen remaining Borderers, all he had left after the demon-flood had melted the glacier, followed him, heads down and grumbling. Only the blind luck of being already on that rocky outcropping had saved them. No one wanted to be here any more.

Persekoi should've turned round and gone home, but those blind sorcerers won't let him. And now Vyre's found a place to defend.

And it was hard to feel they were on the side of right when his daughter and his woman – well, she was *everyone's* woman, but she'd born *him* a daughter – were in that hill-fort.

'Captain Hawkstone,' an aide called, his voice as disdainful as ever, 'Lord Persekoi will see you.'

'What's he want?' Simolon wondered.

'Likely it's to order us to go in first,' Hawkstone muttered, then he told Simolon, 'Keep the lads together and if some bugger tries to commandeer our guns and powder, tell 'em to krag off.'

His Borderers were one of the few units to have got through the glacier collapse with their gunpowder stores intact. He suspected the only reason Persekoi hadn't confiscated it already was because he was punishing his own men for losing theirs. Bolgravs were vindictively principled like that.

As he followed the aide through the ranks, he got a better look at what they faced: a hill-fort at the north end of the plateau, perched in front of a ravine. And beyond was a deep gloom in which one could almost imagine a conical mountain topped with towers and spires.

Must be the low cloud, he decided.

Then the sun dipped below the western hills and visibility plummeted, leaving him still unsure of what he'd seen. He found Persekoi squinting into the murk with his toadies, in confident mood.

'Ah, the brave Hawkstone,' he said sarcastically. 'Finally, we run Vyre to ground, yuz. Now, justice will be served.'

One man's justice is another man's massacre, Hawkstone thought. *How can I save my daughter from this?*

'Do we know what we face, sir?' he asked, carefully deferential.

'A few dozen mercenary scum, some hunters and a nest of vermin,' Persekoi sniffed. 'And Raythe Vyre.' When he glanced at his own sorcerers, the two Izuvei immediately turned their blind eyes towards them and Hawkstone's spine quivered. 'We have special plan for Vyre.'

'Good,' he growled. 'Bastard killed some of my best.'

'One of my men is worth ten of yours and I lost *eighty* in that flood,' Persekoi snapped. 'Speak not to me of losses.' He gestured towards the hill-fort. 'You have not seen this like before, ney?'

'No – even the Krodesh have outgrown wooden forts. It was likely put up by the same primitives who left those carved poles.'

'Yuz, so I think. Is good – Vyre thinks he is safe, but crowded together makes easier kill. We trap them, attack at dawn. Your men – with gunpowder I kindly leave you – will make western perimeter. My scouts take east. No escape for Vyre this time, I think.'

We keep our own powder and we get picket duty – better than it could have been.

'Yes, sir.' Hawkstone saluted before the Bolgravian lord changed his mind.

He hurried back to his men and sent them around the edges of the hill-fort, a few hundred yards from the palisades, motioning each into position until they were all hidden in the rough land before the walls. He took Simolon right to the edge of the ravine – and they both went still, staring through the murk at a ruined city just two hundred yards

357

away, on the other side of the churning waters of the confluence. It was some time before either could speak.

For Hawkstone, those ancient ruins were nightmarish. Such things shouldn't exist. The Aldar were from the Pit, and so were sorcerers, whatever Scripture said.

'Keep your eyes peeled,' he told Simolon. 'If they make a run for it, chances are it'll be along this flank.' He glanced along the ravine at what might be an archway spanning the gorge about a mile further west, but even as he peered, the setting sun plunged the canyon into deeper shade.

'No heroics, Sim,' he muttered. 'If they come, slip away before raising the alarm. Let the Bolgravs do the fighting.'

He turned to go – and froze.

The two Izuvei were some twenty yards away, mounted on horses, and he was instantly paralysed by their sightless white orbs, remembering what they'd done to Vyre's scouts.

'You, Hawkstone,' the aged male called, his Magnian slow and heavily accented. 'This sector is yours, yuz?'

'Yes, lord,' he replied nervously.

The blind sorceress nudged her mount closer. 'There is strong possibility of incursion here.'

'Do you wish me to bring more men?'

'Ney,' the man replied. 'Do not.'

'You will raise alarm and fall back. We will be behind you, with soldiers, to face those who come,' the woman said. 'Vyre and his red-headed *zuké* – you know this woman?'

'Sounds like Kemara Solus,' he admitted. 'A Ferrean woman?'

'Ferrean witch,' the sorceress corrected him. 'We take her, burn her.'

Hawkstone shared a look with Simolon. He'd always rather fancied the healer – she looked like she enjoyed a good tumble, though folk said she had a temper. But if she really was a witch, he was glad he'd stayed away.

'I thought she was just a healer?' he dared ask.

'She was on glacier, aiding Vyre,' the blind man rasped. 'There was a presence with her, seldom felt. She will suffer and die for her sins.'

'So if we see them, do we shoot?'

'Of course,' the blind sorceress sneered. 'Are you soldier? Lead ball kills as well as sword or spell.'

With that, the two Izuvei turned and headed west, which made Hawkstone wonder if perhaps there really was a bridge out there.

If a lead ball can kill a sorcerer, I'd love to put one each into your backs, he thought sullenly.

Then he almost pissed himself, because the sorcerer swivelled his head and stared at him through sightless eyes, before riding on.

'No bombards,' Sir Elgus noted. 'You said they had bombards in the glacier, but I'm not seeing them now.'

Raythe grinned. 'I was thinking the same thing. And something else – no wagons.'

'They must've lost them all in the flood,' Jesco said cheerily, patting one of the monsters carved into the entrance arch. 'Poor buggers have probably been on half-rations too. Apart from the powder in their flasks – no more than a few shots at best, if they managed to keep it dry during the flood – they'll be using those flintlocks as glorified spears.'

'There's still more than three hundred of them,' Vidar noted. 'Trained soldiers, well-used to bayonets and blades. And these palisades won't keep them out.'

'No one's saying it's going to be easy,' Raythe replied. 'But the palisades are going to limit their approach, concentrating them at certain points. If we can whittle them down, then meet them with determined force – and a few tricks – we have a chance.'

Just not much of one.

Everyone was inside the fort, and they'd been pleasantly surprised by how well the place had weathered: although overgrown, there were ditches where men with flintlocks could crouch and shelter from enemy fire, and the palisade fences might be wooden, but they were dug in deep and tightly bound up with durable cords made from a broad-leafed plant Varahana called flax.

Give me a regiment of Otravians and I could hold off an army here, for a while at least. But could a small force of mercenaries, a few able-bodied hunters and villagers and their wives and children stop even one concentrated attack? He doubted that very much.

He made a 'gather in' gesture. 'Listen, we all saw the bridge. If we can punch through their perimeter in the night, we can get everyone across, and that would give us just a single point of entry to defend.'

'It's over a mile away and they've already posted pickets,' Jesco noted.

'That's an easy run,' Raythe noted. 'A small group could slip past the pickets in the dark, get to the bridge and see if it's intact, then be back inside an hour.'

'Foaley reckons he saw two riders in Academia robes heading for the bridge,' Vidar said.

Raythe groaned. 'Imperial sorcerers.' He remembered the pillars of ice in the glacier. 'That bridge is our only chance of escape. I'll have to take them on.'

Jesco frowned. 'Raythe—'

'I'll take Kemara,' he interrupted. 'She and I . . . well, listen, she's no novice. At the glacier, she and I achieved a *meld*. Do you know what that is?'

Elgus Rhamp whistled softly and even Jesco looked impressed. Varahana frowned, clearly feeling Kemara had kept far too much secret, but all she said was, 'Well, aren't you both just full of surprises.'

'Kemara and I can deal with those sorcerers,' Raythe said, more confidently than he felt. 'That's if they're even still there. We'll check the bridge and return fast as possible. If it's safe, we'll slip everyone across before dawn. If they attack in the meantime, Elgus, Jesco – it's up to you to hold them at bay.'

'We'll hold until dawn,' Elgus growled. Then he chuckled and added, 'Unless they actually attack, in which case we're kragged. But we'll try and make it look like they shouldn't. Now go – and come back quick, or we're finished.'

Kemara was working with the Sisters of Gerda to set up her field hospital. It was fully dark now and the Bolgravs didn't appear to be in any hurry to attack; perhaps they preferred fighting in daylight. That was a relief, but it gave everyone more time to be afraid. Then she looked up to see Raythe Vyre making for her purposefully.

'Unless you've got a cache of medicinal herbs on you, I don't have time to chat,' she told Raythe, even though he had that 'I want something' look on his face.

'I need your help.'

Knew it . . .

'You and I can save everyone,' he started. 'We have a meld like no other.'

'That might be true, but each time we do it, it's like dousing myself in oil, then dancing round a bonfire.'

'I know, but if we're to survive this, we *need* that option. I think we can get everyone across that bridge during the night, though I'll need to scout it first – but we've seen Bolgravian sorcerers heading that way. I can't take them on alone, but together, we can. We'll have Vidar scouting for pickets, and you and I can deal with the sorcerers. We can do this, Kemara.'

'You don't know what you're asking,' she protested.

'I do – I *really* do – and believe me, I wouldn't ask if I had any other choice! But those are Izuvei sorcerers out there – I can't take them on alone.'

'And that's supposed to be encouraging? I'm not trained for this!' She looked around angrily and saw the Sisters were assiduously pretending not to listen, but Moss Trimble – *bless him* – was all ears. She threw him a look of appeal, thinking, *Get me out of this, Moss.* 'I'm better off here, healing the injured.'

But when he spoke, the sailor surprised her. 'With respect, I think you should do it,' he said. 'The defence won't hold long enough for us to need healers here. If there's hope of escaping, we have to take it.' He faced Raythe. 'I'm coming too.'

'No, you're not,' Raythe said.

Kemara stared at the two of them. 'I haven't said I'm going,' she started, then stopped. *Do I even have a choice?* 'I'm neither a servant nor a soldier for you to order about,' she said mulishly, then caved. 'All right, fine, I'll do it.'

Moss turned to Raythe. 'I can fight with blade or gun. Let me come.'

'I've got Vidar – he's plenty. The fewer of us, the better.'

'If you meet soldiers, Kemara will need someone to shield her. Let that be me.'

'I'm not helpless,' she insisted, thinking, *All this damned chivalry will get someone killed.*

Raythe was staring at Moss, who was facing him squarely. She didn't know many who'd face down a sorcerer in an eyeballing contest and she wasn't sure if she should be grateful or annoyed. No man had ever looked out for her in her life, and she'd never asked one to.

Maybe he's worth keeping around . . . That was a thought she'd not had in a very long time.

'We don't have time to waste debating this,' Raythe grumbled. 'It's your call, Kemara.'

She looked at both, then said, 'Moss has saved my life at least once. He has my trust.'

Moss gave her a grateful look, but Raythe grumped, 'Fine. Let's move. It's dark enough to hide us, but the ringlight will light our way. Meet me at the western end of the ledge behind this hill in twenty minutes.'

Kemara gave the Sisters of Gerda a few last instructions they clearly didn't need before retrieving the mask from its hidey-hole and hooking it inside her skirts. She scurried through the maze of palisade fencing behind Moss, who revealed a sure sense of direction, and found Raythe already waiting, huddled beside Vidar, who was looking decidedly bearish in his furs. The planetary rings basted the darkness with pale silver.

'No guns,' Raythe said, 'and no sound. There's a gap in the palisade near the ravine; that's where we'll slip out. Vidar goes first to clear the way. If we're seen, we fall back.'

'Retreat, and tomorrow we all die,' Vidar growled.

'Aye, but if the alarm's raised, pressing on would be stupid.' Raythe turned to Kemara. 'Our role is to deal with the sorcerers. Don't be frightened of them, just concentrate on your own spells and you'll be fine.'

He's fought in battles. For all her self-reliance, she'd never done that, so she took the words to heart.

The men looked to their blades and Kemara girded herself mentally for what might be required. Then Vidar led them to the gap and one by one they slipped through, out into the night.

⟁

'Where's my father?' Zarelda asked Jesco urgently.

The Shadran looked up from sharpening his longsword. 'Zar, darling, you just missed him. He's off gallivanting behind enemy lines.'

Her jaw dropped. 'What—? I've been waiting to see him for ages—'

'No one told him,' Jesco said, apologetically. 'He's trying to find out if we can sneak everyone away via that bridge we saw from the viewing ledge.'

'So he's *already* gone?' she exclaimed. This was *typical* of her father, always throwing himself into things and telling her afterwards, leaving her to guess how close she'd come to being orphaned this time. 'I hate him sometimes.'

'He's doing his best, love.'

'Sure, for everyone else,' she snapped, stalking away. Banno, who'd been hovering nearby, came to meet her and they found a place where they couldn't be overheard to confer.

'What do we do?' he asked. 'Talk to my pa?'

She set her jaw, trying to force her anger aside and deal with the

363

problem. *Cool heads win battles,* her father always said. *So, let's think coolly: do those smoke plumes, if that's what they were, really matter now?*

'If Father succeeds, we've still got to slip everyone out of the fort under the Bolgies' notice,' she said, thinking aloud. 'And if he fails . . . then we need a plan. At worst, summoning the grass fires over the hills could be a distraction, but at best, it might save us all. So I still think we should do it.'

Banno looked at her doubtfully. 'On our own?'

'I have a familiar. I know how to light a fire and call the wind. That's all mundeus sorcery – my speciality.' She'd never done anything of the sort in such large scale . . . but she felt certain she could manage.

'Then do you even need to go there? Why not just light a fire outside the walls?'

'That'd never work,' Zar replied. 'It'd be too small and the Bolgravs would just snuff it out. It has to arrive in a massive wave, more than they can deal with.'

'But we don't know what's out there,' Banno answered. 'There mightn't be enough grass on the hills to carry the fire to here. It wasn't even a big smoke plume – perhaps it was the last remnant of an old fire?'

'We'll never find out without looking,' she replied, not in the mood for sensible doubts. 'We have to do *something*. We can go and see, so at least we'll know.'

'But there'll be sentries –'

'It's dark – they'll never see us. Come on, help me, Banno – *please.*'

She couldn't say why, but she felt a real need to be *acting*, not just waiting. Mental images of that awful day when Colfar's rebellion collapsed and the imperials hit the baggage train were etched on her mind for ever. Rape, torture and murder awaited those taken alive, all the horrors of an army unleashed.

I don't want to survive a losing battle.

She looked up at Banno, beseeching him to be the man she needed, the one who'd back her, whatever.

He didn't disappoint. 'Let's do it,' he said. 'But if we tell someone, they'll forbid it. It's just you and me.'

'That's how it should be,' she told him, kissing him with all her strength. 'You're the best – now let's go.'

Larch Hawkstone passed up and down his picket lines all evening, slipping between the men dotted along the half-mile left flank of the hill-fort. His diligence was born of fear: his Borderers were able enough, but Vyre's men included hunters like Cal Foaley, who could move like ghosts. So he took it on himself not to sleep, and to keep his men on high alert. The Izuvei warning rang in his mind; he too was sure that Vyre might try something here.

So why hasn't Lord kragging Persekoi positioned a secondary line behind my pickets? Are they hoping to lure Vyre in? he wondered. If that was the case, then clearly his men were considered expendable, and that thought made his blood boil. He felt a perverse envy for Vyre's people: they might be on the losing side of this war, but at least they were going to die free.

Dead's just dead, he rebuked himself, as he reached the next post and surprised Virgus Boril taking a piss. 'Eyes open,' he hissed at the former trapper, who should've known better.

'It's all quiet,' Boril grumbled.

'O' course it is, and it'll stay quiet after you get knifed.' Hawkstone peered about: Boril had a good spot, in a pile of boulders with a good view of the fort, although now the cooking fires were out, it was just a dark silhouette. 'Stay alert – I'll just pop in on Simolon, then I'll be back.'

He crept out into the dark again, looping behind his pickets and approaching from the rear so he wouldn't be taken for an enemy. He found Simolon in position at the very edge of the ravine, where the churning whirlpool below muffled all other sound. It was clearly the point of maximum danger.

I should move some support in here, he mentally noted.

365

'All good, Sim?' he asked, staying low. They were overlooking the near end of what looked like a viewing ledge, complete with a low fence of wooden poles, most of them broken. The planetary rings lit the wet ground, making the dewy grass glimmer, and revealing the shapes of eerie ruined towers over the ravine – an awe-inspiring sight.

So I wasn't imagining it, he thought, dumbfounded. *What is this place?*

Simolon leaned in and muttered, 'This is where I'd come, if I was Vyre. Right here.'

Hawkstone agreed. 'I'll tell Virgus Boril to come join you and shift the others closer. Has there been any movement?'

'Not yet,' Simolon replied. 'Boss, I don't like this place. I reckon it's haunted.' He peered across the canyon and shivered. 'It's nearly autumn. I'll bet we're gonna be stuck here all kraggin' winter. My wife'll bugger off with some other fella.'

That seemed all too depressingly likely.

Hawkstone clapped Sim's shoulder and started to rise –

– when a feathered shaft of wood slammed into Simolon's eye, snapping his head back. He slid to the base of the crevice where Hawkstone cowered, already dead.

Hawkstone rolled out backwards and went slithering towards a dip where he might be able to hide, but an arrow rammed into his right buttock and lodged against his hip bone. His whole body convulsed in blood-hot agony and he couldn't hold back a sharp cry. He prayed the sound had been drowned by the gurgling water below, bit down on the pain and concentrated on slithering towards a hollow he'd spotted, reaching it just as dark shapes slid into Simolon's post.

Krag it, I should've stayed in camp. I should've stayed in bloody Teshveld.

But he was here and all he could do for now was to lie still. The flint-lock beneath his hand was primed and ready – but that was only one shot, and after that he'd be at their mercy.

Better to let 'em by. I gotta live through this if I'm to save Rosebud tomorrow.

He saw faces lit by the ringlight: Vyre himself, and the bearskin hunter who'd been at his cabin. He prayed again, this time that those yellow eyes hadn't spotted him. Then he saw the hard-faced redheaded healer go by: the blind sorcerers had called her a mizra-witch.

A fourth face flipped briefly into view and he stared at straggly whiskers festooning a face he knew.

That's Toran fecking Zorne – what the krag?

Then he heard stealthy feet coming his way. There was just a chance that they might miss him if he found a dark enough hole, so clamping his jaw against the howling pain of the shaft in his buttock, trying not to think that his life could end right now, in this humiliating, meaningless way, he flattened himself and kept crawling–

–until the ground fell away before him and as he started rolling, the barbed arrow ripped his flesh open, but came free. His whole mind blank with numbing agony, he struck a boulder and blacked out.

'There was someone else,' Vidar growled in Raythe's ear. 'I plugged him, but he's gone.'

'Then he's still alive,' Raythe whispered. Kemara and Trimble had passed on and so should he, but this was a loose end. 'We've got to find him before he raises the alarm.'

'I'll find him,' Vidar replied. 'You need to go on, keep with Kemara.'

Raythe agreed. 'Absolutely: I've got to be with her, especially if those Izuvei show up.' Kemara and Trimble were already out of sight, lost in the gloom. *We're barely over the fence and it's going wrong already.*

They stood at the edge of a small ditch. They could both smell the stink of blood, but the place was full of shadow and there was nothing moving below. *If we could chance some light, this'd be over in moments,* Raythe thought glumly, *but it's not worth the risk.*

After a moment, he whispered in Vidar's ear, 'Find him, kill him, then catch us up.'

He moved silently back to the edge of the ravine and began working his way along. He couldn't be more than a minute behind Kemara and Trimble, but they were invisible in the darkness ahead. As he hurried on, the wind rose, tearing the thick clouds like shredded sails and revealing the greater arc of the planetary rings in their shimmering glory. It also illuminated a pair of figures more than a hundred yards ahead and about to disappear behind another fold in the land.

He sped up, slithering precariously on the wet moss, and now he could see the arch of the bridge, only half a mile or so away, lit by the ringlight dancing on the river below. It was tantalisingly close – and looked to be whole.

It really could be our salvation – as long as those blasted sorcerers haven't stationed a regiment on it.

But they'd seen no sign of anything like that. The Bolgravs thought them pinned in and they'd spotted only the two Izuvei going that way. 'Gerda willing, they're already back in camp,' he whispered to himself.

On a cloudy night with plenty of cover, sneaking out was easy, and Zarelda had had years of practise. Her father had no idea what she got up to some nights. So ghosting past the Bolgravian sentries was child's play, even with Banno next to her.

Once they were through the cordon, they ran, reaching the eastern hills and within ten minutes they were clambering up. From up there, they could see the Bolgravian campfires closing around the hill-fort like jaws. Zar prayed to Gerda that her father was okay and that he'd make it back, then she cast her eyes ahead.

As they approached the ridgeline, the clouds parted and the planetary rings gleamed in an unearthly curve over their heads, radiant platinum lighting the landscape. They crested the hill – and stopped, completely stunned.

There was fire in the valley below: many, *many* fires, and they weren't burning wild. She could see one huge central bonfire, and at least three clusters of what must be cooking fires spread across a wide plain that stretched westward towards more hills.

We're not alone, she thought numbly. *There are other people here.*

368

Before them was a poumahi arch guarding a path down the hill: this one was not only carved in ferocious detail, but the two smoking torches lighting it showed it was painted a fresh, vivid red.

'Deo on high,' Banno breathed, 'is it another expedition? More imperials?'

Before Zarelda could frame an answer, a lone figure stepped between the pillars of the arch and roared out a shrill challenge in a language she'd never heard before.

4

On the bridge

Larch Hawkstone came to his senses as boots above him dislodged dirt and small stones trickled down onto him. His arse felt like a Pitfiend had rammed a burning spear into him, but he gritted his teeth and fumbled at his flintlock, loading just as a dark shape appeared above.

He twisted and pulled the trigger, the hammer slammed down . . . and the powder fizzled out.

Then a body slammed down on him, shoved the weapon aside and a knife flashed. He threw up a hand, somehow managed to catch the wrist of his assailant, moaning as the man's weight crushed his ribs, pushing out most of his wind.

It was the Norgan bearskin – Vidarsson, he remembered – and with his eyes glowing amber and his bestial snarl, it looked like he was already halfway to a blood-fit.

I'm doomed. No one was close enough to save him if he shouted and he was about to lose the battle to keep the knife out of his chest, so he used his last breath to squeak, 'What's a Ramkiseri doing with Vyre?'

'*Hawkstone?*' The Norgan's face went from ferocity to frown. 'What did you say?'

'Please,' he begged, 'my daughter's inside that fort.'

Vidarsson placed the knife against Hawkstone's throat, but he didn't cut. His face was incredulous. '*You have a daughter in our caravan?*'

'Angrit's girl,' Hawkstone panted, terrified, knowing the next second could be his last.

'Little Rosebud?' Vidarsson asked. 'She's *yours*?'

'Yes, yes she is – I gave her mother money, but I couldn't look after them,' Hawkstone blurted. 'I wanted to, but the Governor had me travelling all the time – and Gravis *owned* her. All I ever wanted was a family.' As he spoke, he knew he meant every word.

'You're helping the Bolgies,' Vidarsson rasped.

'No choice – I got commandeered – but I swear to you, I'm only here for my girl.'

'By the Pit, Hawkstone . . .' Then Vidarsson's eyes narrowed. 'What's this shit about a Ramkiseri?'

'That man I saw with Vyre and the Ferrean healer – Kemara Solus, yes? *That bastard's a Ramkiseri agent.* It's him what's led this entire pursuit. We thought he was dead when the frigate went up, but I swear, the man with the healer is him.'

'*Trimble's a Ramkiseri?*' Vidar was having trouble taking Hawkstone's words in.

'Trimble? That's not his name. He's called Zorne – Toran Zorne.'

'*Zorne?*' Vidar had clearly heard the name, presumably from Vyre. 'Are you sure?'

'Please, Vidarsson,' Hawkstone begged, 'I won't raise the alarm, I swear on my daughter's life. Warn Vyre – there are Izuvei sorcerers waiting for him at the bridge. Warn him, so he can get my Rosebud out of this shit.'

His case made, he surrendered his fate to chance and a bearskin with blood in his nostrils . . .

Kemara strained up the next slope, Moss beside her. After five hundred miles, one more hill meant nothing to her travel-hardened body, but somehow, this felt like the most important mile of all. The bridge was growing larger and brighter as the clouds cleared and ringlight illuminated the landscape. Then they entered a dark cleft and found it was lined with more of the ancient, weathered poumahi poles leading down to the bridge.

She glanced at Moss as they went down the defile and onto a platform, to see his normally impassive face was lit with wonder. Before them, at the foot of the giant span, two great statues like dragons of Pelarian myth brooded, but these had an alien cast to them – not Pelarian, but something centuries older. The emerald moss covering them was glistening wet and with the mist wreathing them like smoky breath, she could almost believe they lived.

Beyond them was the bridge they'd seen, rising in a gentle curve that ended at a giant gatehouse protecting the old city. The span was wide enough for two wagons – and more importantly, it looked intact. And above and behind loomed the ruined city and the impossible floating rock on which the chained citadel stood, defying gravity.

It's incredible, she thought, *like stepping into a dream.*

Even better, she couldn't see any enemy soldiers, only dead leaves and windblown dirt clogging the bridge's walls. Nothing stirred on it, or behind them. 'Is it safe?' she murmured, loath to speak loudly in such a place.

'It's safe,' Moss said, with unsettling certainty. She almost didn't recognise the patient, stolid man who'd been flirting gently with her ever since he woke in her cart. This man oozed capability and danger – and all trace of a sailor's rolling gait was gone, which unnerved her somehow.

'We should wait for Vyre,' she suggested.

'He's coming,' Moss replied, stroking the muzzle of the dragon statue on the left. 'The earliest tales I remember were of dragons who took human form and taught us sorcery. Some say all sorcerers are of their blood.'

There was an underlying passion in his voice as he spoke, a cold hunger that suddenly made Kemara glad she'd remained wary of his advances.

'Come,' he said, 'let's walk this bridge and ensure it's safe.' He held out his hand, uncharacteristically masterful, and although she didn't dislike such a trait – certainty was an attractive quality in any man – it wasn't the him she thought she knew.

'Hands free,' she told him curtly. 'We don't know what's here.'

He pulled a wry face and she couldn't tell if he was hurt or amused. Then he spun round and marched between the brooding dragons, and out onto the mighty span. She found herself trailing him, feeling like an intruder, as they crossed the threshold of a lost world.

The planetary rings glowed above the silvery arch of the great bridge Raythe was making for – as Above, so Below. Raythe was running now, gambling that if Kemara and Trimble had passed, it was safe, and conscious that time was running out – if Kemara walked straight into the hands of the Bolgravian sorcerers, she wouldn't stand a chance.

They should have waited, he fumed. *Why the krag didn't they wait?*

He jumped a small stream, clambered up a rise, then leaped down onto what turned out to be an old road that dipped into a poumahi-lined cutting leading right to the bridge itself. Drawing his sword, he emerged on a ledge, where he was confronted by two emerald dragons.

Magnificent, he thought, then turned his attention to the bridge: a hundred yards ahead of him, right at the apex of the bridge's arch, he saw two figures silhouetted against the city beyond. He hurried after them and halfway there, risked a low, urgent call.

When she heard him, Kemara stopped and turned – just as a prickling sensation he knew all too well rippled over him from behind. When he spun round, he saw two robed figures, pale orbs glowing in their cowls, now stood between the dragons, facing him. They started carving blue lines in the air, whispering, '*Fear.*'

No, it wasn't 'fear', it was *Vyre*.

They know my real name.

They were Izuvei, fanatics who sacrificed body and soul for power: the sort who'd ripped apart Colfar's front lines. And they were too strong for him alone.

'*Cognatus, animus – scutum,*' he cried, and a sorcerous shield flared

373

around him as he drew his pistol and took aim, though the range was chancy. 'Don't take another step,' he warned.

'Yield, Vyre,' his target rasped contemptuously. The scorn in the ancient female voice was justified, for he knew he had next to no chance of hurting them from here.

'Raythe,' Kemara called, hurrying towards him. Trimble was close behind her.

But the Izuvei weren't waiting: they unleashed a burst of unseen energy which slammed into him, sending coruscating sparks skidding across his translucent shielding. He staggered backwards, almost falling, but somehow his shield held.

Now the Bolgravian sorcerers started advancing, chanting and carving sigils in the air. They were clearly anxious to prevent him melding with Kemara, although they were likely already wrapped in one of their own.

In an attempt to buy time, he went to fire his pistol, but that same invisible force smashed down on his wrist, almost breaking it, and red hot pain seared his vision as the gun dropped harmlessly to the stone.

But Kemara was close and shouting her own summoning words: 'Kaneska alla mizra!'

His wrist was agony, but Cognatus was in him and he pulled himself together. Carving a rune left-handed, he began, 'Cognatus, impet–' but another unseen blow burst over him, sending him reeling, then a second battered him to the ground. He glimpsed Kemara, struggling against shadows, her eyes bulging at the strain, and Trimble was behind her – but surely he should be in front? And he was holding a flintlock, cocked and ready . . .

Kemara, he shouted through the nebulum, the meld! He reached for her with his mind, even though it already felt too late –

–when something fell like a comet from the darkness and with a ferocious roar, slammed into the back of the male Izuvei. Someone shrieked and Raythe saw a large figure plunging a long, lethal claw into the man's chest.

The sorceress gasped and clutched her own breast, as if she and her partner shared the same heart, but the beast had already turned its attention to her: jaws snapped and wrenched, tearing her throat out, and she crashed to the ground.

Growling, the beast ripped a chunk of flesh from the body and started gorging on the bloody tissue.

Vidar . . . he's lost himself . . .

Then a shot rang out and slammed into the bearskin, knocking him off his feet. Snarling weakly, Vidar tried to stand and failed; his shape was losing definition.

Raythe spun, expecting to see more Bolgravians appearing over the apex of the bridge, but it was Moss Trimble, holding a smoking flintlock.

'*Kragga*,' he snarled, snatched up his own pistol and thumbed back the hammer – but before he could fire, Trimble had tossed his emptied weapon aside and grabbed Kemara, locking her in a chokehold with her body shielding his. He placed a stiletto against her left breast. 'Drop your pistol, Vyre, or she's dead.'

'Vidar?' Raythe called over his shoulder, keeping his gun aimed.

Vidar raised his head and croaked, 'Trimble . . . is Zorne.' Then he fell onto his side and lay there unmoving.

Trimble is Zorne. Toran Zorne.

'So,' Raythe said, his voice surprisingly steady, 'we now have a face to the name.'

'You knew my name already?' Trimble – *Zorne* – said curiously. 'How?'

'I was tipped off by friends in Otravia.'

'I shall be interested to learn who. You still haven't dropped the pistol,' he added, gouging the stiletto into Kemara's breast and drawing blood. 'Next time it goes all the way in.'

Raythe took aim at the spy's face. 'You're going to kill her anyway.'

Kemara tried to speak, but Zorne's forearm tightened, choking off her words. 'Why should I? I'm not finished with her,' he said flatly. 'Five seconds.'

'If she dies, you die.'

'I don't think so. Four.'

Behind Raythe, Vidar groaned faintly. Bearskins took a lot of killing. But healers didn't . . .

'Three.'

Does she have anything? Because I don't. The praxis is too slow for this work . . .

'Two.' Zorne gave a faint smile. 'One . . .'

'All right!' Raythe blurted, lowering his pistol.

'Well chosen,' Zorne said, as if praising a child. 'Drop the gun and back away.'

Raythe looked at the pistol, then at Kemara, thinking, *He's going to kill us both in the end anyway.* For a moment he reconsidered firing, but he was a lousy shot left-handed. He placed the gun down, then backed up towards the unconscious bearskin, telling himself, *While there's life, there's hope.*

'Thank you,' Zorne drawled, reversing his grip on the stiletto – and slamming it up to the hilt in Kemara's chest. She convulsed as blood bloomed on her bodice and Zorne dropped her like she was garbage, pulling out the thin-bladed dagger as she flopped lifeless to the stone.

No . . . Kemara . . . no –

'Poetic,' Zorne remarked in a flat voice. 'I have now killed both your women. Tami is rotting in a mud pool near where you bathed.'

Tami's face flashed before Raythe's eyes as he sagged. *'You bastard . . . '*

'No, I am legitimate,' Zorne said, and his voice remained flat, atonal. 'Good family. Full of love.' It sounded like a fiction. The Ramkiseri agent held up the stiletto and said, *'Mutatio gladius,'* while tracing a complex multi-rune.

In seconds, the stiletto grew into a sword, a feat Raythe had heard of but never seen. And even as he stared at the Ramkiseri, a Bolgravian company clattered down the defile behind him, guns raised and bayonets fixed. The trap slammed shut.

Raythe felt his heart tear with loss: the deaths of Tami and Kemara, and the knowledge that he'd failed everyone, including his daughter – and they would all suffer for his failure.

His despair turning to sudden fury, he snarled, *'Come on, then!'* Reaching across his body, he drew his sword left-handed and gripping it awkwardly, he charged forward.

Zorne spun his conjured blade gracefully and came to meet him.

There came a time when prayers weren't enough, and Mater Varahana had reached that point. Prayer needed faith, and her shallow pool of belief was running dry.

The planetary rings lit her way as she passed from tent to tent, talking to those within, bolstering courage where she could. Frightened wives and grandparents were cradling scared children while the menfolk preparing to fight made their peace with Deo. Everyone made her welcome: they wanted to be reassured that Paradise awaited them, that Gerda loved them and would lift them on high – and that miracles were real and Rhamp and Duretto would be able to out-fight a Bolgravian regiment while Lord Vyre found them a way out of this trap.

It was emotionally exhausting, but it left her no time for her own fears, which was a mercy.

But sometime after midnight, on a lonely path between sentry posts, she ran out of distractions.

She clutched the nearest poumahi and sank to her knees in the sopping wet grass, dry-retching until she regained some semblance of calm.

'I never wanted to be a priestess,' she groaned. 'I just wanted to learn the truths of the world.'

Her old life in the Magnian Royal Library flooded back to her: a pampered existence of parchment and old leather and ancient scholars who knew everything and loved to share it. It had been a brief, golden period in her life – and in the history of Magnia too, before the Bolgravians yoked scholarship to the empire and declared 'dangerous' knowledge must be suppressed. She knew exactly what would come tomorrow: the Bolgrav soldiers would butcher the men, then round up whoever was left and the 'fun' would begin. Those who died would be the lucky ones.

Deo, Gerda, help me . . .

But she was all prayed out. The litanies had never been real to her, for Deo was a lie, every scholar knew that.

But I do believe in peace, and in doing our best for each other. I believe in the goodness of people, even though evil is real too. It doesn't come from Deo or the Pit, it's all our own . . .

When she finally opened her eyes again, she saw that the carving on the poumahi she was embracing was an image of Kiiyan, the Goddess of Mercy. Weirdly, it was the serene, alien visage of the Aldar goddess which gave her the strength to rise.

It felt so unfair that she would never get to explore the city on the other side of the ravine, or learn the lost secrets of the world. *I'll die on the threshold of wonder, a frustrated scholar who spent her last years parroting scripture when I should have been living . . .*

She took a deep breath and resigned herself to her brief future. Right now, people needed her. And she could always find a pistol and choose her own ending.

As she neared the gates, she spied shadowy movement around Rhamp's pavilion, which was lit from within by dim lanterns. She hesitated, doubting her welcome, for Rhamp saw her as a rival and enemy and his men, typical soldiers, were a mix of superstitious need and brutality. She was more likely to face derision and hostility than gratitude.

'It is my duty to spread the love of Deo,' she quoted silently. 'There will always be those who refuse to hearken, but they should not steal my tongue.'

Steeling herself, she approached – and stopped dead when she heard an unfamiliar voice saying, 'Yuz, Kapitan Rhamp, you have seen sense.'

The Bolgrav accent froze her soul.

'You say one third of people follow you?' that voice went on. 'Those others will fight, yuz?'

Varahana went rigid, praying to Gerda that she'd misheard, knowing she hadn't.

'Few of them *can* fight, Lord Persekoi,' Elgus Rhamp rumbled. 'If you let my men keep their weapons, we'll stand aside. When the rest see the way of it, they'll capitulate.'

'Of course,' the Bolgravian drawled. 'But ringleaders must be captured or killed. I have names: Vyre, Duretto, Vidarsson, Solus. And the Mater, of course. She must be made example of. Church belongs to Empire.'

'There's no one on that list we'd mourn,' another voice put in: Bloody Thom.

'Aye,' Crowfoot added, 'but Vyre, Vidarsson and Solus are on their way to the bridge – with Moss Trimble, one of your sailors.'

'They are awaited,' the Bolgrav replied. 'We have Izuvei sorcerers, and soldiers also. "Moss Trimble" is ours. He has done well to bring us here to remarkable place. Empire will reward all.'

Perspiration beaded on Varahana's scalp.

Trimble is a spy? Dear Gerda, and he fooled us all. He must have revealed himself to Rhamp when we were cornered, offering him a chance of survival . . .

'My men control the main entrance,' Elgus Rhamp told the Bolgravian. 'Give me half an hour to prepare and we'll open the gates and join your attack, Lord Persekoi.'

'Excellent,' Persekoi drawled. 'I return to my camp. So we say . . . half of hour, yuz?'

'Done,' Elgus Rhamp answered, and other voices muttered agreement.

She'd heard enough. Before the men left, she was carefully retracing her steps, terrified lest she trip on a tent peg or run into a guy rope and betray herself. The moment she was clear, she pulled up her hood and hurried away, a hundred plans bubbling through her mind. They all came down to one thing.

I have to tell someone . . . But Raythe, Vidar and Kemara were gone. *It has to be—*

That thought was not yet fully formed when a dark shape appeared before her, hard hands clasped her arms and a sharp voice murmured, 'Whoa, there, Mater. Are you all right?'

'*Jesco!*' Varahana blurted, and because there were no unbelievers in a battle, '*Thank Deo and Gerda!*'

Zar and Banno stared at the newcomer in absolute shock.

She was a woman, for one thing – young, perhaps eighteen, but in her prime, muscled like a warrior. There was no doubt of that, because all she wore was a shoulder cloak made of feathers, and a beaded skirt with a narrow bodice.

Moreover, she was of no race Zar knew. She was beautiful: her skin was a deep brown, her frizzy hair black, her nose squat and her lips thick and full, and she had the power and grace of a lioness. Her face was tattooed around the cheeks and chin with the same swirling designs found on the poumahi carvings. She had a two-handed wooden weapon, a strange thing like a spear, which she gripped by the sharpened end, brandishing the long, polished wooden shaft like a blade.

'Re-oko, kono mon kinjuru, sha,' the woman shouted, shrugging off her feather cloak and going into a fighting crouch, her eyes blazing.

'What?' Banno gaped.

'Tata'ki, moshi ma haru,' she snarled, stamping her foot.

'What in the Pit is she saying?' Banno asked nervously.

'I don't know,' Zar replied. 'I've never heard a language like that.'

Banno hefted his flintlock and took aim. 'Back off,' he called. 'Back off, or I shoot!'

The woman didn't appear to understand; she just stamped her other foot, swirling her wooden weapon with astonishing dexterity.

'What do I do?' Banno whispered. 'I don't think she even knows this is a weapon.'

The young woman stalked forward, raising her strange weapon to high guard. She looked magnificent, and utterly alien.

Zar caught Banno's arm. 'Don't shoot her.'

'What do I do if she attacks?' he asked, lowering his flintlock.

'Protect yourself – Oh! I have an idea.' Raising both hands, she called,

'*Animus, Adefar*—' and as her familiar rushed in, her night-sight deepened and she felt a rush of sensations, most emanating from the stranger. Now she could smell the girl; her body had a herbal scent to it, like rosemary. '*Ignus,*' Zar added, and flames burst into life above her hands.

The girl froze, her warlike posture faltered and her mouth shaped a perfect 'O'.

But then she carved a symbol on the air and said, '*Kaneska alla maho.*' A nimbus of scarlet flared around her, then faded as she dropped back into martial readiness.

Zar gasped, 'She's a mizra-witch—'

Banno quickly took aim again, but the girl blurred into motion, darting to one side and gesturing with an open palm – and an unseen force knocked the gun up and aside, just as the hammer clicked down, the firing pan exploded, the weapon spurted flame and the ball went shooting into the sky. The girl stumbled backwards, her eyes wide, her mouth gaping . . .

As Banno gripped his flintlock to strike her with the butt, she recovered and, roaring in fury, brought her weapon flashing round. Moving like a dancer, she slammed the wooden blade into Banno's temple and he dropped like to the ground like a sack of flour.

Gasping, Zar tried to snap off a spell, but before she managed more than a syllable, the blunt end of the wooden weapon hammered into her belly and she folded over, panting for air. Then the girl launched herself at Zar, pinning her on her back in the dirt with one knee on her chest. She gripped Zar's throat – but she didn't squeeze. Instead, her big lustrous eyes stared into Zar's with awe.

'Mahotsu-kai?' she asked, in an incredulous, amazed voice. 'Shiro hada mahotsu-kai?'

Then she snapped off another stream of words, her eyes flashed with light, and then to Zar's amazement, she heard her words in common Magnian. 'You are wizard?'

She's channelling her words through our familiars – they know both languages . . .

Zar felt her eyes bulge, hardly able to breathe with the weight of the young witch crushing her. And Banno was lying unmoving beside them.

'Please,' she gasped, 'we're here in peace.'

They stared at each other, open-mouthed, then the brown-skinned girl moved one hand from her weapon and touched Zar's lips. Staring at her, she said, 'I am wizard, like you. Where you come from?'

But before Zar could reply, a score of men in what looked like boiled-leather armour poured through the poumahi arch. They all wore their hair in complicated topknots and carried polearms tipped with spear-points or axe-heads. Like the girl, they were brown-skinned, with heavily inked faces.

The young woman got up, and only then did the men catch sight of Zar and Banno – they gaped at the strangers and took a step back, their own eyes wide in shock.

Adefar, Zar whispered in her mind, *do you know their tongue?*

In response, Adefar did the unexpected, flashing to Rima's shoulder, where a lizard appeared. The two pressed their heads together, then Adefar returned and when next the warrior spoke, Zar heard him in Magnian, saying, 'Rima, what are these creatures?'

Not 'who'; but 'what'.

The young woman, evidently Rima, was attracting admiring glances from the warriors as she draped her short feather cloak over her shoulders again. 'I was just about to find out,' she said, swaggering over to Banno's flintlock and picking it up curiously. 'Took you old men long enough to get here.'

'What's that?' the burly leader asked, peering at the weapon.

'Fire-stick,' Rima sniffed. 'It looks harmless.' She tossed it to the man and stood over Zar, who was still clutching her aching stomach. 'This one is a wizard, though. She belongs to us.'

Us? Zar wondered. But that could wait. 'We need your help,' she croaked.

The men started at what must have sounded like gibberish to them, but Rima squatted beside her and caught her chin again. 'You must tell me who you are and where you come from, Pale Girl.'

'My name is Zarelda,' she answered, 'and I can show you where I come from.' She rolled over to check Banno was breathing, relieved to find he was, then climbed painfully to her feet. Without waiting for permission, she tottered back to the crest of the hill and pointed down at the valley, where the Bolgravian campfires still encircled the dimly lit hill-fort.

'I come from down there,' she croaked.

Rima and her warriors joined her at the crest of the hill, sucking in their breath when they saw the fires, muttering questions in voices laced with disbelief.

'Are they another tribe?'

'Who are they all?'

'Where have they come from?'

'What are they doing in the forbidden lands?'

Rima turned to Zar. 'These are Tangato lands. To trespass here is forbidden. But you are mahotsu-kai – wizard – so you are safe, if my Master accepts you.'

Tangato? Zar had never heard of such a people. She stared at the dark girl: close up, she could see that the patterns on the woman's chin had been *chiselled* into her flesh, leaving ridges of ink-stained flesh. *Are these savages?* she thought, determined not to show how frightened she was. *I'm an Otravian sorceress: I fear no one.*

'What about Banno – my friend?' she demanded, trying to match Rima's certainty.

'Him?' Rima smirked. 'Him, we will eat.'

Madly beating heart

Light faded and sound went dim, the sound of blade on blade dropping away, leaving Kemara alone with her madly beating heart, punctured and pumping blood where it shouldn't go, and her fury, most of it directed at herself.

You stupid bitch . . . you know never to trust a man . . . not that you'll ever get the chance again . . .

The damp cold of the stone was seeping into her body – until a dark presence overlaid it, filling her, heart and soul, body and mind, and the hole in her heart somehow *inhaled*, sucking the blood in her chest back into itself, then resealed . . . and *thud – thud – thud* – the beat restarted. Her lungs blasted a passage up through her throat, making her silently convulse; she vomited blood, then gulped down a mouthful of air: of *life*.

Inside her mind, a masked face chuckled and whispered, *Child, we're not dead yet.*

Her eyes flew open and her senses exploded back to life.

The chime of steel on steel reached her first: twenty yards away, she could see Trimble – *no, Zorne: Toran Zorne* – hammering at Raythe Vyre, who was fighting hunched over and left-handed, barely keeping to his feet. Even as she watched, Zorne lashed out with his boot, catching Vyre on the side of his right knee, and he crashed to the ground. He desperately threw himself into a roll, barely evading what would undoubtedly have been a finishing blow; instead, Trimble's – no, *Zorne's* – sword clanged off the stone bridge. The Otravian rose again, breathing hard, and lunged, forcing Zorne to back away.

'Nearly,' Zorne noted flatly.

How did I ever let that man get close to me? she wondered. *He's hollow inside . . .*

Beyond them, there were now at least twenty Bolgravian soldiers lined up, the lead men holding torches and the rest with flintlocks raised skywards, watching Zorne play cat and mouse with his victim.

Ready yourself, Buramanaka murmured, and this time Kemara found she could see him clearly in her mind. He was clad in overlapping strips of burnished bronze, like an armoured panther, and wore the scarlet mask she'd plucked from his tomb. He held a long-handled sword, gently curved and shimmering like liquid.

No one noticed when she sat up stiffly; nor could they tell her blood was once again coursing through her. The duellists were locked onto each other; to the onlookers beyond, she was just a dark patch amid the shadows.

Raythe was trying to rally when Zorne stuck him in the side, then kicked him in the groin. He went down in a heap.

'I think the point's been made,' Zorne noted, signalling to the soldiers. 'Bind him.'

And Buramanaka whispered, *Now, my child . . .*

She rose as energy shimmered through her: the blade Buramanaka had been holding in her mind vanished – and reappeared, cold and real, in her hands – and a new part of her brain quivered with knowledge of exactly how to use it. The leering blood-red mask formed over her face, becoming her, as she became it.

She took a step, took two, and then ran, leaped, and soared right over Zorne's head, over the crumpled Otravian and into the advancing Bolgravian soldiers . . .

'Eat him?' *Gerda on High!* 'No –!' Zar stormed, shoving Rima aside and standing over the unconscious Banno, confronting a wall of tattooed dark faces and powerful bodies. 'He's mine!'

Adefar made the words into their tongue and they all paused, looking her over: a pale, skinny, short-haired girl in strange clothing. A few snorted and one, a giant, ferocious-looking man, spat and strode towards her.

She gulped as she faced his fierce visage with all those coiled markings. He jerked into a head-butt motion, and she instinctively gasped and recoiled – straight back into Rima's hands.

The Tangato woman interposed herself. 'Don't be such a porohea, Kamo,' she sniffed.

Adefar translated 'porohea' as 'idiot'.

'Bullying girls demeans you,' Rima went on. 'And this one is claimed for Hetaru.'

The burly Kamo eyeballed Rima, ran his eyes down her body, rolled his massive shoulders and made a mockingly subservient gesture as he backed away.

Zar let out her breath gratefully.

Rima turned Zar around. They were nearly of a height, but the Tangato radiated capability beyond her years. 'I was joking,' she said. 'We haven't eaten prisoners for years.'

Zar stared. 'You were *joking*? At a time like this?'

'There is always time for laughter,' Rima declared, before turning back to Kamo. 'There are invaders in our valley. Why don't you do something about it, as a warrior should?'

The big Tangato warrior touched his chest with his right hand with ironic deference, as if some private joke were at play between them, then he suddenly twisted and poked his tongue at Zar, leering menacingly.

'Don't be such a porohea,' Zar told him.

He snorted as if her defiance was beneath contempt, then sauntered away, snapping orders. But Rima was evidently impressed. 'You and I are going to be friends,' she chuckled, then she stepped in and pressed the tip of her nose to Zar's, who retained just enough control not to pull away. Nose and then forehead pressed together was a strange sensation, almost as intimate as kissing. Rima's breath smelled of mint-leaf and some unknown spice.

'Koni'ka, Zarelda,' Rima said softly. 'Hayeri a mihi.'

Welcome, Zarelda, Adefar whispered. *Come among us in peace.*

'Um, uh, sure,' she replied awkwardly.

The Tangato girl smiled tolerantly, and stepped away. 'We are Tangato, the Ancient and Always, the People of the Land,' she said. 'Come. The men will see to the fighting. I must take you to Hetaru.'

'But you don't understand,' Zar protested. 'There are two sides down there – two tribes. One is in the fort – they're good people. The others, the greycoats, they are evil.'

'That doesn't matter,' Rima replied. 'These are Tangato lands and that valley is a forbidden place, so they must all die. Come, the Master awaits.'

'No!' Zar backed away. 'My father's down there–' She floundered, then inspiration struck. 'He's a mahotsu-kai as well – he's guiding us through these lands – so you have to help us against the greycoats.'

Rima cocked her head, curiously like a bird, looking perplexed. 'Your father also? *Subarashi.*'

Incredible, Adefar fed her. *Fantastic. Unbelievable.*

The Tangato sorceress strode after Kamo and drew him into a rapid-fire exchange, then turned back to Zar and said urgently, 'Come, I must take you to Hetaru, quickly.'

But before they could go, a new figure appeared in the arch of the poumahi and everyone present went absolutely still.

Zar's first impression was of vivid colour – a splash of bold red with gold embroidery so thick that the fabric barely moved. The face was starkly white, as if painted, topped by a tall pile of black hair, carefully braided and coiled atop the head and adorned by gold chains.

Zar couldn't tell if the figure was male or female for the elaborate robes concealed all shape, and the gait made it look like they were gliding. Behind them came more colourful figures, then a group of burly men beside a palanquin which was empty except for an elaborate, glittering throne.

But Zar's eyes were fixed on the figure with the painted face. *Female,* she guessed from the accoutrements, a glittering painted fan and rings on every long, delicate finger.

Rima's switch from strut to subservience was instantaneous. Dropping to one knee, pulling Zar down with her, she unleashed a torrent of words that Adefar translated as, 'Long life to you, Great Queen. I exist to serve.'

Zar kept her eyes lowered for all of five seconds, before burning curiosity – and the thought that Otravians didn't kneel – got the better of her and she looked up.

The newcomer was standing before her and the white face wasn't a face at all, but a mask. Red lacquer lines around the chin were similar to Rima's, but more elaborate. The masked visage was severe, narrow-eyed and covered all of her face, but the eyes were human, gleaming beadily, like a bird's, and focused intently on her.

'Please,' Zar blurted, her words tumbling out in their tongue, 'help my people.'

'Do not speak uninvited,' Rima hissed. 'I'm sorry, Great Lady, she's –'

'Gaikiko,' the lady, interrupted, her voice cold, inflexible. *Foreign, alien.*

Her entourage crowded around. They were clad in a panoply of glittering silks in every bright hue and wearing masks of copper, some fashioned like animals, some human. They murmured to each other as they stared down at Zar.

'Foreign,' Rima agreed, 'but a sorceress.'

'*Ah*,' the courtiers muttered. 'Mahotsu-kai.' *Sacred.*

With a flick of her wrist, the Lady folded her fan to a needle-point, reached down and touched it – it was as sharp as a stiletto – to Zar's chin and lifting it, as Rima had done earlier, she said coldly, 'Yabanhito'– which Adefar translated as 'barbarian'. 'If she is a sorcerer, take her to Hetaru. She belongs to him now. All other foreigners must die.'

'*No!*' Zar shouted, rising to her feet.

The eyes behind the mask bulged indignantly, but before anyone else could speak, Rima rose, grabbed Zar's arm and snapped, '*Kizetsu* –'

Stupefy, Adefar translated helpfully as a fist of darkness scattered her awareness across the stars.

⟁

Sometimes, you must make the hard calls, Elgus Rhamp reminded himself. *It doesn't always feel good, but alive beats dead, and that's the biggest truth of all.*

The lads didn't like it either, and that was understandable: no one liked crawling to the kragging Bolgies – but what choice was there? *We had a good run, we've seen a few sights and now, if Persekoi keeps his word, we'll live to tell the tale.*

That had to be better than being slaughtered so far from home that their ghosts would wander for ever.

He was waiting with Crowfoot and Bloody Thom at the main gate. Banno should be here, but no one could find him, or Zarelda Vyre. *That girl must be quite a lay, to turn his head so.* If he could get his surviving son out of this alive, it'd be a good night's work.

If not, I'll take one of Gravis' whores and make more . . .

Then a greycoat runner appeared. 'Is ready, yuz?' he said, in that hateful accent.

'Aye,' Elgus growled. 'Come ahead.'

Persekoi wanted his own men to lead the attack and Elgus was fine with that. There was too much fellowship now between his lads and the Teshveld folk for this to be easy. 'Set a few men to guide them in,' he told Crowfoot. 'Let the Bolgies do the killing.'

The Bolgravian runner returned a few minutes later with the first ranks of grey-clad men, their uniforms looking ghostly in the ring-light. Persekoi was at the front, his blandly handsome face confident, his mind already on future rewards.

'Sir Elgus,' he said loftily, 'is ready, yuz? You come with me, share in triumph, mmm?'

In other words, if this is a trap, you die too.

Elgus gestured towards the higher slopes. 'My sword is yours.'

Persekoi peered at Elgus' old broadsword, a relic of a time when all soldiers wore armour and guns were too unreliable to be any real threat. 'You keep,' he smirked. 'Put over mantelpiece to show children.'

This is my father's sword, you wanker, Sir Elgus didn't retort. Instead he bowed and fell into step with the komandir, leading the first wave of Bolgravians into the fort. In moments there were dozens of them inside, winding their way upwards to where the villagers slept. Their bayonets were glittering silver, needles of death. Elgus wondered how many would have to die before those left surrendered. More particularly, he wondered if Persekoi could be trusted.

Where are you, Banno? he worried. *Wherever it is, keep your head down . . .*

He clanked along beside the Bolgravians, still boiling over the dismissive jest about his sword, but feeling like an anachronism in his armour. Persekoi was right: the old ways – *his* ways – were dying out. Men didn't fight head to head now, but shot each other from yards apart, without having to look their opponents in the eye. This was war the imperial way: massed slaughter replacing old-fashioned guts and glory.

Like it or not, I have to roll with it. The future belongs to Persekoi and his ilk.

They climbed up through the empty first tier, for the Teshveld folk had bedded down in the old huts on the upper levels, behind the inner palisades. The cooking fires had all died down and no one was around to challenge them –

–until a sudden volley rang out, tearing up the silence: flintlock muzzles were flashing above them, sending balls whistling through the palisades and hammering into the ranks of Bolgravians. He heard shrieks from the wounded, but most folded with little more than agonised grunts, tumbling to earth as a second volley, this time of arrows, sleeted down, skewering the grey-clad soldiers as they scurried for cover – but there wasn't much: they were almost completely exposed to the attackers above them.

Miraculously, he wasn't struck, and nor was Persekoi, who dived in behind the same low earthen bank. Bolgravian voices were clamouring all around them, shouting in fury, but to his bemusement, no one was firing back.

'Shoot, damn it,' he told Persekoi, 'you need to return fire—'

The Bolgrav was scowling fiercely, but now he admitted, 'No powder – was lost in glacier flood.'

Bloody Vyre, Elgus thought, aware of the irony. *He's going to get me killed after all.*

'Obvini—' the Bolgravian officers shouted, '*obvini!*' *Attack – attack!*

Those who could rose and attempted to storm up the hill – which served to reveal the genius of the primitive fort, for they ran straight into the next palisade fence, which afforded no cross-bars for climbing, just spaced poles too narrow to squeeze through, but wide open when it came to defenders shooting from above. More arrows slashed down on the greycoats, and then another volley sent the Bolgravians reeling back, screaming their pain and fear and fury.

Elgus could pick out the voices giving the orders: Jesco Duretto, Cal Foaley and even Mater Varahana. *They knew – but who blabbed? Gerda's Tits, was it my Banno? But how did he know?*

'*Obvini!*' Persekoi shrieked again, and the next wave of soldiers came up and went piling forward – straight into the teeth of another vicious volley, which sent them stumbling back, leaving even more bodies scattered across the killing ground.

Persekoi whirled on Elgus and ordered, 'Bring your men up – join the attack!'

Elgus bit his lip, thinking, *Where are their kragging sorcerers? And where's Vyre?* Suddenly, this plan was going the way of his previous ones. *Am I going to die helping the kragging empire?*

But he saluted Persekoi, then ran down the slope to take charge of his men. 'Thom, Crow, get the lads into line—'

'What the feck's going on?' Bloody Thom snarled.

'Blood and chaos,' Elgus roared. 'We're going in.' Seeing the doubt, he sprayed spittle in his lieutenants' faces, roaring, 'It's do or die: come on!' He whirled, raised his old-fashioned broadsword and shouted, 'Pelarians, forward!'

They didn't like it, but he was proud that they followed him, falling in with the next line of sweating, fearful Bolgravian soldiers preparing to march up the slopes. *Vyre's lot must be getting low on powder*, he told himself. *They'll break.*

The Bolgravs took the slope at a run, stumbling over bodies and slithering on the wet grass as they shouted to Deo and Gerda. They slammed into the palisades and hacked at them with axes – until the defenders opened up again, the rattling, flashing musketry presaging the dark flowers bursting into bloom on chests and faces, followed by silent arrows sleeting down, cutting down more and more of the attackers.

Elgus' mercenaries were up next, but when he hesitated, so did they.

'Obvini!' Persekoi snarled, appearing beside Elgus. 'You will attack!' He had a drawn sabre in one hand, his pistol in the other. The braid adorning his immaculate uniform glowed in the ringlight. 'Get your cowardly savages moving, Rhamp!'

That fecking does it.

His longsword crunched into the crook of Persekoi's neck, smashed his collarbone and severed his throat. The man's face swelled in shock as his legs went.

'Not such a fecking relic, eh?' Elgus roared, kicking him off the blade and bellowing, *'PELARIANS: KILL THE KRAGGING BOLGIE BASTARDS –'*

Mercenaries were used to this sort of *volte-face*; often as not it was the only way to stay alive. They reacted instantly, plunging blades into the backs of the men before them, shouting, *'PELARIA – PELARIA –'*

In moments, the remainder of the Bolgravians were dead or running from Rhamp's men. Those at the rear fell back, spilling out onto the plains. The Pelarians cheered, hollering insults at their backs as they fled into the gloom, and the defenders added their own voices.

But there are still plenty of Bolgies out there, Elgus thought, *and there's the small matter of how I extricate myself from this mess. One step at a time . . .*

For now, he grabbed Persekoi's plumed hat and put it on the end of his sword, shouting, 'Duretto – you there? It's Elgus –'

There was a ringing silence.

Then Jesco Duretto's voice rang out, coolly derisive. 'Sir Elgus? Gracious, is that you?'

'Pretend it was all planned,' Crowfoot murmured in his ear.

'I'm already there,' Elgus muttered, before hollering, 'Lured 'em in and nailed them – just like I said I would.'

There was a pregnant silence. 'Did you just? When was that?'

'*Uh*—'

'The runner must've got lost,' Crowfoot whispered.

'The runner must've got lost,' Elgus parroted, then inspiration struck. 'I sent him to Banno – thought he was with you. Gerda's Teats, tell me my lad's safe.'

It was a gamble: Banno really might be up there, having betrayed his own kin, but he didn't think so. The boy was a love-struck fool, but he was a loyal Rhamp.

This time Jesco's response wasn't quite so sarky. 'Banno's not here.'

'Deo on High,' Elgus shouted, relief flooding him, 'damned boy can't think past his codpiece.' He winked at Crowfoot. 'Are we good to come up? Feeling a bit exposed out here, and the Bolgies are regrouping.'

There was a pause, then Jesco, sounding decidedly vexed, called, 'Come ahead.'

There was still some chance they would get their heads shot off, but Elgus decided to risk it. Waiting here for the Bolgies would be suicide, and Vyre's people had some honour.

Like I used to . . . But his lads were alive, at least until dawn. *No regrets, no looking back.*

'We're coming up with hands raised, so you know it's us,' he called. 'There's still a shitload of Bolgies out there. I killed their commander, but they'll find another and come again.'

Another pause, then Jesco called, 'Sure, all good.'

Crowfoot slapped his shoulder and grinned.

Bloody Thom muttered, 'We gonna feck them over?'

'Nope. That moment's gone, Thom. Persekoi's down and we don't know what his replacement's made of. And you know what? I'm starting to feel that betting against Vyre is a losing wager. Let's see if the prick survived his jaunt to that bridge and how it all shakes down at dawn before we commit again.'

'But some Bolgies escaped; they'll know we backstabbed them.'

'Fog of war,' Crowfoot sniffed. 'Never happened.'

Elgus sheathed his sword, picked Persekoi's beautiful sabre as a trophy – 'For the mantelpiece,' he muttered to himself – before leading his men up the slopes. They picked their way between scores of Bolgravian corpses, until they reached the palisade where Duretto and Varahana had deployed their flintlocks and archers to lethal effect. He went to the gap, where the too-pretty Shadran waited.

'Cleverly played,' Jesco drawled, his tones ambiguous. 'Even I doubted for a moment.'

In other words, he's almost certain we tried to screw them, but he can't prove it.

'I'm sorry the runner didn't reach you,' Elgus bluffed. 'Communication breakdown. Won't happen again.'

'It really had better not,' the Shadran said. 'Come on up.'

Seeing Varahana cradling a smoking gun, Elgus said, 'I thought you a woman of peace, Mater Varahana?'

'Needs must,' the Mater replied, her elegant face expressionless. 'Gerda was also a warrior.'

Looking around, Elgus realised that the only folk here were the best hunters and most redoubtable of the villagers. 'Where're the women and children?'

'By now, halfway to the bridge,' the priestess answered.

'Then you've heard back from Vyre?'

'No, but we decided we couldn't wait.'

'You slipped the cordon on the west side, then?'

'They were all Teshveld folk there,' Jesco replied. 'Hawkstone's men. They had a change of heart and let us through.'

Elgus blinked in surprise. '*Larch Hawkstone?* Don't trust him—'

'Oh, I think I know who I can trust,' Jesco said archly. 'Come on, ladies, it's time to go—'

He stopped suddenly and they all turned and stared as a fresh uproar arose from the plains to the south. The wind carried the sound of panicked voices, screams and battle-cries. Fire flared, setting the Bolgravian tents alight, one after the next, until the whole camp was in flames.

'What in the Pit?' Elgus blurted.

Crowfoot and Bloody Thom were looking as mystified as he.

'There's only Bolgravs out there, right? Have they turned on each other?'

Jesco clapped Varahana's arm. 'Who cares? This is the chance we need. Come on, let's go.'

The first moments were bewildering and glorious. Kemara's vault took her right to the front of the Bolgravian soldiers closing in on the help-less Otravian, and Buramanaka's sword swept round with a power and a precision that was nothing to do with her and everything to do with Buramanaka, who was riding her body with bloodthirsty glee.

Even as she landed, her first blow cleaved through the neck of the leading officer before she unleashed a wave of force that scattered men like dolls, knocking aside bayonets and muzzles, then she was among them, spinning like a top and carving a circle in blood. Her sword sliced through flesh, bone, wood or metal as if they were shadow – five men lay dead in three seconds – then she blurred left, away from lunging shafts of steel, and scythed down three more. Carried along by a wave of fury, she lashed out a foot and broke a man's nose; she lunged and took another in the heart. She found herself crying out in pleasure as a bayonet scoured her back before beheading the man who *dared* harm her. She leaped and landed, going low this time as she spun around, and another foe was downed, his legs severed at the knee.

The remainder, less than half of the original twenty, broke and pelted back towards the dragon statues as if she were the Queen of the Pit.

Perhaps I am.

395

She straightened from her fighting crouch, drooling blood and laughing.

Then something punched into her, knocking her off her feet and sending her sprawling among the corpses. Fluting Bolgravian voices rose as two sorcerers – Karil and Jorl, her familiar told her – emerged over the apex of the bridge. They must have been waiting on the far side to close the trap.

Toran Zorne darted to the edge of the bridge and picked up Raythe's discarded pistol, then throwing wide his arms, conjured a sorcerous shield.

He's Ramkiseri, she realised, *so he's also a sorcerer*. How he must have been laughing inside as he flirted with her. The thought made her blood boil.

But it occurred to her that she should run: three sorcerers against one was suicide.

Inside her, Buramanaka snarled, *Kill or be killed. The Lord of Blood does not flee. Get among them before they can conjure.*

Then Raythe Vyre groaned, rolled over and looked up at her, scarlet-masked and coated in blood. 'Kemara?'

'Get up,' she ordered, her eyes on the advancing sorcerers. 'Get up and fight.'

'What–?' Then he followed her gaze and mumbled, 'Oh.'

'Exactly,' she said tersely. 'Come on, Vyre, let's see what you're really made of.'

Not nothing, evidently, for he rose shakily and murmured, '*Cognatus, animus*,' and then, more strongly, '*Praesemino. Habere scutum.*'

His mind brushed hers, the sensuality of the meld flaring between them, bringing traces of his smell, his heat, his taste. An orb of light encased them, lighting the bridge around them.

The Bolgravian sorcerers instantly attacked, the fire erupting towards them turning the outside of their shield scarlet.

'*Consano*,' Vyre shouted, and the shield was reinforced. The flames faded, revealing the pale faces of their foes a dozen yards away. Zorne darted to one side and took aim.

Kemara, feeling Buramanaka snarling inside her, cried out, 'Cuzka kazei—' and battered the twins with a blast of wind, but her meld with Raythe was weaker than it'd been in the glacier or at the beach and their protections held.

Vyre's wounded and exhausted, and I'm . . . She hesitated, caught between two thoughts. *Am I too much Buramanaka, or not enough?* Previously Vyre had led, but he looked stupefied by injury and blood-loss.

Then the Bolgravian sorcerers shrieked and raised their arms to the sky. Thunder cracked, so loud the stone arch quivered, and Kemara, seeing a flash, grabbed at Vyre's arm and raised her other hand, palm out, denying the blast. An instant before striking, the bolt of lightning visibly *bent*, blasting a pit into the bridge surface instead, sending splinters of rock flying about them.

She saw Zorne stagger, struck by a flying stone, but he kept hold of Vyre's pistol and pulled the trigger at the moment all her protections were down—

Raythe was in the meld and yet not: present and gone. Everything was happening through a haze of exhaustion; it was all he could do to cling to awareness. Kemara's sweat and blood filled his nostrils but she was *over there* when she should be *inside* him.

Then the sky cracked in two, something ripped through the air and blinded him. He reeled back, feeling the light encasing him and Kemara fail, and dropped to one knee. He tried to stand, not even sure which way was forward, and now Cognatus was flapping inside him like a caged bird, shrieking in Old Magnian, *Fight, damn you – it's my life too—*

He opened his eyes in time to see Zorne's pistol bark. Kemara staggered backwards with another hole in her chest and fell onto her back.

'No,' Raythe croaked, picking up his blade left-handed again, hopelessness filling his heart. 'You will not take us alive.'

Zorne looked at him curiously, assessing his risk, then tossed the spent pistol aside and drew his sword again. 'We don't want you alive, Vyre. I just need proof you're dead.'

He's already beaten me once before.

Then Kemara sat up again, coughed blood and said, 'You keep missing my heart, dear "Moss".' She stood and stalked to Raythe's side. 'Perhaps you don't know where I keep it.'

The sorcerer twins halted, their eyes widening, and chorused fearfully, '*Nava!*'

Nava: the Bolgrav word for living corpse.

But Zorne snarled, 'She's sustained by a mizra-spirit. Break the link.'

He stepped aside and a moment later, a torrent of energy blazed from the sorcerers' hands – but Raythe had already reached out and grasped Kemara's hand and this time he held nothing back.

'*Habere, scutum,*' he bellowed, and their shield flared just in time to repel the blast of energy, giving the instant they needed for their souls to lock – and in a burst of vivid clarity he saw Buramanaka was feeding Kemara life while she fed him energy. He saw her truly for the first time: a woman who'd suffered but still loved humanity enough to be a healer. Despite the callous mask she showed the world, she was a fighter, one who stood for what was right.

Like him, then. *Who knew?*

The meld flared between them, but even so, the next assault nearly ripped them from each other. He felt Cognatus and Buramanaka howling: they were like sand castles caught in a gale, flying apart grain by grain – but somehow, the four of them, desperate to live, held on together.

But the assault faded at last and now they countered, impelling themselves forward in a blinding rush, sweeping up the bridge with swords swinging.

Roaring defiance, Kemara went straight for the twins, her conjured blade slashing through both necks in one blow. They remained standing – until the heads rolled off, leaving neck stumps spurting blood, and at last the bodies crumpled to the ground.

Raythe's leap took him to Toran Zorne, standing at the edge of the bridge. His blade smashed down, this time breaking Zorne's in two, and the momentum carried the tip straight into the Ramkiseri's right breast, pushing him backwards.

Zorne struck the stone rampart—

—then flipped off the edge of the bridge and fell, plummeting head over heels into the torrent below.

Raythe gripped the rim and saw Zorne strike the water and vanish below the surface.

He cursed, but right now Kemara was more important. He staggered up to her before whispering, '*Abeo*.' Cognatus left him, taking away all his strength, and the way Kemara slumped into him, he knew her familiar – her *demon* – had been dismissed too.

A trace of the hyper-intimacy of the meld lingered, because he found himself reaching with hands and mouth and soul to consummate the bond they were forging—

—until she punched him, *hard*.

'Hey—' he gasped, stars colliding in his head.

'Don't take liberties,' she snarled, a wounded lioness. 'That bloody meld has *nothing* to do with anything.'

He rubbed his jaw ruefully. 'Oh, come on – we just saved each other's lives.'

'We just danced on a volcano.'

That was true . . .

'But it hasn't erupted yet.'

'There's always tomorrow.'

He noticed that her strangely curved sword had vanished, and so had the mask – and that her chest was a sticky mess of blood. He couldn't imagine how she still lived. 'Don't take this wrong,' he said, 'but I have to know.'

He reached out and pulled open her ripped, blood-soaked bodice, enough to uncover the wounds on her chest. The ringlight showed a triangular wound above her left breast and a circular one above her right. Both were seared shut and looked weeks old.

'Holy Gerda,' he breathed.

She pulled her bodice together and sat up, gazing at the scattered bodies around them. 'Deo on high, what a mess.'

'You did all of it,' he noted. 'I just got beaten up.'

She swallowed, then abruptly turned away and vomited.

'How are you even alive?' he asked.

'Don't know.' She shook her head. 'He – Buramanaka – he said he'd not finished with me.'

'Legends say that the Aldar took a lot of killing. According to what I've read, you had to pretty much behead them, or cut their hearts out, then burn the bodies.'

She looked at him blankly. 'I'm just a woman.'

Raythe laughed. 'You were *never* just that.'

He left her with that thought and limped back until he found Vidar's body. Steeling himself, he checked for a pulse – and sagged in relief when he actually found one. *I've lost Tami, but I haven't lost Vidar. Thank you, Deo, if you're listening. Which I can't imagine you are, being imaginary . . .*

He straightened and peered towards the hill-fort, a shadowy silhouette beneath the rings.

Of course, I may have lost everyone else . . .

Then shouts rang out and he saw Gravis Tavernier leading a straggling line of villagers, mostly women and children, onto the bridge. They stopped abruptly, gaping at the carnage in blank horror.

'Who's there?' Gravis called shakily, seeing their silhouettes.

'It's me, Raythe Vyre. What are you doing here?'

'Jesco told us to come while he held the rear,' Gravis panted, then turned and called, 'It's okay: it's Lord Vyre – thank Gerda, he's cleared our way!'

A ragged cheer rose from the Teshveld folk appearing, bearing their possessions. They stared at him and Kemara, and he noted how many were also making signs against evil.

'Kemara, Vidar's hurt,' Raythe murmured. 'Could you tend him, please? I need to direct things, and–'

'—and you know krag-all about healing,' she finished for him.

'Quite. And I have to find Zar and see what's happened back at the fort, and—'

'Yes, yes,' she snorted, 'go on, Lord Vyre – I'll clean up after you. I'm used to it by now.'

If she was softening, it was imperceptible – but when their eyes met, there was definitely something new there. Perhaps she'd read his soul the way he'd read hers and not hated what she saw either . . .

But they could explore that later. For now, she was already bending over Vidar, while he began directing his people's efforts, as the now familiar weight of responsibility settled on his shoulders once again. There was a lot to do if they were to survive the night, after all. He pulled aside the first group of villagers and set them to work. 'Throw the Bolgravians into the river, then get yourselves across the bridge.'

As he passed him, he clapped Gravis Tavernier on the shoulder: it was the old miscreant's knock on the door that had started all this, after all. The sky had cleared and ringlight illuminated the majestic bridge and the ruins beyond, beneath the impossible floating Aldar castle, tethered by those massive chains.

Vashtariel's city . . . and the greatest motherlode of istariol ever known, if the tales are true.

Then he looked back towards the hill-fort and muttered a prayer that those he loved would make it safely here.

Epilogue

Over the bridge

The sun rose far away above the eastern ranges, and Raythe squinted from his vantage atop the gatehouse overlooking the great bridge that had brought them to this refuge.

At least, I hope it's a refuge and not a death-trap.

Almost everyone was in now: Jesco, Elgus and Varahana had arrived with the rearguard after some kind of action at the hill-fort that he'd not yet been able to get to the bottom of. Jesco and Varahana were certain Elgus had planned betrayal, but the knight was bluffly adamant that he'd tricked the Bolgravs to buy them a chance at survival.

'You can't argue with results,' he'd said heartily.

Well, you can if they're accidental and you intended the opposite, Raythe thought, but proof was another matter. Still, he was used to watching his back.

But he couldn't rest: not with Zarelda and Banno still missing.

He prayed they'd gone off to be alone and now found themselves cut off. *They'll rejoin us soon,* he kept telling himself, but sleep was impossible, which was why he was sitting on the gatehouse, watching the dawn.

'Raythe,' drawled Jesco, whose post it was, 'get some beauty sleep, will you?'

'Too late for that.'

The Shadran looked him over and grinned. 'Oh, not a complete lost cause,' he purred. 'Did you know that we've taken on extra hands? It was Hawkstone who let us through the cordon. He's down below now.'

'Larch Hawkstone? From Teshveld?'

'The very same,' Jesco chuckled. 'He got himself half-killed in the process, but he's been reunited with his family.'

'He has a *family* here?'

'A daughter, by one of Gravis' women – Angrit. Young Rosebud is ecstatic, but Angrit is ... well, less so, but stranger things have happened.' Jesco twinkled. 'Like you and the handsome Kemara, perhaps?'

'Ha! There goes your credibility.'

'Don't deny you admire her,' Jesco chuckled. 'That's plain for all to see.'

'Admire, yes, but it's hardly mutual – and there's a long way from admire to desire.'

'Not in my book,' Jesco laughed. 'I'll say no more, just mark my words.'

'I look forward to throwing them in your face for years to come.'

They faced the dawn, admiring the way the rose-gold light streaked the majestic ruins, rippling in the river below, lighting up the verdant swathe of vines that entangled the lower reaches and glittering on the floating rock above.

Then the light struck the ground on the far side of the bridge and they caught their breath.

There was an army there, ranked and waiting – but not an army like Raythe had ever seen before. Every man looked to be in boiled-leather armour. Their skin was almost as black as their hair and their weapons were strangely primitive – he couldn't see a flintlock among them, just halberds, spears and bows. Strange banners flew above them, long triangular pennants in the brightest yellows, reds, blues and greens. And some were mounted on *phorus birds*.

Amid them brightly clad, masked women passed among the lines, messengers or maybe officers, it was hard to say, while others clustered around a throne set above the defile overlooking the dragon statues and the bridge.

On it sat a white-faced figure in scarlet robes. Raythe drew out his little telescope, focused it on the enthroned leader and shivered. Whoever it was wore an Aldar mask.

Then he saw someone kneeling before the throne and he gasped in

403

horror at the sight of his daughter, her head bared, with a halter around her neck.

Dear Gerda, he groaned inside. *They've got Zarelda . . .*

⟁

Zar woke to numbness. 'Ha . . . wha . . .' she mumbled, opening her eyes, blinking up at orange torchlight. There was a strange taste in her mouth and her chin throbbed hotly, but she was shivering with cold.

She was lying on her back. Dark silhouettes looming over her resolved into a sitting figure: a young woman with a dark visage and a tattooed chin. *Rima,* she remembered. The Tangato woman was sitting cross-legged beside her left shoulder, gazing down at her solemnly. 'Koni'ka modoru,' she said gently.

Without Adefar, Zar had no idea what she meant, but it felt like *Welcome back.*

On her other side sat an old man with a shock of white hair, wearing a skirt of flax. His face was completely covered in the Tangato patterns, as were his bare shoulders and his white-haired chest. He had deep brown eyes that bored into hers, but it wasn't a fierce or frightening face – there were many laughter lines.

He must be Hetaru . . .

Zar suddenly remembered and jerked her head up, crying, 'Banno – Banno?' Her speech came out slurred.

Have they drugged me?

Rima laid a hand on her shoulder and her eyes gleamed as she channelled her familiar. *Her mizra familiar . . .* Then the Tangato woman said in Magnian, 'Your man is in the next dwelling. He is safe, and so are you.'

Safe . . . where is safe here?

Zar tried to sit up and realising that she was naked beneath the feather cloak, clutched it to her chest. 'What about my father, and my people?' she asked, shaking off her lethargy.

'Safe, for now,' Rima told her. 'You will see. Shiazar is coming to take you there.'

'Shiazar?'

'You have met her – she is the empress of our people.'

She remembered the imperious masked woman of the previous night and shuddered.

An empress . . . Have we just traded one evil empire for another?

Hetaru made a comment to Rima, then rose and left. The Tangato woman studied her face and said, 'It becomes you.'

The sudden dread that struck Zar crystallised when Rima handed her a polished metal disk. She lifted it and saw her reflection: a skinny, pale-faced girl *with black marks etched into her chin.* They were still raw, a pattern of spirals and swirls that looked menacing and savage.

'What have you done to me?' she whispered in a cracked voice.

'It is a great honour,' Rima told her. 'And necessary, to protect you. Now all know you are one of us: a mahotsu-kai of the Tangato.'

An hour later, Zar was made to kneel before the throne of Shiazar, Great Queen of Earthly Paradise, Guardian of Death's Threshold, Empress of the Tangato and Serene Divinity of Light, to name but a few of her titles, who sat above her, conferring with her war chief, Kamo, and Hetaru, her high priest.

'One of us' or not, Zar was leashed round the neck like a pet – or a prisoner.

But Adefar was inside her, translating, and ready for more when the time was right. However, when she tried conjuring energy to loosen the leash, the cord itself resisted, and Rima looked at her sharply, shaking her head. She was standing proudly in her feather cloak and little else, more warrior than woman, holding the halter around Zar's neck.

Realising her praxis had been limited, Zar stopped struggling and listened instead.

'Their leader is a sorcerer,' Hetaru was saying. 'We must proceed with caution.'

'But we have his daughter,' Kamo retorted impatiently. 'If he doesn't surrender, kill her.'

'His daughter belongs to me,' Hetaru replied mildly. 'No one will harm she whom the gods have blessed.'

Shiazar silenced them with a gesture. 'You claim her, Hetaru: but can a paleskin really be blessed? Or is she the servant of some nisokami, come to spread evil?'

Nisokami – false god. Zarelda caught her breath as the import struck her. *I'm not safe, for all Rima's assurances. Shiazar could strip me of Hetaru's protection, and then what?*

She looked up at Rima and saw worry in her eyes.

Oh Gerda . . . Blinking back tears, Zar stared across the ravine to the distant figures on the gatehouse roof and whispered, 'Father, *please*, get me out of this.'

THE END

ACKNOWLEDGEMENTS

New series! New hopes, new dreams. New characters to haunt my sleep (or rather, lack of it). New lives to vicariously live, and new rules to play by. Let's do this, Bradley!

Thanks to: Jo Fletcher and the team at JFB and Quercus (especially Molly Powell), for their faith in this series and my writing. Thank you to super-agent Heather Adams for linking us all up (and thanks also to her husband and partner in crime, Mike Bryan).

Thanks to test readers (regular faces Kerry Greig, Heather Adams and Paul Linton, plus a big thank you and welcome to Lee Murray (check out Lee's writing at https://www.leemurray.info/) for their guidance and unflinching opinions. Also thanks to my nearest and dearest, especially my children, Brendan and Melissa, my parents, Cliff and Biddy, my sister Robyn, and all my friends – you know who you are.

But most of all, thanks to my wonderful, patient wife, Kerry, for sharing the highs and helping me through the lows. And of course, hello to Jason Isaacs. Tinkety-tonk and down with the Nazis.

David Hair
New Zealand
January 2020

Read on for an extract from Book Two in
The Tethered Citadel Trilogy

WORLD'S EDGE

Prologue: The Long Road Home

He woke to the sound and feel of words, tumbling from his own mouth, and realised from the dry rawness of his throat that he'd been babbling '*Ruscht, consano, consano a multo, quaeso, lanista . . .*' for hours.

Ruscht – heal me, heal me of it all, I beg you . . . over and over.

And the familiar had been dutifully doing so.

I'm alive . . .

Abruptly he fell silent and just listened to the churning of the river, the moan of wind in trees, the call of birds, the hum of insects and the painful rasping of his own breath. Then taste returned, the bitter tang of blood and river water in his mouth; the smell of damp earth permeated his nostrils.

Then came pain, the agonising damage to his torso, punctured skin and the rending that steel had wrought on flesh – and the exquisite torture of even the subtlest movement. He knew his own body well enough to know that despite waking, survival still hung by a thread.

The worst pain of all, though, was the bitter ache of defeat. He'd been cast down, hurled into the gorge and washed up here to die alone.

But I am Toran Zorne, Under-Komizar of the Ramkiseri, and I am never alone. My empire is with me.

That reminder, that pride, rekindled his endurance. He opened his eyes and found himself wallowing in the shallows of a sluggish river, half in and half out of the current. He crawled forward and collapsed on the stony shore beneath high cliffs.

A river that carries traces of istariol, he remembered.

A river that soon became a lake, that became a glacier, that inched towards the sea before becoming another lake, then another river, flowing through Verdessa into the sea ... a miraculous journey, possible only through the strange geography of Shamaya, where a motherlode of istariol could create pockets of benign, life-supporting climate, even hundreds of miles inside the frozen wastes.

Fragments of memory had started returning. He knew how he'd got here – his last coherent memory was of Raythe Vyre, off his feet and surely dying, and yet somehow the bastard had managed to plunge his sword into his gut.

Toran Zorne rolled over, peeled away the sodden material and examined the wound, still livid, but newly sealed. It should have been fatal, maybe not instantly, but in the hours afterwards. He should have been bleeding out while lying unconscious in the water.

But I have you, Ruscht, and you have kept me alive.

This wasn't unheard of, a familiar keeping their host-sorcerer alive, even without instructions. Familiar spirits might not be terribly intelligent, but some things stuck in their wayward minds, and uppermost of those was that the human they'd bonded to *must not die*. And if there was one thing Ruscht was well-practised at, it was putting his master back together again.

'*Abeo, Ruscht*,' Zorne breathed. *Rest now.*

The familiar squirmed in pleasure at his approval, then left his body. Magic – even unconscious magic – was draining, and what they both needed above all was to rest. As the invisible spirit vanished, Zorne rolled back to the river's edge, lapped at the water until his thirst dissolved, then closed his eyes and let the tranquil sounds sweep him away into darkness.

When he woke again, it felt like the following morning. He found Ruscht inside him again, unable to stay away, and the wound, while still painful, was binding up, thanks to the familiar's presence. Using magic to heal others might be nigh on impossible, but repairing oneself was easier. He clambered to his feet and scouted the area until he found a bit of a trail along the river beneath the cliffs. It took him up and out of the ravine to a low rise at the south end of a plateau. After a while, he managed to get his bearings: he'd been here before, just a few days ago.

He'd been Moss Trimble then, one of the three hundred souls the infamous Raythe Vyre had led here, searching for istariol. A simple man, Trimble had been, with base habits. As Trimble, he'd been courting the midwife, Kemara Solus, while trying to get close enough to plunge a stiletto into her black mizra-heart.

Her familiar saved her, just as Ruscht has now saved me . . . but hers pulled her back from having her heart impaled – and then turned her into a killing machine.

Such was the potency of a mizra-witch – and if she was one, so Raythe Vyre must be too. It wasn't through cunning or skill they'd stayed one step ahead of the empire, but through the deepest evil known.

It occurred to Zorne that for the first time in his life, he was outmatched.

That notion haunted him all morning as he walked north, staying low to the ground, moving from copse to dell towards an impossible city that grew against the northern skyline. *Rath Argentium*: a place he'd never believed existed, let alone thought might have survived the Ice Age. But there it was: Shiro Kamigami, the dreaded citadel of the god-kings, chained and floating above the Silver City. It could be no other.

Finally he was close enough to see the camp his Bolgravian allies had made before assailing Vyre's position, a hill-fort at the edge of the ravine.

As he drew closer, a chill shuddered up his spine.

The Bolgrav camp was *utterly* destroyed, as if a hurricane had blown through it. The bodies of the soldiers were strewn everywhere, lying where they'd fallen, being picked over by thousands of vultures and dozens of the giant flightless phorus birds they'd thought were extinct or even mythic. But there were men present too, brown-skinned, with black hair, carrying what looked to be basic spears and clubs, who were calmly looting the camp. Remarkably, they were being directed by garishly robed women, some of whom were actually *riding* the giant birds.

They've destroyed an entire Bolgravian regiment . . . but who are they?

Shocked to the core, he circled the destroyed camp before heading for the bridge that crossed the ravine to Rath Argentium. He found a low hill where he could survey a troubling scene: arrayed on this side of the bridge, thousands more of the strange warriors were facing the city. They were singing and beating their chests and shaking their weapons, but making no direct attack.

He could see the bridge, where the demonic pair had slain four imperial sorcerers and forced Zorne to throw himself into the river. The greatest concentration of warriors was there, facing across the span – and was that *a throne*? It was surrounded by bright banners and more people.

Across the bridge, in what appeared to be a fortified gatehouse, he saw the distinctive silhouettes of long flintlocks, which suggested Vyre's people were inside. So Vyre and Solus had clearly got their people into the city while this tribe – who must surely be some unsuspected remnant of the Aldar Age – were slaughtering the Bolgravians. He pictured a surprise attack at night against men who'd run out of gunpowder and been taken from behind. It was difficult to believe and harder to stomach.

That leaves me as the only empire man here.

His assignment was to find and kill Raythe Vyre, a mission he'd been working on for two years now. Duty demanded that he find a way into the city and split the man's black heart.

But that no longer made sense – not because he didn't believe he could still do it, but because the stakes were so high that any kind of failure would be unacceptable. He'd heard the tales about Rath Argentium, and now he believed. Moreover, for a patch of warm land to exist this deep into the ice, the istariol lode here must be immense, the kind of power that could change history.

I can most likely kill Vyre, but if I fail, no one will report this place back to my masters – they will never know of this motherlode until the istariol turns up in the hands of our enemies. That cannot be permitted.

Given that, his course was clear: he must leave this place and report back to his Ramkiseri masters, which would mean retracing his footsteps: thirty miles or more following the river south, right to the edge of this patch of unfrozen land where it lapped against a glacier, down that glacier for another fifty-odd miles to where it re-melted in

411

northern Verdessa, then more than a hundred miles through the wilds to Rodonoi, the imperial garrison port. From there he'd have to sail for hundreds of miles more to Sommaport on the Magnian coast – and finally, ride another two thousand miles to reach someone with the rank to deal with this.

It would be a journey of insane proportions.

But Vyre did it, to bring his people here. I can do no less.

He didn't believe in Deo or Gerda, so he didn't bother with prayer. He believed in *empire*, the innate destiny of Bolgravia, and his own superiority. So he turned his back on the incredible panorama of the mythic city, faced south and took one step, then another: one injured man, starting on the long road home.

PART 1

Across the Divide

1

Who are these people?

'Who are these people?' Raythe Vyre wondered, gazing from the gate-house tower in awe at the stone bridge and across the far side of the ravine that was protecting his small group of travellers from annihila-tion. Below him, behind a hastily thrown-up barricade of two wagons and some broken timbers, stood a thin line of mercenaries and hunters aiming flintlocks and bows, while dozens more were in position in a variety of vantage points. Behind them were the women and children and old folk of the caravan, readying ammunition, arrows, bandages and stretchers, and setting up water stations.

There's just three hundred of us – and we don't even know if this is the only way into the city.

For now, all he could do was use his spyglass to try to work out exactly what they faced. These were like no other people he'd ever seen, and he considered himself widely travelled. The fighting men were dark-skinned, with distinctive features, sporting black markings on their faces. Those he presumed to be officers had curved metal swords and elaborate leather and metal helmets, while the rest wore patterned leather breastplates which left their arms bare. Their weapons were mostly bows or long wooden spears. Right now, they were all singing, a warlike chant that involved a lot of thigh-slapping and pulling faces.

The only women present were mostly clustered about the throne of their ruler, some of them mounted on the phorus birds. They wore brightly coloured robes and masks with red and black patterns lacquered around the eyes, cheeks and chin. Their hair was elaborately coiled and piled high and they each carried a multi-coloured fan – he thought they might be using them to signal each other. They reminded him, chillingly, of mosaics he'd seen of Aldar women.

'I count two thousand, give or take,' said Jesco Duretto. The tall, handsome Shadran was cradling a long flintlock, a light breeze teasing the black hair that framed his finely chiselled olive-skinned face. 'And there's nothing but smoke coming from the Bolgrav camp. I reckon these folk have killed the Bolgies for us.'

'They might have killed them, but not for us,' Raythe replied, returning his spyglass to a small figure kneeling before the queen's throne. At the sight of that slender fair-haired girl, his heartbeat skittered.

It was his daughter, Zarelda.

Feeling his anguish, Cognatus, his familiar, perched unseen on his shoulder in parrot form, shrilled angrily.

How Zar could be there, Raythe had no idea; in fact, he had nothing but questions. Was this ruined city actually deserted? Who had lived and who had died in last night's chaos? Were any Bolgravs still alive out there? And maybe most importantly: where had these people come from – and what would they do?

'Is Foaley back?' he asked Jesco. The hunter had set off at first light with a group of scouts to determine the state of the city.

'Just now. He'll be up in a minute,' Jesco replied, looking at the warriors and shuddering. 'This is the strangest place I have ever seen, bar none.'

Raythe followed his gaze, past the ruins of tall stone buildings, many with strange curves and crenulations; they looked somehow more akin to art than architecture. Above them was the greatest wonder of all: a huge rock that *floated* above the city, tethered in place by four giant chains, every link longer than a man. And atop that, mostly hidden by the bulk of the floating rock, was a fortress.

'Rath Argentium,' Raythe breathed. 'The royal seat of the last Aldar king. I never believed it was real.'

Jesco pointed to the citadel above. 'They say that when he realised that his reign was doomed, Tashvariel the Usurper locked himself and his courtiers in the banquet hall and for three days and nights they ate and drank and screwed until they were utterly sated, then they took their own lives, rather than yield. They say he murdered his lover Shameesta before he died, and that he haunts the place still, raging against the gods—'

'Enough with the ghost stories.' Raythe grimaced. 'It's scary enough as it is.'

The song of the warriors ended suddenly and Raythe's people stirred, anticipating attack. But another song began, this one mournful. 'It's got a beauty to it,' Jesco remarked. 'I wonder who they are?'

'The women wear Aldar-styled masks. I believe these must be the remnants of the survivors of the fall of the Aldar.'

'Then why aren't they in here?'

'No idea.' Raythe turned as boots thumped on the stone steps behind them and Cal Foaley, a lupine hunter with weather-beaten skin and tangled grey hair, his flintlock slung over one shoulder, appeared.

'Boss, all the scouts are in.'

'And?' Raythe answered, matching Foaley's gruff tone.

'Everyone's accounted for, except your daughter and Banno Rhamp. We lost six, with thirteen wounded, in the hill-fort engagement with the Bolgies. All the gear we could carry is inside, including some larger items people managed to haul over in their handcarts. We've got enough powder and shot for half a hundred volleys, and about as many arrows. We've food for a week, but no fuel for fires and very little water. But we've found steps to the river below and Varahana's already organising water containers. My cousin Skeg swears he's seen fish, too – big 'uns, he reckons.'

'Do we have any way of catching them?'

Foaley grinned wolfishly. 'Skeg was a fisherman – he's onto it.'

'Excellent. So what about the city? Is it secure? Is it empty? Are there other ways in?'

'Gan Cobyn's already ridden the outer wall. There was another bridge on the far side, but it fell down ages ago; this bridge is now the only one, and the rivers completely encircle the place – it's actually an island. The cliffs are sheer, with only half a dozen manmade stairs carved into them, for drawing water, I reckon.'

'Station guards above each set of steps down to the river,' Raythe

415

ordered. 'The only advantage we have is that we're inside and they're outside. Let's not lose that.'

'Ahead of you, boss. I've put some of Rhamp's mercenaries at each vulnerable point.' His tone said exactly what he thought of Sir Elgus Rhamp and his mercenaries.

'About them—' Jesco began.

'Later,' Raythe interjected.

Jesco and Foaley both scowled, then the hunter went on, 'Most of the houses might look wrecked, but there are enough intact to shelter us, many times over. Kemara's set up her infirmary a block behind us and Gravis Tavernier has found what he reckons is an old inn – it's got ovens and furnaces he thinks he can get working. And Matty Varte has found an old garden – it's run wild, for sure, but there's fruit and veg; some we recognise, others we don't. At any rate, there's enough food for the short-term, if they're safe to eat.'

Raythe grinned at him. 'That's encouraging. Show them to Mater Varahana – she's a scholar and might know what's safe to eat. How're Vidar and the other wounded doing?'

Foaley looked down. 'Vidar's the worst – he's at death's doorway. The other injuries are mostly minor, except Fossy Vardoe, who took a bayonet in the chest. Kemara reckons he'll make it, though.'

'I'll visit them when I can,' Raythe said, then he stopped as the latest song ended. 'Hold on, what's this?'

There was a ripple of movement among the warriors across the ravine, who were forming up behind a figure wearing a long cloak of what on closer inspection turned out to be red, green and brown phorus feathers. As they started advancing onto the bridge, Raythe leaned over the battlements and called down to the men aiming weapons at them, 'There's a small group moving onto the bridge. Don't shoot unless I order it.'

He watched the tribesmen advance, training his spyglass on their leader: surprisingly, a young woman, with lustrous black hair and strong, attractive features. Her face had similar markings to the men: war-paint? Or even tattoos?

'It's an embassy,' he called again. 'Don't shoot.'

'Aye, we hear you,' a gruff voice called from below: Sir Elgus Rhamp. They all watched in silence as the group crested the apex of the bridge and stalked towards them. They were holding their spears in a strange way that made Raythe wonder if that was what they actually were: the thick hafts were shaped, and the men held them close to the bronze heads, which was odd. They looked apprehensive, but the young woman appeared completely calm.

'All right, listen,' he called out, 'Jesco's going to fire *one shot* in the air, as a warning. It is *not* a signal to open fire – is that understood?'

'Understood,' the voices chorused.

Raythe nodded to Jesco, who pointed his flintlock skywards and pulled the trigger. The hammer dropped and sparked and the gun shot flame and a ball into the sky, the sound reverberating throughout the valley, making the circling birds scatter.

The men on the bridge visibly flinched, looking round in alarm, which confirmed Raythe's suspicion that they'd never seen a gun before. But the woman spoke to them sharply and kept walking. A low murmur rose from his men below and he couldn't blame them. She was an impressive sight; her feather cloak blowing out behind her revealed just a beaded kilt and bodice, leaving her waist and calves bare. She had the shapely limbs of an athlete.

'Do I shoot again?' Jesco asked, reloading swiftly.

'Wait,' Raythe said. When she was a hundred yards from the gate-house, he called out, 'That's far enough–' although he had little hope he'd be understood.

But to his surprise, the woman halted, and a moment later something flashed from her hand and became a bird that circled above him, unseen by anyone else, shrieking at Cognatus.

Something passed between the two spirits, then Raythe heard a whisper in his ear.

'*Are you . . . Rat Weer?*'

He blinked in surprise. 'I am Raythe Vyre,' he shouted back. 'Do you speak Magnian?'

He saw the woman mutter to herself, then she called back, her words slow and awkwardly pronounced, but understandable, 'I do not speak Maneeyan, but my familiar does.'

Below him, Raythe's gunmen hissed, 'She's a sorcerer.'

Or a witch, Raythe thought grimly. *The Aldar used mizra, not the praxis.* These people clearly had memories of the Aldar, judging from the masks the women wore. *This isn't a conversation I want to have in front of my men,* he decided.

'May I approach you?' he called.

She frowned, shifted her weight from foot to foot, then called, 'Ae.'

He descended to the barricade, admonished his men not to shoot *anyone* without his express command, then, feeling very exposed, he clambered over and walked out onto the span.

The girl came to meet him, stopping ten yards away. Up close she was a picture of vitality, with an expressive, ever-changing face. She wrinkled her nose at him.

I wonder what kind of legend I've stepped out of, in her people's mythology?

'What's your name?' he called.

Disturbingly, she ignored him, instead focusing on Cognatus, and again, something passed between it and her own familiar, a lizard sitting on her head. He was troubled by her skill – he had no idea what she doing or how she could get Cognatus to comply – but she was nodding in satisfaction.

In Magnian Common, she said, 'I am Rima.'

His heart thumped: had she just pulled the knowledge of his language out of Cognatus?

'I'm Raythe Vyre,' he said. 'I seek a truce. We don't want to fight you.'

Her lips moving, she silently translated his words, then said, 'The city is tapu.'

'Tapu?' It wasn't a Magnian word.

She scowled, conferred with her familiar, then clarified. 'Sacred and forbidden. You must leave.'

'We're not leaving,' he replied firmly. 'I wish to speak with your ruler.'

She lifted her chin and said, equally firmly, 'She who leads us is Shiazar, Great Queen of Earthly Paradise, Guardian of Death's Threshold, Empress of the Tangato and Serene Divinity of Light. You are not worthy to speak to her.'

Raythe doubted that even the Emperor of Bolgravian claimed that many titles. 'I am Lord Raythe Vyre, Earl of Anshelm, in Otravia. I have met with rulers of larger nations than your own. Let me speak with your queen.'

'We have your daughter,' Rima announced – for a young woman, she clearly had no shortage of self-confidence. 'You do not set the terms.'

'The life of one is not worth more than those of the many,' he retorted. 'Do not threaten my daughter.'

Rima glared, but mellowed her tone. 'Your daughter is not threatened. She has been adopted by my tribe.'

What? Raythe was momentarily stunned. 'She's on a leash at your empress' knees.'

'No unknown may bear weapons before the throne – her magic is a weapon. The cord resists sorcery; it is necessary for any sorcerer with unproven loyalty.'

Raythe was impressed: such artefacts took skill to make. *They might have primitive weapons, but that doesn't mean their sorcery will be backward,* he reminded himself. 'Release her, and we can talk.'

Rima shook her head. 'A sorcerer is sacred. She must serve Her Serene Majesty. She will learn our ways and live as one of us.'

'No, she will not.'

Rima lifted her chin again. 'The alternative was to put her to death. Would you prefer we had done so?'

'I warn you–'

'Do not "warn". You have come as thieves to a sacred place, to steal that which belongs to us. Go home, never return, and give thanks that your daughter's gift of service has obtained this for you. You have three days.'

With that, Rima turned on her heel and walked gracefully away, as if three dozen flintlocks weren't trained on her back – although Raythe suspected she didn't even know what a flintlock was. The more he replayed her words in his mind, the more they revealed – about her and her people.

'Wait,' he called.

She turned, head held high. 'Yes?'

'Was my daughter alone?'

The girl pulled a thoughtful face, then said, 'Her husband is with her. He is also safe.'

Husband? Raythe went to speak, then realised that Zar wouldn't claim to be married for no reason. His face impassive, he asked instead, 'What is required for me to meet Queen Shiazar?'

Rima considered. 'Her to desire to meet you. Perhaps it may occur.' Then she turned again, and strutted away.

'She's a heck of a woman,' Cal Foaley breathed when Raythe got back to the barricade.

'Wild and wonderful,' Jesco agreed admiringly.

Raythe stared after her as the men began to relax and chatter. 'Right,' he said eventually, 'we need a leaders' meeting. Cal, take charge here.'

Foaley saluted offhandedly and sauntered away.

Jesco plucked urgently at his sleeve. 'Listen, before we do, you need to know that last night Elgus Rhamp tried to change sides, then covered it up when the Bolgravian attack failed. You've got to deal with him, once and for all.'

Raythe considered Jesco's words, then breathed in his friend's ear, 'It'll have to keep. For now, we need every man, and if I turn on Elgus, his men will defend him. But when the time comes . . .'

Sir Elgus Rhamp stared along the bridge, quietly simmering. This expedition was cursed. *I should have cashed in Raythe Vyre back in Teshveld.*

But the promise that had drawn him was hanging over his head: five hundred yards above the highest ridge of this mountain-city, tethered to the ground by massive chains, was a floating rock *riddled* with istar-iol, enough wealth for many lifetimes, which meant the mines below would also be full of the blessed, cursed stuff. The scouts said this city was built on the slopes of what had once been a mountain, until the rock above broke away. Now the middle was like a hollow volcano: a miraculous place.

But this expedition has cost me two of my sons – maybe three, 'cause no one knows where Banno is – and it'll probably be the death of me.

Raythe Vyre wanted a meeting, but he needed the thoughts of his two lieutenants before that. He picked a random gate into a courtyard and waved in grey-bearded, calculating Crowfoot and swarthy, belliger-ent Bloody Thom.

'How're the lads?' he asked the pair.

'Truth, boss, their heads are spinning,' Crowfoot replied. 'Floating castles, lost tribes, Aldar ruins? It's like we've fallen off the edge of the world.'

'But most of all, the lads don' know what side we're on,' Bloody Thom added. 'Last night, we were about to help the damned Bolgies, then we kragged 'em instead. Deo knows we hate them bastards, but Vyre needs to go down. So damned right, our heads are spinning.'

That was all fair, but Elgus had been right beside that Bolgie commander when the attack fell apart. Changing sides twice in one night was a first for him, but it had been a crazy situation – and as it turned out, the right choice.

'You were there: Jesco Duretto and his lot had the Bolgies cold – and then those savages hit their rear. We'd have gone down with them if I hadn't two-stepped us out.'

Crowfoot scowled. 'You didn't know that was coming, Elgus. You made that call purely on gut.'

'And my gut got it right,' Elgus retorted, slapping his ample girth. 'Sometimes it ain't the logic but the *feel*, and that attack din't feel right. Those Bolgies were messing up and Vyre's people had the high ground. They wanted us to go into the teeth of their guns, uphill in the dark. So damn right I pivoted, and I was right to.'

Thom got it – he understood that while large battles were decided by numbers and firepower, skirmishes like last night got settled by luck and cosmic energy. And three times now, Vyre had led his caravan out of the empire's jaws.

The gods are with him, my Pa would've said.

Focusing on Crowfoot, who was all about numbers and tactics, Elgus said, 'Vyre has the upper hand and Duretto suspects us. We play along and wait our moment.'

Crowfoot snarled in frustration. 'Elgus, even if that Bolgie force was wiped out last night, they must've told their superiors where they were going. We have to be gone – with a shitload of istariol – before the empire returns.'

'Maybe – but it's just as likely they were operating in the dark, and who's to know if they left adequate directions? Verdessa is a new settlement and things are loose in such places. And in case you've not noticed, there's an army out there – so until we know what we face, we play along. Got it?'

His men grumbled into their beards, but they grunted assent.

'Look, I'm chewed up over this too,' he told them, 'but I'll see us right, lads. I always have.'

With that he headed for Vyre's meeting, readying the lies he'd need to hide what he'd done last night – but his thoughts constantly returned to his one remaining son.

Banno was last seen with Zarelda Vyre. If she's a prisoner, where's my boy?

'Well?' Crowfoot growled.

Bloody Thom hunched over, seething. 'Elgus is deluding himself. We've got two, maybe three months before the empire arrives, I reckon. By then, we've gotta be gone.'

Crowfoot considered. 'A month for anyone who escaped to reach Rodonoi, a month to get their shit together – I reckon they emptied the garrison, so they'll need reinforcements – then a month to return. So aye, three months.'

Thom leaned in and whispered, 'You reckon Elgus's still got the balls for this?'

'I don't know,' Crowfoot said, and that was painful to admit. They'd all been through so much together, all the chaos of the imperial conquests and the rebellions. 'He's got to assert himself with Vyre or that slimy Otravian will sell us all out, you watch. When we strike, they've all got to fall, Vyre and his ringleaders.' He enumerated their enemies, finger by finger. 'Jesco Duretto. Vidar Vidarsson. Kemara Solus. Mater Varahana. Cal Foaley. Vyre himself. Six backs, six knives.'

'And maybe seven, if Elgus don't see us right,' Thom growled after a moment.